D.W

Look for the new novel from Loretta Chase . . .

# *Mr. Impossible*

Other Regency Romances by Loretta Chase

*Isabella*
*The English Witch*
*Viscount Vagabond*
*The Devil's Delilah*

Historical Romances by Loretta Chase

*Miss Wonderful*

# The Sandalwood Princess

### and

# Knaves' Wager

### Loretta Chase

A SIGNET BOOK

SIGNET
Published by New American Library, a division of
Penguin Group (USA) Inc., 375 Hudson Street,
New York, New York 10014, USA
Penguin Group (Canada), 10 Alcorn Avenue, Toronto,
Ontario M4V 3B2, Canada (a division of Pearson Penguin Canada Inc.)
Penguin Books Ltd., 80 Strand, London WC2R 0RL, England
Penguin Ireland, 25 St. Stephen's Green, Dublin 2,
Ireland (a division of Penguin Books Ltd.)
Penguin Group (Australia), 250 Camberwell Road, Camberwell, Victoria 3124,
Australia (a division of Pearson Australia Group Pty. Ltd.)
Penguin Books India Pvt. Ltd., 11 Community Centre, Panchsheel Park,
New Delhi - 110 017, India
Penguin Group (NZ), Cnr Airborne and Rosedale Roads, Albany,
Auckland 1310, New Zealand (a division of Pearson New Zealand Ltd.)
Penguin Books (South Africa) (Pty.) Ltd., 24 Sturdee Avenue,
Rosebank, Johannesburg 2196, South Africa

Penguin Books Ltd., Registered Offices:
80 Strand, London WC2R 0RL, England

Published by Signet, an imprint of New American Library, a division of Penguin
Group (USA) Inc. *The Sandalwood Princess* and *Knaves' Wager* were previously
published by Walker and Company and by Avon Books in separate editions.

First Signet Printing (Double Edition), January 2005
10  9  8  7  6  5  4  3  2  1

*The Sandalwood Princess* © Loretta Chekani, 1990
*Knaves' Wager* © Loretta Chekani, 1990
All rights reserved

℗ REGISTERED TRADEMARK—MARCA REGISTRADA

Printed in the United States of America

PUBLISHER'S NOTE
These are works of fiction. Names, characters, places, and incidents either are
the product of the authors' imagination or are used fictitiously, and any resemblance to actual persons, living or dead, business establishments, events, or locales
is entirely coincidental.

# The Sandalwood Princess

*To my husband, Walter*

# Prologue

## *1811*

THOUGH THE HOUSE Hemu had so nervously entered was finer than any he could aspire to, it seemed at first far too modest for the powerful woman who dwelt here. Yet perhaps her secluded abode did suit the Rani Simhi. She was the princess of secrets. Even her true name was no longer spoken. The great Lioness, the most dangerous woman in all India, might live precisely where and as she chose. So her humble messenger Hemu meditated as he stood, head bowed, patiently awaiting her pleasure.

Moments passed. The fan her large manservant held swayed languorously over her head, and the smoke of her hookah curled and shuddered in the lazy current.

At last she spoke. "You bring me news, Hemu."

"Yes, princess."

She gestured to him to speak.

"My master but two days ago composed a letter to his friend in England," Hemu said. "My master expressed his sorrow that the friend's wife is no more."

The rani raised her index finger a fraction of an inch. Instantly, every servant vanished from the room, except for the great, hulking man who continued dragging the fan back and forth in the heavy air.

"Is it the name I gave you?" she asked Hemu.

He produced a piece of paper on which he'd painstakingly copied the English letters: Hedgrave.

The princess glanced at the paper, then up at her servant.

"This is an intelligent man, Padji," she said. "We will give him five hundred rupees."

Hemu's jaw dropped.

"You see the advantages of literacy," she told the messenger. "You are a rich man now. I advise you to leave your master."

As she spoke, the fan stopped moving. Padji drew out a bag of coins and gave it to the stunned Hemu.

Hemu left, showering hysterical blessings upon the wise and generous rani whose life, he prayed, would continue a thousand thousand years. When his footsteps died away, the rani rose.

"Padji," she said, "we go to Calcutta."

# 1814

In England, in the richly furnished study of Hedgrave House, the Marquess of Hedgrave trembled with fury. "It is incomprehensible to me," he raged. "At last the she-devil comes out of hiding, and you tell me we can't touch her."

"Politically, her timing was perfect, as usual," Lord Danbridge answered. "Ranjit Singh is bound to capitulate, sooner or later, and he's not above selling his supposed allies. She had sense enough to move before he did. She knew Bengal would be a deal safer than the Punjab for her, especially with the Company's protection. Rightly so, I must say. Whatever you think of her, the Rani Simhi's invaluable. The Ministry could do with a few more minds like that. Why, her spies—"

"I know. The whole damned subcontinent's infested with them." Lord Hedgrave stood up and stalked to the fireplace. Glaring into the flames, he said, half to himself, "I had them offer her twenty-five thousand. It's *mine*, curse her, but I was willing to pay. I might have known that wouldn't work. She knew who wanted it. Who else knows she's got it but the man she stole it from?"

Hedgrave had always had a bee in his bonnet about the Indian woman, his friend thought. In the years since Lady Hedgrave's death, however, the thing had grown into an obsession. Masking his concern, Lord Danbridge said gently, "Maybe she hasn't got it any longer. It's been a long time."

"Then what's she hiding?" his host snapped. "You sent the news yourself. Six different agents assigned. Three now incapacitated, two mysteriously vanished, one dead."

"India can be a dangerous place."

"Precisely." Lord Hedgrave turned back to his guest. "That is why I want you to contact the Falcon."

As Danbridge opened his mouth to protest, the marquess shook his head. "I know what you're going to say, Danbridge. Don't waste your breath. I happen to know he's working for us."

"I merely wished to point out that this is not the sort of enterprise he's accustomed to undertake."

"He'll undertake anything, provided the reward is high enough. You may offer him fifty thousand pounds—in addition, of course, to expenses. He'll get his money as soon as he puts the object into my hands."

"Here?" Danbridge asked incredulously. "You want him to come to England?"

"Into my hands. We're a long way from Calcutta, and the woman's fiendishly clever. Too much could go wrong along the way. I won't have him passing it on to anyone. He is to get it—I don't care how—and put it into my hands," he repeated, as though it were an incantation. His blue eyes glittered with an odd light.

Lord Danbridge looked away uneasily as he considered his friend's demand. Certainly, Hedgrave had, when required, moved mountains. Dealing with India—which was to say, the East India Company—was generally a case of moving mountains: Board of Control, Secret Committee, Directors, Council, Governor-General, and General Secretariat, not to mention Parliament itself. A lot of stubborn men, precious few of whom truly considered the well-being of the vast subcontinent England now reluctantly managed, thanks to Clive and Wellesley and their ilk.

Except in this one disturbing matter, Hedgrave at least acted disinterestedly. He was one of the few who truly grasped the difficulties of overseeing India's internal affairs and strove to accommodate the contradictory demands of the British and the many differing cultures of India.

Considering Hedgrave's unstinting political labours, one could hardly begrudge him a favour in return.

The Indian woman had apparently stolen from him an object of considerable value. Now that she was out of hiding, Hedgrave wanted it back. Given the previous failures, the Falcon was their only hope. In any case, he was the only man Danbridge could rely on not to get killed in the attempt.

Lord Danbridge met the feverish blue gaze. "I'll contact him," he said, "but it will take some time."

"I've waited thirty years," was the taut answer. "I can wait."

# === 1 ===

## *1816*

THERE WERE WORSE places to live in Calcutta, and better. Here in the crowded quarter, as elsewhere, the streets flooded in the monsoon season and the price of a palanquin soared in consequence. Fever, too, struck here, just as it did in the great palaces of Garden Reach and in the meanest slums.

The place stank, as all Calcutta stank. Indoors, the odour of ghee blended sickeningly with the reek of bug flies. Out of doors, the stench of death overpowered even that of animals and refuse, as the smoke of funeral pyres on the Hooghly riverbank thickened the broiling atmosphere. Incense only added to the miasma. In the near one-hundred-degree heat of midday, the noisome compound curdled and churned like some foul sorcerer's brew. All the perfumes of Arabia would not sweeten this place and make it fresh again, had it ever been.

All of India was not like Calcutta, Philip knew. Places existed where the breezes blew sweet and pure. He had long since learned, however, to close his senses to what could not be mended or amended. Fifteen years in India had taught him, if not an Oriental patience, then a sufficient Occidental stoicism. The climate, the stench, were beyond his control. Thus he simply accepted them. As to the neighbourhood—admittedly, one might have lived more luxuriously, but then, not so anonymously.

His rented stucco cottage suited his current role as a hookah merchant. In this busy quarter, his comings and goings aroused little interest. His command of the language was flawless, as was his grasp of etiquette. The fierce Indian sun had darkened his complexion, and an application of nut oil did the same for his fair hair. Even the blue of his eyes did not betray him. Eurasians were scarcely rare in this place.

Calcutta's founder, an Englishman named Job Charnock, had married a Brahmin lady. Like Job, the British who came in earlier times mingled freely with the natives. One found their progeny not only throughout the subcontinent, but at Eton and Oxford as well.

Thus Philip Astonley, youngest son of the Viscount Felkoner—blue-blooded and unequivocally British—easily passed in India as a mongrel. This was no great transformation, in Philip's opinion. In the process of ejecting his youngest son from the family, his lordship had called the eighteen-year-old an ungrateful cur. Philip perceived small difference between Nameless and Anonymous. In any case, if he ceased at present to be anonymous, he would very likely cease to live.

The thought was not an idle one. As he turned the corner into the narrow street, his finely tuned instincts stirred in warning. The street was deserted, as it usually was in the sweltering afternoon, when most of Calcutta slept. Yet he'd caught a movement, a glancing shadow at the opposite end of the street. His steps quickened.

He had the house key in his hand when he reached the door. Before he opened it, Philip glanced about once more. The street lay empty and still. In the next instant, he'd slipped through the door and locked it behind him. The small house, shuttered against the glaring sun, was dark, but not altogether quiet. From the room beyond came a strangled moan. Silence. Then another moan, higher pitched.

Philip drew out his knife and crept noiselessly to the bedroom. A wail of agony tore through the stillness, and he saw a man on the floor beside the bed jerk convulsively. Muttering an oath, Philip hurried forward, and dropped to his knees beside his servant's knotted body.

His face was hot and soaked with sweat, his pulse frenetic. As soon as Philip touched him, Jessup jerked spasmodically and began to babble. The words, half English and half Hindustani, spilled in a steady, chattering stream, punctuated by strangled cries of anguish. It looked like fever, but it wasn't.

"Damn you," Philip growled. "Don't you die on me, soldier."

Grasping the servant under the shoulders, Philip hauled him onto the bed. The body twisted and trembled, then knotted up once more in pain. The hysterical litany—of scorpions, cobras, bits of the Book of Common Prayer, fragments of battles, women's names, oaths—was broken only by choked wails of agony.

The poison evidently acted slowly, bringing hallucinations as well as pain. Without knowing exactly what sort of poison, Philip dared give his servant nothing, not even water.

He squeezed Jessup's hand. "I'll have to leave you for a minute, old man," he whispered. "I'm going for help. Just hang on, will you? Just *hang on*."

The old woman Philip sought lived across the way. Silently praying she'd be home, he threw open the door.

He found her waiting on his doorstep.

He was not altogether surprised. The aged Sharda was the local midwife and doctor. She could probably smell illness and death.

"My servant, mother—" he began.

"I know," she said. "You have great trouble, Dilip sahib."

7

*Sabib?* Though Philip bowed his head respectfully as she entered, his eyes narrowed with suspicion.

"Jasu—" he began again.

She gestured him to be silent. "I know," she said.

In the room beyond, Jessup screamed, then subsided again into demented babbling. The latter was worse than the screams. Philip gritted his teeth. It was all he could do to keep from dragging the old woman to the sickbed. She had her own ways, however.

He felt her gaze upon him.

"I will go to him," she said. "Have patience."

She studied the small space which served as kitchen, living room, and dining room. A plate of pastries sat upon the table. She took one, broke it in half, stared at the fruit center, then sniffed it.

"Figs, you see," she said, pointing to the dark paste. "To add another sort of seed is not difficult, and the flour, I think, was tainted. He has terrible visions?"

"Yes," Philip said tightly, "and pain. Yet I hesitated to give him anything."

"Opium we can give him for the pain," she said. "The other must run its course, I fear."

Her examination confirmed the preliminary diagnosis. Accordingly, she measured out a dose of the laudanum Philip handed her. After what seemed an eternity, Jessup began to quiet somewhat. He still babbled, but more like a drunken man, and the spasms and strangled cries ceased. Perhaps he would sleep, Sharda told Philip. At any rate, the servant would not die, though he may wish it. His recovery would be very long and very painful.

"A fiendish mixture it is, to bring both madness and maddening pain," Sharda said as they left the sickroom, "and no relief of death. But it was not meant to kill him." She patted his arm in a sad, kindly way. "Only to cause great suffering, so that you would heed the warning."

He had known, hadn't he? He'd felt it as he'd entered the street, and seen it in the vanishing shadow.

While the old woman was examining Jessup, Philip had put on water to boil. Now he courteously offered tea, and made himself wait until she was ready to enlighten him.

She sipped and nodded her approval. Then she looked at him.

"A little while before, a man brought me a message," she said. "I must tell the blue-eyed merchant he is known, as is his intention. And so, he will die if he does not depart Calcutta before another day passes."

Not only known, but his mission known as well. Gad, the woman was incredible. "And this, I take it," Philip said calmly, nodding towards the sickroom, "is what I might expect?"

"You know of whom we speak. Your death will come slowly, only after many times Jasu's sufferings. Go away, as you are told, and *live*."

Philip Astonley was not a reckless man. He never underestimated his adversaries. If the Rani Simhi said she'd kill him, she'd do it, and, naturally, in the ghastliest way her evil imagination could devise. He'd known she'd penetrate his disguise sooner or later. He had not, however, dreamt this would occur quite so soon. What had it been? Less than forty-eight hours. Still, he should have been prepared. It was his fault Jessup lay in the room beyond, mad with pain and hallucination.

He met Sharda's anxious gaze. "I will heed the warning," he said.

Minutes after, her grandson, Hari, set off with a message to Fort William. Two hours later, Hari returned with the Honourable Randall Groves. A trio of servants and a pair of palanquins followed them.

Every window and door in the street promptly filled with curious onlookers. This was perfectly satisfactory. The rani would speedily receive word the merchant was departing.

Philip was already packed when Groves entered, looking exceedingly put out. He grew even more put out when

Philip led him into his own room and quietly explained what was expected of him.

"Confound it," Randall snapped. "This is your specialty, ain't it? How the devil do you expect me—"

"However you can," Philip said. "Bribe, lie—I don't care. The *Evelina* is scheduled to sail tomorrow, and Jessup and I have to be on board." He thrust a packet of papers into Randall's hands. "Don't use them unless you have to. I'd rather not bring his lordship into this, and he'd rather I didn't as well, for obvious reasons."

"Philip, the ship's loaded to the limit, and Blayton don't even want the passengers he's got. The Bullerhams, Cavencourt's sister, Monty Larchmere, and all their servants. You expect me to throw a couple of 'em overboard?"

"If you must. I'd talk to Monty first. He's a greedy devil. For a hefty bribe, he'll probably agree to wait through the monsoon season for another ship." While he spoke, Philip was winding a turban about his head.

Randall stared at the turban a moment. Then a horrified understanding widened his eyes. "Good grief," he said. "*That's* why you sent for me. You're still meaning to do it, ain't you? For God's sake, Philip, the curst woman knows who you are!"

"Exactly. As I so carefully explained, she means to kill me if I'm not gone by tomorrow, so I'd better work fast, hadn't I?"

Philip slipped his knife into its sheath and fastened it to the sash he wore under his long muslin *kurta*. With the loose shirt he wore muslin trousers. For the evening's endeavour, these would be less encumbering than the *dhoti*'s complicated draping. His toilette complete, Philip returned his attention to the now grim Randall.

"Don't mope, Randy," he said. "I don't plan to get killed. The lady wants me gone, and I'll oblige her. But I'm damned if I'm leaving without it. I've never failed yet, and a man must consider his reputation."

"You're mad," said Randall.

The blue eyes flashed. "Have a glance in the other room, my lad," Philip said in a low voice. "Have a look at what the witch's done to Jessup. I can't pay her back as I'd like, because the curst female's too precious to our superiors. But I'll repay her as I *can*, that I swear."

The Rani Simhi resided in a vast mansion on the banks of the Hooghly at Garden Reach. Though the English had built these Palladian palaces exclusively for themselves, the Indian princess was an exceptional case. The Governor-General, Lord Moira, had personally overseen the previous resident's eviction, in order to provide the enigmatic Indian woman a domicile befitting both her status and her usefulness to His Majesty's government.

This night, she celebrated her fifty-fifth birthday. The palace was packed with guests both British and Indian. She appeared briefly, to receive the company's good wishes, then, according to her custom, retired to her private rooms. Though in so many ways unlike other native women, she chose to imitate them in leaving the responsibilities of hosting to her sons.

Since the party was held in her honour, she might have lingered if she chose. This night, however, she had one visitor whose company she wished to enjoy privately. So she explained to Amanda Cavencourt when the latter voiced regret about keeping the princess from her guests.

"You leave tomorrow for England," said the rani. "We may never meet again. Besides, they are all idiots, and tiresome." She made a slight gesture with her hand, and a large, jewel-encrusted hookah was brought forward.

"Your brother, for instance," she went on, as she examined the mouthpiece. "Generally not a stupid man, but he has married foolishly an ignorant woman. If she were not so ignorant, she would love you. Instead, she hates you, and drives you away. I detest her."

"Two women cannot rule one house," Amanda said

calmly. "My presence is a constant irritant. Or perhaps embarrassment is more like it. My ways aren't hers and never will be, so there's always friction. You understand," she added.

The rani studied the silken-clad woman who sat cross-legged opposite her. "I understand she would fly into a rage, could she see you now. I am told she considers the sari indecent."

Amanda grinned as she took up her mouthpiece. "She'd certainly drop into five fits if she saw me smoking this." She gave a defiant shrug, and drew on the hookah with practised ease.

She knew her erratic attention to deportment merely aggravated her sister-in-law's dislike. In time, Eustacia might have nagged her wayward relation into more acceptable behaviour. Unfortunately, no lessons, no reminders, however regular, could change Amanda's appearance.

Her light complexion resembled too closely the mellow ivory lightness of the natives of the northern Ganges. Glossy dark brown hair, rippling in thick waves, framed the oval of her face. Thick black lashes fringed large eyes of a peculiarly light, changeable brown. The bones of her countenance strongly defined, the nose straight and well-modeled, the mouth wide and overfull, Amanda's face was far too exotic for European beauty. More mortifying to Lady Cavencourt, both Europeans and natives regularly mistook Amanda for an Indian.

"I comprehend well enough," the older woman answered, "but I object. We will speak no more of her. She is tiresome. I have a story for you, much more interesting than your foolish new sister."

Nothing could be so pleasurable as this, Amanda thought. How she would miss the sultry Calcutta evenings spent with the fascinating princess . . . the languorous clouds of smoke and incense that filled the room with shifting spirit-shadows . . . the rani's clear voice, smooth as a running river, coiling through the twists and turns of ancient legends. Amanda forced back the tears filling her eyes.

The rani smoked silently for a moment. Then she raised a finger. All the servants scurried from the room, save the large Padji, who stood still as a statue by the door. When the rest were gone, she began:

"Tonight, I tell you of the goddess Anumati, she from whom the childless women of my native kingdom besought sons and daughters. When she answered their prayers, the women would bring her gifts, as rich as their means permitted. But whether rich or poor, the new mother must always bring as well a carved figure."

From the cushion beside her, the rani picked up a small wooden statue. Amanda had seen it before. Normally it stood upon a shelf, along with other statues and talismans in the rani's vast collection. It was about ten inches tall, a beautifully carved sandalwood figure of a smiling woman whose belly was swollen with child.

"Many lifetimes ago," the rani continued, "such figures filled Anumati's temple, and precious stones adorned her magnificent statue. In her forehead was set a large ruby, and in her right hand an immense pearl in the shape of a tear. These were the gifts of a prince and princess of ancient times. The ruby, from the prince, symbolized the blood of new life: the son Anumati had given the previously childless couple. The pearl, his wife's gift, represented the tears of happiness she'd shed at her son's birth. This stone, more rare than even the ruby, was called the Tear of Joy."

By the doorway, Padji shifted slightly, and threw his mistress a glance. Her eyes upon the statue, the rani went on.

"Many lifetimes later, marauders came and ransacked the rich temple. The chief of them must have the greatest jewels, of course. With difficulty, he removed the ruby. The pearl, however, was more deeply set. To get at it, he must break the hand from the statue. He beat upon it with an altar stone and at last the arm began to crack. At that same moment came a great rumbling. The temple walls shuddered and the ground beneath trembled. His terrified companions fled, some dropping their loot in their haste. He remained, still struggling for the pearl. Just as he broke the hand away, the temple roof collapsed."

"Anumati was very angry," Amanda murmured. "I don't blame her."

"Her revenge was greater than that. Mere hours after the temple's collapse, several of the marauders returned. The new leader, as greedy as his predecessor, determined to have the two great stones. They dug through the rubble— a tremendous task—and at last, by the next day, found the chief's crushed body. The ruby lay in his hand. The pearl was gone."

She looked at Amanda. "What do you make of that?"

"The logical explanation is that the pearl was crushed to powder," Amanda said thoughtfully. "Yet Anumati's worshippers would probably conclude she took away her treasure because, instead of Life and Love, death and destruction filled her temple."

The princess nodded. "It was said Anumati had abandoned the defiled place and taken all joy with her. The temple grounds were considered accursed. My people followed the advice of their priests, and did not attempt to restore either the temple or their ravaged town. Instead, they built new houses a safe distance away."

Gently she stroked the figure's forehead. After a moment she said, "Now I come to my own lifetime."

From the doorway came a long, drawn-out sigh. The princess affected not to hear it.

"I was many years younger than you when a Punjab prince conquered my father's kingdom," she said. "When this conqueror investigated his new domain, he made two discoveries. One was myself. To strengthen his political position, he took me as his wife. He also discovered the temple ruins. His greed being far greater than his fear of curses, he ordered the temple excavated. Thus he unearthed all the treasure the robbers had left behind in their terror. Also, he found the skull of the chieftain, and within it"—she paused briefly—"the Tear of Joy."

Amanda stifled a gasp. "In the skull?" she asked incredulously. "How did it get there?"

The rani shrugged. "Who knows? There it lay, undamaged after nearly a century. My husband gave it to me, before all the town. He was a pig, but politic. Before them, he gave it to me. In private, he took it back—for safekeeping, he said. He permitted me to keep a few baubles, and this figure, the only one which had not been destroyed in the temple's collapse. I was not pleased," she added with a faint smile.

There came a loud sniff from the doorway.

"What ails you, Padji?" the princess asked.

"Nothing, mistress."

"Then be silent." She turned back to Amanda. "Once and only once in my life have I loved," the rani said. "I speak not of ordinary love, which I have possessed in abundance. I speak of a great, all-consuming love, such as most persons merely read of or see performed in drama, but never experience in their lives. In your legends, it is the love of Tristan and Isolde. In mine, it is that of Krishna and Radha."

After a moment's consideration, Amanda said softly, "You mean sinful love, I think." She blushed as she spoke, not for any missish reason, but because to speak of sin to the rani was ... oh, absurd, really. Her morality was not defined by the Church of England or English society.

"Yes," the Indian woman answered calmly. "Sinful love." She lazily drew upon the waterpipe.

While she awaited the rest of the story, Amanda gazed about her, trying to memorise her surroundings, for it would be the last time, perhaps. Thick with smoke and incense, these chambers would have frightened the ladylike Eustacia, and most gently bred British ladies. They would have perceived the place as a den of iniquity. Certainly it fit their image of the Rani Simhi as a dangerous woman whose history comprised one long career of sin.

Perhaps it *was* sin, Amanda reflected. Nonetheless, the princess's world was fascinating, and Amanda had been happier here than anywhere else she could remember. Whether legend or history, the universe her Indian friend revealed was a dream world, captivating as a fairy tale. It was also just as safe as one, for Amanda could never enter its pages.

A light breeze wafted from the garden, carrying the scent of flowers and the fresh fragrance of the carved vetiver entryway. Something else, Amanda thought, drawing an appreciative breath. Agarwood?

"My husband became one of the most powerful princes in India," the rani continued. "Thus the British soon arrived, to persuade him to accept their protection rather than that of the French. Among them was one, tall and fair. In his hair gleamed the golden light of the sun, and in his eyes the glistening sea. I saw him and love consumed me. This passion caused me to risk death, the punishment for adultresses. Richard Whitestone became my lover, and in time, I ran away with him."

Padji cried out, "Oh, mistress, would that I'd cut out the dog's heart!"

"Hold your tongue," said his mistress. "My friend does not wish to hear your ignorant babbling." She turned back to Amanda. "He is like a child sometimes. He thinks everything may be resolved by cutting out hearts. One cannot explain to him. He is not a woman."

Amanda's gaze slid from servant to mistress. She understood. "Your lover betrayed you."

The princess shrugged. "Men are easily confused. One night I awoke, and found my lover gone."

"He took everything," Padji growled. "The jewels—"

"He took from a thief," his mistress corrected. "Merely to abandon my husband was insufficient payment for his selfish cruelty. I stole from his treasures, took what he held truly precious, gold and jewels. Yet this was not entirely revenge. My lover and I must live on something, and he was not a wealthy young man."

"Still, he took everything? Abandoned you and left you destitute? Whether you'd stolen the treasures or not, that was a despicable thing to do," Amanda said indignantly.

"There is more to be unfolded," the rani answered, "as it was unfolded to me. I later learned my husband had persuaded the Englishman to seduce and take me away."

Amanda's mouth fell open.

"My husband had grown to fear my influence. He was eager to be rid of me, but dared not kill me, for fear of an uprising. If I committed adultery, however, my own people would pursue me and put me to death, while he stood by, innocent, the injured spouse."

"Good heavens."

"As I told you, he was politic. Still, he also betrayed his English ally. He'd promised Richard Whitestone a considerable reward, which he failed to deliver. Thus my lover took his payment from me."

"That hardly excuses him," Amanda said, rubbing her forehead. "I know you believe each matter also contains its opposite, but all I see in this is villainy."

"So it is, memsahib," Padji solemnly agreed. "I might have caught and killed him, but my mistress would not permit it. Even then—"

"I was betrayed. What of it?" the princess interrupted. "Women are always betrayed. Yet I prospered. Did not this Englishman show me the Fire of Love, which so few experience? Did he not release me from my husband and carry me to safety? Within months my husband lay dead of fever—and I was spared the *sati*. Instead of burning on his pyre, I was free, many miles away. Did I not find another husband, worthy and loving, who gave me strong sons and showered me with wealth?"

All while she'd spoken, her voice calm and cool, the rani had continued stroking the statue.

After a moment's silence, she said, "Though he took all else, Richard Whitestone left me this figure. One night, as I lay weeping for him, Anumati came to me in a dream. In time, she said, I would discover the meaning of this suffering, and its end. The one object my lover had left me was her gift to me, which she would fill with all her blessings. This was her promise, and she kept it."

She must have observed dissatisfaction in Amanda's face then, because she laughed. "Ah, my young friend, the matter of love still troubles you."

"You speak as though you forgive him," Amanda said, "yet he behaved abominably in every way. He behaved like a—a prostitute. Then he stole all you had."

"Merely the acts of a desperate man. Yet I have no doubt he loved me. Such passion cannot be feigned. Perhaps that made him most desperate of all, for ours was the love that is madness and rapture at once."

"If it *is* a sort of madness," Amanda said reflectively, "then no wonder it is treacherous. As you said, most of us only read about it—yet the stories are always tragic, as yours seems."

"What tragedy?" was the cool response. "I found happiness after."

"But destructive, at least," Amanda argued, without quite knowing why she needed to argue. "I don't know about Krishna and Radha, but what about Tristan and Isolde? What about Romeo and Juliet?"

"Ah, yes," the princess said. "*Romeo and Juliet.* I have read this work of your great poet many times. A fine scene, that in the garden. She calls to her lover, as I called to mine in my sorrow and loneliness." In English, then, she quoted as she gazed towards her own garden, " 'O! for a falconer's voice, / To lure this tassel-gentle back again.' "

The Rani Simhi was still a beautiful woman. As she softly uttered the longing words, her face softened, too, and for an instant, Amanda saw in her profile the young girl who'd known rapturous passion. For that instant, Amanda almost envied her. Almost.

"Would you lure him back?" she whispered.

The princess's gaze, dark and liquid, came back to her. She smiled.

Padji shifted restlessly.

"We bore Padji beyond his little patience," his mistress said, her voice brisk again, "and I keep you overlong with my tales. Yet he understands," she added, throwing her servant a warning look, "that you must know the story, because now the statue belongs to you, my dear friend." So saying, she held the sandalwood figure out to Amanda.

Stunned, Amanda took it.

"Anumati's is a woman's gift, to be passed from mother to daughter. I have no daughters of my blood, but you have become the daughter of my heart. Thus I pass the Laughing Princess to you. May all her blessings enrich your life, as you have so enriched mine, child."

There was no holding back the tears then, a monsoon flood of them, so that Amanda scarcely saw the heap of gifts Padji began piling before her, barely comprehended the rani's affectionate words of farewell. Silks, kashmir shawls, perfumes, and incense—a rajah's treasure. In vain Amanda protested this largess. The princess waved away all objections.

"If you remained with me, my daughter, thus would I adorn you," she said. "Also, I would find you a fine husband, tall and strong and passionate. Unfortunately, I could find no one worthy in time."

Amanda gave a watery giggle. Indian women were often wed at puberty. At six and twenty, even by English standards she was at her last prayers.

"That is better," the rani said. "We part with smiles." She embraced Amanda, then added, "If I find you a husband, I shall dispatch him to England, never fear."

In the flurry of gift giving and leave taking, they did not hear the soft rustle in the dark garden beyond or the featherlight footsteps fading into the night.

# === 2 ===

AMANDA THOROUGHLY LOATHED the palanquin. She objected on principle to human beings used as beasts of burden. However, the rani always provided a palanquin to collect her English friend and bring her home again. Rather than professional bearers, who were notoriously untrustworthy, four of the rani's own sturdy, well-armed servants carried it.

They made their way speedily through the dark streets, Padji at their side to terrify any prospective evildoers with his muscular hulk and monstrous sword. Amanda doubted even Queen Charlotte's safety was so well provided for.

All the same, Amanda had never travelled with so much wealth, and the jewels in the lacquered box made her anxious. Still, who could know what she carried? Spies. Spies lurked everywhere. Not to mention that everyone by now had heard of the master thief, the Falcon. His vision, it was claimed, penetrated stone walls.

Roderick called the stories typical native nonsense. Certainly, he admitted, India abounded in cutthroats and thieves. Nonetheless, no man could turn himself into the night breeze and slip through keyholes. No man slithered into gardens in the guise of a snake, or flew through windows in the form of a dove. That, supposedly, was how the Falcon had made off with one woman's ruby necklace, and another's diamond bracelets. More likely, Roderick told his sister (when Eustacia was not nearby), the women had bestowed the jewels upon their lovers, and accounted for the missing gems as supernatural thefts. Lately, everything was blamed on the Falcon.

Yet Amanda had heard other tales—of documents, letters, political secrets bought or stolen, then sold. Always, one name was whispered: the Falcon. Only one name, but she little doubted it comprehended a vast network of spies and mercenaries, as likely controlled by the East India Company as by an Indian mastermind.

She sighed. She would miss India, but not its atmosphere of suspicion and treachery. She had grown accustomed to the stench, heat, and din of Calcutta, yet she would not miss those, certainly. Apart from the rani, her one friend, what would she miss, really?

A cry sheered the night, like a dying bird song, and the palanquin halted. Amanda heard Padji's voice in sharp Hindustani: "What message?"

"For the woman," an unfamiliar voice answered in the same language.

Amanda peered through the shutters.

In the darkness she made out Padji's immense form, then a flash of metal, whistling as it swooped to his neck, so swiftly she had no time to cry out a warning before the gleaming blade lay upon the servant's throat. Amanda blinked. That must be Padji's own sword, because his hand hung empty now. How had the man done it?

"Lay down your weapons," the strange voice commanded the bearers, "or he dies."

"Run, fools!" Padji cried. "Take her away. I die for—"

"No!" Amanda cried, before the bearers could move. "Do as the pig says."

"A wise woman," the voice said softly. "Down on your knees, my elephant," he told Padji.

"I kneel to no thieving pig. Cut my throat, then, fool, and the others will fall upon you."

"No!" Amanda screamed.

Too late. Silver gleamed as it swept through the air, and Padji crumpled to the ground. Instantly, the bearers set down their burden. To Amanda's amazement, the intrepid attacker fled, pursued by four shrieking avengers.

Amanda pushed open the palanquin shutters and scrambled out. She stared at the dark heap on the ground. "Oh, Padji," she whispered. Shaking in every limb, she crept towards him. Gingerly, she reached out to his shoulder, then jerked her hand back. What was she thinking of? The thief must have cut his throat. He'd be covered with blood . . . sticky . . . ghastly.

She scuttled back hastily, struggling to control the spasm of nausea. One . . . two . . . three deep breaths. Then she looked about her, while her heart seemed to pound in her ears. She was not far from home. Even if she could have endured touching the body, she certainly could not carry it with her. She returned to the palanquin and quickly collected her belongings.

The robber had chosen the site well. Large gardens sprawled on either side of the dark, narrow passageway's high walls. The houses' inhabitants were too far away to hear cries for help. Normally, the gates at both ends of the passage were kept locked. Tonight, though, with virtually all Calcutta's upper crust at the rani's celebration, it must have been more convenient to leave the way open. Or else the thief had broken in. Alone? Amanda glanced anxiously about her. A risky business for one man, wasn't it?

She held her breath, but the only sounds she made out came from a great distance: hoofbeats and voices. Nearby she heard only her own heart thundering.

Clutching her awkward bundles to her, she hiked up the skirts of her sari, ran blindly to the end of the passage, and turned the corner.

A dark form swept out of a gateway, a hand covered her mouth, another wrapped round her waist and dragged her backwards into the shadows.

"Drop it."

To her shock, it was the same voice she'd heard only minutes before.

She dropped the lacquered jewel box, then drove her elbow into her attacker's stomach and tore away from him. A foot shot out, tripping her. She stumbled, and the packet of silks slid out from under her arm. Still tightly clutching the Laughing Princess, Amanda regained her balance, only to be hauled up against the robber's body. The hand closed over her mouth again, choking her.

"Drop it, curse you!" he gasped.

Amanda squirmed, frantically trying to break free of the suffocating embrace. One strong hand pressed painfully over her mouth. The other crushed her rib cage. She stomped on his foot, pushed, kicked, and elbowed, all the while clutching the sandalwood figure as though it were her firstborn. That was all she wanted. Why wouldn't he take the rest and let her go? But he was pulling at her hands now.

Again she jammed madly with her elbow. This time he abruptly released her, and her own force unbalanced her. She fell against him, felt him dropping with her. They crashed to the ground . . . and she found herself pinned beneath him.

"Foolish woman," he said, panting. While the weight of his hard body held her down, he began prying her fingers loose from the figure.

"No!" she shrieked, as he wrenched the statue from her grasp. "You bastard! No!"

There was a heartbeat's pause, and Amanda realised she'd cried out in English.

"A thousand pardons, memsahib," he said.

Then he leapt to his feet . . . and vanished into the night with the Laughing Princess.

White hot, it churned round her, blinding her: Rage. Amanda dragged herself up onto her knees and screamed, "You filthy bastard! You bloody, thieving swine!" Silence answered. She pounded her fists into the dirt in impotent fury.

Something else pounded, somewhere beyond the vast,

surrounding wall of rage. Footsteps? She raised her head, just as a figure staggered into the narrow entryway.

"Oh, missy, what has that pig done to you? Fiend. A hell-fiend. We will find him. We will tear him in pieces and rip out his heart while it yet beats. We will—"

"Padji?" she croaked, disbelieving.

He fell to his knees beside her. "Aye, it is Padji, the worthless slave who has failed you." He took her hand and pressed it to his lips, repeatedly, while he muttered inarticulate lamentations.

Amanda pulled her hand away. "You're alive," she said. "I thought he'd murdered you."

"A blow only. Half a breath's less force and I should not have sunk under it. A moment less in blackness and I should have caught him and killed him, and thrown his polluted head at your feet. Ah, we have been tricked, and it is my folly. Aiyeeeeeee," he wailed. "I am a dead man."

"Do be quiet," Amanda snapped. "There's no point staying here moaning about it. We've got to get home."


The servants were all abed, and Roderick and Eustacia were still out when Amanda and Padji reached the house. This was exceedingly fortunate, for Roderick would have made an international incident out of the attack—after, that is, his wife had finished dropping in and out of fourteen fits of hysterics.

Mrs. Gales, Amanda's companion, possessed a less turbulent disposition. A tall, ample-figured woman in her mid-forties, the auburn-haired widow had small use for emotional displays. India was a treacherous, incomprehensible place, and the natives were, in general, demented. If one made a fuss about every objectionable episode that occurred, one would live in a constant state of fuss. This, to Mrs. Gales's mind, constituted a prodigious waste of time and energy.

Though distressed by her employer's shocking experience, the widow perceived no reason to compound the unpleasantness with swoons or hysteria. Instead, she calmly advised Amanda to wash and change. Mrs. Gales meanwhile saw to Padji's facial injuries in her usual efficient manner, ordered him to sit quietly in a corner, then set about making tea.

With the removal of grime and the resumption of proper English attire, Amanda discovered she didn't look nearly as ghastly as she felt. Her modest yellow muslin frock concealed her few outer bruises. Her mouth was sore, her jaw ached, and her ribs felt as though she'd been run through a gristmill. Nonetheless, her looking glass showed nothing obviously amiss.

As she entered the parlour, she found Padji in a considerably more colourful state. His face was bruised and cut where the paving stones had scraped it, and a large lump had sprung up on the back of his head. The villain had aimed beautifully, he grimly admitted. The man had struck with the sword hilt just below the cushioning turban.

"Indeed, the fellow sounds remarkable," said Mrs. Gales as she handed Padji a cup of tea. He shook his head and commenced to rocking to and fro in a melancholy manner. Mrs. Gales shrugged and placed the cup on the floor beside him.

"I can scarcely credit it," she said to Amanda. "That one man should attack so large and well-armed a party. How could he have robbed you while he was running away from four bearers? There must have been two robbers at least."

Amanda shook her head. "It was the same one. He must have tricked them somehow, then doubled back for me."

"So it was," Padji grumbled. "A master of deceit. How did he know my mistress's signal?"

Amanda put down her teacup and looked at him. "Is that what the strange bird sound was?" she asked. "Is that why you stopped?"

Padji covered his face with his hands. "I am a dead man. She will tear my tongue from my throat. She will flay my flesh and pour burning poison into the wounds. 'Protect my daughter,' she told me, and I failed. She will bury me alive and sing curses over my grave."

"She'll do no such thing," Amanda said briskly. "The man merely robbed me. I wasn't raped or murdered. Calcutta is filled with thieves. I shall send a note, explaining."

"No!" he shrieked, jumping up. "You must not tell her. She will know soon enough. My mistress learns everything. But there is time. I will go with you on the ship, and when she discovers, I will be far away."

"Go with us!" Mrs. Gales echoed. "Are you mad?"

"I must go. There is no place in all India I can hide. Her spies will find me out. They will put out my eyes with burning brands, because I was a blind man who did not see the Falcon as he swept down upon her beloved daughter. They will—"

"The Falcon?" Amanda cut in before he could commence another litany of horrors.

Padji covered his mouth with his hands.

Amanda rose from her chair and approached him. "That was the Falcon?"

"Forgive me, precious one. I am mad with grief. I know not what I say."

"Do you not?" Amanda responded. "Very well. I shall send to the rani for servants to guide you back, lest you lose your way in your confusion."

Padji fell to his knees before her. "No, missy, no, I pray you. She will make me die a thousand times."

"Then tell me what the Falcon wanted with me. He might have taken the jewels and silks easily enough. Why did he want only the Laughing Princess?"

"O beloved of my mistress, there are matters I do not understand. I have followed her since I was a child, slept in mud and eaten maggots when I must, yet even to me she does not reveal everything."

"If he wanted the statue, it must be of great value," Amanda said.

"Aye, so he must have believed." He raised his head to gaze at her. "You told me you dropped the box of jewels and the silks, but you fought him for the Laughing Princess. So what must he think, but that this statue is of the greatest value of all?"

"Damn," Amanda said softly. Padji was right, of course. A cleverer woman—the princess, for instance—would have instantly dropped the object she most valued and fought over trinkets. Amanda had lost her most treasured gift because she'd let emotion rule instead of reason. "It is not others who betray us," the rani had once told her, "but we who betray ourselves."

Amanda had lost only a wooden statue, perhaps a hundred years old, perhaps much less. As antiquities went—and India was thick with them—the Laughing Princess's monetary value was slight. To her, though, it was a piece of legend, a piece of India. More important, it was a gift of sentiment, the only treasure the rani's false lover had left her, the only physical reminder of one brief, intense passion . . . and betrayal. It was a gift to her "daughter," she had said. That word was perhaps dearest of all.

Amanda's own mother had existed briefly, a figure in a haze, a beautiful princess forever locked in the prison of her own fairy tale world. Smoke . . . and incense . . .

Amanda shook herself out of her reverie to find her two companions staring at her.

"What's done is done," she said. "Perhaps it will turn up. If the thief was the Falcon, and if he's as clever as reputed, he'll realise the figure's worthless and discard it. You may even find it on your way home," she told Padji. "If, that is, your knees haven't frozen into that position. *Will* you get up?"

"But I go with you," he said, gazing up at her with misty brown eyes.

Amanda stared back incredulously.

"You most certainly do not," Mrs. Gales said. Then, as though recollecting he was a native, and therefore congenitally irrational, she patiently explained, "We could never arrange your passage at this late date, even if Lord Cavencourt permitted it, which I strongly doubt. The end of our long war with Napoleon has left a great many former soldiers in need of employment. Lord Cavencourt cannot in good conscience pay a foreigner for what an English servant can do."

"Unless, of course, the foreigner is French," Amanda put in dryly, "and an excellent chef."

"My dear girl, you know I never meant—"

"I know, Leticia, but that argument won't wash."

"I can cook," Padji cried, still gazing soulfully up at Amanda, his hands now folded in supplication. "I am an excellent cook, even the English food." He launched into a staggering list of his gastronomic accomplishments, down to the art of soft-boiling eggs.

"I'm sorry," Amanda said gently. "Truly—because I'll miss you dreadfully. But even if we could arrange it—which I know we can't—to take you would be most unwise, and not fair to you at all. This is your country. You'd hate England. It's cold and damp, and many people will treat you unkindly because you're a foreigner and your skin is dark."

"I will be despised," he said. "I will live as an untouchable, a leper. But I will serve you faithfully. And my mistress will not fill my mouth with scorpions and—"

"Lud, but you have the most ghastly imagination, Padji. Oh, *will* you get up? What are you thinking of, to be grovelling in this way, a great strong man like you—and at your age."

Padji rose. "Then you will take me with you?"

Amanda sighed. "The ship sails tomorrow. To arrange passage at the last minute requires a great deal of money and influence. That means my brother must arrange it, and I assure you he won't."

"But if it can be arranged, you will let me serve you?"

"It can't be," she answered, her gaze flickering from the

huge Indian to Mrs. Gales. "Roderick would never permit it, let alone help."

"Never fear, mistress, O beautiful and compassionate one, whose eyes burn with golden flames and—"

"Padji, you must—"

"Tomorrow. I will arrange it all, and tomorrow I will commence a new life, as your adoring slave."

Oblivious to her half-hearted and Mrs. Gale's emphatic protests, Padji commenced a speech on the thousand ways he'd serve his new mistress. He'd just begun soaring to improbable heights of self-sacrifice—the eating of flies being deemed somehow necessary to satisfactory service — when the Cavencourt carriage was heard at the gate. Padji promptly crawled out a window and escaped through the garden.

# === 3 ===

RODERICK ACCOMPANIED HIS sister, her companion, and her
maid on board ship, dutifully saw their belongings properly
arranged, repeated for the hundredth time what Amanda
must do upon reaching England, checked for the fiftieth
time the papers entrusted to her, gave her a peck on the
cheek, and departed.

Not ten minutes after he'd gone, one of the mates appeared, requesting Miss Cavencourt's appearance in the
wardroom. The captain wished to speak with her.

"Miss Cavencourt has scarcely had time to catch her
breath," Mrs. Gales said reprovingly, with a glance at the
weary, unhappy Amanda. "Is the matter so urgent it cannot
wait?"

The man apologised, but declared they could not weigh
anchor until the problem was resolved.

Alarmed and puzzled, Amanda went with him, Mrs. Gales
following with stiff disapproval.


As soon as Amanda entered the wardroom, her heart
sank. Beside Captain Blayton, Padji stood at proud attention.

"We have a problem, Miss Cavencourt," said the captain
after a brief, apologetic preamble. "In fact, we have had any
number of problems in the last twelve hours," he added
irritably.

"I do hope Padji has not created difficulties for you, sir," said Amanda.

Captain Blayton's stern countenance relaxed slightly. "Ah, so you *do* know him. When he claimed to be your cook, I must admit I was—well, that is neither here nor there. The case is this: my own cook failing to report for duty last night, I ordered a search. Just before dawn, this fellow—Padji, as you say—appeared, and led us to a certain tea shop, where we found Saunders in a state of delirium."

"Terrible fever," Padji said gravely. "I heard his cries. I have heard that terrible sound before."

Amanda threw Mrs. Gales a glance. The widow must have grasped the situation just as quickly, for she glared at Padji.

Sublimely oblivious to Mrs. Gales's sulphurous expression, Padji bent his own innocent gaze upon Amanda.

"I tell the great ship's master I have no more heart to cook for the family when my gracious mistress is gone," he said sadly. "My heart breaks because she leaves forever. In the night, I run away to see the ship that will bear her away across the world. I weep many tears into the waters, to send a part of me with her. It was Fate led me to the place, mistress, that I might find the poor man, my brother cook, in time to save his life. I carry him, gentle as one holds a baby, to the shop of a good friend. This friend recognises the man, Saunders. And so myself I seek out the wise captain, and myself do his bidding and find the doctor. With my own hands, I make a healing broth, which the doctor himself tastes."

"Yes, well, there's no question you were helpful," the captain interjected. "But we ought to get to the point, oughtn't we?" Turning to Amanda, he said, "The doctor has pronounced Saunders unfit to travel."

To move him from his bed would be death," Padji solemnly agreed. "I see at once the hand of Fate. The gods lead me to this man. Why? Inscrutable are the ways of the Eternal, yet this riddle is soon unlocked. The man is a cook. What is Padji? A cook. It is plain I am summoned in order to take his place, and continue near my beloved mistress."

"The point is," the captain said impatiently, "this fellow proposes to cook for us in exchange for passage to England. It is true I need a cook. On the other hand, I cannot possibly harbour runaway native servants. I considered speaking to Lord Cavencourt himself, but—well, I was reluctant to get your cook into difficulties, after he'd made himself so useful. He seemed exceedingly alarmed at the prospect of confronting your brother."

"Dear me," said Mrs. Gales sympathetically. "How awkward for you."

Amanda found her own sympathy inclining to Padji. He had done a terrible thing, but he was obviously desperate. She could not abandon him.

"How I wish I'd known sooner," she told Captain Blayton. "Had you spoken to Lord Cavencourt, you would have learned he'd have no objections. Padji has simply spared my brother the unhappy task of discharging him. You see," she quickly explained, before the captain could wonder what horrendous crime the Indian had committed, "the rest of us had grown accustomed to Padji's hearty style of cooking. Unfortunately, Lady Cavencourt found it too robust for her delicate palate."

An expression of relief washed over the captain's lined face and a greedy gleam appeared in his eyes. "Hearty?" he repeated eagerly. "Robust?"

"Oh, yes," Amanda said. "Padji's style, I'm afraid, is a deal better suited to keeping a fighting army—or navy—in trim. Plain English food, enlivened with a dash of Indian spice."

From that point on, the captain was hers. Amanda had only to assure him she'd take charge of Padji when they reached British soil, and the matter was settled. The captain agreed to allow Padji to cook his way to England.

Padji expressed his gratitude in his usual fashion. He

dropped to his knees and kissed the hem of Amanda's frock. "Oh, generous mistress. Oh, kind and wise—"

"Get up," Amanda snapped. "Don't grovel. You disgust the captain."

Padji scrambled to his feet.

"Furthermore," Amanda went on, "while we are on board this ship, I am not your mistress. Captain Blayton is your master, and you will obey him absolutely, or he will flog you. He has been exceedingly kind to take you on, considering the difficulty you've caused him. You will cause no further problems, do you understand?" She could only hope Padji understood that poisoning crew or passengers must be considered a problem.

Padji nodded, all humility, then turned to the captain. "Oh, wise and generous master," he said, "how may I serve you?"

Amanda stood at the railing, watching Bengal dissolve into the distance, and with it seven years of her life. So had she watched England recede on the grey, late spring day she and her parents had fled financial ruin and humiliation.

Not that they'd been entirely ruined. Roderick had managed to salvage the manor house in Yorkshire at least, and it would be awaiting her. Humiliation, too, was perhaps an exaggeration. Mama was oblivious, as she was to virtually everything. Papa, who'd spent most of his life pretending all was well—regardless what facts loudly contradicted—had evidently come to believe it. At the time, Amanda had felt she alone was aware that her mother was hopelessly ill, her father had just lost a fortune, and she had lost her betrothed in consequence.

Though nothing at all was wrong, in Papa's view, India and Roderick were expected to set it all right. Papa had made his fortune there, and met his wife. He must have believed he could return to a happier past. He returned, and India killed first his wife, then him, in less than a year.

Though Amanda had mourned them, she could not say

she missed them. All the life before their passing seemed too much like a troubled dream. She had simply looked on, always outside, always helpless. When they'd gone at last, the sad dream had ended.

Amanda would miss the rani though, for she was solid and real, the product of a harsh Oriental reality. She'd embraced and welcomed Amanda into her world, where Amanda had found a friend, a sister, even a mother. Padji formed part of that welcoming world. No wonder that, after the first moment's stunned dismay, Amanda's heart had soared with relief. In a moment, the huge Indian had become her bulwark, and she no longer felt so alone and vulnerable.

Oh, certainly she had her companion and her maid, Bella. Both were fond of her, but they could never understand how afraid she was of England. She'd needed Padji, and he, needing her, had come. Perhaps it was Fate, as he claimed.

One could only hope the princess would forgive both her friend and her servant. Yet she must. She knew how difficult it was for mere mortals to manage Padji. The princess herself had said that once he got an idea into his head, no power on earth could get it out again.

He'd seemed uncharacteristically restless the whole time his mistress had related last night's story, and very unhappy when she'd given Amanda the Laughing Princess. Or had Amanda only imagined that? She was no longer certain what she imagined, what was part of the story and what was not. The goddess Anumati, the marauders, the vindictive husband, the false lover—layer upon layer the tale had unfolded, like the petals of a lotus. Even at the end, Amanda had felt there must be more.

The robbery brought more. It had seemed another piece, another unfolding petal, opening and drawing Amanda towards the dark centre of its heart . . . dark, like the passage last night, and dangerous.

She winced, recollecting the strong fingers relentlessly prying hers loose from the figure. Of course the thief must

34

be strong. The masculine form she'd watched through the palanquin shutters had seemed so slender next to Padji's bulk, yet the robber had felled the muscular servant with a single, well-aimed blow. When he'd fled before the pursuing bearers, the thief had moved with cat grace, leaping lightly into the shadows. Then, out of the shadows he'd leapt upon her, and she had felt his taut, merciless strength.

Why had he not knocked her unconscious as well? Surely that would have been simpler than wrestling with her for a piece of wood. Moreover, he would have ensured her silence . . . and oblivion.

Smoke and the scent of agarwood . . . rough muslin and the crushing trap of hard muscle . . . a long body pressed to her back . . . and the confusion, black and hot. Amanda shuddered at the recollection. Turning from the hypnotic sea, she found an intent, blue-eyed gaze upon her.

The man looked away to the ocean.

*In his hair gleamed the golden light of the sun and in his eyes the glistening sea.* Amanda smiled. The rani's description of her English lover would aptly describe a considerable portion of the British male population. In any case, this man's eyes were not the shifting, unreliable colour of the sea, but deep, deep blue. Even at a distance of several yards, Amanda had not mistaken that. He wore no hat, and the ocean breeze tumbled and tossed his thick, dark gold hair.

His profile ought to have been sculpted, she thought with critical appraisal: the high forehead and clear ridge of brow, the aquiline nose, the firm, well-shaped jaw. She sensed a slight movement then, and hastily withdrew her gaze.

He was undoubtedly handsome, but that was no excuse for staring at him as though she were a cobra intent upon her next meal. Furthermore, any man so splendidly attractive must surely be vain, accepting as his due the admiring gazes of scores of stunning women, which Amanda most assuredly was not. Not to mention it was silly at her age . . . Lud, she must be overtired.

Without sparing him another glance, Amanda made her way back to her cabin.

*Bloody hell.* Over a million square miles of subcontinent, vessels swarming up and down the coasts, and the curst Indian was aboard *this ship.*

Not until early afternoon, when the *Evelina* had sailed out into the Bay of Bengal, had word trickled down from crew to passengers about the cook's replacement. Not until very late in the day had Philip discovered who the new cook was.

Philip had, wisely, he'd thought, kept within the cabin until they'd sailed well beyond reach of Calcutta. He knew the rani's spies must be mingling among the crowds at the docks. He knew better than to let them catch a glimpse of him in daylight.

Escaping the cramped cabin at last, he'd come above for a preliminary scout of the deck. He'd scarcely taken in his surroundings when his gaze lit upon a turbaned giant, standing by the ship's bell. The massive brown being gravely listened to a mate, who explained the six four-hour watches and pointed out the inadvisability of tardiness in producing the daily ration of grog. The few words the giant spoke merely confirmed his identity. Philip never mistook a voice.

Luckily, he'd been staring at the Indian's broad back, and Padji hadn't seen him. Philip had slipped away to the stern to weigh his options. He considered stealing a lifeboat, but instantly discarded that notion. He couldn't leave Jessup behind, and he certainly couldn't take him along. They were trapped.

Philip glanced about him. The woman had left. She must be Miss Cavencourt. The Bullerhams and their staff had boarded shortly after he had, and he'd helped their servants with the trunks. That left three female passengers, and the one standing by the rail seemed far too young to be the widowed companion Randall had described. She was also, obviously, not a servant. Her dress would have told him so, even if Philip hadn't noted unmistakable signs of breeding in her profile and carriage.

He'd sensed something else, though, and he'd stared at her overlong, trying to determine what it was. Some nagging recollection. He swore again. If it nagged, it must be attended to, whatever it was. As if he hadn't enough to cope with already.

"My dear," said Mrs. Gales, "Bella is perfectly capable of seeing to your frocks. You'd do better to nap. This morning you looked as though you hadn't slept a wink, and our interview with the captain cannot have been restful. Padji was most thoughtless to oblige us to tell falsehoods. My conscience is most troubled." Troubled or no, Mrs. Gales continued steadily with her needlework.

Amanda was bent over her trunk. She'd been examining her frocks, trying to decide what she'd wear for her first dinner at the captain's table. The blue was more fashionable, but the rose was more becoming ... She flushed and pulled herself out of her fantasies. "You weren't the one told all the fibs, Leticia."

"I didn't contradict you, though, did I? And poor Captain Blayton. Such a dreadful morning he must have had." She sighed.

Amanda looked up. "He seemed happy enough about replacing his cook so speedily. Nor did he seem remotely displeased to be talking with you near a whole hour after," she added slyly.

"My dear, I do not find endless miles of ocean nearly so fascinating as you do. We shall see enough of it, I daresay, and there is no harm in allowing a harassed gentleman to unburden himself."

Older gentlemen did tend to confide in Mrs. Gales. She was well-rounded and comfortable in form, and equally comfortable in personality. Having no pretensions to beauty, the widow was neither vain nor flirtatious, but a sensible, well-bred, and tolerant female. Perhaps that was why so many mature men were drawn to her. One could not be amazed to learn the captain had, so soon after meeting her, commenced confiding his woes.

Amanda frowned at a crease in the bodice of the blue muslin. "I take it more than Padji harassed him, then?"

"I'm afraid so. Captain Blayton has apparently fallen victim of the whims of the aristocracy. He was obliged to leave Mr. Larchmere behind in order to take on an invalid solicitor and his valet. The Marquess of Hedgrave's solicitor," Mrs. Gales added significantly. "Naturally, a mere 'Honourable' must give way."

"How sick is this man?" Amanda asked. "He can't be seriously unwell if he undertakes a long sea voyage."

"But that is just the point, my dear, and no wonder the captain is so provoked. Mr. Wringle was carried on board and, according to Captain Blayton, looked even worse than the cook he hadn't dared move from Calcutta! Did you ever hear the like?"

The blue-eyed man was the valet, then. Miss Cavencourt's colour rose once more. She let the lid of the trunk fall shut. "It seems most inconsiderate to me," she said, ruthlessly squelching a flutter of disappointment. "This is hardly a hospital ship, and I daresay we'll all be tried enough with Mrs. Bullerham's digestion."

"Mrs. Bullerham's only problem is a revolting tendency to overeat," said Mrs. Gales with a sniff. "I expect she'll be running Padji ragged demanding special teas and broths, and complaining the whole time. When I heard the news, I was nearly as irritated as the captain. Though Mr. Larchmere is rather full of himself, he does relate the most charming anecdotes, and I had counted on him to relieve the tedium of our mealtimes at least. Not that the captain is tedious," she added, "but he is responsible for everything. One cannot expect him to carry the entire burden of entertainment. I do not blame him a whit for feeling as he does. I should feel put upon myself. Yet, as I told him, the Whitestones have always been high-handed. One might as well complain of the ocean being damp, you know."

Amanda sat back on her heels. "I beg your pardon," she said. "Did you say Whitestone? Whom do you mean?"

"Richard Whitestone, Marquess of Hedgrave, my dear," Mrs. Gales said patiently. "Very high-handed they all are. Or were, since he's the last of his branch of the family. His heir presumptive is a distant cousin, I believe. There is the marquess, half a world away, yet the commander of an East Indiaman must do his bidding, regardless who is inconvenienced. Not that one is surprised, when most of the East India Company dances to Lord Hedgrave's tune." She shook her head. "Really, Amanda, I must insist you lie down and rest. You are as white as a sheet."

"He's far too sick to undertake a voyage of any sort," the ship's surgeon said brusquely as he followed Philip out of the cabin. "Just as I told Mr. Groves last night. If it's fever, it's not like any I've ever seen." He paused. "Well, not since this morning, actually. Our cook showed similar symptoms."

For a moment, Philip felt ill himself. So that was how the murderous Indian had gotten on board the ship. But Jessup would not die, Philip told himself. He would *not*.

"The physician in Calcutta seemed to think my master risked greater danger in remaining," he said, in as placating tones as he could manage. "The climate had already weakened his constitution, and the doctor believed he'd not survive the monsoon season. Surely his case isn't hopeless, Mr. Lambeth. I was given to understand the present ailment resulted from ingesting tainted food."

The surgeon continued on towards the upper deck. "No surprise, that. Confounded Indian food," he muttered. "Spiced so hot you never know what you're eating." He scowled. "Blayton's a damned fool, hiring that Indian. Miss Cavencourt herself admitted her sister-in-law couldn't stomach the man's cooking."

The queasy feeling washed through Philip again. He blamed the rolling vessel.

"The Indian was employed by Miss Cavencourt's family?" he asked with no more than ordinary polite curiosity. "I wasn't aware of that."

"*Was.* Unreliable, like all of 'em. Not a native you could trust as far as you could throw him. A sneaking runaway, that one. Admitted it himself—boasted, even. Should have been flogged, to my way of thinking. But the lady stood up for him, and who's going to contradict Lord Cavencourt's sister?" Mr. Lambeth hesitated a moment, then added reluctantly, "Still and all, she don't seem a fool, and the Indian seems to worship the ground she walks on. Whatever he gave Saunders seemed to do the man some good. Maybe you can get him to mix up one of them messes for your master. Worst it can do is kill him, and he's not likely to last more than a week anyhow."

On this uplifting note, the surgeon took his leave.

*Cold-hearted swine.*

Philip returned to the cabin. Jessup lay upon his stomach, moaning faintly.

"Is it very bad, old man?" Philip asked softly.

"Unh."

"Are you thirsty? Can I give you some water?"

"Nunh."

"You have to take something. You've got to keep up your strength, soldier," Philip said with an attempt at heartiness.

Under the rusty brown stubble, Jessup's normally ruddy flesh lay flaccid and damp, a jaundiced green. The whites of the eyes he painfully opened had turned pale yellow, webbed with spidery red lines, and the brown irises were cloudy, unseeing. He mumbled something. Philip bent closer.

"Throw . . . me . . . over," came the gasping words.

Philip swallowed. "Can't," he said. "They'll keelhaul me. Just isn't done. You're going to have to hang on. But of course you will," he added encouragingly. "Fifty thousand pounds, and half that's yours, my lad. There it waits, safe and snug in the bottom of the trunk. You're not going to pass up twenty-five thousand quid, are you? We'll get you a pair of roly-poly tarts, one for each arm. And we'll dress you like a lord—shining boots from Hoby, one of Locke's hats, and Weston's best cut of suit. It's Weston now, you know, for the Beau's brought him into fashion . . ."

On through the long afternoon and into the twilight, Philip sat by his servant and talked until he was hoarse, because words were all he could offer. He must give the man reason to live, to hold on. If Jessup held on this night, if he managed to sleep a bit, perhaps he'd wake stronger tomorrow. Perhaps he'd swallow a bite then, and grow stronger yet.

If and if, perhaps and maybe. Philip Astonley had never felt so helpless since the day, fifteen years ago, he'd made his decision. Was this the end of it, of the dream that never quite came true, but never quite proved false, either? Trapped on a ship bound for England, his one friend in the world about to die, his worst enemy about to kill him? The Falcon had always known he'd be murdered one day. He was not afraid to die. He was simply curious: Would Padji snuff him out quickly, or would the giant take his time, to draw the thing out with supreme, unruffled Indian patience?

However the end came, it would be his own damned fault, Philip reflected disgustedly. Rage edged to the surface again. The rani . . . imbecilic Randall . . . the woman . . .

Jessup groaned. Banishing his growing fury, the Falcon focused mind and energy on keeping his servant alive.

# == 4 ==

MORNING CAME AT LAST, and Jessup finally fell into exhausted sleep. He was sinking, though. His colour had deteriorated to grey.

Philip recalled the surgeon's words: "Maybe you can get him to mix up one of those messes for your master." He'd have to hazard it. There was a chance the Indian would recognise him. On the other hand, Jessup at present had no chance at all.

After all, Philip—in the disguise of a plump, prosperous hookah merchant, complete with beard and thick padding—had merely passed Padji briefly in the hallway of the rani's palace. For the robbery, he'd shaved and foregone the padding. Thus Padji was unlikely to equate the merchant with the robber. Would he note a resemblance between Mr. Brentick, valet, and the thief, though? Perhaps not. Philip had, as usual, disguised his voice that night. The Falcon could mimic virtually any masculine voice he heard, and more than a few feminine ones. What Padji had heard was an excellent imitation of the Bhonsla Raja.

His decision made, Philip dressed quickly but carefully, discarding any garments that still bore traces of agarwood. The expensive incense was too distinctive. He would have to adjust his posture and stride. He'd imitate Monty Larchmere's stiff and graceless valet.

That left one's countenance, but it was too late for cosmetic adjustments. Virtually everyone on board had already seen him. In any case, Padji could not have seen the robber's face in the unlit passage. Even the rani— who was aware the merchant was the Falcon or the Falcon's accomplice— would recognise the eyes only. Padji hadn't her opportunity to study the ersatz merchant at close hand. Had they ever seen Jessup, though? Philip swore under his breath. Never mind. The Indian might make the connexion. He might not. Half a chance, then.

Philip headed for the upper deck and turned towards the forecastle, hoping to find the cook there. A confrontation in plain view of others was vastly preferable to a private one in the galley's hot confines.

Philip had scarcely taken five steps before something struck the back of his head. Instinctively, the Falcon's hand went for the knife under his coat, and he whirled round. His glance darted about, seeking his attacker . . . and lit on a woman. Miss Cavencourt. He drew his hand, empty, from the coat. She hurried towards him, her face flushed, and her coffee-coloured hair whipping in the stiff sea breeze.

Something tapped at his leg. He glanced down and saw a bonnet, which the wind knocked against his leg. He'd stepped on one of the ribbons. He snatched up the hat and held it out to her.

"I take it the missile is yours, miss?" he said, then cursed himself. Servants didn't make facetious remarks to their betters.

The colour rose higher in her cheeks. Dusky rose on mellow ivory.

"Yes. Thank you." Gingerly she took it.

"I'm afraid I accidentally trod on the ribbon," Philip said with great deference while his brain clawed and scratched, trying to place her voice. It wasn't enough. He needed another few words, and he'd already said more than he ought. Ladies didn't speak to strange gentlemen, and he wasn't even supposed to be a gentleman. Drat that idiot, Randall.

She'd turned away slightly to examine the bonnet. Now her gaze slid slowly up to meet his. Her eyes were very unusual, large and amber-coloured.

"Oh, it doesn't matter," she said. "I'm—I'm sorry it hit you. I'd taken it off, you see, because the wind was knocking it about, and then I forgot I had it . . . Oh, well. At least it didn't fly into the sea." She flashed a nervous smile. "Thank you." She turned and made quickly for the forecastle.

*No.*

Not possible.

Not the same woman.

But he was already following, calling out, "Miss? I say, Miss Cavencourt!"

She halted and turned around.

"I beg your pardon, miss, but you can't go there," Philip said, his brain working rapidly while he schooled his features to a proper servantlike blank.

Her surprise stiffened into chilly hauteur. "Indeed," she said coldly. "Are you a sentry?"

"No, miss, certainly not," he answered, his tones humbler still. "I only guessed you might not be aware the forecastle is no place for ladies."

Though her expression remained chilly, he discerned a shade of indecision in the glance she threw behind her.

"That's where the off-duty crew customarily take their leisure," Philip explained. "They may be about soon, and you'll find the company a bit rough, miss, especially without an escort. I rather think the commander would prefer you kept away, escort or no."

She stared at him as though he were foaming at the mouth.

"That is quite absurd," she said. "That is, I realise it was kindly meant, but I assure you I have nothing to fear."

Definitely the same woman. The same height, the same form, the same voice, with its husky overtones.

At that moment, Padji emerged from the galley. His gaze swept the deck and flitted past Philip without a glimmer of interest before lighting upon Miss Cavencourt.

She turned to Philip. "That man is my servant. As you see, I can have nothing to fear, on the forecastle, or anywhere upon this vessel." Again she began to walk away.

Crushing the wild urge to heave her arrogant person over the rail, he followed. Jessup first, he reminded himself. The woman could provide a less risky way to get what Jessup needed, if Philip could but control his temper.

"I beg your pardon, miss," he managed to choke out. "I meant no offence."

"None taken," she said dismissively, still walking.

"I didn't realise the cook was your servant," he said hurriedly, as the immense form loomed nearer. Philip kept his eyes downcast. "I was about to speak with him myself. You see, I need his help."

Miss Cavencourt paused.

Philip didn't grovel, precisely, but near enough, while he explained "Mr. Wringle's" condition and the surgeon's estimation of the invalid's prospects.

"Mr. Lambeth sounds monstrous disobliging," she said when he was done. "He should have spoken to Padji directly."

"I am in no position to make demands of anybody, miss. I regret to say we caused considerable inconvenience to several people, and I understand Mr. Groves handled the emergency less diplomatically than one could wish."

Imbecilely was more like it. Had Groves allotted Philip the role of master, he'd not be in this humiliating position. He'd have had them all running briskly at his beck and call. He'd learned that, if nothing else, from his overbearing sire. Small good it did him now. Leave it to Randall to behave like a blithering idiot at the first hint of difficulty.

*Aye, but you left it to Randall, didn't you?* nagged a sardonic voice in his head. *Had to dash off like an adolescent hothead, didn't you, wild for revenge?*

Miss Cavencourt's low, crisp tones broke through the red fury in his brain.

"I shall speak to Padji, of course," she said, "but it would be best if he examined your master himself."

"There's no need to put him to the trouble," Philip said smoothly, "though you're most kind to offer. I've told you exactly what the surgeon told me. I listened very carefully, you may be sure. My master does need to eat something and—and I can scarcely get him to swallow water."

He felt her studying gaze upon him then, even as he watched the Indian out of the corner of his eye.

"I see," she said, her tones less frosty. "You are very anxious, Mr.—Brentick, isn't it?"

"Yes, miss."

"I shall ask Padji to prepare something as quickly as possible, and he'll send for you when it's ready."

Except for the sentry, the forecastle was deserted. Nonetheless, Amanda took no chances. In Hindustani she repeated Mrs. Gales's revelations and voiced her own suspicions.

Padji shrugged. "What did the servant want of you?" he asked.

"Haven't you heard a word I've said? Mr. Wringle, who was hurried on board in the dead of night—the night I was robbed—works for the Marquess of Hedgrave, who happens to be *Richard Whitestone*."

"What did the servant want of you?"

"Gruel—broth—I don't know. Something for that wretched, thieving master of his. Did you poison him, too?"

"A healing broth. I see. I shall make it now." Oblivious to Amanda's look of outrage, Padji turned and descended into the galley. She followed.

The brick-lined space was as hot as Hades. Padji promptly began crushing herbs. Amanda perched on a cask and glared at him.

"You can't poison him, you know," she said. "I'm not saying I'd object if you did, but you can't. You'd be the first suspect, and you've nowhere to hide."

"Why should I poison this man? He has done me no ill."

46

"It's obvious what happened. The Falcon turned the statue over to Mr. Wringle, who hastened aboard the first ship bound for England."

Padji shrugged.

"There's no need to get inscrutable with me," Amanda said irritably. "You said yourself the Falcon stole my statue, and the more I've considered your explanation, the less sense it makes. He always steals for *someone else*."

"May you cut out my tongue for contradicting, mistress, but I know nothing of that. He's a thief."

"He's a professional—or one of a group of professionals—and you know as well as I that the services are hired out."

"I am but an ignorant servant, O adored one. I know nothing," Padji said imperturbably as he mixed the herbs into hot liquid.

This approach, obviously, would lead nowhere. Amanda considered. "I see," she said after a moment. "You know nothing, ask no questions, merely follow orders. Is that correct?"

"Such is my lowly ability, O daughter of the moon."

"Then who ordered you to poison the cook, you deceitful creature? I know you poisoned him, so you needn't waste breath denying it. I know, in fact, precisely the mixture you used. Did your mistress not tell me of her old family recipe? A fungus, is it not, which grows on—"

"It is unseemly for the mistress to speak of these matters," Padji cut in reprovingly. "They are the concern of the lowly slave."

"Is it seemly to tease and mock your mistress?" Amanda retorted. "Is it honourable to keep secrets from me, when I risked my honour,.and that of my family, to save you? Did I not tell monstrous falsehoods on your behalf?" She drew out her handkerchief and wiped her perspiring forehead. Then, recollecting her irritating sister-in-law's methods, she dabbed at her eyes. "This is my thanks for taking pity on you," she said in a choked voice.

"Aiyeeee," Padji wailed softly, pushing the bowl aside and gazing at her in anguish. "She is the true daughter of my mistress. With a word she stabs at my heart."

"Your own mistress would have cut out your heart by now, if you so vexed her," Amanda answered. "But you know I am soft-hearted and sentimental, and so you take advantage of my weakness and mock me."

Instantly, Padji dropped to his knees. "No, beloved, no mockery. It is not so. Ah, I am a man torn between two lionesses. 'Protect her from all danger,' my princess orders me, and so I do my lowly best. Yet her too-wise daughter sniffs trouble and wishes to throw herself into it. What is to be done with such women?"

Amanda withdrew the handkerchief from her eyes. Trouble, he'd said. Then she was right.

"For a start," she said briskly, "you might tell me the truth. The rani left something out of her story, did she not? The value of the statue, for instance. Why should the Falcon steal a piece of carved sandalwood? And *will* you get up?"

Heaving a great sigh, Padji rose. He would tell her, he said, and she would not believe him, but he was a man beset on all sides.

Miss Cavencourt expressing impatience with a brisk tapping of fingers upon the cask, Padji hurried on to offer what he called his humble theory. He was unaware of any great monetary value to the statue. Still, he knew someone wanted it. Offers had been made, thefts had been attempted. These were all quashed, of course, for Anumati's wishes must be consulted, and the goddess had not at that point named the heir.

"Never mind that," Amanda said, disregarding dreams and visions and settling to facts. "Who wanted it?"

"What other but the man she told you of?" Padji asked sadly. He shook his head. "Why will they not leave each other in peace? He abandoned her. I might have killed him and put an end to it, but she will not have an end to it. She puts a curse upon him and writes the curse down in a letter, that he will know who has done it. He took her heart, she writes in this letter, and so she takes in return the new life from his loins. He shall sire no sons, and his name will be forgotten, as he's forgotten her."

While this threw an interesting light on the rani's response to seduction and abandonment, it hardly answered the question.

"That was a suitable curse, I admit," Amanda said, "but what has it to do with the statue?"

"He has no sons, and his wife has been dead five years now. Perhaps he wishes to wed again," Padji answered.

Amanda stared at him. "Are you trying to tell me he wants the statue back because he thinks it will undo the princess's curse?"

Padji nodded. "Did she not tell him in her letter that he had left the thing of most value behind? Did she not say he would know nothing of true happiness until—" He stopped short, his brown eyes wary, his stance alert. "No more," he whispered. "These matters are not for others' ears."

His hearing must be prodigious acute. Hard as she listened, a long, tense moment passed before Amanda could hear the approaching footsteps over the noise of the crackling stove and the endlessly creaking timbers. A moment later, the ship's surgeon descended the steps into view.

As soon as he spied her, Mr. Lambeth's heavy features knit into a frown. "Galley's no place for ladies, Miss Cavencourt," he growled.

With slow dignity, she rose from the cask. "On errands of mercy," she answered coolly, "one regards the errand first, and the surroundings not at all." In a few crisp words, she informed him that she'd come to compensate for his neglect of the ailing solicitor. While she lectured, Amanda covered the bowl of broth and set it on a platter.

The surgeon's countenance darkened. "The man's done for," he answered defensively. "My time's better spent with those I can help."

"Indeed. Attending to Mrs. Bullerham's indigestion— a

permanent condition, as all of us who know her will attest—is of far greater importance than attempting to make a dying man's last hours endurable."

On this self-righteous note, Amanda took up bowl and platter and stalked out.

Not until she'd marched halfway across the deck did she recollect she was to have sent for the valet. Just as well, she told herself. She wanted a look at his master, didn't she?

The door opened immediately in response to her resolute knock, and the tall form of Mr. Brentick promptly blocked it.

"Miss Cavencourt," he gasped.

A mere fraction of a moment passed before he schooled his features to polite blankness, yet that was time enough. She spied the sorrow and anxiety in his countenance, and simultaneously recalled the edge of bleakness in his voice earlier, when he'd asked for help. He was genuinely distressed about his conniving employer. Amanda experienced an irrational twinge of guilt. She promptly smothered it.

"Padji had the broth ready while I was there," she said. "It seemed foolish to let it cool while someone came to fetch you, especially when I was returning this way. Or nearly this way," she amended with strict regard for accuracy. Her cabin was at the stern, well-lit, large, and luxurious. This, she saw as she peered past the tall, dark-coated figure, was a tiny, dark cell.

"That was very kind of you, miss." Mr. Brentick tried to take the broth from her, but she held fast and raised one autocratic eyebrow in perfect imitation of her brother. The valet retreated to let her pass.

"Oh, dear, the poor man," she said softly, involuntarily, as she approached the invalid. He looked ghastly. "No wonder you are so alarmed." She looked up to meet a stony blue gaze.

Amanda decided to disregard Mr. Brentick's facial expressions. "Can you prop him up a bit?" she asked. "If you will hold him, I can feed him."

The valet hesitated, his face stonier yet.

"It wants two people, Mr. Brentick," she said impatiently. "While you dawdle, the broth grows cold."

Under the stiff mask, he seemed to struggle with something, but it was a brief combat. Then, his piercing blue gaze fixed on her as though in challenge, he moved to the cot to do as she asked.

Before she'd left the cabin, Amanda had promised to send Bella on the same errand in two hours. Mr. Brentick had protested, citing the needless trouble to herself and her servant, and he had got an unpleasant glint in his eyes. Amanda had firmly ignored both words and look, and in the end, she'd won the skirmish.

She waited until Bella was gone before taking Mrs. Gales into her confidence. Then Amanda quickly outlined the rani's tale, her own suspicions, and the information Padji had so reluctantly offered.

Mrs. Gales listened composedly throughout, occasionally interjecting a calm question. When Amanda was done, the older woman shook her head.

"Five years in India may have disordered my reason," she said. "On the other hand, it has taught me to accept the possibility of such mad goings-on. Once one has seen a man—of his own free will—swinging from a hook, which has been inserted into the flesh of his back, one is prepared to see or hear *anything*."

"Then you do believe it's possible Lord Hedgrave hired the Falcon to steal my statue?" Amanda said with some relief. She had feared Mrs. Gales would think she'd taken leave of her senses.

"It's possible." Mrs. Gales took up her needlework once more. "I will not pretend to understand the Rani Simhi," she went on. "She is an Indian, and therefore incomprehensible. She most certainly ought not have told so lurid a tale to an unmarried young lady. On the other hand, at least she did not pretend to virtue, and one must respect her honesty. As to Lord Hedgrave, I'm obliged to admit I would not put it past him. My late husband had dealings with him, as did many of his colleagues. When the marquess wants something, he goes after it with all the inexorable force and disregard of obstacles of the Juggernaut. Whatever or whoever lies in his path is simply mowed down."

"Would he go to such lengths for a wooden statue?" Amanda asked. "That's what bothers me most of all. It hardly makes sense, does it?"

Mrs. Gales hesitated, her usually smooth brow knit. After a moment, she said, "In England, more than one gentleman has paid a large sum for the privilege of lying in Dr. John Graham's Celestial Bed. If they believe a bed will instantly correct their inability to beget offspring, why should not Lord Hedgrave believe in the efficacy of a wooden statue? I suppose a marquess might be as superstitious as the next man. When it comes to these matters, my dear, otherwise sane and sensible men can prove amazingly irrational." She smiled faintly. "What an extraordinary woman the rani is. Her letter must have acted on him over the years like slow poison. One ought not admire her, to be sure, yet it is so seldom a woman can achieve so effective a revenge for ruination. With words only. How very clever of her! Wicked, of course, but clever."

"I should say lucky, rather," said Amanda. "If he had produced an heir, her curse would have been a joke."

"I daresay she'd have found some other means of torturing him," Mrs. Gales answered dryly. "In any case, they are both quite wicked creatures, which makes it difficult to choose between them. Still, my sympathies naturally incline to my own sex, and it *is* your statue. I do not see why Lord Hedgrave should have it. The idea! To set a murderous Indian thief after a British subject—an innocent young lady, no less."

"If the theft *is* Lord Hedgrave's doing," Amanda reminded her. "We don't know that for certain, any more than we know Mr. Wringle's got my statue. But I mean to find out. I'll speak to Padji again, tomorrow." Her colour rose slightly and her folded hands tightened in her lap. "I expect we shall have to be underhand, but I see no alternative. Mr. Wringle comes with a deal of influence. Randall Groves himself, no less, escorted him on board, and all the Marquess of Hedgrave's power looms behind him."

Mrs. Gales looked up from her needlework. "You are quite determined to have it back, my dear? Are you sure?"

"Yes." Amanda met her gaze squarely. "I cannot explain, but the statue means a great deal to me."

"You needn't explain. As I said, I do not see why that arrogant man should have it, especially via such abhorrent methods. You ought be able to simply demand what is rightfully yours from this Mr. Wringle."

"He has only to deny it," Amanda said, "and if I demand a search—"

"Yes, my dear, we both know how the world works. Unfortunately, I also know how Lord Hedgrave works." Mrs. Gales paused, a shadow of concern crossing her countenance. "He can destroy you, Amanda. He can ruin Roderick. Even for a wooden statue."

"I know," Amanda answered quietly. "I intend to be careful."

# === 5 ===

THE PLUMP, DARK-EYED maid appeared five times a day with
the odd-smelling broth. Five times a day, Philip propped
Jessup up, while Miss Jones patiently spooned the liquid
into him. By the end of a week, Jessup seemed marginally
better. By the end of the second week, he'd definitely improved. During this time, Miss Cavencourt also supplied
plump pillows and fresh linens from her own stores.

Philip was none too happy to find himself under so great
an obligation to her. Still, he reminded himself, she had
saved Jessup's life.

Accordingly, Philip sought her out that afternoon to thank
her. He found her, as he'd expected, above, standing at the
rail and gazing out at the sea. She spent most of the day at
the rail, it seemed, sometimes with Mrs. Gales or Bella, but
most often alone. Time and again he'd come up for a five-
minute breath of air, and find Miss Cavencourt standing so.
An hour later, he'd be back for another hasty gulp, and
behold her there yet, apparently lost to all the world, her
gaze fixed upon the water.

At his polite greeting now, she started, and, as though
she had been someplace very far away, a long moment passed
before her golden eyes brightened with recognition.

Halfway through the proper little speech he'd prepared,
Philip became aware of a new scent mingling with the salt
air. Patchouli. But light, only a hint. It must be in the
shawl. Kashmir was often stored in patchouli, to ward off

insects. Nothing ominous about that, he thought, as he continued somewhat distractedly to describe Jessup's improved condition and express his gratitude.

"It's very pleasant to be applauded," she said when Philip finally ground to a halt, "but most of the credit goes to Padji. It's his secret receipt, you know."

"Indeed. We are most fortunate you brought him with you," Philip replied stiffly.

"You seem devoted to Mr. Wringle," she said, her gaze upon his left lapel. "Have you been long in his employ?"

Now it begins, he thought cynically. Still, expecting an examination sooner or later, he'd prepared his answers. As usual, he'd offer no more truth or falsehood than absolutely necessary.

"I have been acquainted with Mr. Wringle some time," he said, "but came into his employ only very recently, thanks to Mr. Groves." Mr. Groves the incompetent. Jessup a solicitor and Philip the valet, when it was supposed to be the other way about! But that wasn't all Randall's fault, was it? With Philip unavailable at the time, Jessup had to play the master. They'd hardly chuck Monty Larchmere out on account of a mere servant, regardless how desperate the case.

"Then your loyalty is all the more admirable." Her gaze swept upward, and he found himself gazing into golden light, where shadows flickered. "You've scarce left his bedside this fortnight."

"Naturally, one would wish to be at hand if the master needed anything."

"All the same, you will not wish to wear yourself out. You'll be no use to him if you sicken as well, and your pallor tells me you haven't enjoyed a decent night's sleep—or a proper meal—the whole time."

Until that moment, Philip had not felt the least unwell. Abruptly he became aware of his aching muscles, and with that awareness, weariness began to steal through him. It was as though he'd been an automaton these last two weeks.

Now she'd said the words, the mechanism proceeded to disintegrate.

"It can't be healthy for you to remain so long in that close space," she went on, ignoring the denial he murmured. "At least when Bella is there, you might leave with clear conscience, and take a stroll in the fresh air."

Fresh air. Damn her. But she couldn't know about *that*. She only wanted him out of the way.

"I appreciate your concern, miss, but I'm afraid the nursing still wants two people."

"Oh . . . yes . . . naturally. In any event, you are here now, aren't you? How silly to tell you to do what you're already doing. Sillier still to make you stand and endure a lecture, when I have just recommended exercise. Pray don't let me keep you." She turned back to the sea.

Philip hurried back to the cabin, certain one of Miss Cavencourt's minions was nosing about. That he found no minion, nor a single article disturbed, did not appease him. He crawled into his uncomfortable hammock and tried to nap. Too late. She'd killed sleep, hadn't she?

For Jessup's sake, Philip had clamped down his own feelings, locked and sealed them away. He hated the cabin. Monty Larchmere was as hard up as everyone suspected, or he'd never have settled for this miserable hole. The place was narrow and dark, and the air was stale at best, but mostly foul. Philip would have slept above on deck, if he dared. He didn't. He couldn't leave the cabin unguarded at night, even locked. What was a lock to the sly Indian, curse him. Curse her as well—Pandora, with those deceitful golden eyes. She'd uttered the words and the demon he'd locked away had sprung out to smother him.

It was early afternoon, but light scarcely reached this place. It was dark, rank, suffocating. Too familiar.

That was all a lifetime ago, he told himself as he forced his eyes closed. Another life, a child's, and he was a man. How many times in the last fifteen years had he hastened fearlessly towards certain death? He was no longer a weak, helpless little boy. He was not afraid . . . of anything.

All the same, he felt it steal over him in a slow, icy stream: Dread. Groundless, irrational, his adult mind insisted, even as it sank under the cold horror.

In minutes, Philip was out of the cabin, hurrying blindly through the passage. Then he was into the light at last, into the air, gulping it greedily until his mind rose out of the icy trap and his heart returned to its normal, steady beat. Damn her to hell.


Jessup's recovery continued at the same faltering pace, and the ensuing week was slow torture. Of course one must eat and rest and exercise. Philip was not a fool. Yet his appetite dwindled, suffocated, as his reason was, by the endless watching in the hot, tiny cell. The sight of food sickened him, and he grew bone-achingly weary, so that climbing to the upper deck this day was like scaling a thousand-foot cliff.

Catching sight of him, Miss Cavencourt marched across the deck and commenced another lecture. Philip stared at her, utterly unable to comprehend a syllable. Then something began to buzz very loudly in his ears, his muscles jerked crazily, and Miss Cavencourt and all the world were submerged in a heavy black blanket.


A child was screaming, sobbing, somewhere. A door, thick and heavy . . . and oppressive, stifling darkness. He couldn't breathe. His little hands burned, raw with pounding on the immovable barrier. "Please, I won't do it again, Papa. Please, Papa. I'm sorry."

Something cool and wet touched him then, and a gentle hand brushed his forehead. Philip's eyes opened to golden light shimmering amid the shadows. Autumn at Felkonwood, safe in the forest. The light fell warm, and the breeze blew sweet with . . . patchouli?

His mind shot back to the world and discovered a woman

bent over him. He tried to pull himself up.

"No, Mr. Brentick, not so quickly," Miss Cavencourt said softly. "You'll make yourself sick."

Nausea rose in a dizzying wave. He lay back again and took a long, steadying breath. "What happened?" he asked. His voice seemed to come from miles away.

"You collapsed," she said, "under the weight of my disapproval."

A disconcerting warmth overspread his face. Devil take it! He'd swooned at her feet—he, the Falcon—and now he must be blushing like a schoolboy.

A faint smile curved her full mouth, but her gaze softened to smoky amber. "You should have listened to me, Mr. Brentick. But that will be my only 'I told you so,' " she added, the smile fading, "so long as you follow my directions henceforth. Fortunately, there is no fever. You are simply overtired and weak from hunger. I want you to try to sleep. When Bella comes by later to feed your master, she'll bring you some broth as well. You must try to finish it. Even if you feel a bit queasy at first, it will do you a deal of good, I promise."

She rose, and only then did he realise he lay, not in the hammock above Jessup's cot, but on a narrow mattress on the floor. How the devil had she managed that? As she moved away, Philip glimpsed a large brown shoulder at the corner of the open doorway. Padji. So that was how.

Gad, how long had he lain unconscious? They might have ransacked the entire cabin by now.

Philip waited patiently until the pair had departed and their footsteps faded away. Then he sat up slowly, fighting the urge to vomit, and crawled onto his hands and knees. The trunk was still wedged against the wall, and his mattress had been pushed against it. He fumbled in his coat, found the key, and unlocked the trunk. His arms seemed to be made of blancmange. He needed three attempts to get the lid up.

A few endless, stomach-churning minutes later, he sank

back onto the mattress. They'd touched nothing. The tiny telltale feather lay exactly as he'd placed it, upon the small rug in which the Laughing Princess still nestled. He'd made certain all was as it should be before replacing all as it had been.

What the devil was she about? A golden opportunity, and she and the Indian had ignored it. Why did she bother with him, with Jessup? Why hadn't she let Jessup die? That would be one obstacle out of the way. And today—an ideal opportunity for Padji to eliminate Philip himself. Easy enough to render a swoon fatal, with the mistress by to create any needed distraction. Why had nothing happened? Was it possible she didn't know, after all? Or was she more cunning than he imagined?

He couldn't think any more. Not now. Later. His head fell back upon the pillow, and in minutes he was asleep.


"It's in the trunk," Amanda said. With trembling hands she brought the tumbler of wine to her lips and sipped. She and Mrs. Gales sat on the cushioned banquette under the row of windows.

Mrs. Gales's needle was not so steady as usual. "You promised to be careful," she said. "That was foolhardy, Amanda. Suppose he or Mr. Wringle had wakened?"

"Padji saw to that. I don't know what he used. At any rate, I had the cloth over Mr. Brentick's eyes, and Padji was very quick. He'd got the keys when he was carrying Mr. Brentick to the cabin. Then we had all the bustle of carrying in the mattress. I made sure to ask whether there were clean linens. If either had awakened, that would have been our excuse for rummaging." Amanda swallowed a bit more wine before adding, "Padji was in and out of the trunk in about a minute. I'd hardly turned my head before he was done."

"Indeed. Practice makes perfect, I suppose," Mrs. Gales said dryly. "Still, *your* aptitude in the matter is a surprise. Your presence of mind seems nothing short of miraculous."

"Hardly. If Padji hadn't been nearby, it would never have occurred to me to take advantage of the situation. When Mr. Brentick fainted, I nearly did, too, I was so . . . taken aback."

Frightened, half to death. Every day she'd watched his brief ventures above, and her heart had gone out to him, so sick and miserable he seemed.

At first she'd told herself this was just as he deserved for associating with a low criminal like Mr. Wringle. But Reason had promptly pointed out it was fully possible the valet had no idea what his employer had been up to. Why should Wringle tell his servant? If he had, why should the valet risk his own health to care for such a man? Just suppose Mr. Brentick were of the same dishonest ilk. Wouldn't he do far better to let his master die, and collect the reward himself? There must be a reward—a considerable one—to drive Wringle from Calcutta in his condition.

The more she'd reflected, the more evidence Amanda found to make the valet an innocent bystander. And today . . .

How she wished she'd not remained in the cabin to nurse him. She should have summoned Bella. As yet, the maid knew nothing about the statue, except that it had been stolen in Calcutta. *Her* conscience would not have shrieked while she listened to Mr. Brentick's delirious mutterings. The poor man had cried out to his papa.

Some childhood terror must have seized him. Amanda could understand that. She had her own nightmares. Everyone did. Yet her heart had ached at the pitiful pleas, and again later, when his eyes had opened. Horror lingered in those deep blue depths, and in the fleeting moment before he came fully awake, they'd seemed the innocent, terrified eyes of a little boy. She had wanted . . . really, how stupid. He was a grown man, and ill. He'd simply had a nightmare, or a hallucination brought on by exhaustion—or by whatever Padji had used on him.

Mrs. Gales was saying something, and looking at her rather strangely.

"I beg your pardon," Amanda said. "I fear my mind wandered."

"I asked why you didn't take the statue when you had the opportunity."

Amanda thrust the valet's image aside. "Far too risky," she answered. "Padji, Bella, and I are the only outsiders who've entered that cabin, which would make us prime suspects. The instant the theft was discovered, the commander would have to comb every square inch of the vessel. Eventually they'd find the statue, and then it would be only my word against Mr. Wringle's that the Laughing Princess is rightfully mine."

The widow sighed. "I see. The captain would probably leave the matter to be settled in England, and—"

"And the Juggernaut—Hedgrave—would crush me." Amanda swallowed the last of her wine. "The task, you see, wants subtlety, cunning, and patience, at the very least. It wants the Falcon, actually, but as we haven't got *him*, we shall have to make do with Padji."

"Beg pardon for mentionin' it, guv, but a body'd think you was turnin' into a fusspot is what," said Jessup as he hauled himself up to a sitting position. "Ain't the damned thing hid good enough? Don't I have this here pistol under the pillow? Don't I keep a sharp lookout the whole time the gal's here? Not to mention which, they do say two's company, if you take my meaning."

"You're in no condition to dally with ladies' maids," Philip said. "And do I have to remind you the abigail belongs to the woman I robbed?"

He'd already had an unsatisfactory discussion the day before with Bella, who'd taken umbrage at his offer to relieve her. Two months they'd been at sea, and Jessup, though still weak, was sufficiently alert to take note of his surroundings. That was the trouble. He'd taken note of the plump Bella—and she of him, evidently, for the two were at present behaving like a pair of moonstruck adolescents.

All by himself, Jessup had contrived an explanation for his lowly speech and coarse manner, because, he said, he was tired of giving one-word answers. He had only to "confess" that Mr. Groves had exaggerated his position—he was merely a solicitor's clerk. Bella would pass along the revelation. Thus, when Jessup at last became well enough to venture among the others, no one would expect anything but the common sort of fellow he was. Meanwhile, he wanted more privacy.

"I ain't like to forget when you call it to my attention every other word," Jessup answered grumpily. "Like I ain't been through half a hundred battles with you, not to mention we been through a deal worse since we left off soldierin' for thievin'. Leastways in a battle, a fellow gets his leg shot off or his arm, or something clean-like. He don't get poisoned and drove all the way to Bedlam and back with no hope of dyin' and bein' done with it."

When all else failed, Jessup was not above applying guilt. He was entitled, considering his master was to blame for his condition. The poison had so weakened Jessup's constitution that many months would pass before he was his sturdy old self again. Now his employer wished to deny him the comfort of a woman: a plump, amiable maid with gentle hands and a soft, soothing voice.

In Jessup's place, Philip would have wanted the same. Besides, this was a man of five and thirty summers, not a callow youth. While perhaps unequal to the rani's fiendish tricks, Jessup was nonetheless up to every other sort of rig. He knew the wooden statue's value. He'd not risk his share of the reward for a tumble with any female.

"I suppose I am behaving like a fussy nursemaid," said Philip ruefully, as he commenced pacing the tiny cabin space.

"Worse," his servant answered tactlessly. "I never seen such a case of fidgets in my life. Whyn't you go run about the deck and leave me in peace?"

"I do not fidget," Philip snapped. "And I have been 'running about the deck' as you say, the whole curst afternoon. There is not one thing for me to do, and not one person to talk to except sailors, and they'd prefer spending their leisure jabbering at each other in their incomprehensible argot. Why can't they say 'right' and 'left' like normal people? What's wrong with front and back, forwards and rear? Do you know how many sails are on this ship? A least a thousand, and each with a different name, I expect," he concluded in exasperation.

"Is she pretty?" Jessup asked.

"What?" Philip whipped round so quickly that the top of his head grazed a beam. "What the devil are you talking about?"

"Miss Cavencourt. Is she pretty?"

"Are your wits wandering again? What has that to say to anything?"

"Just askin', guv. No need to get your innards in an uproar. I was too sick to notice when she was here, and I ain't seen her since I been better. Just wonderin' if she's plump like her maid."

"She is not plump at all, so you needn't drool over both of them."

"Aye, one of them scrawny ones, I expect. A spinster, I think you said she was?"

"I did not at any time say she was a skinny old maid. Not that it's any of your concern."

"We got her statue, so she's some worry, ain't she?"

"It was hers for less than an hour. It was Her Royal Hellcat's for a curst eternity. Or, to be more accurate, it was in her possession. We both know Madam Fiend stole it from Hedgrave."

"That's so, but Miss Cavencourt don't seem the same kind, do she? From what I hear, she was worritin' over you like a mother hen."

"Certainly. The lady of the manor always looks after the ailing peasants," Philip answered irritably.

The servant rubbed his eyes. "Well, I don't blame you

for feelin' the way you do. Bound to stick in your craw, it is, havin' to bow and scrape and be ordered this way 'n' that. Still, it's in the way of business, and you won't hurry this ship any faster, for all your fussin' and fidgetin'." Jessup sank back into the pillows. "I never seen you so jumpy, like a cat in a tub o' water. Wears me out, just watchin' you."

"What sticks in my craw," Philip gritted out, "is being trapped on a ship with a carved figure worth fifty thousand pounds, an Indian as like to murder us in our sleep as not, and the woman, supposedly his employer, I robbed. Think, man. She's breached the security of this cabin. You're infatuated with her fat maid. Do you wonder that I'm *jumpy*?"

"No, I don't wonder, guv," was the weary reply. "I just wish you'd go be jumpy somewheres else."

# === 6 ===

HE WAS NOT avoiding her, Amanda told herself as she dragged her gaze from the tall, golden-haired figure prowling the deck. Mr. Brentick was a servant, and he knew his place. Her only excuse for talking with him was to enquire after his master, which added up to no excuse, since he must know Bella would report to her.

Certainly Amanda had no need to lure the valet from his cabin and occupy him in conversation while Bella did her own part. The abigail had at last been taken into confidence. Once she understood what Amanda required of her, Bella had made short work of the valet.

All the same, one could not help feeling uneasy about him, or sorry for him, perhaps. So restless he was, roaming the vessel like a caged cat in the Royal Menagerie. He did remind her of a cat. At first he'd seemed so stiff and formal, even awkward. But that was only on the rare occasions they spoke.

When he wandered, as he did now, it was with the lithe grace of a tiger. He even seemed to exude the same aura of power . . . or danger. Amanda was not sure what it was, exactly, only that now and again it seemed to lurk in his eyes as well, and it fascinated her, even as she instinctively shrank from it. Well, really, what had that to do with feeling sorry for him?

Amanda fixed her gaze firmly on the choppy sea. More than three months had passed since they'd left Calcutta. If the weather held, they'd reach Capetown in another week or so, according to the commander. Then, in as little as a month—though more likely longer—they'd reach England. East Indiamen had been known to sail all the way from China to the Thames in a bit over three months, but that was rare. One storm could drive a vessel far off course, or damage it severely enough to require months of repairs at the nearest port. Furthermore, the *Evelina* had been becalmed twice and could be again. She must not think about time, Amanda chided herself.

The wind seemed to grow stronger as morning gave way to grey afternoon. Certainly Mrs. Bullerham's usual complaints had increased significantly in volume. Two servants had hauled the obese harridan up, as they did nearly every day. She had, as usual, found fault with them throughout the process. Now, outraged with the ship's rocking, she was venting her displeasure upon her spineless spouse.

Amanda moved some distance aft, where she wouldn't be able to hear them—or at least not so clearly. The clouds thickened and the vessel rose and fell on the choppy sea. Ten minutes later, Mrs. Bullerham's booming tones rose suddenly, audible even over the wind and the moan of the timbers. Blast the woman! Why the devil didn't she go below if a hint of rough weather so overset her?

Amanda glanced back and drew a sigh of relief. The Bullerhams were preparing to descend. Amanda strolled back to her preferred spot and, gazing idly about, saw Mr. Brentick scowling after the clumsy parade. Abruptly, he looked towards Amanda, meeting her curious gaze before she thought to withdraw it. He bowed—no, it was more like a nod—and equally unthinkingly, she smiled. He hesitated a moment, then, to her surprise, crossed the deck to her.

"Does the smoke sicken *you*, Miss Cavencourt?" he asked.

"The smoke?"

"From the galley. The cooking odour and smoke, Mrs. Bullerham declares, is intolerable."

"Mrs. Bullerham's toleration is of exceedingly limited quantity," Amanda said.

"I wish I'd been warned. I had the temerity to suggest she move farther aft, away from the smoke."

"Did you? I hope you didn't suggest how far aft. In the vessel's wake, for instance."

"Swimming is reputed a healthful exercise," he said blandly.

"Indeed. I wonder no one's recommended it to her ere now."

"Evidently, no one recommends anything to Mrs. Bullerham, as my still-tingling ears will attest."

Amanda glanced up. His face was devoid of expression, except for those unreasonably blue eyes. The glint she discerned there was not entirely humour. Mrs. Bullerham must have been exceptionally vindictive today.

"Oh, dear," she said. "She gave you a nasty dressing down, didn't she? I hope you will not regard her. Discontent has poisoned her mind long since, and the boredom of the voyage makes her even more beastly, though it hardly seems possible."

"I fear there was too much truth in what she said to be disregarded. She wondered I had nothing better to do than idle about the livelong day, and no better sense of propriety than to accost my superiors with my unsolicited opinions." He paused, his face stiffening. "As I seem to have accosted you, Miss Cavencourt. I do beg your pardon."

"You needn't," she answered, instantly wishing Mrs. Bullerham at the bottom of the sea. "Whenever she provokes me, I stomp off to vent my feelings to Mrs. Gales or Bella. Otherwise, I should probably throttle her. Rage all you like, Mr. Brentick. You'll feel better after."

His blue gaze swept her countenance in a swift, cool assessment that left her unaccountably flustered.

"Thank you, miss," he answered quietly. "Your indignation on my account is sufficient. Mrs. Bullerham would say 'excessive,' in that it has led you to tolerate an impropriety."

67

Amanda flushed. She'd considered only his injured feelings, not their relative stations. Now she wished she'd left him to stew.

"Mrs. Bullerham would likely add that my grasp of etiquette leaves a great deal to be desired, and I wouldn't know an impropriety if it bit me on the nose," she answered tartly. "Though I don't see why it is ill-bred to commiserate with another human being. I wasn't inviting you to—to flirt with me, Mr. Brentick, merely to relieve yourself of the string of oaths burning your tongue." She could have bit off her own tongue then, but it was too late to recall the infelicitous words. Mortified, she turned back to the sea.

"I beg your pardon, miss," he said after a long, tense moment. "Naturally, the thought of flirting never crossed my mind."

She understood the words well enough. It was his tone that puzzled her. Was he laughing at her, a plain, aging spinster who talked of flirting?

"Actually, I wish you hadn't mentioned it," he went on. "It's rather like opening Pandora's box, isn't it?"

She threw him a scathing glance. "I was not trying to put ideas into your head. My temper got the better of my reason, perhaps, or I should have chosen less absurd phrasing."

"It's too late," he answered hollowly. "The damage is done. I can't think of a single remark that would not be construed as flirtatious."

Incredulous, she turned around full to stare at him. She'd always found him painfully handsome, but now, with that amused gleam in his eyes, he was . . . devastating. Gad, what had she done? Was it the ship rocking so hard, or her heart? She drew a steadying breath.

"Well. Then. At least I have taken your mind off Mrs. Bullerham," she said.

"Entirely."

"She's bored, you know, and when some people are bored, they become ill-tempered—in her case, more ill-tempered than usual. Bella, on the other hand, becomes a fiend for work," she went on, nervous under his unwinking cobalt stare. "She will clean the cabin a dozen times a day. Mrs. Gales merely switches from knitting to crochet or embroidery."

"And you, miss? What do you do when you're bored?"

She dropped her gaze to his lapel. "I'm never bored," she said.

"I envy you. I am—*was* bored out of my wits. Apparently, it makes me . . . impertinent. I have nothing to clean, because Miss Jones won't let me. She cleans our cabin as well. I have never learned needlework of any kind and—*ahem!*"

Her head shot up. "I beg your pardon?"

His countenance remained blank. "The rest was flirtatious, Miss Cavencourt. I suppressed it."

"Oh. Are you an accomplished flirt?" she icily enquired.

"Yes, I regret to say."

"I wonder you regret acquiring such a skill. To me it has always seemed a most difficult art to master."

"In that case, I applaud your *instincts.*"

Heat washed over her face once more.

"That blush, for instance," he remarked soberly, "could be fatal to a faint-hearted man."

She quickly recovered. "Pray do not put fainting into your head, Mr. Brentick. You seem overly susceptible to every stray remark, and I know you are inclined to swoon on occasion."

"Touché, miss. Very well aimed, that one."

"I was not *practising,*" she said, exasperated. "You needn't congratulate me, as though I were an apt pupil. Don't you know a setdown when you hear one?"

"Yes," he said. "Fortunately, I am a stoic."

Not a wisp of a smile, only that provoking glint in his blue eyes. She ought to box his ears. She ought to, at the very least, put him firmly in his place. Yet she felt he was daring her, goading her to do so, and she refused to be manipulated. Her own eyes opened wide and innocent. "Are you indeed, Mr. Brentick? I wish you had mentioned that earlier. I might have spared my sympathy for a more needy object."

For more than a week after that exchange, Philip kept a decorous distance from Miss Cavencourt. He felt certain he hadn't misjudged. The beckoning smile he'd responded to was of a kind familiar to him. He knew what she wanted: to win him over, allay his suspicions, distract him with a bit of flirtation. He was quite willing to play. He'd played the game too often to fear distraction. His senses might respond to an alluring countenance and a slim, shapely figure. Why not, after so many months without feminine companionship? Nevertheless, his mind would remain alert, as always.

No, he'd not misjudged, precisely, merely overstepped a shade too far, moved a bit too quickly for her. Very well. He could wait. Plenty of time.

So he reminded himself as he stood at the rail, his gaze fixed on Capetown. They'd drop anchor soon, and all the port's diversions would offer themselves to his needy senses: fresh meat, vegetables and fruit, drinkable wine, and women—scores of lively, accommodating tarts.

About damned time, too. These last few days had passed with intolerable slowness, each more provokingly tedious than the one preceding. Hardly surprising, in the circumstances. Now he'd no need to worry about Jessup, Philip's restless mind found no other important matter to occupy it. Thus that mind had taken hold of minor matters. Such as how long he'd been without a woman.

Capetown neared, and the deck swarmed with fleet-footed seamen, while the air rang with a babel of commands. Philip smiled. These hardened sailors were as impatient as he for dry land and all its pleasures.

In a tremendous hurry to get his enormous cargo home, Captain Blayton had refused to linger long at any port. Here, however, he'd remain two days at least, replenishing supplies while his passengers tasted the delights of Capetown's brand of civilisation.

Delight, indeed, Philip thought happily. A proper bath and proper food . . . and improper women . . . at last. As he surveyed the deck's activity, his glance fell upon the fore-castle. There Padji stood, gazing about as well, his round, brown countenance sublimely indifferent.

At that moment, the door to pleasure and freedom swung shut with a deafening clang. Philip closed his eyes and uttered a low stream of oaths. How could he have been so stupid?

How the deuce could he think of leaving the *Evelina*? What better opportunity for the Indian but then? Padji might make off with the statue and easily lose himself in the crowds. The Indian might find it difficult, but certainly not impossible, to make his way back to Calcutta, devil take him.

Seething, Philip watched the passengers and most of the crew disembark, then stomped back to his cabin.

"You ain't goin' ashore?" Jessup asked, astonished.

In a few curt sentences, Philip outlined his concerns.

Jessup was affronted. "*I'm* here, ain't I?" he demanded. "You think I'd let that scurvy Indian get anywheres near it?"

"I think," Philip said tightly, "that scurvy Indian would have the pillow over your face and the breath crushed out of you before you could lay one finger on your pistol. We don't have a prayer unless we're both here—you exactly where you are, and my humble self at the door."

Thus they spent three interminable days and nights while their fellow passengers ate, drank, shopped, and toured by day, and ate, drank, and danced by night. That Padji never came within a mile of their cabin the whole time was a circumstance nicely calculated to drive Philip into a mur-derous rage.

On the fourth day, the vessel once again set sail.

"Should've gone ashore like I told you, guv, and got a

woman," Jessup said, shaking his head. "Won't be no livin' with you now."

"Go to blazes," Philip snarled. He stalked out, slamming the cabin door behind him.

As he emerged into the sun, the first person his eyes lit upon was Miss Cavencourt. She stood at her usual place at the rail, leaning on her elbows and gazing at the sea. She'd given up her bonnets weeks ago, and the wind tossed and tangled her coffee-coloured hair and whipped it against her cheeks. Philip glared at her.

The temptation to heave her over the rail was well-nigh irresistible. Unfortunately, at the same instant this prospect beckoned, the mischievous wind began gusting about her, driving her skirts up to reveal, for one devastating moment, a pair of elegantly turned ankles and slim, shapely calves. Philip's gaze slid up to her narrow waist and on to the agreeably proportioned curves above. At that moment, the urge to mayhem gave way to one equally primitive, though less homicidal.

His glance swiftly took in his surroundings. He spied Mrs. Gales at the stern, talking with the captain. Philip's face smoothed, his narrowed eyes gentled, and his muscles relaxed. With the unconscious grace of a stalking cat, he closed in upon his prey.

Miss Cavencourt may have sensed his approach, for she turned while he was yet some distance away. She didn't smile this time. When he neared, she responded warily to his greeting.

"I hope you enjoyed your visit ashore, miss," he said obsequiously.

"It was interesting," she said. "Yet I rather wish I hadn't gone. I scarcely got used to walking on solid land before I was back on the ship. Now I must grow used to that again."

"By tomorrow you'll have forgotten what solid land is like. It's amazing how swiftly the human bod—being adapts." *Ob, nice slip there. Try thinking with your brain, Astonley.*

"I collect you decided to spare yourself that exercise,

72

Mr. Brentick. Bella tells me you elected to remain with your master. Your devotion is commendable."

"I perceived no alternative at the time," he answered. "In any case, we got along well enough by day. At night, though, when he was asleep and I came above, I felt as though I walked a ghost ship. It was so quiet—a mere handful of seamen aboard. Just the creaking timbers and the waves plashing against the hull."

"How peaceful it sounds," she said softly. Her eyes, focused somewhere past him, softened, too, from sunlit gold to smoky amber. "I rather envy you."

"I thought you enjoyed Capetown, miss."

"I found it interesting. I'm not partial to—to crowds and social gaieties. I am rather a recluse, I'm afraid."

The teasing breeze lifted her scent to his nostrils, only to sweep it away again in the next instant.

Instinctively, he moved a step closer. "Then had you been in my place, you'd not have wished for company, as I did."

The shadowy amber glance flickered to his face. "Solitude and loneliness are not the same thing," she said.

"Perhaps not. Perhaps I was just bored. I think there was one mad moment when I actually yearned for a dressing down from Mrs. Bullerham," he said ruefully.

She smiled then, disarmed. Finally. "You make yourself sound desperate, Mr. Brentick, yet I cannot believe you could sink to so pathetic a state."

"No. What I actually wished was far more audacious. I wished I had not trespassed on your kind nature." He dropped his voice. "Among other regrets."

She turned away and fixed her gaze on the sea. "Is that an apology?"

"Yes."

"Oh."

He saw her hand tighten on the rail. Small and slim it was, its mellow ivory deepened to burnished gold by weeks in the sun. He wanted to touch its softness. His own fingers curled frustratedly into his palm. What the devil did he think he could accomplish in a few minutes? He had a rift to mend, and that wanted a clear head. Very well. He'd already made better progress than expected. After all, she could have chosen not to understand.

"Am I pardoned?" he asked.

"That depends on what you're apologising for."

"For having the effrontery to flirt with you, Miss Cavencourt, and insult your intelligence by pretending I wasn't," he answered boldly.

To his surprise, she didn't colour up.

"Gad, so that's what it was," she said wonderingly. "Mrs. Bullerham overset you more than I thought that day—or you are, truly, bored out of your wits." She turned an amused countenance to him. "They say the insane have flights of genius, though, and I must say your performance—well, you are very subtle, or I am very thickheaded. But you must not do it again."

"Oh, I know I mustn't," he said.

"Of course not. You would be casting your pearls before swine."

"Miss Cavencourt, I must beg leave to protest that choice of phrase, figure of speech or no."

"Mr. Brentick, you are all that is gallant, but if you do not dismiss yourself on the instant, I shall choke myself laughing." She bit her twitching lip and turned away again. What, he asked himself crossly, was so hilarious


"But, my dear, he admitted he tried to flirt with you," Mrs. Gales said as she knotted a silk thread. "You cannot wish to encourage him."

"I'm certain I discouraged *that*," Amanda said, smiling at the memory of his bemused face. "My experience of men is limited, I admit, but I'm sure they don't care to be laughed at. Yet it seemed so funny, or perhaps I was relieved. I'd thought he'd been mocking me that day. Now I realise he was—or is—quite desperate. His days must seem to him like solitary confinement. His sole company is a cross, recuperating invalid—whom Bella has monopolised."

"You feel *sorry* for the valet?"

Amanda recalled the terrified muttering she'd heard one day, and the nightmare lingering in deep blue eyes. Yes, that made her feel sorry for him, but it was the restlessness, too. His inability to be at peace with himself made solitude—which she welcomed—lonely and dreary for him. She pitied as well his intolerable boredom, which drove him to flirt with an ape leader like Amanda Cavencourt.

There was more, and that she could voice. "I think he's overbred and overeducated for his station in life," she said slowly.

"I think he is far too handsome." Mrs. Gales deftly guided her needle through the linen. "I expect he wreaks havoc with the maids, wherever he goes."

Amanda grinned. "More than the maids, I'll wager. I guessed today he's a rake of sorts. That seemed funny, too—a rakish valet, a self-proclaimed accomplished flirt, in such desperate case as to practise his skills on *me*. I shouldn't be surprised to learn he'd thrown one of those luring looks at Mrs. Bullerham, and that was what hurtled her up into the boughs."

Mrs. Gales's steady hand arrested midstitch. "What sort of look was that, my dear?" she asked mildly.

Amanda was staring into some distance beyond the cabin walls. "I once saw a painting of Krishna as a young man. He stood, surrounded by women, in a stream. He had his arms about two of them, and gazed at one in just that way. Intently." She shrugged, and her tones lightened again. "In any case, Krishna was quite the rake, was he not? The look must be commonplace enough, if the painter knew precisely how to convey it."

"A great deal too common, if you ask my opinion. If you catch the fellow gazing at you in such a way again, Amanda, you are well advised to box his ears."

"For a *look*?" Amanda laughed. "I daresay the poor man

can't help it. For a flirt, it must be an uncontrollable habit, rather like a nervous tic."

"Amanda," said Mrs. Gales, "overeducated, overbred, he remains a servant. Pray recollect as well, he is also a *man*. I shall say no more."

# === 7 ===

THOUGH SHE UNDERSTOOD well enough what the widow left unsaid, Amanda's common sense told her the warning was ludicrous. Long ago she'd learned she was not the sort of woman men wanted. All her one beau had desired was Papa's wealth. Thus, the following day, when the valet paused in his perambulations to greet her, Amanda saw no harm in leading him into conversation.

She soon learned he'd been a soldier, and had spent most of his service in Central India. He treated her to a few military anecdotes, and she found him both witty and surprisingly knowledgeable regarding Indian ways.

When he joined her at the rail the day after, the discussion continued where it had left off. Every day thereafter they met at the same place, at the same time, and talked. By the end of a week, their half-hour conversations had stretched into an hour, and even that time began to seem far too short.

Mr. Brentick was clever and very amusing, yet she'd met scores of clever, amusing men. The difference was that he appeared to find her so, too. When she lapsed into Hindu philosophy, one of her pet topics, he seemed fascinated. He asked intelligent, perceptive questions, and never hesitated to debate if he questioned her opinion. Amanda was accustomed to blank stares or, worse, condescending indulgence of her unwomanly and most un-British interests.

She found Mr. Brentick not simply superior to the common run of manservant, but a superior, rare species of man. Most important, she felt she'd found a friend. At the end of a fortnight, she felt as though they'd been friends all their lives

Amanda was on her way to the upper deck when the door to the Bullerhams' cabin opened, and Mrs. Bullerham, leaning heavily upon her cane, lumbered through. Her mind elsewhere, Amanda didn't notice the massive figure emerging until she was upon her. Then she stopped short, missing a collision by mere inches.

"This isn't a race course," Mrs. Bullerham announced in booming tones, "though one should not be required to remind you that ladies do not run. Did your mama not tell you it was unseemly?" Moving farther into the passage and thus blocking it, she boomed on, "But I forget. Your mama was ill-equipped to oversee your education."

Amanda's face set and her heart began to pump with hurt and rage, but she said not a word, only waited for the detestable woman to move out of the way.

"I am, of course, aware of your awkward situation," the heavy voice went on. "You are not entirely to blame for your ignorance. I'd hoped Mrs. Gales would drop a word in your ear, but she, evidently, is preoccupied with the captain. I have held my own tongue out of pity. But it will *not* do."

"I have often found that holding one's tongue does well enough," Amanda answered tightly.

"You are pert, miss, as I have remarked before."

"Then I wonder you wish to speak with me at all."

"Duty calls louder than personal feelings. As it should in your case," Mrs. Bullerham rumbled. "Your brother is a peer as well as a justice. Whatever your mother was, noble blood runs in your veins. Even if you are without self-respect, you ought consider your family."

"I would appreciate it, ma'am," said Amanda, "if you would step aside and permit me to proceed."

"So that you may hasten to your rendezvous? Are you

afraid the cit's valet will make off with your maid if you dally?" came the taunting reply. "Have you no pride?"

"Too much, ma'am, to respond to ignorance." Amanda turned away.

A fat hand clamped upon her arm. "Don't be a fool, girl. You're no beauty, but you can't be so desperate. Certainly you don't wish others to speculate that you are so starved for masculine attentions you must stoop to dallying with servants. You will become a laughingstock."

Amanda reached up and pried the fat fingers loose, then jerked her arm away. "I trust you are finished."

"I'm not, Miss Impertinence—not by—"

"Ah, Mrs. Bullerham," a cool, deferential voice interposed. "Did you wish assistance ascending the steps?"

Amanda's head whipped round, and her face flamed as she saw Mr. Brentick striding towards them. The blaze in his blue eyes seemed to crackle through the dim passage.

"Or had you rather," he went on in more ominous tones as he neared, "return to your cabin to *rest*?"

Mrs. Bullerham opened her mouth. Mr. Brentick took one step closer. Mrs. Bullerham shut her mouth, turned, and scuttled back into her cabin.

The blazing blue gaze fell upon Amanda then, and her heart seemed to clench into a hard little fist. She couldn't breathe.

"Miss Cavencourt, may I invite you above, to relieve yourself of the string of oaths burning your tongue?"

He'd heard. What burned then was her face.

"It seems the Devil also makes work for idle tongues," Mr. Brentick said as they reached the rail. "Mrs. Bullerham has the true instinct of a killer."

"It would be more gallant to pretend you'd heard nothing," Amanda said, forcing a smile.

"I thought that would be cowardly. I'm already disgusted with myself for not intruding sooner, but I was caught between Scylla and Charybdis, you see."

She was far too hurt, bewildered, and mortified to see anything at the moment, and her smile felt like a hideous facial contortion. Looking away, she inhaled deeply of the brisk salt air.

"I thought at first that if I dashed to your rescue, it would make matters worse," he continued. "I didn't realise my presence was unnecessary to accomplish that."

"If you will not be gallant," she said, "then please don't be kind, either." She swallowed, and made herself meet his sympathetic gaze. "Is it true? Is that what others think?"

"As you told me a while ago, Miss Cavencourt, her mind is poisoned. It was all venom."

She shook her head. "No, and that's the worst of her. However venomous, there's always truth in what she says. What enrages everyone is that she's insensitive enough to say it. It *is* what others think, isn't it? That I'm so desperate—"

"Why would anyone but a miserable, dyspeptic old cow think anything like that? Her mind is as sick as her infernal liver," he answered angrily.

"Do *you* think it?" she asked.

He stared at her a moment incredulously, then, to her confusion, he smiled. "If you'll pardon the impertinence, miss—are you mad?"

"What do you mean?"

"She said you were at your last prayers," he answered with the excessive patience usually offered the mentally enfeebled. "Whatever other twisted 'truths' she may have uttered, you cannot be so overset as to credit *that*."

Amanda stared at him blankly.

He returned the stare. "You aren't," he said. "It's quite impossible. Do strive to collect your wits."

"I wish you'd collect yours, Mr. Brentick. I most certainly am at my last prayers. I am *six and twenty*."

"And?"

She coloured. "And—and I have a looking glass."

"If you can't gaze into it in a rational manner, I can't imagine what possible good it does you."

Her eyes narrowed. "I hope you are not trying to persuade me I am some sort of *femme fatale*."

"I should not presume, miss."

"If that is your notion how to appease my wounded dignity, I must point out you are altogether off the mark." As she met his expressionless gaze, another suspicion arose. "You aren't—you aren't flirting with me again, and pretending you're not, are you?"

His eyes opened very wide. "I wouldn't dream of it, miss."

"I should hope not. You did promise you wouldn't."

"If memory serves, I said I *mustn't*."

"And so you mustn't," she said, growing flustered in quite a different way. "It makes me most—most uncomfortable."

"I'm painfully aware of that, miss. It is most provoking." His tones were aggrieved, but a devil danced in his blue eyes.

She answered the devil. "Oh, I nearly forgot. No doubt you fear your skills will grow rusty from disuse."

"That is not what concerns me," he said. He paused a moment. "I perceive a refreshingly independent spirit abruptly cowed by the perverted utterances of a foul-minded rhinoceros. I do all in my humble powers to distract you, and you do not attend. Instead, your beautiful eyes dart about, as though you were a hunted creature. It *is* provoking."

She caught her breath. "My what?"

"Of course there's no point reminding you your eyes are beautiful, because you're irrational. Your abigail has probably told you a hundred times, not to mention your beaux, but all those sensible voices are drowned out by the noise of that squealing sow."

No. He didn't really think she was . . . no, certainly not. He spoke so out of kindness, because he pitied her or felt obliged to smooth her ruffled feathers. Or it was mere habit. *I daresay he wreaks havoc with the maids.*

"*Do* you wreak havoc with the ladies' maids?" she asked.

"I beg your pardon?"

"That's why Mrs. Bullerham claimed it was a rendezvous, you know. Because you're so handsome," she said brazenly. She was rewarded. The mask of assurance faltered. She had disconcerted him. "And also, probably, because there's a devil in your eyes, Mr. Brentick."

His confusion lasted but an instant, and he flashed a wolfish grin. How white his teeth were, gleaming in his lean, tanned face.

"Your recent ordeal has overheated your imagination," he said. "She's made you see evil everywhere."

"No, not evil," she answered thoughtfully. "Krishna, rather. Are you familiar with the Hindu deities?"

"I know some of the thousand names, though I can rarely keep them straight," he said, obviously puzzled by the abrupt turn in the conversation.

"How long were you in India?" she asked.

Philip remained nearly another hour at her side. Never had they conversed for so long a time. More important, this was the first time the talk ventured near the personal, and what he learned was puzzling and troubling. He'd experienced niggling doubts before, but in recent weeks, they'd swelled to daunting proportions. He listened to her today, and watched her expressive face, and wondered whether it *was* possible she knew nothing, made no connexion at all between him and the man who'd robbed her.

He considered the evidence again later, when she'd gone. She hadn't let Jessup die, for one. Furthermore, after four months, Philip was still alive. To eliminate him without awakening suspicion would be difficult, he admitted. Still, the task was not beyond the wily Indian's powers.

But nothing. Not even a glimmer of recognition. That left a few alternative interpretations. For instance, Padji may have latched onto Miss Cavencourt for his own purposes. The Indian may have played on her kind nature and convinced her to take him to England.

He could have several reasons for doing so. Fear of the

rani's rage when she learned of the theft was one excellent reason, although it needn't drive him all the way to England. Another, more in character, was a vow of revenge upon the rani's true enemy, Hedgrave.

Philip knew the Laughing Princess was not worth fifty thousand pounds, let alone the additional thousands previously expended to retrieve it. He was aware the Falcon represented no more than a very expensive tool in an ugly game: two vicious children squabbling over a toy each wanted only to spite the other. He could not be greatly shocked to discover the game had become deadly.

In that case, Miss Cavencourt may not be, as he'd originally believed, a cunning disciple of the ruthless Rani Simhi. She might be merely another tool, though an innocent one. Or was that simply what he wanted to believe now, because he'd been trapped too long on this damnable ship? Had the long months of abstinence twisted his reason? Was he making excuses for her simply because he desired her? How absurd. He didn't need to *like* her to want to bed her—or any attractive woman.

Yet she'd played havoc with common sense from the start, hadn't she? She'd aroused him when he'd attacked her that night in Calcutta, and found himself grappling with a she-cat. Only recently, however, as he'd come to know her better, had the memory returned to haunt his dreams: the swish of silk and the tinkle of thin golden bangles . . . the scent of patchouli mingled with smoke . . . darkness . . . and a fierce struggle with a warm, slender body, lithe and so pleasingly curved.

He'd thought she was a native, until she'd cursed him in those crisp, well-bred accents. He smiled wryly. The unladylike epithets had aroused him as well. He'd known one fleeting, utterly mad urge to return, to join battle with her again . . . and conquer.

That, however, was four months ago. Now? Now, he admitted silently and with no small self-mockery, she was driving him crazy.

*   *   *

Despite Mrs. Bullerham, Miss Cavencourt stood conversing with Philip the following day, at their usual time and place.

"You said you ran away to be a soldier," she observed. "But you've never said why you had to run away, or what you were running from."

When he hesitated, her earnest gaze flitted away. "Or is that too personal a question? Roderick tells me I always ask awkward questions, and that's one reason I— But he's a solicitor, you know, and never likes to tell anyone anything."

"Force of habit," Philip said. "Men of law must be discreet regarding clients' affairs, and secrecy becomes a way of life. My case is no secret, though. I ran away because my father and I did not see eye to eye on my future. He'd reared and educated me to follow in his footsteps as a schoolteacher. He even sent me to public school. He had some dream I might one day soar to the dizzying heights of a university position."

"From what I've glimpsed of your knowledge, Mr. Brentick, I should say it might have been an achievable goal."

"My father had certain infallible methods for ensuring obedience and diligence." *Torture, for instance. Torture works very well*, he added silently. "These were administered sufficiently early and consistently to remain effective, even when I was away at school and no longer under his unique tutelage. I did attend to my studies. All the same, by the time I was eighteen, I knew I could no longer obey his wishes."

*Papa had a perverse sense of humour, you see.* That was why Lord Felkoner had forbid the military career his youngest son most desperately desired. His lordship had chosen the Church with the same fine sense of irony. Incorrigible Philip might look forward to more years of the grinding studies he detested. After would come the eternal tedium, the steady drip, drip of hypocrisy and meaningless work, years of pious chores which bore not even the saving grace of vigourous physical activity. Lord Felkoner, obviously, had wanted his son walled up permanently, and the airless catacombs of clerical life would do very nicely, thank you.

Philip saw his frown reflected in anxious eyes, and quickly smoothed his features. "Hardly unusual," he said lightly. "Hotheaded youths run away every day to become soldiers or sailors. I was lucky. I got to India, and the young officer I served led me to all the excitement and adventure my naive young heart could have wished for."

"You were lucky to survive," she said somberly. "India's is not the most amenable climate for Europeans. Even my parents, who'd lived there many years before, didn't survive the second visit."

He remembered something Mrs. Bullerham had said. "Fever?" he asked.

"I suspect my mother was dying before she ever got on the ship," she answered. "I think England had already—" She caught herself, and went on in brisker tones, "Yes, the fever took her first. Within another month, my father was gone as well."

"I'm sorry. That must have been terrible for you, especially in a strange country, away from your friends and relatives."

"I had Roderick." She was silent a moment. When she spoke again, only the slightest quaver betrayed her. "Would you be very much shocked, if I told you it was a relief?"

"No."

"I was relieved," she went on more steadily, "because I didn't have to worry any more. I didn't have to wonder what I could do, or feel helpless because I'd never find an answer. Nothing could be done. My father returned to India because he was ruined, and needed Roderick to look after us. Papa was broken, you see, and couldn't be fixed."

Her eyes glistened. As Philip watched her slim hand rise up and dash a tear away, something tightened within him.

"That is what Mrs. Bullerham meant about my lack of proper supervision," she continued. "My parents were broken. They weren't living, really. They were like a pair of smiling dolls propped up on a shelf."

To play a servant was a confounded nuisance. He ought to be able to hold her in his arms and let her cry away the hurt. He certainly wished he could stomp down to Mrs. Bullerham's cabin and choke the life out her. Sentence after sentence, she'd cut and slashed. She'd even probed what must be a very old though still tender wound. Gad, but she and Lord Felkoner would have made a splendid pair.

"Miss Cavencourt," Philip said gently.

She dashed away another tear and looked at him.

"Shall we get up a petition?" he asked. "To have Mrs. Bullerham keelhauled? It is accounted an infallible cure for digestive complaints."

A watery smile rewarded him.

"I wish yours were not such a sympathetic countenance," she said. "I'm not a watering pot. I rarely weep unless I'm thoroughly enraged."

"I thought you were enraged. You have every right. Not a syllable that woman utters but is calculated to wound, and cruelly. She deserves her liver. I hope she chokes on it."

"That's hardly charitable."

"I'm not a charitable man. Moreover, I recognise the type. My fath—my family contains a few such vipers, and I've met more than enough in India as well, native and otherwise." Too heated. He was letting words slip. Philip collected himself. "Let us not discuss these dispiriting topics. You'd promised to help me sort out some of the major Hindu deities. Let's dwell on the gods, shall we, and consign the Mrs. Bullerhams of this world to—"

"Obscurity," she quickly supplied. Then, to his relief, she laughed.

# === 8 ===

THE STORM STRUCK a few days later. It swept down suddenly upon the *Evelina* in a gale-driven, whirling mass of black clouds that swelled and churned round the lone vessel, heaving up the waters beneath her.

With startling efficiency, the crew took in the sails just as the storm roared down upon them. It was already raging when the top-gallant yards were sent down and the masts struck.

Philip, who'd never experienced a major storm at sea, stayed after the other landlubbers had fled below, but not long. A tremendous swell sent the vessel lunging perilously to port, and Philip skidding across the wet deck toward the raging waters. One of the mates grabbed him, and, in no polite language, ordered him below.

Philip staggered towards the companionway, and the heavens cracked open to light the ship blazing white for one wild instant. As he ducked below, the white flame was doused by heavy black, and a deafening crash rent the air and seemed to shake the very ocean bottom.

Another crash and heave threw him from the bottom step. He tumbled forward and cracked his head against a timber. Along with the blast of pain came an onrush of bile. He staggered on to the cabin, hurriedly unlocked the door, and dove for a basin in the very nick of time.

Though the storm was over by late morning, the sea continued violent, heaving and tossing the twelve-hundred-ton vessel as though it were a child's toy boat.

For three days Philip clung to his mattress. He scarcely possessed the strength to cross the few feet to the cabin door. He was utterly unable to do anything for Jessup, barely able to look after himself. Luckily for the sorry pair, Miss Jones was immune to *mal de mer*. The indefatigable Abigail appeared twice a day, bearing bowls of some bland but sustaining mixture. With her came a cabin boy, whose unenviable task it was to empty basins and chamber pots for the seasick landlubbers.

By the fourth day, the buffeting had subsided somewhat, and agony dwindled to mere misery. Able at last to observe with some degree of lucidity Miss Jones's nursing methods, Philip soon ascertained precisely where all her sympathies lay.

Philip she simply handed his bowl and spoon. Then, turning away, Miss Jones devoted herself to Jessup. She lovingly fed and fussed over him. She fluffed his pillows, straightened and tucked his blanket, and tenderly held his hand until he sank into a doze.

By the conclusion of this operation, Philip was again beset by doubts. Had fifteen years of India, the last five spent dodging treachery at every turn, entirely poisoned his mind? Was it possible he saw intrigue and conspiracy where none existed?

As she turned back to him at last, Miss Jones must have remarked Philip's frown, for she said comfortingly, "Don't you worry now, Mr. Brentick. This pesky weather's just set him back a bit. But I do tell you, and I hope you won't take it amiss, as you'd better help him change his ways. He can't go back like what he was, you know."

"I beg your pardon?"

She moved nearer, and spoke in lower tones.

"My pa was just like him, strong as an ox. Drank gin like it was rainwater and never felt it. Then the influenza got hold of him, and he was never the same after. The littlest chill'd keep him in bed near a fortnight. Finally, the leech just told Pa straight out if he didn't want to be a pitiful wreck all the rest of his life, he'd got to mend his ways."

"My master spent half his life in India," Philip answered defensively, as she stood, hands on her hips, fixing him with a reproachful look. "Consider the climate's effects."

"Mr. Wringle'd do better to consider his wenching and drinking and stuffing himself," Bella answered with a sniff. "Don't tell *me* that ain't a man likes his carousing, because I won't believe you. An ignorant country maid I may be, but I wasn't born yesterday. Nor I ain't seeing all my tending go for nothing, and so I mean to tell him, soon as he's feeling more himself again."

Having delivered this lecture, her face softened. "There now," she said somewhat abashedly, "don't mind me. It's just the worry. He scared me half to death when I seen him get so horrible sick again, after all these weeks doing so good, too."

"I'm sure your careful nursing will not go for naught, Miss Jones," Philip said. "My master is aware, as I am, that he owes you his life. In fact, I'm sure he owes it twice now, for I've been no good to him at all."

She blushed and attempted to make light of his quite genuine praise.

"Goodness, Mr. Brentick, it's but a bit of soup now and then, and I'd go clean mad if I'd to stay in one place all the day."

"Yet Miss Cavencourt and Mrs. Gales need your services as well," he said. "You must be exhausted, running back and forth."

"Miss Amanda don't like to be fussed over when she's sick. She gets cross, you know, and wants to be let alone. And Mrs. Gales is only the tiniest bit under the weather. When I left, she was setting up in the bed, just knitting away, like that was the only cure for anything."

"Is—is Miss Cavencourt very ill?" Philip asked.

Bella appeared to consider. "Well, she's green enough," she said after a moment. "Greener than you are, Mr. Brentick. You look a deal better than yesterday, I'm happy to say. All the same . . ." She eyed him thoughtfully. "Mr. Wringle's whiskers make him look more distinguished, but I can't say the same for yourself. You look like a sailor what's been on a five-day binge."

Philip stroked his rough chin. "Raffish, Miss Jones?"

She shrugged her plump shoulders. "Whatever that is. Where's your shaving things?"

"Thank you, but I don't feel up to shaving at the moment. Perhaps later."

"Well, don't I know that?" she answered indignantly. "I got eyes, don't I? I'll shave you," she added, to his astonishment.

His shock grew to horror as her gleaming eye lit upon the washbasin, where his neglected razor lay.

"Thank you, but that will not be necessary," he said firmly. "Nor advisable. The ship is not altogether steady at present."

"I was shaving my pa since I was twelve years old, and I done Lord Cavencourt time enough when his valet was too drunk to be trusted with even a towel. My hands is perfectly steady."

"No one has . . . *ever* . . . shaved . . . me," Philip said, picking out the words with all the cold deliberation of his sire at his intimidating best. "*No one.* Not even J—no one!"

She drew her hand back from the razor and sighed. "Oh, very well, if you're going to get all in a roar about it. I was just looking for something to do."

Swiftly recollecting himself, Philip assumed a mask of penitence. "I do beg your pardon. Illness appears to make me cross, as well. But it is a quirk of mine. I can't bear to be shaved." He thought quickly. "If you truly want something to do . . ."

"Well, didn't I just say so?"

"In that case, I would be immensely grateful if you'd sew the button back on my coat. It came loose the day of the storm. When I fell ill so suddenly, I tore my coat off, and the button came loose," he explained. "It's dangling by a thread."

Bella's round face brightened. "Well, that's more like it, then." She retrieved the coat, then glanced about. "Got anything else? I expect you don't care much for mending, and there's no tailors near to hand."

When the door at last closed behind her, a choked guffaw broke the silence. Philip's icy blue gaze fell upon his servant, whose shoulders were shaking.

"Are you experiencing convulsions, soldier?" he asked frostily. "It would serve you right, for pretending to sleep, only to eavesdrop."

"Bless me, guv, if the wench wasn't gonna shave you. *You*," Jessup chortled. "I never heard your voice go so high like that afore. Lawd, did y' think she meant to nick up somethin' else for you?"

"You know perfectly well I let no one come near me with a razor. Not even you, you decrepit old budmash. She's taken *your* measure, hasn't she? You heard her, lad. Miss Jones means to see you mend your wicked ways. She'll do it, make no mistake, even if it kills you."

Jessup chuckled. "Well, and mebbe I might let her. She do make salvation look sweet enough, that one. And pluck to the backbone, ain't she? I seen brave soldiers near wet themselves when they heard that tone from you, and she didn't so much as blink. Damme but I thought I'd bust a gut, tryin' to stifle myself."

"Why don't you try again?" Philip answered, taking up a pillow. "Or would you rather I *helped* you?"

Bella returned to the Cavencourt cabin bearing one coat, one shirt, and two pairs of trousers.

Amanda had dragged herself up to a sitting position. She gazed dully at the pile of clothing.

"What is that, Bella?"

"Mr. Brentick decided to come off his high ropes and let

me mend his things." Bella took up her sewing box and deftly threaded a needle. "He took it ill when I asked to shave him," she added, grinning. "I was afeard he'd jump clean out of bed and whack his head on the ceiling."

"I suppose most men wouldn't trust a woman with a razor," Amanda said.

Bella's grin broadened. "I wish you could have heard him. And seen him. For a minute there, he almost had me quaking in my slippers. I never in all my life seen anyone get so high and mighty. Looking down his nose at me, he was—and there I was standing practically on top of him, as there ain't room enough in that cabin for a cat to wash its whiskers. And he got this little twitch in his jaw and his nose pinched up, and his voice just—just *dripped* out, like pieces of ice. '*No one shaves me*,' he says. And I fair near dropped a curtsey and said, 'No, Your Highness, no they don't, I'm sure.'" She giggled. "Oh, he is a one, that one."

"I expect it was being so seasick," said Amanda, baffled by the strange flutter within her. *Mal de mer.* Would it never end? "No doubt he was out of sorts."

"He was in a temper fit is what. He don't like being sick, I can tell you. Hates it worse than you do. Still, who can blame him, such a nasty little place it is, and him with them long legs." She shook out the trousers and gazed at them in shrewd appraisal. "And who'd think, skinny as he is," she said, "any man could have such a small bottom?"

Amanda's face grew unpleasantly hot. She glanced at Mrs. Gales, but that lady remained serenely asleep. The widow slept as steadily as she plied her needles and hooks. A cannon blast might wake her, but nothing less, once she'd composed herself to slumber.

"He asked after you," Bella said, after a moment. "He seemed very worried. Maybe that's why he got so grouchy. Poor man, it don't seem fair, do it? Him so fine and handsome as a prince in one of your fairy tales. Why, he might have been a gentleman, miss, and then—"

"Bella."

The maid looked up enquiringly at the unaccustomed sharp tone. "Yes, miss?"

"My head is aching like the very devil. Do you think you can mend *silently* for a little while?"

By the end of the week, though the sea continued choppy, the deck was sufficiently safe for perambulation. Late in the day, Philip made his way above.

Bella had said her mistress was fully recovered, but the mistress did not appear. He waited an hour at their customary place, then spent another two hours prowling the vessel from stem to stern. Perhaps she'd come earlier, and the exertion had tired her after the strain of illness. Perhaps she'd taken to her bed once more.

He would *not* think about beds. Not her bed. Nor was it wise to consider his own narrow mattress. That had seemed a deal too much like a coffin, and the airless cell in which it lay seemed to reek of illness and decay. So Bella must have noticed as well, for she'd arrived today with bucket, mop, and cloth, and the hapless cabin boy in tow. With Jessup alert and vigilant, Philip had happily fled, leaving the maid and her slave to scrub the living daylights out of every square inch of offending surface.

Not that her efforts could possibly make the space tolerable to Philip. Falling asleep would continue to be an ordeal. To linger there at all when it wasn't necessary was needless torture. *Ah, thank you, Papa.*

"There now, Miss Amanda, it's all right."

Amanda's eyes flew open, and she jerked upright . . . to utter darkness. Panic seized her, and she tried to shake off the hand grasping her wrist.

"It's all right, miss. You had a bad dream," Bella said soothingly.

That was all. A dream. A very long one. She must remember it. Padji ought to know. But she wouldn't forget, not this one. Not one detail.

Amanda sank back upon the pillows, and patiently accepted Bella's fussing and fluffing and tucking. "Thank you," she said softly. "I'm sorry I woke you. Do go back to sleep. I'm all right now."

In a few minutes, Bella was lightly snoring. Her mistress, however, remained painfully awake.

Amanda turned restlessly.

Seven bells. Eleven-thirty.

Eight bells. Midnight.

Squelching a sigh of exasperation, Amanda slid from the bed. She fumbled about, found her clothing, and managed to dress without waking her companions. Then she crept from the room, closing the door gently behind her.

Above, a full moon lit the deck with soft, eerie light. There were sailors about, but they were busy with their tasks, their voices muted. Amanda automatically headed for her usual place at the rail. Then she hesitated. It was one thing to wander about unattended in broad day, with Mrs. Gales at the stern keeping discreet watch. It was quite another to stroll about alone after midnight.

Amanda was about to turn back when the cool breeze carried a familiar scent to her nostrils: Tobacco smoke. She saw a tall, slim figure move from the shadows of the mizzenmast to the rail. His hair gleamed silver in the moonlight. He leaned upon the rail, half-turned from her. She could just make out the tiny red glow of his cigar when he drew upon it.

She told herself she ought to leave before Mr. Brentick became aware of her presence. She was amazed he hadn't noticed already. His senses always seemed so acute. Yet she smelled the smoke and a great, empty place seemed to open within her, and she knew only that she didn't want to be alone.

She'd taken but two steps when his posture tensed and his head swivelled in her direction. Too late to retreat.

Heart thumping, Amanda continued, though the space between them seemed to have grown to an immense stretch of cold and hostile plain.

His greeting was warm, however, when she neared. "Miss Cavencourt," he said softly, surprised. "For a moment I thought you were a ghost."

"You'd better pretend I am," she said, abashed by his wondering stare. "Or that I'm sleepwalking. I'm supposed to be slumbering like a good little girl, but I couldn't, and I thought I'd go mad trying to keep quiet about it."

"With all due respect, miss, you *are* mad, you know. We have settled that question long since."

He looked down at the cheroot he held, and frowned. As he raised his hand to toss it into the water, she cried, "Oh, don't throw it away on my account. I don't mind at all. In fact, I rather like it," she added. "It reminds me of Calcutta."

His eyebrows went up. "You miss the stench?"

She smiled and, unthinking, leaned upon the rail, and inhaled. Her entire being seemed to relax. "Not that, exactly, but the smoke. The rooms filled with incense, and the stories. My friend, the Rani Simhi, would smoke her hookah and relate myths and legends," she explained, looking away from him and towards the moon-dappled ocean. "I felt like a little girl, transported to a mysterious place where fairy tales were real."

"After what we've endured recently, I shouldn't mind being transported to mysterious places. Will you take me?" he asked. "Will you tell me a story?"

She bit her lip. "I really ought to return. I shouldn't be out at this hour."

"No, you shouldn't," he agreed, "and I shouldn't ask you." He paused a moment, his eyes very intent upon her face. "But I am monstrous selfish. I wish you would stay . . . long enough to tell me one of your stories."

She thought he must hear her heart thumping so stupidly, even above the moan of timbers and the splash of waves against the vessel. But he only looked at her in that strange, fixed way. Part of her wanted to run, for it reminded her of the steady gaze of a jungle cat, or a bird of prey. Yet another part of her—mesmerised or stunned, she knew not which—could not bear to go away. She thought she could look into his beautiful face, its chiseled planes silver and shadow in the moonlight, for all her lifetimes. "Earthly beauty is a glimpse of the Eternal," the rani had said. "Earthly love is a glimpse of transcendent love."

Eternity and transcendence, indeed. Smiling at her folly, Amanda returned her focus to the glistening blue-black water, and let her mind sink into the smoky, warm, scented rooms where the stories lived.

"When he was a young man, as I've before mentioned, Krishna was a devil with the ladies," she began. "When he was a boy, he was full of mischief. One day, he stole some butter.

Philip took the story with him when he returned to his cabin, just as he took with him her voice and scent, and the dreamy, faraway glow of her eyes. The story made him smile yet, for he saw the several characters in her mobile face, and heard their voices in hers. He'd laughed helplessly when she revealed Krishna's triumph, and her face had expressed the child-god's ineffable ennui as he learned of the miracle he'd performed. Miss Cavencourt had touched something more, though, and Philip found it uncanny she'd chosen precisely that tale.

In punishment for stealing the butter, Krishna's mama had tied him to a heavy mortar used for grinding and crushing food. When at length he grew bored with his situation, Krishna had dragged the mortar between two huge trees and heedlessly uprooted them.

In the roots of the trees were two princes an evil sorcerer had entombed. They'd been buried alive, but the child-god had inadvertently returned them to life.

Did it haunt them after, Philip wondered, as he sank back upon his pillow and closed his eyes. Or had Krishna freed their spirits as well? He wished he might have asked her. He wished he might ask her now. But if she had been with him now, he wouldn't care to talk, would he?

Numskull. If only he'd got himself a tart in Capetown. At this rate, he'd be a dithering imbecile by the time the ship entered the English Channel.

# == 9 ==

"I DREAMT OF the robbery," Amanda said. She sat this
morning upon her customary cask in the blistering galley.
Perspiration trickled down her neck, though she'd arrived
scarcely five minutes before.

"A troubling dream," Padji said as his large hands
dextrously kneaded dough. "I heard you cry out three times,
and my heart ached for your trouble."

"You heard me?" she repeated incredulously. "From the
other end of the ship?"

"I lay by your door, O beloved, as I do each night. So I
slept by the door of the great Lioness. Such is my duty."

"By my door? But you couldn't have been. . . . You
must have been dreaming as well, because—"

"I moved from the place when you rose," Padji said,
"lest you stumble over my lowly person."

"Where did you go then?"

"Above. The hour was late. The mistress must move
where she chooses, fearlessly, in confidence her servant is
near to protect her. I was near, O daughter of the sun and
of the moon."

"Indeed. You are . . . most conscientious, Padji."

He shrugged. "It is my *dharma*. I am of no significance.
Tell me of this dream that so troubles you."

"I know it was only a dream," she said uncomfortably,
"yet I remembered what the rani told me."

"The eye observes mere appearance, which the mind

gives name to. The heart sees into the darkness and discerns truth. In dreams, the heart speaks to the eye and mind. So she tells us in her endless wisdom."

"So she tells us." Amanda sighed. "In any case, a great deal of it seemed obvious, but part of it—well, I didn't know what to think."

"Tell me the whole of it."

"It was the robbery," she said in Hindustani. "Just as it happened, except at the last. The thief had knocked me down and run off with the Laughing Princess. But this time, I jumped up and chased him. Miles, it seemed, down one long passage, then a turning, then another passage. The night was utterly still and black."

"You saw no moon?" Padji asked.

"No moon, no stars. It was like a maze in a great void. Then I came to the final turning, and felt the breeze, which carried the scent of the sea. I stopped suddenly and looked down, and saw the sea beneath me, churning and sparkling, coal-black. I screamed."

"That was your first cry," Padji said, nodding.

"A voice answered me," Amanda went on. "The moon, enormous, white and full, broke past the clouds and shone down upon him. He wore a jewelled turban, and the rich garb of a prince, but his face remained in darkness. His voice was the robber's voice."

Padji gave her one brief glance before he returned to his kneading. "He called to you?"

"He said, 'Come to me. My boat will bear you safely.' But I was afraid of him," Amanda said, looking down at her hands. "I turned to run away, but the passage had vanished, and I stood on a narrow ledge, the sea before me and the sea behind me. Then the ledge itself vanished, and I fell a great way. That, I expect, was the second time I cried out in my sleep. He caught me, and his cloak enfolded me." She paused, her cheeks burning. "I had rather not describe the details."

"He took you as a lover," Padji said without looking up from his work.

99

"Certainly not!" Amanda's cheeks flamed anew. "I would never dream such a thing."

He shrugged, and she recommenced. "I struggled, *needless to say*," she added, glaring at him, "and he laughed. When the laughter died, he'd vanished. I was chilled. I picked up his cloak to put around me, and found the Laughing Princess at my feet. I tried to pick it up, but it was too heavy. I was weary and hungry and cold, and all alone on this great, black sea, so I wept, and called to the moon—to Anumati—to help me. Then the breeze blew. It came warm this time, filled with the scent of agarwood. The air grew thick with smoke. I raised my hand," Amanda said, lifting her arm as she had in the dream. "A dark form swept down from the heavens. It was a falcon. It circled my head three times, then alit upon my wrist. 'I will serve you,' he said."

Padji paused, his brown eyes alert. "The hunting falcon is female. This spoke to you in man's voice?"

"The robber's voice, again. At least, so I believed in the dream, because I told him he was false, and a thief. I shook my wrist, but his talons gripped painfully, and I cried out."

"The third time."

Amanda nodded. "That last cry must have wakened Bella, because she woke me. I was too agitated to go back to sleep. That's why I went above," she added without meeting Padji's gaze.

Padji threw the dough into a bowl and placed a cloth over it. "The dream is plain enough," he said. "Anumati sent it to you. She knows you grow anxious and impatient. She warns you the statue cannot be moved until you are no longer upon the endless sea. You understood that wisdom, for we spoke of it many weeks ago."

"Of course I understand. That isn't what bothers me." Her finger traced the outline of a bud embroidered on her skirt. "I only want back what's mine. But sometimes, when I think about what must be done, I wonder if it's wrong." She glanced up. "You promised not to—not to hurt anybody, you know."

"I obey your wishes in all things, my golden one."

"I am not . . . convinced Mr. Brentick knows anything about it," she said, unconsciously lapsing into English. "It's possible his master has not confided in him. Mr. Brentick has not been long in his employ and—and men of law are very secretive. My brother certainly doesn't confide in *his* valet. It's even possible Mr. Wringle objected to his own role, but hadn't any choice. Or maybe he doesn't know the statue was stolen. It may have come through another intermediary. Lud, even Randall Groves."

"One cannot know. One cannot look into another's heart," Padji agreed.

"In fact," Amanda went on with more assurance, "if either were truly dangerous men, Anumati would have warned me, wouldn't she, in the dream?"

"You did not see the man's face in the dream."

"But I heard his voice," Amanda reminded. "It was not Mr. Brentick's. And Mr. Wringle hasn't the same form. He's too short and square." She glanced away, frowning. "Why did I dream of a prince and a falcon, though? Can there be some other on this ship? But that doesn't make sense at all. What the devil did it mean?"

"Thrice he changed his form," Padji said reflectively. "A thief, a prince, a falcon, each held you by turns. One robbed, one loved, one brought pain." He shrugged. "Most strange. A prophecy, perhaps."

Amanda shook her head. "No. Dreams may help explain what is, but I am still too English to believe they can tell what will be. I am certainly no oracle. Nor do I wish to be." She shivered, despite the heat.

Amanda certainly never *intended* to return to the upper deck at night. The trouble was, the closer they got to England, the more anxious she became.

Two months passed, during which more than one night lengthened into morning while she lay broad awake in her bed. She didn't venture above every time she was restless, only when it became intolerable. That added up to a mere half-dozen late night rambles. She found Mr. Brentick there every time.

Still, he could not possibly get the wrong impression. Amanda had let him know, the second time she'd crept above, that Padji was lurking about. Padji must have let others know as well, and in his own inimitable way, solicited discretion. Certainly, not one whisper of Miss Cavencourt's nocturnal wanderings reached Mrs. Gales's ears, even though Captain Blayton told her everything.

The *Evelina* was at long last approaching the Channel. She'd probably be sailing up the Thames in a matter of days, if the winds held favourable. In a matter of days, the Laughing Princess would be Amanda's at last . . . if all went well. But she would not think about that, she chided herself this night as, for the seventh and positively last time, she escaped her cabin and sneaked up to the deck.

Mr. Brentick looked round at her approach, his countenance half surprised, half—was it pleased? Amanda recollected that in a matter of days, he would be out of her life forever. Well, what did she expect, she asked herself crossly. Did she think that, like Padji, the valet would suddenly develop an irresistible need to abandon his employer and follow her to Yorkshire? If he looked pleased, it was because he liked her Indian stories.

"Another difficult night, Miss Cavencourt?" he enquired sympathetically. "I suppose you long to be home, and its being so near makes you restless."

"It's good to hear some rational excuse," she said. "I simply felt wild to get out of the cabin. Now I shall sleep the morning away again." She glanced up. "Are you always here?" she asked. "Are we seized by similar demons at the same time? Or do you never sleep?"

"Old habits die hard. In the military, I grew accustomed to a few hours' rest snatched here and there."

"Oh."

He glanced about. "I suppose Padji is of similar habits."

"I wonder if he sleeps at all." She, too, looked around her. "Where is he? I told him there was no need to skulk about. Everyone knows he's there."

"Evidently, he's well schooled in discretion."

"Yes."

"He's been with you a long time, I take it."

She considered briefly how to answer. Perhaps it wasn't wise, but if she told the truth, Mr. Brentick's response might tell her something. She wanted reassurance. Not that it mattered, really, whether he was innocent. She'd never see him again. But how unpleasant to part, suspecting him, feeling unsure . . .

"I might as well speak frankly," she said. "We're nearly home and I doubt the captain would have Padji tossed over at this late date, even if he could find anyone audacious enough to attempt it." She stood a bit straighter, her posture half-defiant. "Padji wasn't my servant. He ran away from the Rani Simhi. He'd committed an offence, and was terrified of what she'd do to him. You may find that difficult to credit, considering his size and strength. So did I. But I got on this ship and there he was . . . and so I told the captain a clanker."

"What hideous crime did the fellow commit?" Mr. Brentick asked.

With some relief she discerned only genuine curiosity in his tones. "I was attacked . . . and robbed one night, and he was supposed to be protecting me."

"The rani sounds monstrous unforgiving."

"That's what Padji would have one believe. Nonetheless, I'm happy to have him with me. He *is* an excellent cook."

"And an excellent watchdog." He sounded peeved.

"Does he make you uneasy, Mr. Brentick?"

"My dear lady, the fellow is over six feet tall, big as an ox, and strong as one. Only a nitwit would not be uneasy." After a short pause, he went on, "Do you know, I'm terrified to move a muscle when you're by, lest it be interpreted as an unfriendly act, and result in my immediate demise."

"Padji is big, but he's not stupid," she defended. "I'm sure he can distinguish an unfriendly gesture from a friendly one."

"Can he distinguish friendly from too friendly, Miss Cavencourt?" he asked.

Her face grew warm. "I don't think I wish to know what you mean," she answered firmly. "You're getting that tone in your voice, Mr. Brentick."

"What tone is that?"

"Your flirting one."

"And you find it disagreeable."

She threw him a sidelong glance. "You know perfectly well that women find it agreeable. I'm sure you practised for years to get it just right."

"Practised? For *years*?" he echoed aggrievedly. "You make me out to be thoroughly unscrupulous."

"Not at all. You told me you'd developed diligent habits of study. One might naturally assume you applied them to more than Cicero's orations."

"Natural philosophy, for instance?"

"Call it what you like. I only request you not do it with me," she said nervously. "I know I shouldn't be here, but you needn't make me feel I've sneaked off to an assignation. I realise flirting is practically an addiction with you, Mr. Brentick, but you must try to show it who is master. If I were a man," she added in earnest tones, "you wouldn't try to flirt with me, would you? Why not just pretend I'm a man?"

He gazed at her a moment, then laughed.

"Miss Cavencourt, the moon offers little light tonight, but even in this near Stygian darkness, the task you propose is quite impossible."

Amanda raised her chin and turned her own gaze to the black water. "Then you shall just have to flirt all by yourself, because I most assuredly will not help you."

"You are exceedingly kind," he murmured. "*That* task is merely onerous."

"Excuse me. I am not well-versed in these matters. I was under the impression that flirting, like quarrelling, takes two."

"I said it was onerous," he answered gravely. "Yet I am not frightened by the enormity of the challenge. On the contrary, if I don't flirt, and very soon, something terrible might happen. I'm filled to bursting with double entendres and leading questions. If I don't let them out, I might . . . explode. I don't mind exploding, really, if I must, but you might be struck by a flying limb, and that would be most *improper*. Not at all the thing. Mrs. Bullerham would never countenance it."

A half-strangled laugh escaped her, floated upon the sea breeze . . . and sank into a taut silence. She hadn't noticed he'd moved, but he was much nearer now. His presence, dark and oppressively masculine, seemed to enclose her.

"You don't know you're provocative, do you?" he asked, his voice low, puzzled.

Alarmed, Amanda swung round sharply. That was a mistake. She came up short mere inches from his chest. Her glance flew to his face. It seemed a long way up. She felt very small, vulnerable, and trapped. "What are you doing?" she demanded.

"Flirting. All by myself."

"You are not. It's—it's something else entirely." Where the devil was Padji, confound him? The air was quite cool. Amanda felt feverish, and her heart seemed to shrink very tight in her breast.

Shadows veiled the valet's expression, and in the darkness his blue eyes gleamed black, unreadable. Yet her other senses had grown painfully acute. She was conscious of a faint, lingering aroma of tobacco and some light cologne or soap. Her ears caught the quickened sound of his breathing. Or was that her own? She retreated, and felt the rail dig into her back.

"It *is* something else," he said, more softly still. "I'm trying to pretend you're a man." He face bent closer. "I'm

105

trying to remember my place." His arms brushed hers as his hands clamped down on the rail on either side of her. "It's not working," he whispered, his breath warm on her face as his mouth descended to hers.

A hairsbreadth from contact, his head jerked back abruptly. Amanda blinked, then saw two large brown hands gripping the valet's shoulders.

"The mistress is sleepy," Padji said sweetly. "It is time for her to retire."

Nearly seven curst months, Philip raged silently while he stood at the rail and pretended not to watch Miss Cavencourt chatting with her companion. Seven months and not even one miserable kiss. Seven months on this vessel with the same woman, and he hadn't so much as touched her. Nor would he. He'd seen to that, hadn't he?

Two days had passed since his ill-fated attempt, and Amanda Cavencourt had not come within fifty feet of him, curse her. But he couldn't curse her, really. Though she might break a few rules, ignore a few conventions, she wouldn't break them all. India and the rani hadn't possessed her entirely. England's oppressive morality maintained a hold.

Philip ought, actually, be grateful he was still alive. He didn't deserve to be. An unforgivable lapse, that. He'd known the Indian was standing guard, and the Falcon had simply . . . forgotten. One moment he was aware, as always, of every detail of his surroundings, of every sound. The next, he was aware only of her, of her husky voice and unconsciously sensuous movements and the maddening scent of patchouli. He'd wanted to lose himself there, in her.

Now she wouldn't even speak to him.

"Portsmouth," Padji repeated stubbornly.

"He said Gravesend. Even Captain Blayton said Gravesend. Mr. Wringle and Mr. Brentick will disembark there with the rest of us," Amanda said, for the fifth time.

"The mistress troubles her mind with the duties of her slave," Padji reproached. "I speak to the sailors. They tell me many things of England. They are patient with the ignorant black man and draw him maps. The two will leave us at Portsmouth, for that way is quicker."

It was quicker, Amanda had to admit. Lord Hedgrave lived in Wiltshire. "Then you are saying Mr. Brentick lied to me."

Padji shrugged. "Sometimes the servant must say what the master tells him to say. Sometimes the servant is told lies, and believes them. I am fortunate. My mistress utters only golden truth to me."

Amanda gazed unhappily about the galley. "Do you realise what you're saying?" she asked. "The captain expects to reach Portsmouth *tomorrow morning*."

"I have told the maid. She is prepared. There is naught for you to trouble with, mistress. All is in readiness."

"All? What about me?" she demanded. "Am I supposed to stand about idly the whole time?"

"Yes, O beloved daughter of the great Lioness."

Nothing to do. Nothing to say. Not a word. Not even good-bye. All the same, it was better she said nothing. After the other night . . . when he'd almost kissed her.

Amanda knew she was not the most decorous woman. She would never be altogether a lady—at least not the conventional sort. Still, she wasn't a lightskirts. It was one thing to treat servants as human beings and friends, for her servants had always been her friends. It was quite another to be kissing someone else's servant. One was not supposed to kiss any man, even a gentleman, unless one were betrothed to him.

So it needn't have anything to do with rank at all, rather with what was right and what was wrong. Except, Amanda reflected sadly, she'd never entirely accepted all her culture's rights and wrongs. Except, she added more sadly, she had wanted that beautiful, naughty man to kiss her, more than anything else in the world.

# === 10 ===

"WELL, LASS, WHAT'S this?" Jessup asked as Bella set the tray down. "Not spirits, is it?"

Bella grinned. "My mistress don't know, and she'll be fit to be tied if she finds out. But you been complaining how thirsty you was, so I thought, no harm in a drop. But mind," she added, shaking a finger at him, "only a drop. You don't want to end up a sick old wreck like my poor pa, do you? Like I told you, Providence gave you another chance to mend your wicked ways."

"I was hopin' I didn't have to mend *all* of 'em," he said meaningfully. "A man needs somethin' to look forwards to. Like a bit of a cuddle now and then with a pretty lass," he added with a wink.

"Well, I can't think what pretty lasses you could find just now," Bella answered, eyes downcast.

"Can't you?" he asked. He took hold of her hand. "Mebbe you'll think clearer when you're not so thirsty."

"Only a taste for me, Mr. Wringle," was the prim answer. "Spirits always make me act so foolish."

"Do they now?" he answered cheerfully as he released her hand to take up the bottle.

The crew members who weren't sensibly sleeping were very non-sensibly engaged in jollity upon the forecastle. The noise carried but faintly to the stern, where Philip stood.

He was half tempted to join them, to spend this last night blind drunk.

It was the first night of the full moon, which was partially veiled now by a thin cloud. Yet it shed light enough to dance upon the water, which shimmered blue-black in the night. The Indians, Philip recalled, attached some deity to every phase of the moon. Whose night was this? *She* would know, of course. Miss Cavencourt meant to write a book about the myths and legends she'd so assiduously collected during her sojourn in Calcutta. Perhaps he'd read it one day. By then he'd have forgotten her, very likely, or would recall just enough to make him wonder at how susceptible a long voyage could make one. He doubted he'd remember later how very much he wished for her company now.

Her hair was merely brown, he reminded himself, and hazel was an apt enough label for her eyes. She wasn't pretty, nor even attractive, really, unless one had cultivated a taste for the darkly exotic. Nor was she so fascinating a companion . . . unless one preferred contradiction and secrets and was helplessly drawn to a woman who must be unravelled, like an endless puzzle.

His muscles tensed, conscious of an approach. Barely audible, the footsteps, yet he recognised them immediately. Philip didn't move, didn't so much as turn his head. He didn't want to look at her when it must be only to watch her walk on past as though he didn't exist.

The footsteps drew nearer. A few feet away, they paused. A moment later, she stood beside him, her hands upon the rail.

"Several deities are connected with the full moon," Miss Cavencourt said, just as though they'd been speaking this last hour. "Anumati personifies the first day. She and the others are fertility deities. She in particular, though, brings her worshippers inspiration and insight, wealth and longevity, as well as offspring."

Slowly, disbelieving, Philip let his eyes turn to her at

last. She was gazing at the moon, and in the silvery light her uplifted profile seemed to belong to some ancient goddess.

"Does she bring me a pardon?" he asked. "I'm rather in need of one."

He waited through what seemed an interminable silence.

"The trouble with you, Mr. Brentick, is that you don't understand me," she said at last. "When I talk, I talk. When I take a walk, no matter what time it is, I take a walk. It's quite simple. There's no need to make it complicated. That's so—so curst *English*." She turned to meet his bemused gaze squarely. "I know I don't behave altogether properly. That doesn't mean *I'm* improper. Only that sometimes I do what I like. Do you understand?"

"I understand perfectly, Miss Cavencourt."

"Are you sure?"

"Yes. The trouble is, sometimes I do what *I* like. Regrettably, I not only behave improperly, but I *am* improper. Sometimes."

She considered this, and must have comprehended, for her expression grew exasperated. "Then what am I supposed to do?"

"I doubt you need worry yourself about that. Whatever need be done, we can be quite certain Padji will do it," he said mournfully. "I'm only amazed I'm not at present the main course at some aquatic family's dinner."

She gave a soft chuckle. "Then I may take it you've learned your lesson."

"Yes, miss," he answered meekly.

"Because I'd rather continue friends, you know."

Something seemed to squeeze his heart. "Are we friends?"

"Something like, don't you think?" she said, her gaze earnest. "You're so easy to talk to, and your stories are quite as good as my own."

"That is high praise, indeed, coming from you. If you write a fraction as well as you speak, the British public will be enchanted with your tales. I am," he added. "When you tell a story, I'm transported to my boyhood. Every adult care vanishes, and the world becomes the world you reveal. You have a remarkable gift."

"Perhaps that's because I never altogether grew up." A hint of mischief curled her mouth, and she looked back to the sea. "Like a child, I am also partial to being terrified. Shall I tell you a gruesome tale tonight?"

He grinned. "I should like that above all things."

"Very well—but only because you've flattered me." She glanced up at the moon, as though for inspiration, then back at him. "Once upon a time," she began, "a group of pleasure-seeking travellers ran aground off the Indian coast."

She gave each traveller a character, and detailed with relish the charms of the alluring maidens who rescued them. She described the feast these beauties served, and made his mouth water. She made him long to sip the magical wine the guests tasted. Philip could hear the whisper of silk and the tinkle of bangles, smell incense and jasmine, feel the velvet softness of the sirens' skin.

Just as the travellers were seduced by their hostesses, Philip was seduced by his companion's low, sensuous voice. He heard her voice bidding him sample the food and wine, just as he felt her hands caressing his face and playing in his hair, her arms encircling his neck, her mouth, soft and ripe, warming and teasing his. He sank, with the guests, upon silken cushions, and gave himself up to pleasure.

"On through the golden afternoon into twilight, the guests dwelt in this garden of earthly delights. At last, darkness crept upon them." Miss Cavencourt's throaty voice dropped and cracked, grew raspy, and a tiny, delicious chill of anticipation crept up his neck. "The first of the guests, lying in the arms of one beautiful maiden, opened his eyes to gaze into those of his lover. . . and saw hers . . . cold as ice. Before his horrified gaze, she changed. Her skin darkened and shrivelled. Her thick, silken hair frizzled up as though a flame had been set to it. She laughed, and the horrible, hungry sound froze his heart. Then she smiled, and that was more ghastly still. Her hands, like claws, grasped a gleaming blade. He, immobile with terror, could only watch helplessly as the knife descended, ever . . . so . . . slowly . . . to his throat."

The smiling sidelong glance she threw Philip was quite evil. She was enjoying herself, bloodthirsty wench.

"She cut his throat," Miss Cavencourt went on in sepulchral tones, "and drank the blood. Every one of the travellers met the same fate. You see, this was not a paradise of sensual pleasure, but a demons' lair. The alluring maidens were ogresses, who seduced men only to feed on them." She shook her head sadly and sighed. "The wages of sin."

He'd remained a respectful distance away, though his lounging stance as he leaned back upon the rail, his body half-turned to her, was hardly decorous.

Nonetheless, he remained as he was, taking her in, trying to drink his fill of her, all the while knowing this could not possibly be enough. He told himself it must be enough. The enchantingly evil story was her farewell gift to him, though she couldn't know it was farewell. Nor should she. He made himself speak normally.

"A moral tale," he said. "Yet puzzling. I'd always thought the Hindus celebrated pleasure. What of your favourite, the blue-skinned Krishna, who played his flute and drew women by the score?"

"Earthly love, in all its many forms, offers us a glimpse of transcendent, spiritual love. That, apparently, is how the Hindus accommodate it, as they seem to accommodate all aspects of life. This story was probably some sort of warning not to let physical pleasure blind one to evil. Or, the tale may simply have been composed by a misogynist," she added, grinning. "Actually, it's rather mild, when you compare it to Adam and Eve's fall from grace. *All* our earthly woes are blamed on one naive female."

He laughed. "You lived too long in India. It's made you a skeptic."

"And a heretic and a cynic. But not consistently. My brain is not nearly well-regulated enough."

"Consistency is boring. To me it bespeaks a narrow mind. There are far too many predictable people in this world, Miss Cavencourt. Be thankful you are not one of them. I am." He paused a moment. "I shall miss you."

"I shall miss you as well," she said lightly. "You're an exceptionally good listener. Still, I have a few days left to tax your patience, have I not? I promise to treat you to one or two more grisly tales, for you seemed quite taken with tonight's."

"I was a soldier. Murder and mayhem are quite in my line."

"Then murder and mayhem it shall be." She stepped back from the rail. "Now, however, it's time to say good night. I got away early because Mrs. Gales was dining with the captain. I'd best return before she does. She rarely lectures, but I should hate for her to discover how disreputably I've been behaving."

"Others may consider it disreputable. I consider it kind." Philip straightened and moved a pace nearer. "You were especially kind to pardon me. You don't know how grateful I am."

She smiled. "To be alive, certainly. Still, it wasn't all kindness, Mr. Brentick. To encounter a kindred spirit is rare, and I hated to lose the few days we have left. I wanted us to part with pleasant memories. As friends," she said, putting out her hand.

So simple a gesture. So trusting. She thought him a servant, yet she offered her hand to him as a friend. Even the Falcon's cynical heart was touched. Because she was so very alone, he realised. What a pity that was.

He took the proffered hand, and as he felt the cool, soft, slim fingers close about his, his heart constricted within him. His hand tightened as well. *Good-bye*, he said silently.

Then, because a polite handshake could not be enough, he held it a moment longer, and another. His eyes scanned her moonlit countenance, memorizing her as she was this last night, all silver and shadow, her eyes widening in surprise or perhaps alarm, he knew not which. It hardly mattered. He raised her hand to his lips, and heard her sharp intake of breath, but more important was the light tease of patchouli about him, the scent and velvet softness of her skin against his mouth. He felt her hand tremble. Reluctantly, he released it.

"Good n-night, Mr. Brentick," she said in a tiny voice.

"Good night, Miss Cavencourt." *Good-bye, Amanda*.

She turned and began to move away.

No.

*No.*

"Damnation, not like this," he muttered.

In one swift flash of movement, like the Falcon he was, he'd closed the distance between them, lightly caught her shoulder to turn her back to him, and pulled her into his arms. One sure hand clasped her neck, the other pressed her back, preventing escape. Swiftly, too, his mouth descended to hers, covering it before she could cry out, and taking before she could think not to give.

He was a thief, after all, and he'd steal this, too, if he must.

Four bells. Ten o'clock. Amanda heard the sound distinctly just as she was moving away. After that, nothing was clear. She was aware of a blur of motion, a hand on her shoulder. Then the world, or some mad wind, sent her spinning into his arms.

It could not be happening.

Automatically, her hands went out to break free, but they were trapped against his chest, and she was imprisoned in the hard strength of his arms. She looked up, alarmed and confused, only to watch his face blur into darkness as his mouth crashed down on hers.

It was not happening.

Her trapped hands knotted into fists, and she squirmed

against the unrelenting snare of his body, only to strike muscle and heat. Shocked to the core, she shuddered and ceased struggling.

She didn't know what to do. And then she didn't want to do anything, because the insistent pressure of his mouth eased. The kiss grew gentler, more coaxing . . . and more dangerous. Far more dangerous, for he tasted of the sea, yet more of himself, and that was sweet and heady like opium. Her lips answered and, like a drug, the taste and scent of him stole through her in a stream of languorous warmth that sapped the strength from her muscles and left longing in its wake.

Her hands opened against his coat, crept up the sea-tinged wool to his shoulders, and on, to curl around his neck. The air was filled with the salt sea, and with the scent of him, of smoke and spicy soap, and she nestled into the warmth and the strength of him. It wasn't happening. It was a dream. She'd dreamt it before.

Helplessly, her muscles answered every light pressure of his hands, turning into each caress as though his touch were music. Mad, sweet music, irresistible. She became a serpent in his arms, a cobra moving to some enchanted flute. Dark and dangerous the spell, too, for at its edges something wild waited.

His fingers tangled in her hair. His tongue, cool and feather light, teased her lips, tempting and tantalising until they parted.

The waiting, wild demon sprang then, and the dream became another world, fierce and dark and hungry. His tongue invaded and demanded, sending fiery shocks through her. Her fingers tightened about his neck, while her body strained against his, and her heart raced so she thought it would burst from her.

His lips left hers to trail teasing kisses upon her brow, then down along the bones of her cheek, and on to her neck and the hollows of her ear, where he lingered to torment until she moaned. Then his mouth found hers again, and drank possessively, while his hands dragged from her shoulders down the length of her body to her waist and hips, moulding her to him.

That was when it crackled within her, the fear. She heard a low, choked cry—her own. Yet it was not happening. It was a dream.

He broke the kiss, but his hands moved to clasp her waist tightly. His breathing was laboured, as hers was. When he spoke, his voice was low, hoarse.

"I really . . . don't want . . . to let you go," he said, striving for breath between words. "But you are driving me mad and . . . " His eyes were dark, hot, intent. Damp tendrils clung to his forehead. The hands at her waist gripped harder.

Numbly, she looked about her. Not a dream. Good God.

She snatched her hands from his neck.

"Stay with me," he whispered.

She pushed frantically, then pulled at his fingers, trying to loosen his grip of her waist. "Let me go," she gasped. "Please. Oh, Lord, please let me go."

He exhaled a long sigh and his hands released her.

Tears sprang to her eyes. "I'm sorry," she blurted out. "I didn't mean—oh—" Then she fled.

Philip watched her slip away into the shadows, and willed himself not to pursue her. He couldn't bring her back. Even the Falcon could not swoop down and make off with this prize. He smiled ruefully. Make off where? He hadn't any place to take her. What had he thought—that he might ravish her here, on the deck, in some dark corner amid the casks and ropes? *Idiot*.

He returned to his eternal position at the rail and stared down at the water.

Any lingering doubts he'd entertained had vanished the instant he'd kissed her. She was innocent. Her mouth had told him so. Hers was not the response of a practised seductress—he'd had enough of that kind to know—but of the child she partly was, utterly untutored in lovemaking.

Shocked, he'd very nearly stopped it as soon as it had begun. Another moment's struggle, surely, and he'd have released her, for unwilling women were not to his taste. He would have stopped it, certainly, were it not for those confiding hands, creeping up to his neck, and were it not for her ripe, trusting mouth's willingness to follow his lead. That had quite undone him.

She'd succumbed too quickly, and so sweetly. Her slim, beautiful body had curved so naturally and so warmly to his. He'd wanted to wrap her around him, to lose himself in her erotic innocence, even as he taught her.

Oh, he'd lost himself all right, in needless torment. He knew perfectly well he couldn't seduce a naive gentlewoman, yet that was exactly what he'd commenced to do. The temptation had been, quite simply, quite completely, irresistible.

Even now, his heartbeats refused to steady. Even now, the taste of her mouth, of her skin, lingered, along with the scent of patchouli and the sweet heat of her slim body. He glanced down at his fingers, white-knuckled, clutching the rail.

He told himself it was but a kiss. A prolonged one, admittedly, but at most no more than a passionate embrace. He'd embraced countless women, Asian as well as European, and bedded scores of them. This painful arousal was simply the result of seven months' enforced abstinence.

Tomorrow he'd be free of this accursed ship, and of her, and there would be other women. He could buy half a dozen tomorrow, in Portsmouth. He need simply endure this one night, a few hours, and it would be over at last.

Accordingly, since only a few hours remained, the intrepid Falcon headed for the forecastle, with the very sensible intention of drinking them away.

Amanda felt reasonably steady by the time she entered

117

the cabin, though she rested her back against the closed door for a moment.

Mrs. Gales looked up from her needlework. A shadow of concern swept her calm countenance, and she rose.

"Are you ill, my dear?" She crossed the cabin to take Amanda's arm.

"N-no."

"You were above?"

"Y-yes. Talking to Mr. Brentick. I thought it best to—to keep him occupied."

"Poor dear, you must have been quite uneasy."

"I'm fine," Amanda said. Her glance flew to the cot, where Bella lay, snoring. "Is *she* all right?"

"Certainly. It was only a bit of laudanum, after all, and I'm sure she was careful how much she drank."

"And Padji?"

"He carried her in, then said he was going above," Mrs. Gales answered, as composedly as though Padji's carrying in an unconscious Bella were an everyday event. "He did not want to be absent overlong."

"D-did he get it?"

"I presume so. He was grinning like a naughty boy."

"Where is it?" Amanda's legs would support her no longer. Shakily, she lowered herself onto the banquette.

"I don't know. He only put her on the cot and left, with that smug grin on his face."

Never one to waste words herself, when action was more efficient, Mrs. Gales quickly found her brandy flask and pressed it into Amanda's hand. "There's no more to be done now, my dear," she said gently, "and no point in worrying. Have a sip. You'll feel better. Then you must try to get some sleep. We have an anxious morning ahead of us, I daresay."

# === 11 ===

PHILIP DID NOT return to the cabin until shortly before day-break. Getting dead drunk had taken an unconscionably long time.

He'd scarcely fallen asleep when a cannon blast shot him upright, and twin blasts of pain shot through his eyeballs. He gazed wildly about. Seeing no evidence of destruction, he finally realised that what he'd heard was some inconsiderate brute banging on the door and shouting.

Philip dragged himself from the mattress. An anchor had, apparently, fallen repeatedly upon his head, and his mouth was redolent of low tide. He'd not brought himself to so revolting a state in years.

The knocking and shouting recommenced with renewed vigour. Philip staggered to the door and unlocked it.

One of the mates with whom he'd dissipated stood in the passage looking abominably fresh and alert.

"Time to be off," the mate announced. "Captain's on fire to be gone, and I better warn you—in his mood he's not like to give you more than a quarter-hour."

Philip bit back a profane retort. The commander had not taken yestereve's last-minute request well. In wartime, East India men customarily stopped at Portsmouth, for they travelled in convoy. England was not at war at the moment, however. The wind having risen briskly, Captain Blayton had adamantly refused to make the unscheduled stop.

Philip had been forced to invoke the Marquess of

Hedgrave's power and, this receiving scant respect, had finally thrust the last of the documents into the captain's hands. According to these, Messrs Wringle and Brentick were on a secret government mission. Captain Blayton at last, and with very ill grace, had consented to drop his unwelcome passengers at Portsmouth. Evidently, that meant he would drop them into the harbour if they could not disembark within the next fifteen minutes.

"A quarter-hour it is, then," Philip said. He fumbled in his coat—in which he'd slept, or tried to sleep—and found his purse. He thrust a pile of coins into the mate's hand, asking for help with the baggage.

The hefty bribe elicited the assistance of four strong seamen, which was fortunate, as it turned out, for Jessup proved to be in worse state than his master. A brawny sailor had to carry him down the ladder onto the boat waiting to take them ashore. Throughout the short trip, Jessup's head hung miserably over the rowboat's side.

After depositing their passengers and flinging their belongings haphazardly about them, the crew members hopped back into their boat and rowed feverishly for the *Evelina*.

Jessup dutifully took up one carpetbag. Clutching it with both hands, he managed to stagger about three feet. Then he slumped down upon a trunk and gazed blearily about while Philip took his own throbbing head and aching body in search of transportation.

Some hours later, after being jolted in a stinking coach from one low hostelry to another—and arguing with the driver at each stop—the two were at last comfortably disposed in the large chambers of a commodious inn.

Jessup immediately fell upon his bed, where he sprawled, groaning.

Philip glared at him. "What the devil's the matter with you? You weren't up roistering with the rest of us, and you seemed well enough all yesterday." His eyes narrowed. "May I take it Miss Jones stopped in for one of her visits?"

Jessup moaned.

"What in blazes did the wench do to you?"

"Nuthin', guv." Jessup dragged his hand over his face. "Leastways, I don't remember. I must've had a drop too much. She brung a bottle and—"

"And you haven't touched liquor in seven months. Damned fool. You know your liver isn't what it was. Didn't I tell you that, a score of times? Confound it, didn't your chubby reformer tell you?"

"Aye, she tole me."

"But you didn't listen. I suppose you emptied most of the bottle yourself."

Jessup nodded wretchedly.

"Oh, good work. Very intelligent," Philip said. "After what your poor belly's been through, you're lucky it didn't kill you."

A tap at the door interrupted the lecture. Philip answered it, to learn from one of the inn servants that his bath awaited him in the adjoining chamber. His mood instantly lightened.

"That's what I like," he said, turning back to Jessup. "Prompt service. Fawning attention. Someone bowing and scraping to me, for a change. Gad, seven months, and never a proper wash the whole time. Don't look for me for at least a week, soldier," he said as he headed for the connecting door.

Jessup grumbled something unintelligible, then buried his face in his pillow.

Philip chuckled. "I do hope you got some pleasure from her last night," he said, shaking his head, "seeing you're paying so handsomely today."

Soap, gallons of fresh, hot water, towels that weren't damp and scratchy with salt: paradise, Philip thought as he sank into his bath. The throbbing in his head subsided and his taut muscles at last began to relax.

More than half an hour later he climbed out, dried himself off, and went to the trunk to unearth the dressing gown he'd forgotten to take out before. It was near the bottom, for he hadn't bothered with it during the voyage. He'd not felt inclined to linger in the tiny, stale cabin, even if life aboard ship had accommodated a long morning's dawdle over newspapers and coffee.

The dressing gown lay carelessly folded upon the rolled-up rug which contained the Laughing Princess.

Philip stared at the robe, then at the open door between the two rooms.

Wine. Jessup drunk, unconscious. And Philip above, lost in an embrace . . . that never should have been allowed to begin. Where had Padji been?

The heavy haze which had filled Philip's mind all morning abruptly cleared, and an unpleasantly familiar warning chill trickled down his neck.

In that moment, every piece of the game came together in his brain.

He took out the rug, though he didn't need to. He unrolled it, though he knew what he wouldn't find.

Naked, he knelt by the trunk, gazing down at the rug's contents: a jar of incense.

He closed his eyes and laughed. It was an ugly sound that made Jessup jump up from his bed and hurry to the open doorway to stare at his master.

"That bitch," Philip said softly. "That treacherous, scheming bitch. Seven months." He turned to meet Jessup's baffled gaze. "Seven months," Philip repeated. His mouth warped into something like a smile. "Is that not Oriental patience for you, soldier?"

"What—" Jessup stopped short as his employer held up the jar of incense.

"Seven months they've played us for a pair of fools. Whored her maid. Whored herself—or would have, I've no doubt. I hope you got a tumble out of the maid, my lad. I, you see, was too much the gentleman to attempt the mistress . . . because she's a *lady*," Philip spat out.

Jessup moved into the room, his horrified gaze fixed upon the jar of incense.

"You see it now, don't you?" Philip said in deceptively cool tones. "Why should you suspect her that last night, after all those days and nights, weeks, months? No one knew—or so we smugly believed—it *was* our last night. Why should you dream there was anything in the wine? Did it taste odd in any way, soldier? Would you have noticed? Or would you have put it down to your ailment, and going so long without?"

"But she drunk it, too," Jessup said, dazed. "I seen her. I wanted to get her drunk."

"Of course Miss Jones drank it. Why shouldn't she? She might lie there in a stupor, for she'd no more to do. The Indian slips in, picks the lock as neat as you please, takes out the statue, throws the maid over his shoulder, goes out and, moments later, deposits maid and statue at the feet of his mistress. Then he proceeds to the forecastle to join our dissipations and watch me drink myself into stupefaction." Philip's fingers closed about the neck of the jar. "I couldn't have done it neater myself . . . if I'd such a pair of clodpates to deal with."

Abruptly he flung down the jar, then ripped a shirt and a pair of trousers from the trunk. "Sorry," he muttered. "Aye, you'll be sorry, sweetheart."

Five minutes later, he was dressed and out the door.

An hour after, he stood at the pier, clenching his fists in impotent fury. The *Evelina* was long gone, driven swiftly by the most accommodating wind she'd encountered since leaving Calcutta.

One might hire a speedier vessel, and very possibly overtake her. But then what? Board the ship and demand that Lord Cavencourt's sister be flogged? Keelhauled? Tried and hanged as a thief? What the devil had he been thinking of?

Murder, Philip answered silently. A nice, satisfying little murder. He would take her smooth, slim neck in his hands . . . and choke the life out of her. He merely wanted to strangle her, that was all. With his bare hands.

"But that would never do, miss, would it?" he murmured.

123

"What would Mrs. Bullerham think? Most improper."

Stories. All those lovely stories. The seductive voice and scent. The ridiculous, contradictory innocence and vulnerability, and the pity he'd felt because she was so utterly alone.

"Oh, Amanda," he whispered. "You miserable . . . little . . . scheming . . . *bitch.*"

In one particular, the Falcon had erred. Padji had not placed the statue at his mistress's feet. He had concealed it for the remainder of the journey in an exceedingly elaborate and lofty arrangement of turban.

He did not reveal this until they were all safely ensconced in their hotel in London. Only then did he present to his mistress, with all appropriate ceremony, the Laughing Princess. In the event the theft had been discovered too soon, he explained, it was best the statue not be in his mistress's possession. Equally important, she ought not know where it was. Thus, only Padji would suffer for the crime.

Amanda was far too weary to point out that she'd never have let Padji be punished in her place. She'd barely the strength to thank him. She'd spent these last days in a frenzy of anxiety and guilt. Even in Gravesend, she'd expected Mr. Wringle to pop out of every door and alley, screaming for a constable. More appalling was the prospect of seeing Mr. Brentick's shocked, reproachful face. He would have concluded Amanda Cavencourt had toyed with his affections purely for her own criminal ends.

Which was absurd, she told herself now, as she crawled into bed and pulled the blankets up over her head. She was quite certain he could know no more of the Laughing Princess at present than he ever had. Even if he did, she could not be the only suspect.

As to what had occurred that last night—well, that had nothing to do with his affections, did it? Such things were not unheard of. Lady Tewkshead had eloped with Sir Rodger Crawford's groom. Miss Flora Perquat had been exiled to

Calcutta because she'd had a child by her father's gardener. Mr. Brentick must have kissed any number of gently bred ladies—and bedded at least some of them. One embrace would mean little to him. Furthermore, he'd kissed Amanda only because there was no one else conveniently at hand.

He would not break his heart on her account. Men had a different attitude about physical intimacy than women did. It was laughable to imagine she'd led him astray. Men went astray by nature. The difficulty was in leading them otherwise.

Amanda's hand slipped under her pillow and closed around the sandalwood figure. It didn't matter, she told herself. It was done and the princess was safe. Nonetheless, long hours passed before the tears abated, and Amanda Cavencourt, thief, fell asleep.

# ==12==

CAVENCOURT? THE ELDERLY solicitor mumbled, while his trembling hands sought to make order of the documents his visitor had exasperatedly flung back upon the desk.

"Lord Cavencourt's sister," Philip repeated, for the third time. "She lives in Yorkshire. I want to know where."

Coming here, clearly, was a mistake. Mr. Brewell had nearly succumbed to apoplexy at the sight of him. The old lawyer had no sooner recovered from the shock than the argument had commenced, and with it a blizzard of legal documents that might have papered the dome of St. Paul's, with plenty to spare for Westminster Abbey.

Unfortunately, when one had been out of one's native country for fifteen years, and had scarcely set foot in London previous to that, useful acquaintances were few and far between. When, moreover, one preferred one's presence not be known, the list of possible information sources shrank even further.

The Falcon had contacts in virtually every corner of India, persons whose discretion could be relied upon in the interests of the Crown or, more often, Profit. London, on the other hand, might have been the moon, so alien it was. Actually, one might have tracked down Miss Cavencourt a deal more easily on the moon than in the chaos of this infernal city.

Three weeks he'd wasted, searching on his own, hanging about hotels and inns and questioning tradesmen. He'd gone in disguise to clubs and gaming hells, even managed without invitation a few visits to Society affairs. He'd learned little.

He heard no mention of the Cavencourts in the gossip he eavesdropped upon. Not wishing to draw attention to himself, he'd dared do little more than listen. As it was, he encountered far too many former fellow officers and company men. To attract their notice was to court recognition, and word might easily reach Hedgrave.

The Falcon had far rather have slivers of bamboo jammed under his fingernails and set on fire than find himself under examination by Hedgrave or any of his colleagues. Only yesterday, in Bond Street, Philip had narrowly escaped Danbridge's shrewd scrutiny . . . and the inevitable humiliation of admitting that yes, the intrepid Falcon, whose name was feared throughout India, had got the statue . . . and had it stolen from him. By a twenty-six-year-old spinster.

All of which left Philip with his family solicitor. At present, Philip could have cheerfully applied the bamboo method to Mr. Brewell. The lawyer was older than Methuselah, and his chambers had most likely been built—and not cleaned since—the Flood. One glimpse at the musty old office, and Miss Jones would have flown at it with mop and brush. Very likely she'd have taken the dusty old lawyer, in his rusty black coat and breeches, out of doors and given him a vigourous shaking.

"Cavencourt. Cavencourt." The watery grey eyes looked up from the papers. "Would that be the Baron Cavencourt? The eighth, isn't it? Or is it tenth? Odd family. Something about his—or was that the other one? But they're in India," he concluded, much befuddled.

"Lord Cavencourt lives in Calcutta," Philip said patiently. "His sister is recently returned to England. We were on the same ship. She mentioned Yorkshire. What I want to know is *where*."

Mr. Brewell shook his head sadly, and his wrinkled, grey face assumed an expression of reproach. "With all due respect, this is hardly the time to be racketing about the countryside after women. There is a great deal to be settled. In any case, you ought think first of going home. The family—"

"Can go to blazes," Philip snapped. "We've discussed all that at unnecessary length."

"But at least—"

"I owe them nothing. They've lived quite comfortably without me more than fifteen years. I daresay they'll manage to endure another few days. I came for information," he continued in taut tones. "If you can't provide it, I shall seek elsewhere. Good day." He turned and headed for the door.

"But my—"

"And not a word," Philip ordered. "Not one word."

"That will considerably complicate matters."

"I don't give a damn."

"Might one at least mention you're alive?" the solicitor pleaded. "I need only say I received word from trustworthy sources."

Philip paused, his fingers on the handle. "Very well. But no more than that." Then he left.

Philip returned to the inn to find his bags packed, and Jessup reading a sporting journal.

"What the devil is all this?" Philip demanded.

"I thought you'd want to be goin'. You was just complainin' this mornin' how we'd been wastin' time and you was sick o' the sight o' London."

"I've spent the better part of three weeks scouring every inn and alley of the curst place. You think I want to try the same exercise through all of Yorkshire? Brewell, like everyone else in this confounded warren, hadn't the foggiest idea where the Cavencourts reside," he added angrily. "I daresay he'll be another ten years muddling and stumbling about, trying to find out. If he does try. Which he'd rather not. He doesn't approve my racketing after women, you see."

Jessup picked up a valise. "Kirkby Glenham," he said.

"What?"

"She lives in Kirkby Glenham," Jessup said expressionlessly. "I've paid our shot and hired a carriage. Did you want to have a bite before we go?"

Philip stared at him. "Are you sure? How did you find out?"

Jessup looked away and mumbled something.

"What?"

"Debretts, sir. I looked 'em up in Debretts. Kirkby Glenham. Lived there since the time of the second Baron. There's a map on the table." Jessup nodded in that direction. "It's a manor house on the moors."

Mr. Thurston, the Cavencourts' London solicitor, had warned Amanda that the manor house was not quite ready for her, because his agent had been unable to fully staff it. She, however, had no wish to linger in Town, where she might collide any moment with an irate Mr. Wringle or a murderous Lord Hedgrave.

Thus she arrived at her family home to find the interior entirely shrouded in dust covers, and mould and mildew growing everywhere. In addition to an apparently competent bailiff and an elderly gardener, she found one maid of all work feigning, in a lackadaisical manner, to do the work of a staff of twelve.

At the end of a fortnight, thanks mainly to Bella, dust, mould, and mildew had been scoured away. During this same period, thanks to Padji, the maid of all work had fled, and the gardener threatened to do likewise. After three weeks, Miss Cavencourt had acquired one housekeeper and one scullery maid, while the bailiff had given notice. During this period, a number of servants had come, and quickly gone. They came because the wages were good. They left—usually within twenty-four hours— because Padji was not.

"I have told him a hundred times," Amanda complained to Mrs. Gales, "but he won't listen, or he doesn't understand."

They were in the estate office. Seated in her father's

huge, ugly chair, her elbows on the great desk, Amanda gazed mournfully at a ledger. Opposite her, Mrs. Gales calmly knitted.

"It is a considerable adjustment for him," the widow said.

"But he expects everyone to adjust to *him*. How is one to make him comprehend that English servants do not, and are not expected to, behave as Indians do? No one is humble enough or attentive enough, he thinks. Why in blazes must Mrs. Swanslow taste my food for poison when Padji himself has cooked it?"

Amanda closed the ledger with a thump. "He has her in such a tremble, I cannot make heads or tales of her writing. I cannot tell if these are household accounts or Persian songs of prayer. And now I must replace the bailiff, which is Padji's fault again. He had no business shadowing Mr. Corker about the grounds."

Mrs. Gales laid her knitting aside. "You want a cup of tea, my dear."

"I want a bailiff," Amanda wailed, "and a butler, and maids. Bella should not be looking after the chambers, and the scullery maid should not be doing the laundry."

"Jane had better not do the laundry," Mrs. Gales said. "She doesn't know the first thing about it, and all your lovely frocks will be ruined." She rose. "Do quit this room, Amanda. You only upset yourself here. I shall see about the tea and bring it to the library."

When Amanda hesitated, the widow added, "We shall go to the employment agent in York tomorrow. Until then, there's no point fretting yourself. It will all come about in time, dear. We must be patient."

Amanda obediently trailed after her into the hallway, while wondering, not for the first time, how the widow managed to remain so consistently unruffled. A full eight hours' sound sleep each night no doubt contributed. Amanda slept, but not soundly. Hours passed before she could drive her worries back into the recesses of her mind.

The library was a sensible idea. Amanda would read, and blot out this whole dreadful morning—these last wretched weeks, preferably—with one of the half-dozen bloodcurdling Gothic novels she'd got from York. Chains and dungeons and headless corpses were just what she needed. Come to think of it, a dungeon and chains might be just what Padji needed, bless his interfering heart.

She'd hardly settled into her favourite chair when the door-knocker crashed. With a sigh, she rose to answer it. The employment agent knew she was desperate. He may have sent along an applicant. Mrs. Swanslow had gone to the market, and it would be best if Padji were not the one to open the door. One prospective laundry maid had fled at the first glimpse of him.

Padji, fortunately, was nowhere in sight when Amanda reached the vestibule.

Belatedly, she realised a servant would not come to the front door. Who could possibly be calling? Not any of her neighbours, certainly. She'd given up expecting any sort of welcome from them, not that she had, really—

Amanda's meditations came to an abrupt halt as she opened the door and looked up . . . into the stony, blue-eyed countenance of Mr. Brentick.

"Oh," she gasped. Then, her brain offering no further help to her tongue, she simply stared at him.

"I beg your pardon, miss," he said. "I was not welcome at the servants' entrance, and so, had no choice."

"N-not welcome?"

"Not to put too fine a point on it, Padji closed the door in my face. Very firmly."

"You mean he slammed it, I suppose." The first shock subsided, only to be swamped by chilling anxiety and confusion. "I cannot think why he would be so rude—but he—he's not himself—quite—lately—at least, I hope not. He is not—adjusting. Oh, dear." She backed away. "Please come in."

He threw her a searching look as he stepped over the

threshold. "I expect you're surprised to see me," he said.

"Surprise is hardly adequate to the occasion." Desperately she tried to collect her wits. She'd almost forgotten how very blue and piercing his eyes were, and how tall he was. Or did it merely *seem* that he towered over her? "What on earth are you doing in Yorkshire, Mr. Brentick?" She glanced past him at the empty doorway. "Where is Mr. Wringle?"

This earned her another searching glance.

"Is something wrong?" she asked.

"Yes," he said. "Something is very wrong."

Amanda's face went hot and cold as the colour rushed over it and drained away.

At this moment, a shadow darkened the hallway. She glanced behind her, to see Padji's massive bulk advancing.

"Never fear, mistress," he growled. "I shall see to him."

"Miss Cavencourt, I must speak with you," the valet said quickly. "I am in great difficulty and—" He sidestepped neatly as Padji's huge hand shot towards him.

Amanda hastily stepped in Padji's way. "Enough!" she said. "Did I ask for your assistance, Padji?"

"I only anticipate, mistress," came the low Hindustani response.

"There is no need to manhandle visitors," she answered in the same tongue. "Everyone who comes to the door is not an assassin."

"Actually, your competent assassin rarely comes to the front door," Mr. Brentick politely pointed out. In response to her startled look, he added, "I am acquainted with the language, miss. Fifteen years in India, recollect."

She glanced from him to Padji, her mind working as rapidly as it could in the circumstances. "Padji is surprised to see you, as I am. I'm afraid he doesn't care overmuch for surprises."

"There is a perfectly reasonable explanation, Miss Cavencourt, if you'd be so kind as to indulge me a hearing."

Padji's eyes narrowed. "Send him away, mistress. This man is trouble for you. Also, he stinks like a pig."

Mr. Brentick's blue eyes flashed in his pale face. Unnaturally pale, Amanda now realised. He looked ill, despite his fiery gaze. And thin.

"I beg your pardon," he said stiffly. "I have been upon the road nearly four days, and my lodgings have not been of the most luxurious. I should never have presented myself in this condition, had I any other choice. I spent the last of my funds on coach fare, and came here on foot from the last posting inn."

Amanda's hand flew to her breast. "Good heavens, what on earth has happened?"

His blue gaze seemed to skewer her. "I have been discharged," he said. "Without notice, without a character, without a farthing."

"Oh, no."

"Also, I may add, without explanation. We were in Portsmouth scarce two hours, when my employer flew into a rage. I have no idea what set him off. I know only that he called me an irresponsible incompetent—among other names I shall not sully your ears with—and discharged me."

Padji gave a disdainful snort.

"That is monstrous," Amanda said, disregarding her watchdog. A suffocating wave of guilt washed over her. She knew what had happened. Mr. Wringle had discovered the theft, and taken out his rage on his hapless servant.

"I cannot apologise sufficiently for intruding in this inexcusable way, miss." The valet shot one darkling glance at Padji before returning to the mistress. "I should never have dreamt of doing such a thing, but I had nowhere else to turn."

A low, rumbling sound came from Padji's throat.

"Stop growling," Amanda snapped. "You are not a savage, I hope, and in any case, you are not blind. It's obvious Mr. Brentick is tired—and hungry as well, I'm sure. Take him down to the servants' hall and— No, on second thought, I shall come with you." To the valet she said, "Let us find you something to eat. Then, when you're feeling better, we'll discuss this further.

They'd found Mrs. Gales in the kitchen and, luckily for Philip, the widow had supervised his meal. Padji, he had little doubt, would have blithely poisoned the unwanted visitor, if left to his own devices—and if, that is, Philip were halfwit enough to remain alone with him. Padji had not troubled to disguise his hostility. Miss Cavencourt's reaction was far more puzzling.

The Falcon had, as was his custom, arrived armed with several strategies. For instance, he'd fully expected Padji's attack. Which meant a quick move to grab Miss Cavencourt and hold a knife to her throat, and thus obtain the statue under most undesirable circumstances. As soon as she'd stepped between him and Padji, Philip deduced that the lady was a most incautious and inefficient adversary. Accordingly, he'd mentally shredded Plan A. In another few minutes, he'd begun to feel disagreeably inefficient himself, because she did not react properly.

Philip warily eyed his nemesis now, as he followed her into her office. Padji stood in the open doorway, arms folded across his chest, his round, brown face eloquent with disapproval.

"Mr. Wringle's behaviour seems most unaccountable," Miss Cavencourt began slowly.

He watched her flit past him to take up her position behind the great barricade of a desk. In her pale blue frock, amid the dark, masculine surroundings, she seemed smaller and more fragile than Philip remembered. Not quite real. But that was because she was so false.

"Also most ungrateful," she added, "when one considers your devotion during his long illness. He gave you no explanation beyond what you mentioned?"

"No, miss. At the time I suspected something else displeased him." He hesitated.

"Yes?"

"I regret to say he was beside himself," Philip continued

carefully. "He tore through all my belongings— as though he believed I'd *stolen* something." He lowered his gaze from Miss Cavencourt's startled golden one. "Of course you have only my word I hadn't."

Padji sniffed.

Miss Cavencourt's face grew paler.

"Do you think something *was* stolen, Mr. Brentick?"

He pretended to think hard before answering, "It's possible, though I can't imagine what. He had clothes and legal papers, and a few trinkets and souvenirs—some carved objects, that sort of thing. Nothing of value to a thief, as far as I could tell. He had money, naturally, but he never searched my pockets, and he had plenty to toss about at the inn. It's a puzzle to me, miss."

"If you had taken anything of value," she said, "you'd hardly have arrived here on foot, half-starved." She moved a piece of paper from the right side of the blotter to the left. "I collect you need a loan," she said without looking at him.

Padji scowled.

Philip transformed his expression of innocence to one of embarrassment. "I didn't come for charity—not of that sort," he answered. "I need employment. I've been trying to find work nearly a month now, but with neither references nor friends, there's nothing. Except, that is, to take the King's shilling. I'm no coward, miss, and I'll do that if I must, but—"

"So you must," Padji averred, nodding his head. "So it is fated."

"It most certainly is not!" said Amanda. "Mr. Brentick has served his country near half his life. He seeks work. I do not see why we should not assist him." Her gaze returned to Philip. "The trouble is, I don't know any gentlemen hereabouts you might serve."

"I don't expect the same position, miss," Philip said with appropriate humility. "I'd take anything, so long as it's honest work."

She moved the sheet of paper from the left side of the

blotter back to the right. Then she pushed the inkwell one half inch to the left. She picked up a pen and laid it down again. She bit her lip, and a tiny crease appeared between her brows. Philip waited patiently through the growing silence.

She was a terrible actress. Her guilt, for instance, was too clearly evident, even now. Everything was too evident. Her surprise and curiosity in response to his hints about the theft were too obviously feigned. Her pity for the ill-used valet, in contrast, was unnervingly genuine. Gad, for a moment, she'd even made him feel guilty about the lies he told. Only for a moment, though. Matters were not precisely as he'd assumed, perhaps. Nonetheless, he had no doubt she had the statue, and that was all he need concern himself with.

Thus he waited, his brain ready to provide a suitably manipulative response to whatever her ineptly lying tongue uttered next.

"Would you be willing to accept the work of ten people?" she said at last in a hesitant voice.

His brain screeched to a halt. "I beg your pardon, miss?"

"I am short staffed," she said more firmly. "We're having a devil of a time finding employees . . . and keeping those we do find. My bailiff has given notice and I need a replacement. I also need—oh, lud, *everybody*."

The gears began grinding again. Philip assumed a mask of sympathy while Miss Cavencourt proceeded to pour out her domestic anxieties, with Padji interjecting his own opinions every few sentences.

When she was done, Philip neatly simplified the issues. "What you want first of all, are two reliable people: one to manage matters out of doors, and one for indoors. I am not properly equipped to handle the former, but I'd be grateful for a chance to take on the latter."

"The mistress is confused," said Padji. "Her slave is by, to see to all her wishes. She has no need—"

"I need a staff," Miss Cavencourt said sharply. "I realise

this house is not half the size of the rani's palace. Even so, it wants servants, and *you* certainly don't manage them. You overset everyone who comes. You have driven even Mr. Corker—the most forbearing man I've ever met—to give notice. Whatever possessed you to ask him where I bury the servants who displease me?"

Philip's mouth twitched. He quickly frowned instead.

"Well, he did," Miss Cavencourt told him aggrievedly. "And just this morning, Jane—that's the poor scullery maid— dropped into hysterics because he found a cobweb in the pantry, and threatened to cut off her finger."

"A mild rebuke," Padji said, "for so grievous an offence to the mistress's sight."

Exhaling a sigh of exasperation, Miss Cavencourt sank into her chair. Sank quite literally, that is, for the enormous carved monstrosity swallowed her up. She appeared about ten years old. "Oh, Padji, I am at my wits' end with you."

Padji gazed sorrowfully at her. "My golden beloved is displeased," he said. "I have offended. I shall cut off my own worthless finger to appease her." His hand closed over the knife at his sash, and Philip tensed.

"You most certainly will not, you wicked creature," she said crisply. "I will not have you bleeding all over the carpet. Put your knife away and behave yourself. You have distracted me from my discussion."

"But, mistress, you cannot wish this false, stinking creature in your sublime abode."

Squelching an insane urge to draw his own knife, Philip calmly intervened before the beloved mistress could respond.

"If Miss Cavencourt would be kind enough to outline her needs and direct me to my quarters, I should be happy to clean my offensive person to everyone's satisfaction."

She stared at him. "Are you quite sure, Mr. Brentick? That is, you must be aware what a Herculean task I propose—and we haven't discussed it, really—"

"If you are willing to try me, miss, I am willing to do whatever you require. As I've indicated, I need work."

She coloured, and got that irritatingly guilty look in her eyes again.

"Yes, of course. And I need help, obviously."

"But, mistress—"

"Please hold your tongue, Padji."

"But this man is a vile seducer!" Padji cried. "Not once, but—"

A wash of brilliant rose spread over the lady's cheeks and neck. "That is quite enough," she snapped. "Please leave this room, Padji, and close the door after you. I wish to have a private word with Mr. Brentick."

Padji folded his arms over his chest and stood firm. "It is unseemly. This man is not to be trusted."

Seducer? Was that all? Impossible, Philip decided. That was merely the Indian's excuse for his hostility. But why need he make excuses . . . unless the mistress didn't know the whole truth. Was it possible she believed Brentick ignorant of the whole business? Could she possibly be so naive.

Ten minutes later, Padji had finally retired in high dudgeon. With his exit came rising panic. Still, Amanda chided herself, the thing must be got out of the way now.

Accordingly, she stood up, raised her chin, and plunged headlong at the mortifying subject. "I know you are not a seducer," she said, "and I will not accuse you of behaving improperly when I gave you so much reason to think that I—well, that I was not—that I was *fast*."

Mr. Brentick's blue eyes opened very wide, and he blinked. Twice.

Amanda went on doggedly, "I've had time to reflect upon my actions, and now see that for all my protests and so-called explanations, they would lead people to—to certain conclusions. The voyage was long and the company limited. It was a circumstance conducive to intimacy and—and . . . confusion. We were both confused, apparently." She paused.

He said nothing.

"And so, we made a mistake," she said.

"A mistake," he repeated.

"But I am not fast, and you are not the villainous seducer Padji thinks you, and so we shall not repeat the error, naturally."

"Naturally."

"Then you understand?" She tried to read his expression, but all she found were fathomless blue depths.

"Yes, miss. Quite. The entire episode is to be forgotten."

"Yes." Oh, certainly. That embrace—had it been only a few weeks ago?—was merely carved into her memory like an inscription upon a marble tombstone. It would wear away in a millennium or two. Sooner, if she could remember not to look at his mouth. Or his hands. Sooner still if he'd only stop gazing at her in that watchful, intent way.

# ===13===

THE FOLLOWING DAY, Philip met with Jessup in a York public house.

"It's going to be difficult," Philip admitted. "She's deposited the thing in a bank vault, drat her."

"You sure?" Jessup asked in dismay. "How'd you find out so quick?"

Philip dropped him a disdainful look. "Have you forgotten who I am, soldier?"

"Not likely, guv. But I been wonderin' now and again if *you* forgot," was the blunt reply. "Been wonderin' if you picked up a touch of fever."

Philip ignored this tactless slur on his abilities.

"I had a thorough tour of the house yesterday," he said patiently. "The statue wasn't displayed. Which means Miss Cavencourt believes someone may come after it."

"Which he done."

"Naturally, being the vexatious female she is, she must make my task as difficult as possible. Accordingly, the first place I visited today was the bank, where a talkative clerk confirmed my worst suspicions. I swear," he said exasperatedly, "the Old Nick himself set that woman in my path."

"Then it's gone," said Jessup. "And I say good riddance. Nothin' but trouble since we started on this business."

"For fifty thousand quid, one expects trouble."

"You don't need the money. You done good enough these last five years. Enough to set yourself up like a proper gentleman. And I done good enough with you. Let the lady keep her piece of wood. She worked hard enough for it. She deserves somethin'—no one ever outsmarted the Falcon afore."

Philip glared into his ale mug. "I'm not outdone yet."

"Oh, give it over, guv," Jessup urged. "Ain't you had enough? I have. The jolliest armful I ever run across, and so sweet and kind she was, fussin' over me like I was a baby. She done for me, that one. I ain't goin' near another female, long as I live," he added sorrowfully. "I could've swore she liked me. Why, I'd watch her tidyin' and dustin', and listen to her scold, and I thought I could do that all the rest o' my days. She got me thinkin' 'bout a little cottage, and flowers, and a square of vegetable garden . . . and fat babes, squallin' and crawlin' on the floor. And everythin' would shine and smell so clean. And her with them snappin' black eyes, layin' out my supper—"

"You're maudlin," Philip interrupted. "Get a grip on yourself."

"I do. I had enough. It were a damn fool job to take in the first place, on account of some damn fool lord with a maggot on his brain. It never were your kind of job. One thing to work for king and country, but this— it's just common thievin'," Jessup said, dropping his voice. "Besides, the lady stole it back, fair and square, and never done neither of us no harm. Which she could of, which you know good as I do. Leave her alone, guv."

"I will not," Philip gritted out, "leave her alone. I agreed to a job—whether it's entirely in my style or not—and I have *never* failed anybody, at any time. You think I can retire with this humiliating fiasco as the last act of my career?"

Jessup sighed. "You stole it, didn't you? She just stole it back is all. You didn't fail, exactly."

"One either fails or succeeds. There's no part-way about it. I'll get it back," Philip said tightly, "however long it takes. Meanwhile, I've work for you."

* * *

Like the long-suffering Jessup, Mrs. Gales, too, experienced qualms. Hers, however, were of a more delicate nature, and thus more cautiously expressed.

She and Amanda sat in the library.

"My dear, do you think this altogether wise?" the widow asked as she handed Amanda her tea. "You really don't know the man. It is possible, is it not, that Mr. Wringle sent him to recover the statue?"

"I thought of that," Amanda answered. She took her cup and carried it to the window seat, so she could gaze out at the withered garden. "Padji was so hostile, I supposed he was thinking the same thing. But he wasn't. He'd got it into his head that Mr. Brentick had come for the sole purpose of ravishing me." She smiled faintly. "Which is thoroughly absurd, even if the poor man hadn't been too weak and hungry for such an exertion. You saw him, Leticia."

"Yes." The widow sighed.

"Besides, the statue is quite safe now. I'm the only one who can claim it. Poor Princess, locked away in a cold, dark vault," Amanda said wistfully. "It hardly seems worth all the trouble and anxiety, when I can't even look at her or touch her. I'd wanted to keep her here, nearby while I worked on my book, as . . . well, as inspiration, perhaps. Instead, all I can do is travel into York occasionally to visit her. Poor princess."

"Only for a while, dear," Mrs. Gales consoled. "Just until we feel reasonably certain the marquess hasn't traced it to you. Not that I think for a moment he could," she added in hasty reassurance. "If I were Mr. Wringle, I certainly should not wish to inform his lordship that the statue mysteriously vanished—in Portsmouth, of all places. If Mr. Wringle has any common sense at all, he'll make for the West Indies, or New South Wales, with all due celerity."

Amanda turned to look at her. "Now that might explain it," she said thoughtfully. "If Mr. Wringle wanted to disappear, he must get rid of his servant. Mr. Brentick is far too striking not to be remarked."

"Indeed," Mrs. Gales murmured. "Far too striking."

Amanda returned to the dreary landscape. "Still, he ought at least have *paid* him. But then I should not have a butler. He may not have all the necessary experience, but at least Padji doesn't intimidate him. Perhaps Mr. Brentick will remain more than twenty-four hours."

Mr. Brentick could boast nothing remotely approaching the necessary experience. His ideas of a butler's duties were vague, to say the least. He'd quickly ascertained, however, that his new employer's comprehension of the position was equally dim. A master storyteller Miss Cavencourt might be. A household manager she decidedly was not. She must make all the servants her friends, and setting friends to the weary business of domestic drudgery presented a contradiction her intellect could not untangle. Oddly enough, the only servant she commanded with anything like authority was that great Indian hippopotamus, and that was only when Padji had vexed her past all bearing.

This much Philip had discovered long before he'd swung into his saddle to ride to York. A subtly probing discussion with the employment agent clarified numerous other domestic issues.

Philip returned to the remote manor house armed with some basic information. For the rest, he'd rely upon his natural resourcefulness.

At eighteen, dismissed and disowned, he'd left Felkonwood with but five pounds in his pocket. Three months later, by a combination of work and wagers, he'd acquired the money to purchase his commission. He'd not, as his father confidently assumed, entered the military in the lowly position of an enlisted man, but as an officer. From that point on, Philip Astonley had proved to himself, repeatedly, that he was fully capable of achieving any object he set his sights upon.

When he'd proved to his satisfaction and his superiors' astonishment his genius for command, Philip soon sought a new and more dangerous proving ground. In the last five years, he'd astonished all of India. He'd become a legend.

Now he need only prove himself as a servant, overlord of a handful of men and women. One who'd commanded regiments could certainly command one small household. As to his inept general—he'd merely to win her trust.

With smooth military efficiency, Philip set to work.

Immediately upon his return from York, he met with the bailiff and persuaded Mr. Corker to stay on.

The following day, a parade of maids appeared before Mrs. Swanslow. Padji stalked in to scrutinise them. Two of the maids shrieked, and one fainted. Mr. Brentick entered and revived the unconscious girl, then calmly introduced Padji as a brilliant though temperamental *French* cook.

Thus reduced from supernatural monster to mere Gallic lunatic, Padji was endured with a proper British stoicism. Nobody fainted again, no one even threw her apron over her head. A few giggled—then quickly stifled themselves as their eyes met the butler's imperious blue gaze. With his subtle guidance, Mrs. Swanslow selected two housemaids.

By the end of the week, with the acquisition of some daily servants and one footman, James, the house was adequately staffed, though certainly not as fully as it had been in the last baron's time. Still, Miss Cavencourt expressed no desire to entertain—rather the opposite—and her butler saw no benefit in accumulating a pack of idlers, merely for appearances' sake. The lady had a book to write. She needed quiet and calm, not an army of minions stumbling about the place and quarrelling in the corridors.

Accordingly, Mr. Brentick ordered the library cleaned first thing each morning, hours before the mistress arrived to work. After that, no one but Mrs. Gales or Bella was permitted to intrude upon her. Mr. Brentick noiselessly carried in her tea, and noiselessly took away the remains. He slipped in like an efficient, well-mannered ghost, and vanished in the same manner.

Within a month, his staff became ghosts as well: smiling, cheerful, but quiet and quick. In a month, he'd converted an assortment of sturdy Yorkshire workers into an army of amiable, discreetly attentive wraiths.

Thus a damp October passed, to be succeeded by a wet and cold November. Fortunately for its India-acclimated inhabitants, the manor house was of modest proportions. It would, in fact, have nestled quite comfortably in the east wing of Felkonwood Castle, with room to spare. Years before, Miss Cavencourt's grandfather had enlarged and modernized the manor with an eye to comfort rather than grandeur. Here, no great hallways swept chilling draughts into vast, echoing, chambers. Once properly cleaned, the chimneys performed flawlessly. Even in late autumn, the rooms were snug enough.

The intimate dining room and cozy library faced west, looking out onto a sadly neglected garden. Twigs and dead leaves clogged the ornamental pond at its centre, for, despite Philip's efforts, Padji and the gardener had collided once too often. The latter had departed in a huff several weeks ago. Still, the garden would be restored in the spring.

The house nestled in a shallow dale. Beyond the garden, dark, wooded slopes reached towards the brooding moorland beyond. Nonetheless, even now, at twilight, he did not find the world beyond the library windows altogether dreary. Dark it was, this place, cold and remote, yet with the darkness and remoteness of a secret, quiet in its moody mystery.

Philip stood, the drape pull forgotten in his hand as he drank in the lowering night.

"I suppose it must seem very gloomy to you," came Miss Cavencourt's low voice, startling him.

He quickly pulled the drapes closed.

"All the better, miss," he answered. "In contrast to the chill and gloom out of doors, indoors seems the warmer and brighter." He frowned at the small figure huddled over the writing table. "Your tea will grow cold. Tomorrow we must move your table. I do believe you are working in the draughtiest corner of the room."

She looked up. Miss Cavencourt's method of composing her thoughts, he'd learned, was to discompose her coiffure. Over and over again, while she worked, her nervous fingers would rake back her hair, heedlessly loosening pins and steadily reducing her businesslike chignon to a wanton tangle of coffee-coloured tresses.

Her butler's hands itched to make all tidy and efficient again, so that he might view her coolly as a professional problem. At present, unfortunately, she presented another sort of riddle—an old one, which he was strongly tempted to solve in the time-honoured manner of his gender.

When he'd first arrived, seduction was the very last thing on his mind. In a matter of weeks, it had relentlessly thrust its way forward again. Occasionally, it did reach first place, whence he found it increasingly difficult to dislodge.

"I think it's better this way," she said. "The fire is too cozy and inviting, and the warmth would probably make me drowsy. I find it hard enough to concentrate as it is."

Philip told himself he experienced not the least difficulty concentrating. If she appeared a lonely waif, sadly in want of someone to take her in hand, that was not his problem. He didn't care if her aristocratic nose turned red and her fingers blue with cold. She could freeze if she liked. It was nothing to him.

He removed the tray from the small table by the fire and carried it to the large one where she worked. Finding no clear surface space available, Philip simply set the entire tray upon the manuscript page before her.

"Mr. Brentick, I was working on that!"

"Yes, miss," he said. "I discerned no other method of persuading you to stop."

Her amber eyes lit with annoyance. "Does this not strike you as a shade overbearing? To drop the entire tray under my nose?"

"You ate nothing at midday," he said. "If I bring back another untouched tray, Padji will commence to weeping, and that inevitably throws Mrs. Swanslow into one of her spasms. Then Jane, in sympathy, will go off in one of her fits. We are of tender sensibilities belowstairs. When the mistress neglects her tea, we are inconsolable, and consequently, break out in violence. I realise your work has precedence over such mundane matters as rest and nourishment, miss. Regrettably, the rest of the staff lack my philosophical detachment. What are we two," he concluded, sadly shaking his head, "against so many?"

"We two, indeed," she said with a sniff as she watched him pour. "I can see whose side you are on."

He handed her the cup. "As I understand it, a butler's primary aim in life is the maintenance of domestic order and peace. It wants a firm hand to sustain the battle against chaos," he said, with a meaningful glance at the disaster representing Miss Cavencourt's literary masterpiece.

Ink-spattered pages lay strewn about in gay abandon. Upon table and floor scores of books—most with bits of paper sticking from their pages—stood in forlorn heaps.

She followed his gaze and flushed. "I am not very organised, I'm afraid," she said.

She was not organised at all. Her working methods were as tumbled and disordered as her hair. Ink smudged her fingers. He observed a dark smudge between her fine eyebrows. He wanted to rub it away with his thumb. He wanted to repair her hair. Then she looked up, and the defensive embarrassment in her countenance made him want more than anything else to kiss her.

"Yours is a creative soul," he said, manfully ignoring the patchouli scent teasing his nostrils. "Neatness and organisation want a more pedestrian intelligence."

"I suppose that is a kind way of telling me I'm addled," she muttered.

"No, miss. I was about to provide an unanswerable argument for your acquiring a secretary's services."

147

"Of course I need a secretary," she said indignantly. "I'm not that addled, Mr. Brentick. Naturally, the idea occurred to me. But you forget that many of the works I consult are in Sanskrit, and the rani's notes are all in Hindustani. I should have to scour the entire kingdom for the kind of secretary I need, though it's far more likely he or she lives in India. Furthermore, by the time I did find this paragon, I might have already finished the book, even in my *chaotic* manner."

He sighed and took up her copy of the *Bhagavad-Gita*.

" 'There never was a time when I was not,' " he translated, " 'nor thou, nor these princes were not; there never will be a time when we shall cease to be.' "

"Oh, dear," she murmured.

He looked at her and grinned.

Mr. Brentick assumed the role of secretary in the same quietly efficient manner he'd assumed every other responsibility connected with his employer. The following morning, he accompanied her to the library, where he devised a system for organising her notes. Then he collected the reference works she'd need that day, placed markers in the appropriate pages, and arranged them neatly within easy reach.

He remained with her until noon, reviewing what she'd written previously, and making notes. He stood by patiently to answer every question, fetch books or papers, mend quills, and clean up ink spills. In that curious way he had, he made himself invisible, for the most part, though he became visible the instant she needed him. Every morning thereafter he spent in the same fashion.

Mrs. Gales joined them at the outset. Invisibility, she soon found, was not nearly so much to her liking as it was to the butler's, and the mornings passed slowly indeed, though she had her needlework to keep her busy.

One morning, after a week of this quiet chaperonage, Mrs. Gales rose from her usual seat by the fire and, quite unnoticed, left the room, rubbing her aching head. She met up with Bella in the hallway, and frowned.

Bella nodded in quick understanding, and led the widow to the servants' hall, which at this hour was deserted.

Over a pot of tea, Mrs. Gales expressed her disquiet.

"Sometimes," she said, "a body can be *too* perfect, Bella."

"Well, I don't like 'em quite so skinny myself," said Bella, "but I'd say his face is perfect enough."

Mrs. Gales raised her eyebrows. "I referred to his behaviour. He has made himself indispensable to an alarming extent."

"He do have a way about him, don't he? Not a one of us but does exactly what Mr. Brentick wants—and he don't have to say a word, do he? Only has to look at you and, I declare, whatever he's got in mind, why, it gets right into yours, too—and sticks there pretty tight."

"Indeed." Mrs. Gales refilled her cup. "The question is, what is he putting into *her* mind?"

Bella considered. "Just them heathen gods, I expect," she said. "They don't talk about nothing else, do they?"

"No. That wicked Krishna it was today, and his legion of females. Small wonder she can't keep track of the wives and mistresses. Other men's wives, no less," Mrs. Gales added disapprovingly. "Yet they discuss it in so scholarly a fashion, one feels a fool to intrude."

"It's only for the book, ma'am."

"Yes. I suppose these so-called gods' doings are quite tame compared to the Rani Simhi's biography. Still, *he* will never hint that Amanda ought know nothing of these matters, let alone write of them. All he ever corrects is her syntax. Really," the widow added in vexation, "the man is a deal too much an enigma for my tastes. And I am not at all easy about the way he looks at her." She rubbed her head again. "Bella, I do fear . . . yet he is so very *attentive*," she said helplessly. "So kind, so considerate. He makes her laugh. He makes her—"

"Happy," Bella finished for her. "There's the nub of it, ma'am. Maybe there's more in it and maybe not, and maybe it ain't the properest sort of doings. But all I can think is how things was before. She had to grow up too fast—and Lord knows nobody ever laughed much here."

Mrs. Gales sighed. "Yes, I imagine it must have been so. Her mother was ill many years, was she not?"

"She weren't never right, ma'am. Not since Miss Amanda was a babe. Leastways, that's what my ma told me. I was hardly more than a babe myself then, so I never knew her ladyship when she wasn't . . . sick."

The hesitation in the maid's tones made Mrs. Gales look at her sharply. "What ailed her, Bella? Amanda seldom mentions her mama, and I never met the lady."

"I weren't no lady's maid then, ma'am, and folks wasn't like to tell me everything, now, was they?" came the evasive answer.

Loyalty Mrs. Gales respected. If Bella disliked to gossip about the family's past, the widow possessed sufficient loyalty herself to refrain from pressing.

# =14=

The LIBRARY WAS still, but for the scratching of Miss Cavencourt's pen and the hiss of coals in the grate. Philip stood at the window, his white-gloved hands clasped behind him, his attention fixed upon the wooded slope that rose at the garden's edge. Yesterday's dark blanket of sky had lightened this morning to pearl grey. Here and there faint rays of light struggled through to drop fitful sparkles upon the pond. Trees and shrubs trembled in the wind, and dry leaves danced feebly upon water and ground.

The scratching stopped, and a muttered oath broke the quiet.

Philip turned. "That is your fifth 'damnation' this morning," he said. "I'm not surprised. You might spend your next five lifetimes explaining the *shakta* cults."

She looked up. "If I talk about Kali, I ought to explain that she's just one of the manifestations of Shiva's wife. Everyone thinks the worst of Kali, yet she's simply one element—like one personality trait among many. Personalities are not always consistent."

"You want to defend her because you are partial to bloodthirsty females, miss."

"She is the most important goddess for Calcutta," Miss Cavencourt returned. "You know perfectly well the city's original name was Kalikata. I can hardly ignore her. Besides, if I speak only of agreeable matters, the book will be boring."

He shot her a smile. "Certainly it will—to those with a penchant for severed heads and ghastly vengeances."

He moved to the worktable, which, in less than an hour, his employer had reduced to mind-numbing disorder. "You work too hard and take no rest. Once, I recollect, you sternly recommended exercise to me, miss. I think you ought heed your own advice." He gestured towards the windows. "The wind is not nearly so sharp today. A walk will do you good."

He listened patiently while she fussed that she could not afford to give up time now, when she very nearly had the thing in hand, and that, furthermore, she was quite well and didn't need exercise—not to mention it was *freezing* out there.

Philip let her sputter on. When she had done explaining the error of his ways, and taken up her pen once more, he left the room.

A quarter of an hour later he returned, carrying a woolen cloak and scarf, a thick bonnet, gloves, and sturdy shoes. He had donned a dashing black, many-caped coat.

Miss Cavencourt looked at his coat and the heap of clothing in his arms and sighed. "I collect you mean to haul me out of doors, whether I will or no. I might have known, when I got not a whisper of argument. You are very·managing."

"And you are cross from spending too much time in one overheated room, with your nose stuck in a heap of papers," he said disrespectfully.

"My nose, for your information—"

"Has a spot of ink upon it." He produced a large, brilliantly white handkerchief.


Her butler having expressed a desire to tramp upon the moors, Amanda led him up a familiar though barely discernible path through the wood to the top of the slope. Away from the valley's shelter, the wind blew fiercely, but the slow climb up the hill stirred her sluggish blood, and she found the cold exhilarating.

Amanda inhaled gratefully as they paused at the top to survey the surrounding scene. Occasional scatterings of stunted trees dotted a landscape composed mostly of furze and jagged rock. The land rose and fell roughly, divided by stone walls into large, irregular rectangles.

"Is it all yours?" he asked.

"It was. If it hadn't been for Roderick, we'd have lost everything. Yet the acres we managed to keep are productive enough," she said. "I could get by on the income, but Roderick wouldn't hear of that. If he could, he'd have me living permanently in London in idle luxury."

Mr. Brentick threw her a curious glance, then looked away again. "Still, you'll want to spend time in Town eventually, at least after you finish your book. I realise Society would be too distracting now."

"I'm not going to London."

"Not even for the Season?"

"No," she said firmly. "I want no more Seasons."

"That's a pity," he said. "I rather fancy the challenge of managing a host of lazy, untrustworthy, city-bred domestics. These Yorkshire labourers are so very conscientious," he complained.

"That is your fault, Mr. Brentick. I left all the hiring to you. There was no one to prevent your employing a pack of idlers and thieves if you liked. If you are bored, or lonely for company . . ."

"I am not bored, miss. I am learning that solitude and loneliness are not the same thing."

It was disconcerting to discover that he seemed to recall every syllable she'd ever uttered to him. Equally disconcerting was his mention of London. He had a knack for coaxing people to do precisely as he wished. He changed others' minds as easily as he changed the wine goblets at dinner. But not in this, Amanda hastily reassured herself. She would never again, for as long as she lived, spend another Season in London.

"You understand, then, how and where I acquired my

taste for solitude," she responded calmly. She made a sweeping movement with her hand.

"Yes, the place broods and yearns before us, dark and mute. It does not distract us with pretty, idle chatter. Yet in its own unassuming way, it is treacherous." He glanced round and smiled at her. "For instance, if we remain much longer, mesmerised by the romantically moody landscape, you will freeze into a solid block."

He took her hand to help her down the steep, rough incline, only to release it as soon as the way became easier. Another mile's walk brought them into a corner of the dale sheltered from the winds' force by rocks and a stand of scarred trees.

After investigating the rough boulders, Mr. Brentick selected a suitable resting place. He withdrew from his pockets two flasks and two linen-wrapped bundles. Then he removed his coat and, quite deaf to Amanda's protests, spread it out for her to sit upon. The flasks, she discovered, contained cider. In the bundles nestled neat slices of cheese and thick hunks of freshly baked bread.

"You think of everything," she said.

"I was concerned you might faint of hunger on the way back. While you are fashionably slender, miss, I could not view with equanimity the prospect of carrying you home over nearly four miles of rough terrain."

Amanda hastily averted her gaze, and the warmth blossoming in her face subsided.

They dawdled over their meal with the easy camaraderie they'd enjoyed aboard ship, and had only recently revived during the weeks of working together in the library. Not until she'd consumed the last crumbs of bread and cheese did Amanda realise how probing his questions had become. She glanced up warily when he asked where she'd played as a child.

"Not here," she said quickly. "I seldom ventured so far from the house, except when Roderick was home. He and I rode here often. While he was at school, though, I had to keep within the garden bounds."

"That was wise. If you fell and hurt yourself, you might not be found for hours. I only wondered who your playmates were. You must have had to travel a good distance to visit one another."

She snapped the cap of her flask back into place. "Roderick was here," she said tightly. "He spent every holiday at home."

Mentally she braced herself to deflect the inevitable questions, but none came. Mr. Brentick merely nodded, and neatly gathered up the remnants of their picnic. As they turned homeward, the conversation turned as well, she found with relief. They spoke of Kali.

One day in late November, Philip accompanied his employer and Mrs. Gales to York. Miss Cavencourt had business at the bank, she said. He fully understood she meant to visit her statue, though she'd never once uttered a word about the Laughing Princess.

While entertaining small hope she'd actually take it home with her, Philip was prepared, in the event she did, to relieve her of it. As usual, he'd devised a foolproof plan for doing so without arousing suspicion.

The plan dropped into his mental ashbin when, after half an hour, his employer left the bank empty-handed.

Nevertheless, not a glimmer of frustration ruffled his polite demeanour as, like a lowly footman, he followed her down the street and on to the bookseller's. There he awaited the summons to carry her parcels. Miss Cavencourt spent as much on books as other ladies did on bonnets.

Philip stood by the door, his hands clasped at his back, his countenance blank and incurious as he gazed upon the passing scene. Miss Cavencourt's general factotum did not wear livery. This doubtless explained why more than one passing lady required more than a fleeting glance to ascertain that the fellow by the bookshop door was a mere servant. Some continued gazing, even after settling this matter to their satisfaction. The butler, however, very properly reserved his acknowledging nods for females of the lower orders, who rewarded him with blushes and an occasional giggle.

He'd been amusing himself in this fashion for twenty minutes when a gentleman stopped nearby to glance into the shop window. He was as tall as Philip, his build a degree broader, yet trim and athletic. The hair beneath the elegant beaver was black, and the visage dark and rugged. Philip guessed the man's age at near forty, though the dissolute eyes and mouth may have added a few years.

Though Philip kept his eyes fixed, ostensibly, upon the street, he was aware of the stranger's scrutiny moving to him. At that moment, a signal flashed to Philip's brain, eliciting a response common among the lower species when a rival male trespasses territorial boundaries. His heartbeat quickened and his muscles tensed for battle.

The stranger coolly strode past him to enter the shop.

With stiff fingers, Philip withdrew his pocket watch and stared blindly at it a moment before turning slightly to peer into the window.

The stranger, hat in hand, was speaking to Miss Cavencourt. Clutching a book to her chest, she stared at him. She appeared to answer, then turned away, dropped the book upon the counter, and hurried to the door.

She darted through the entrance and on down the street, utterly oblivious to Philip, who hastened after her. Her mysterious accoster made no attempt to follow, Philip saw with a backward glance, yet she continued hurrying down the street. She was about to cross— directly into the path of an oncoming cart—when Philip ran up and grabbed her arm. He pulled her back from the road and into a narrow alley.

Her bosom was heaving and her face was flushed, her eyes sparkling with unshed tears. He drew her deeper into the shadows, lest curious passersby remark her agitation.

"I want to go home now," she said quaveringly. "I want to go *home*, Mr. Br—" The rest caught on a sob.

She turned to him and pressed her hot face to his chest.

Automatically, his arms went around her, to hold her as her control broke and the sobs racked her slim body.

Philip stared over her bonnet at the grimy wall opposite. He tried to make his mind blank and hard, because that must harden his heart as well. He silently prayed she'd calm soon, before he weakened.

He could not kiss her tears away, nor permit his hands to stroke her back. That sort of unservantlike behaviour would, when she was herself again, create difficulties. He'd spent too much time winning her trust, making her dependent upon him, to risk any awkwardness now. He would not let himself succumb to pity . . . or to the coaxing warmth of her slender body.

Drat her. If she didn't stop soon—

To his unutterable relief, she abruptly drew back. He released her and produced his handkerchief.

"You think I'm mad," she said brokenly into the linen.

"That's nothing new," he said. "I've always thought so."

Her automatic but feeble attempt at a smile sent a darting ache through him.

"Who was the blackguard?" he asked.

"Nobody. One of my moth—my parents' friends."

"A friend, I take it, you didn't like overmuch."

She stared at the handkerchief she was twisting into knots. "No, I didn't—don't."

"I hope he was not disrespectful, miss."

"Oh, no, not at all. Mr. Fenthill is the very soul of courtesy," she said tightly. "But I am not. It is very difficult for me to behave politely with people I—I dislike. Impossible, actually. And so—and so I made a cake of myself. Really, I am sorry. Now all of York will pity you for having a lunatic as your employer." She thrust the crumpled handkerchief into her reticule.

"Not if they learn how grossly you overpay me," he said with feigned lightness. "Are you sufficiently composed to depart this filthy alleyway, miss?"

She nodded, refusing to meet his gaze.

"Very good. Let us extricate Mrs. Gales—forcibly, if need be—from her debate with the linen draper, shall we? You will both want a cup of tea and a bite to eat before we start back."

The night was cold, but he'd become accustomed to that. Or perhaps Philip merely ignored it, just as he'd ignored the noisome heat of Calcutta. Idly he paced the garden walkway, smoking his cheroot while he turned the puzzle over in his mind. He perceived a problem, a major obstacle, and he was certain today's episode formed a part.

No one visited Miss Cavencourt except the vicar, who had called once only. The villagers Philip had encountered were wary and tight-lipped. The few who asked after her employed the mournful tones of those enquiring after the mortally ill. He scented scandal or tragedy of some kind, yet none of his spy's skills could elicit the information he wanted. The villagers might gossip among themselves, but with strangers they were stubbornly aloof.

Exceedingly frustrating that was. Until he had the facts, he could not deal with the problem, and until he dealt with it, she'd remain here, hidden, while her statue remained inaccessible in the York bank.

Philip was aware of the light before he actually saw it. He glanced back at the house, his quick survey showing none but darkened windows until . . . ah, the old schoolroom.

"Oh, miss," said Bella softly as she closed the schoolroom door behind her. "I knowed you was restless. Another bad dream, was it?"

Amanda sat huddled in a child-sized chair. She pulled her dressing gown more tightly about her. "No. At least, not tonight. It was today, and I was wide awake."

"Miss?" Her round face creased in bafflement, Bella crossed the room to join her mistress. The abigail pulled a low stool forward, sat, and took Amanda's hand. "Lawd, you're cold as ice," she said as she chafed the frigid fingers.

"I saw Mr. Fenthill."

Bella's busy hands stilled.

"Actually, it was more than seeing him," Amanda said. "He spoke to me."

"Oh, miss, how could he? But there, ain't that just like him?" the maid added indignantly. "Never did think of anybody's feelings but his. No wonder you come home so pale and not like yourself at all. And hardly touched your dinner, either, Mrs. Gales said. She thought it was—" Bella caught herself up short. "Well, you was working too hard, is what she thought."

Amanda's fingers tightened round her maid's. "She doesn't know, does she? I know you'd never tell her, but she may have heard from others."

"She don't know, miss, and she's too much a lady to pry, so don't you go worrying yourself. Not that you should, anyhow. Because she's likewise too much a lady to judge you on account of what your poor ma did."

"But it wasn't Mama's fault, either." Amanda disengaged her hand, then rose and moved to the window. After a moment she said, "It wasn't. I don't think it was anyone's fault."

"Mebbe so," was the doubtful response, "but he could of let her alone, couldn't he? Her a married woman, a mother, and old enough to be *his* ma."

"She could not have been a mother at the age of ten, Bella. In any case, perhaps if he had been more mature, Mr. Fenthill might have found the will to keep away." Amanda sighed. "But that's all 'if,' and Mama was all 'ifs' and 'might have beens.' If only she'd had an easier time bearing me, if only she hadn't had the accidents . . . Lud, sometimes I think, if only Papa had let her go when she begged him. She was so miserable, and there was the opium to make everything go away. If he'd let her go, and Mr. Fenthill had taken her away and made her happy, she might have found the strength to break her terrible habit. Mr. Fenthill loved her. He might have helped her."

"He only helped her to more of her poison, Miss Amanda, which you know as well as I do. Don't you be making excuses for him. I declare, you'd find some excuse for the Devil himself."

# ═══15═══

THE FALCON STOOD motionless by the door, his body poised for flight, his ears alert to sound on every side, even as he concentrated upon the conversation within.

So that was it, simple and sordid. Her mother an opium addict and adultress. The affair with a man ten years her junior had evidently been neither the first nor discreet. A long and ugly series of scandals explained Miss Cavencourt's firm refusal to reenter Society.

Gad, she'd not been blessed in her parents, had she? What had she said so many months ago? She'd told him her parents were broken. Philip understood now that financial ruin had simply struck the final blow. He could only marvel that her wretched life hadn't broken her as well.

In the room beyond, the two low, feminine voices continued. Or rather, it was mainly Bella's voice now, gently scolding and comforting by turns. She was quite right. Amanda was too soft-hearted. Nothing was her mama's fault, or her papa's, or the doctors', or even that scurvy Fenthill's, according to her. The next you knew, she'd be inviting the filthy libertine to tea.

Why not? Her dearest friend in Calcutta had been the notorious Rani Simhi. Her devoted cook was one of the deadliest men in all India. Her butler was a master spy and thief. Amanda Cavencourt befriended the people most likely to use and betray her. She was a trusting little fool. A hard life had taught her nothing.

On the other hand, Philip hastily reminded himself as his conscience made ominous noises, she had stolen the statue. Never mind that she'd stolen it *back*. She'd been as deceitful and underhand as the rani, had even employed accomplices. Hardly the behaviour of a helpless victim.

Philip had just got his conscience in a stranglehold when he heard soft footsteps ascending the stairs. For all his bulk, Padji could tread lightly enough when he chose. Drat the fellow! The Indian spent most of his nights roaming the countryside. Tonight, of all nights, he'd decided to skulk at home instead.

The schoolroom was tucked into the far end of the dark hall. Padji was swiftly climbing the main staircase, which meant one must pass him to reach the backstairs.

Philip moved to the wall opposite the schoolroom and found a door handle. He opened the door and slipped inside, just as Padji reached the head of the stairs.

Philip heard the light tread approach, then pause inches away. He held his breath as the door handle moved. An instant later, he sensed the Indian moving away, then heard the tap upon the schoolroom door.

"Come out, mistress," Padji said. "Why does the foolish maid keep you in that cold place?"

Philip heard the door squeal faintly as she opened it. James should have oiled it, he thought automatically.

"She doesn't keep me," came Miss Cavencourt's annoyed voice. "Don't blame Bella for my odd starts. What are you doing, skulking about the house at this hour?"

Padji answered he'd thought he'd heard intruders.

"Well, it was just us, and we were about to return to bed anyhow."

The three passed Philip's hiding place. Their low voices faded to a murmur as they descended the stairs.

He waited several minutes after the house fell silent again, then drew a long breath of relief. He'd not moved, had scarcely breathed the whole time Padji had stood by, for the Indian's senses were as acute as his own.

Now that he could breathe properly, Philip found the air in the room exceedingly close and stale. He stepped back a pace and encountered a solid wall. Gad, no wonder. He'd entered a closet of some sort.

His heart was already pounding when he grabbed the door handle. It didn't budge. He tried again. Nothing. The latch was stuck—or some part was stuck. In the utter blackness he couldn't see, and his agile fingers played over the parts to no avail.

Fighting down panic, he reached into his coat for his trusty lock picks . . . and found nothing. He'd changed coats on his return from York, and neglected to transfer his tools. Bloody hell. Not even his knife. What the devil was wrong with him? He'd never been so careless before, never.

This was all her curst fault. He'd been so preoccupied with that swine in York and her hysteria—

He couldn't breathe. Not enough air here for a mouse, let alone a grown man. A man, he reminded himself, as panic rose in a chilling wave. A man, not a child.

Any fool could deal with a closet door. One need simply think it through in a calm, logical fashion. He'd find a way out. He must. He would not be trapped here all night. Good God, not all night!

He raised a fist to pound on the door, then stopped. He couldn't scream for help. He wanted another deep breath to steady himself, but didn't dare. Soon no air would remain. He'd suffocate. Better to scream and let them release him. He needn't explain. Let her discharge him. He'd find another way. Another way, but that would take time— weeks, months perhaps, and all these past weeks' work would go for naught.

He tore his neckcloth from his throat. He could always throttle himself, he thought wildly. But that was madness. *Think, Astonley.*

He couldn't think. He never could when this one unreasoning terror caught hold. He couldn't think and he couldn't scream, and he would just die here by inches.

No, he would not. Of course he could breathe. He was trapped only. He would go mad, but he would endure.

He leaned back into the corner and slid slowly to the floor. Then he drew his knees up to his chest, just as he had so many times so many years ago, and lay his pounding head upon them.

Amanda gritted her teeth, set down the candelabra, and inserted the key in the lock. She had to twist it back and forth a few times before it caught properly. Then she yanked the door open, and her heart wrenched so sharply she had to cling to the frame for support.

For one chilling instant she beheld a death's head. His face cold white and rigid, Mr. Brentick stared unseeingly straight ahead as though she weren't there. She wanted to hug him, hold him close, and comfort him. She knew, though, she must not, for that would shame him. She knelt to meet his blank gaze and tried to pretend she found nothing out of the way.

"Mr. Brentick," she said gently. Her hand crept out to touch his, to call him back to the world.

He blinked, and looked down in a puzzled way at her hand.

"How long have you been here?" she asked.

"I don't know." His voice was weak, distant, a stranger's.

"Do you think you can move your limbs? If you can, I can probably help you up."

He pulled his arms away from his knees and slowly, with obvious pain, straightened his legs. "It's all right," he said. "They've merely gone to sleep." He shook off whatever had seized him and managed a rueful smile. "Not rigor mortis, as I'd thought."

"Don't joke about such things," she said sharply. "You've frightened me half to death."

After a few failed attempts, she managed to pull him upright.

"My legs are like jelly," he muttered.

"Just lean on me." She caught him tight about the waist. He was practically a dead weight, but somehow she got him the few feet across the hall to the schoolroom, then onto the window seat. He slumped against the window and bit his lip. He was definitely in pain.

"Muscle cramps," she said, making her tones firm and matter-of-fact, though she could have wept for him. Wept for him and killed the monster who'd so cruelly tortured a helpless little boy.

With businesslike resolution, she took hold of one leg and began kneading the knotted muscles.

He gasped.

"Trust me, Mr. Brentick. I've had years of practice. Mama suffered terrible muscle spasms. They made her scream. This always helped."

She determinedly wrestled first one, then the other taut calf into submission. When she was done, she looked up to find him gazing warily at her.

"How did you come to rescue me?" he asked.

"I will tell you that," she said, stepping away from him, "after you explain how you came to be in the closet."

"I suppose it's no good to say I was sleepwalking?"

She shook her head.

He swung his feet to the floor, but did not stand up. He simply sat there, studying the floor. She was just opening her mouth to demand an answer when he spoke.

"I was in the garden, smoking, as I do every night, weather permitting. You know I'm not a great one for sleep."

She didn't respond.

"I saw the light in this room. It was one o'clock in the morning, so I thought I'd best investigate."

"I see. Padji suspected intruders as well."

"Just so. I crept up as quietly as I could," he went on. "Hearing only your and Miss Jones's voices, I was about to leave, when I heard someone else coming. I was standing in front of the closet door—not that I knew it was a closet—and so, I slipped behind it, thinking to take the intruder unawares. When I realised it was only Padji, I felt a perfect fool, hiding there. I waited until you'd all gone—then I couldn't get the door open."

"You should have called for help."

"I didn't want to alarm the household."

"Indeed? You had rather spend the night in a very small closet?"

"Perhaps I was not thinking clearly," he said.

She sighed. They could go on this way forever, skipping about the subject, and that she couldn't bear.

"Padji thought you were spying on me," she said bluntly. "He said he locked you in to teach you a lesson."

In the tight ensuing silence she heard his breath quicken. Her heart ached for him, for his masculine pride. Yet she had her pride, too. She knew he'd overheard—perhaps intentionally, perhaps not. In any case, it was too late for pretense on either side.

"He doesn't know," she said, "but I guessed. That day on the ship when you fell ill, you were delirious. Without realising, you told me a secret. I didn't entirely understand then, but tonight, when Padji told me what he'd done, I guessed that's what your father had done and . . . well, I didn't want Padji to be the one to release you."

He turned his head away slightly, to the window. The flickering candlelight threw fitful shadows over the rigid planes of his face.

"Thank you," he said, his voice barely audible.

She understood what it cost him to say that, and hastened to salvage his pride as well as her own. "I imagine you couldn't help overhearing tonight any more than I could that day," she said. "I don't know what you heard, but it must have been quite enough, else you'd not have hidden. I suppose you wanted to spare me embarrassment. You didn't want me to guess you'd heard my—our family secret. Not that it's much of a secret. I should have told you the truth today. I'm not ashamed, not really. I just . . . I didn't want you to pity me. I've had enough of that to last seven lifetimes, I think."

Another lifetime seemed to pass before he looked towards her. His mouth eased into a faint smile. "In the circumstances, Miss Cavencourt, I don't dare pity you. You might retaliate in kind. I've never been pitied, yet I suspect it must be worse even than that curst closet." He rose. "The truth is, I was an incorrigible child. A birching only made me laugh. I was afraid of nothing, you see—except, that is, being trapped in a small, closed space. It was the only punishment that worked."

"I'm not surprised," she said calmly, though the very matter-of-factness of his explanation made her heart ache. "I'd guessed you were a little devil. Still, that is a monstrous cruel way to discipline a little boy, no matter how wicked."

"What would you have done?" He moved closer, and in the unsteady light she discerned a familiar, intent gaze. "I know you'd have tried to understand me, because you try to understand everybody, from the great god Shiva to Jane, the scullery maid. Still, you'd have to *do* something. What, then?"

Too easy to answer. She knew she would have covered that troubled, angry little boy's face with kisses, cosseted him, spoiled him, loved him with all her heart.

"I should not have tried to make a scholar of you," she said carefully. "If you were a very restless child, you'd have been happier boxing, fencing, riding. There's discipline in sports, for both mind and body. Also, vigourous physical activity would have tired you too much for mischief. Your papa tried to make you what you were not. Children should be permitted to be what they are."

"You think my mischief was the common sort," he said. "It wasn't. In addition to the usual boyish pranks, I was insolent, told lies constantly, and *stole*."

She ought to be shocked. She wasn't. The moment she'd opened the closet door and seen his face, she'd understood. "Because you were angry and unhappy."

He was still studying her face. "You are bound to find a kind excuse, Miss Cavencourt. Can't you believe a human being might be born bad?"

"I can believe that, but not of you. Surely that must be obvious," she added hastily. "If I'd thought you intended any ill, I should have left you in the closet, or to Padji's tender mercies. I know everyone thinks me too forgiving, Mr. Brentick. All the same, I do not always turn the other cheek. Martyrdom is not in my style."

"No," he said softly. "I realise you're not a saint."

His tone made her face heat. Belatedly she became aware of her bedtime attire. Despite a flannel nightdress and a robe of serviceable wool, she felt undressed and unsafe. He seemed too near, and also too much undressed. His neckcloth was gone, and his shirt had fallen open to reveal a triangle of flesh that gleamed bronze in the candlelight. She wanted to move to him, touch him. She wanted to hold him, and be held. She shivered.

"You must be chilled to the bone," he said. He began to pull off his coat.

"No!" She quickly retreated. "I don't need it. I'm going back to bed. You can take the candles. I know my way blindfolded." She moved to the door. "Good night, Mr. Brentick," she said. Then she fled.

Philip could have spent the night merely writhing in mortification, but Miss Cavencourt's knowledge of his weakness seemed the least of his troubles as he climbed into bed.

He sat back, rubbing his throbbing temples, wondering how she'd managed to make everything so deuced complicated.

Delirious, she'd said. He felt delirious now. He could not believe he'd admitted the truth, so much truth. He could have simply pretended not to understand what she was talking about. If pressed, he need only deny.

Yet he'd found himself trapped once again, entangled in undeserved kindness and compassion. She'd rescued him herself to spare his pride, and had not left until she'd made him well again. She'd lifted him out of the chilling darkness into sanity. With her own surprisingly strong hands she'd even wrestled the pain from his frozen body.

Gratitude had weakened him and made him incautious. Stunned and grateful, he'd found himself unable to deny, scarcely able to manufacture a fraction of a lie.

That wasn't the worst, though. She'd not only explained and absolved him, but dressed him in shining armour. Of course Mr. Brentick hadn't been spying on her. He'd bravely come to battle intruders, had accidentally overheard, and then sacrificed his own peace of mind to spare hers.

"Oh, Amanda," he muttered. "How could you believe that? Was there ever such a trusting little fool?" He'd wanted to shake her, had tried to do so verbally. Yet even the truth about his character only elicited more of her unendurable *understanding*. "Angry and unhappy," she'd said. *Fool*, he'd answered silently. Bella was right. Miss Cavencourt would make excuses for the Devil himself.

Perhaps she was not entirely credulous, though, Philip thought, as he sank back upon his pillow. She hadn't altogether spared his feelings, had she, for all her compassion? She'd told him plain enough she knew not only what he'd suffered in the closet, but why, and where the terror came from. Gently though she'd worded the admission, Philip had perceived her warning as well. For now, she sympathised. Should he lose her sympathy, however, she'd not hesitate to use his weakness against him. Or rather, she'd let Padji use it. She was not naive in every way. She knew the Indian's character and his uses. Hadn't she used him before?

Very well. The game had grown a shade more complicated and dangerous. He'd need to revise his plans.

Unless someone persuaded Miss Cavencourt to end her self-imposed exile, the Laughing Princess would remain in the York bank indefinitely. She must be got to leave, and take the statue with her.

Her ever-so-kind and understanding knight, Brentick, would *never* venture upon the tender subject of London Seasons again. Knowing the sordid truth, he'd respect her wishes to remain hidden in this remote place.

Yes, she'd tied his hands in that. Frustrating it was, for he could have persuaded her easily enough in a matter of weeks. Now he must manipulate others to do the job for him.

Cool and calculating once more, Philip clasped his hands behind his head, and prepared to spend the remaining night contemplating the tools currently at his disposal.

# ═16═

NOVEMBER SWEPT AWAY on icy winds and December whirled in amid a snowstorm that transformed the harsh, grey landscape to shimmering white.

The snow brought Amanda mixed relief and disappointment. She and Mr. Brentick had taken long walks through the moors nearly every day of the last month. She knew the exercise did her good, for when she returned to her manuscript, she always felt fresh and clearheaded.

On the other hand, to spend so much time privately with him boded ill for her peace of mind. Away from the house, he relaxed, and their conversations were those of friends, rather than mistress and servant. This was what she preferred, usually; she'd always disliked the barriers rank created. Nevertheless, she found herself wishing, in this one case, for the safety of such barriers. Feelings warmer than mere friendship had again surged to the surface. As the days passed, she found it increasingly difficult to maintain a levelheaded detachment. The snow would bring a few days' respite, time in which she might talk herself round to common sense.

On the afternoon following the storm, therefore, Amanda beheld with surprised dismay her butler's entrance into the library. He wore a woolen overcoat, and carried in his arms a heap of clothing. Also boots, she saw with foreboding. Her boots.

"I am not setting foot out of doors," she said resolutely, "until *June*."

Half an hour later, she was trudging up the path that led to the moors. Mr. Brentick followed, dragging a sled.

When they reached the top, one large, vivid anxiety immediately swamped all Amanda's other worries. She looked at the sled, then down at the incline before them. This side of the hill seemed to have grown exceedingly steep since their last walk. She turned her panicked gaze up to him, while her heart churned with terror.

"Haven't you ever gone sledding before?" he asked.

She shook her head and darted another glance at the endless, nearly perpendicular drop.

"There's nothing to be afraid of, Miss Cavencourt."

"I'll watch," she offered.

"You'll freeze, standing here."

Mr. Brentick positioned the sled, then, very firmly, herself upon it. When he took up his place behind her, fear compounded with a flood of other sensations. Two people could share a sled in only one way, apparently, and that placed her between his legs, her back against his chest. Her heart crashed crazily at her ribs, and every muscle in her body petrified into hard knots.

As the sled began to move, a scream rose in her throat, but caught there. She could no more scream than she could breathe. Then the world went whipping past in a flash of white and dark, while the wind blasted her face, making her eyes stream.

Terrified, she leaned back into the hard security of his chest, her mittened hands frozen to the sides of the sled. It was awful. It was . . . wonderful, she discovered in the very next instant.

This was rapture—to fly down the hillside, the cold beating at her, while the warm, strong, reassuring body held her safe and secure. Her scream broke free, but it broke into a cry of joy and breathless laughter.

She heard his shout of laughter mingle with hers, and she felt as though he surrounded her with happiness. He seemed to vibrate with her in the wild joy of wind and speed, as they plunged headlong into the dale's depths.

They reached the bottom an instant or a lifetime later, and the sled glided gently to a stop. Amanda was still laughing. Her body tingled yet with the sheer joy and excitement of the ride. She gloried in the warmth of her quickened blood, and relished the delicious stinging in her cheeks.

As their merriment subsided, she felt his chin drop to the top of her muffler-wrapped head. His arms tightened about her. Unthinkingly, she let go of the sled to relax against him while she caught her breath.

She felt him tense. Turning her head, she saw the laughter ebb from cobalt-blue eyes and a darker emotion take its place.

Amanda knew an instant's flash of recognition, then came an ache within that built swiftly to unendurable pressure. The white haze of their breath mingled in the narrow space between them. His head bent lower, his eyes dark as midnight, intent and mesmerising. His mouth was a breath away . . . and an eternity away.

She turned quickly, and pulled herself forward.

After a brief hesitation, he rose and helped her up.

He became himself again in that moment, ironically polite as he brushed snow from her coat and mittens. Amanda could not collect herself so quickly. They'd nearly reached the top of the hill before her churning brain had quieted, and her pulse steadied.

When they reached the summit and it appeared Mr. Brentick intended to continue towards home, Amanda ought, certainly, have been eager to return to the safety of the library. But her gaze reverted to the steep incline, and she remembered the rush of joy and the thrilling speed. She'd never before experienced anything like it. She heard herself cry out, like a child, "Oh, Mr. Brentick, aren't we going to do it again?"

He'd got ahead of her. He stopped abruptly and waited

until she'd caught up. "Haven't you had enough for one day?" he asked.

She shook her head.

He grinned. "Very well, miss." He dragged the sled round.

They'd climbed up and sledded down that curst hill at least fifteen times before Miss Cavencourt would admit she'd had enough. Thank Providence for the climb, Philip thought. Had any alternate means of ascending offered itself, they'd likely be sledding until Judgement Day.

He threw her an exasperated glance as they staggered through the garden. Four times her weary legs had given out, tripping her headlong or sideways or backwards into the snow. Four times she'd tumbled, and each time she simply lay there and laughed. He'd wanted to strangle her. He'd wanted to close his hands around her lovely throat . . . and kiss her senseless.

*Idiot*. Sledding, he'd thought in all his sublime smugness, would keep her amused while also keeping her far from the house. Mrs. Gales wouldn't like it. The widow was hardly lunatic enough to chaperon them, and risk frostbite while she stood and watched them play. No, she wouldn't like it, and must eventually grow sufficiently alarmed to separate the pair. She'd have to take Miss Cavencourt away from Kirkby Glenham.

A perfect plan it had seemed, better even than the long walks. He'd believed so until the end of today's first descent.

He'd known she was terrified, yet knew as well she'd trust him to keep her safe. Consequently, he was not surprised when she'd succumbed almost immediately to the thrill of speed and danger. It was the rest undid him. She'd hurtled down with him, shrieking, laughing, and the sound of her happy excitement had made him wish they'd never reach the bottom. For those moments, he'd wanted only to plunge recklessly and endlessly through eternity with her. All the same, there was an end—there must be—and at the end was a woman snuggled trustingly against him: Amanda, rosy cheeked and breathless in his arms. She'd looked up at him, her eyes shining pleasure and gratitude, golden trust and . . .

He wouldn't think about that, Philip told himself as he held the door open and answered automatically whatever it was she said. He'd forgotten himself, but only the once, and only for a moment. It wasn't such a terrible plan, as long as one were fully prepared.

"She has missed tea again," Mrs. Gales said grimly as she moved away from the sitting-room window. "There is still no sign of them, and it will be dark soon."

Bella flicked a speck of lint from the chair, and plumped up the cushion. "Your own tea'll get cold, ma'am, and worrying won't bring her home any faster."

Mrs. Gales sighed and took her seat. "They've gone out nearly every single day this month. Yesterday, again, she came home soaking wet. It's a wonder she hasn't caught her death."

"Yes, ma'am, but I heard Mr. Brentick scold her about that himself. And he did send her right up to get dry and change her clothes."

"Why must she spend so much time out of doors in the first place?" was the sharp response. "Sledding, indeed. What on earth possessed him?"

Bella took the seat opposite. This was not the first time in recent weeks that the widow had invited her up to share a pot of tea and Padji's delectable sandwiches. The usually imperturbable Mrs. Gales had grown increasingly agitated as the days passed and Miss Cavencourt's intimacy with her butler increased.

"It ain't healthy for her to spend the whole day hunched over her papers, he says," the abigail responded. "I do think he's got the right of it, ma'am. Why, she looks so bright and rosy, I'd hardly know it was the same Miss Amanda. And for all she do come back fairly dripping, she's laughing, too."

Mrs. Gales's lips tightened into a rigid line as she poured

a cup of tea and handed it to the maid. "She gave him a silver cigar case for Christmas," she muttered.

"Yes, ma'am, but she always was generous that way, you know. Not enough to load me up with frocks and underthings, but she give me a gold bracelet, she did, just as if I was a fine lady had somewheres to wear it."

"Also cigars," Mrs. Gales continued as though she hadn't heard. "And permission to smoke in the library."

"She found out he was going outside at night, ma'am, and said there was no point his freezing. Her pa always liked to smoke his cigar in the library."

"Brentick is not her father, or her brother, or even a gentleman caller. He is her *servant*." The widow set her cup down. "I don't like to interfere. She is no green girl, but an independent young woman, and I am not her governess. I have tried to drop a hint, but she refuses to understand me."

"Well, ma'am, Padji talks plain enough, and she don't want to understand him, either. Not but what it ain't his place to say anything, no more than it's mine. Now she won't hardly speak to him, and the way he looks at Mr. Brentick—I declare, it gives me goose shivers, is what."

Mrs. Gales frowned at the tea sandwiches. "It's not how Padji looks at him that worries me, Bella."


"Not there," Amanda said, horrified. "I won't have the entire household watching me stumbling about and falling on my—"

"Ornamental pond," he finished for her as he wrapped the muffler about her head. "Very well. But it's a good hike to the next nearest one."

"Can't we go sledding instead?" she begged. "I had much rather sit and let you do all the work."

"You'll like skating," he promised. "It's like dancing."

"On ice. Balancing on a couple of blades. I was never a good dancer."

"Obviously, you never had a good partner."

"But suppose the ice breaks? It's been warmer, hasn't it? Suppose it breaks and swallows me up and—"

"It is a very shallow pond, miss. Furthermore, the temperature has soared nearly to the freezing point. Hardly a heat wave."

She fussed and worried as usual, and as usual, Mr. Brentick ignored her. Still, Amanda reminded herself, she'd been frightened of sledding at first. Now he had to devote all his energies to persuading her home again, because she couldn't get enough of it. Winter sports had played no part in her childhood—playing formed virtually no part—and she'd no inkling what she'd missed. She felt as though she'd never been truly alive before, never, certainly, so tinglingly, vibrantly alive as this man made her feel.

Yes, he made her feel like a child again, but not the child she'd been. Instead of that wistful, lonely little girl, he'd conjured up a noisy, giggling brat who always demanded more, and *more*.

All the same, when they reached the pond, Amanda wasn't certain she wanted *any*, let alone more.

"Perhaps Mrs. Gales was right," she said. "I really ought not keep you so much from your duties. Perhaps we should return."

He was kneeling before her, fastening her skates. "Mrs. Gales objects to my idling, I take it," he said without looking up.

"Good heavens, not at all. She says I expect far too much of you. I think she's right. You should not have to entertain me, in addition to everything else."

"Please quiet your conscience, miss. I'd far rather play than work. In any case, I haven't nearly enough to do." He sat beside her to fasten his own skates.

Amanda folded her gloved hands and watched him in silence. So quick and capable he was, always, his hands deft and efficient at every task. Never a wasted motion. He was bound to be an excellent skater. She wished she might simply watch him. He moved so beautifully, so lean and

177

lithe he was, easy and assured, smooth and graceful as a cat. To look at him, to hear his voice . . . She suppressed a sigh. She'd commanded herself a thousand times to be content with what he gave.

He stood and held out his hand.

"Maybe I should just watch first," she said. "Can't you give me a demonstration?"

He shook his head. "It's too cold for you to sit still."

"Please?"

He grinned, his beautiful blue eyes teasing. "Coward."

"Well, yes, I am," she admitted ruefully. "I really hate falling down."

"You love falling down, Miss Cavencourt. You think it's quite the most hilarious experience in all the world."

She stared mistrustfully at her skates.

"Don't just stand there, Mr. Brentick," she heard him cry in a familiar feminine voice. "Help me up."

Amanda's head shot up.

"Oh, lud, how stupid," he continued in the same voice. Then her tall, capable, *manly* butler broke into girlish giggles.

Her mouth fell open.

He stared blankly back.

"That was *me*," she said wonderingly. "How the devil did you do it?"

He shrugged. "A skill I was apparently born with. I thought it might divert you from your unreasoning terror."

"Can you imitate anybody you want to?"

"Virtually anybody. Women are difficult, but your voice is low enough." He put out his hand. "No more procrastinating."

She ignored the hand. "How clever you are," she said. "Do someone else."

"Miss Cavencourt, I haven't come to perform tricks. We have a skating lesson ahead of us."

"I'd rather a lesson in mimicry," she coaxed.

"That will not get your blood circulating. Nor will you

find it nearly so amusing as skating."

He grasped her hands and hauled her upright. Her ankles wobbled ominously.

She looked down at her feet, then up at him.

"Just so," he said soberly. "We are in for a most diverting afternoon."


"You see?" said Amanda. "He'd rather be outdoors. He insists it doesn't make more work for him. He says the house runs so smoothly he has too much time on his hands."

Mrs. Gales set her knitting aside and folded her hands in her lap. They'd retired upstairs to Amanda's sitting-room after dinner. The chilly January afternoon had turned into a bitter cold evening. Upstairs was warmer, cozier, and, Mrs. Gales may have silently added, farther from the omnipresent butler.

"Why, do you think, my dear, he devotes virtually all his time to you?" the widow asked quietly. "He works with you all the morning, then he spends all the afternoon, far from the house, alone with you. He seems to have a most peculiar notion of a butler's responsibilities."

Amanda flushed. "What are you driving at, Leticia?"

"Need you ask me, dear? Doesn't your own heart tell you what troubles me, and all those who care for you?"

Amanda looked away, to the fire. "I see," she said. "Padji has been talking to you now. That doesn't surprise me. But I am astonished you'd credit what he suggests. You know he's disliked Mr. Brentick from the start."

"I have not discussed you with Padji. I observe with my own faculties, Amanda. You are falling in love with your butler," was the blunt conclusion.

The world went black, but only for a moment. The tiny, sharp ache in Amanda's breast vanished in a moment as well. Even when she lay in her bed, defenseless because the night offered no distraction, the ache eventually subsided. Her days were full and busy, and longing had simply come to be a part of them, a trickle of sadness amid the joy. The night loomed empty, though, empty and hopeless because he was not by to light and fill it for her, to make her come alive as he did by day.

Falling in love . . . if it were merely that, she'd stand a chance. But she must have fallen in love lifetimes ago. Now she simply lived with it by day, and died a little of it, by inches, every night.

She turned bleak eyes to her companion. "It's all right, Leticia," she said calmly. "I promise you've no reason to be uneasy. I'm quite safe with him. We've had all the privacy anyone could want, and he's never tried to take advantage. He doesn't want me, you see. But he is too kind to hurt me."

Mrs. Gales's look of shock quieted to compassion. "Amanda, my dear—"

Amanda put out her hand to stop further words. "Please, let it be. Just let me be as happy as I can for a bit longer. Let me live with it my own way, please."

She rose and left the room.

# ═ 17 ═

THE LETTER ARRIVED on the first of February.

Philip found it in a locked drawer of the estate office desk. The lock was an utterly futile precaution, and another testament to Miss Cavencourt's credulity. He might have picked it in twenty seconds. Sometimes, just to keep in practice, he did, though a duplicate key reposed in his pocket.

This day he used the key, though he certainly wasn't in any hurry. Mrs. Gales had prevailed upon Amanda to accompany her to the village, and Padji had gone as well, claiming business with the blacksmith.

Fearing no interruption, Philip leaned back in the huge, ugly chair to peruse the letter at his leisure. He'd no sooner scanned the greeting than he sat up sharply. He flipped the sheet over to check the signature, and uttered a low series of oaths.

The epistle came from the Rani Simhi and, as one might expect, constituted a fascinating mixture of truth, lies, and needless evasions.

She claimed she'd received a note from the Falcon, thanking her for the Laughing Princess. He'd never written such a note, curse her. The Falcon would never behave in such an adolescent way.

The rani also maintained that she'd sent her agents in pursuit, but the thief eluded them. It was believed he'd left India altogether. Then she offered several lines of apology for 'unwittingly'—oh, very likely—placing her 'beloved daughter' in danger.

Philip turned the sheet over and frowned. Padji's departure a shock, was it? He quickly scanned the next paragraph. She forgave Padji . . . she was comforted, knowing he'd guard Amanda with his life . . . utterly devoted . . . to be trusted implicitly . . . fated to be.

Then an interesting switch, from submission to Fate, forgiveness, and loving kindness to narrative a deal more in character:

> All the same, I know the Laughing Princess
> cannot be fated to remain in the hands of my
> betrayer. I have prayed to Anumati and begged
> help. She answered at last in a dream: the man
> who possesses her statue will become but half a
> man, incapable of taking pleasure with a woman.
> So she has promised me, beloved daughter of my
> heart, and Anumati has always fulfilled her prom-
> ises. The curse will not be lifted until the
> Laughing Princess is restored to you or to a
> daughter of your blood. The princess is a
> woman's gift and a man's curse. Remember this,
> and be comforted.

Philip returned the letter to its place, closed the drawer, and turned the key in the lock.

By the time the rani had written, she must have obtained an accurate description of him. She'd have learned he and Jessup had boarded the *Evelina*. She would have deduced exactly what had happened—except, of course, for the second theft. Amanda's first letter could not have reached the Indian woman before this one was written.

The Rani Simhi knew, yet didn't describe him. Why not? Why keep her "beloved daughter" in the dark?

Philip drew a deep breath. Suppose she *had* described him? Where would he be now? Slowly asphyxiating somewhere, no doubt. From now on, he'd better have a look at the post before his employer did.

\* \* \*

"This is not Calcutta," Philip patiently repeated. "Collecting the post is a lower servant's duty. You lose face with the others when you so demean yourself."

"So have I done from the beginning," Padji answered. He poured steaming broth into a saucepan. "To lose face is nothing. I am an insect beneath the heel of my mistress."

He stirred the rice briefly, sprinkled in some seasoning, then added vegetables, and covered the saucepan. He turned to face Philip. "If it is nothing to me, Brentick sahib, I beg you will not trouble your tender heart with the matter."

Philip elected another tack. "It isn't my heart that's troubled, but our footman's. If you won't consider your pride, you might consider his. James has been with us more than four months. He'll think we don't trust him."

"No other menservants did you hire but this ignorant boy. You trust him with nothing that concerns the mistress. Always it is Brentick sahib who arranges the fire. Brentick sahib who carries the tray. Brentick sahib who lights the candles. Always it is Brentick sahib who follows her about like a little dog." Padji folded his arms across his chest and surveyed Philip from head to toe. "Or perhaps like a lovesick little boy."

"Very amusing," Philip said calmly, though the blood rushed to his face. "I see this is no time for a rational conversation. You are in one of your perverse humours."

He turned to walk away.

"Poor Brentick sahib," Padji said sadly. "What can be in these letters that troubles him so? Tender words from a lover, perhaps, a noble prince who is *worthy* of the mistress? Or perhaps her brother writes of a fine match he has arranged? What will become of you when she weds?"

The world grew dark, suddenly, and wild, as though knocked from its axis. Philip's fingers fell away from the door handle as he caught his breath and his balance. The sick sensation passed in a moment, though, and he answered with forced lightness, "In that case, I should find a less arduous position."

"Indeed, that is so. Brentick sahib labours so hard, and the night gives him no rest. All in this house see how he burns for the mistress, and all pity him."

Philip turned abruptly. "Pity?"

"Even Padji's heart aches," the Indian said charitably. "I have heard you cry out her name in the night, begging her to come to you—"

"You filthy swine!"

"Pitiful, like a lovesick boy—"

In a flash, Philip leapt, with force enough to hurl any other adversary to the ground.

Padji never flinched. He pulled Philip's hands from his throat as easily as if they'd been bonnet ribbons. Instantly, the giant had him in a stranglehold.

"I know you, Brentick sahib," Padji whispered while Philip fought for breath. "Not a garden snake, but a cobra. Yet you must strike more quickly to strike me. We understand each other, I think?" His forearm pressed a degree more firmly against Philip's throat.

"I would have killed you long since," Padji went on in the same soft, sweet tones, "but the mistress would not permit it. She is a child in many ways and, foolish like a child, she trusts you. Do you give her any pain, little cobra, and you die . . . slowly."

He let go, and Philip crumpled to the floor.

Amanda gazed in blank astonishment at the brown giant as he carried the soup tureen into the dining room.

"What are you doing here?" she demanded, disliking the innocent expression on his face. The more cherubic Padji looked, the greater the mischief he'd perpetrated. "Where is Mr. Brentick?"

He calmly ladled soup into her bowl. "Brentick sahib is indisposed."

"Ill?" Mrs. Gales enquired. "How odd. He seemed fully in health this afternoon."

"The ailment came upon him suddenly, memsahib."

Amanda leapt from her chair. "What have you done to him, you wicked creature?"

"Amanda!"

Ignoring the widow, Amanda ran to the door, but Padji backed up, blocking it.

"Let me by!" she shouted. She tried to push him out of her way. She might as well have tried to move a stone mountain. Tears sprang to her eyes. "What is the matter with you?" she cried. "Who is mistress here? Get out of my way!"

She started to move to the other doorway, but Padji clasped her arm.

"No, mistress. It is unseemly."

"He's quite right, for once," Mrs. Gales put in before Amanda could retort. "You cannot go to the man's room, my dear. Brentick would be mortified."

"For God's sake, Leticia, he might be dead, for all we know—and you speak of *embarrassment*?"

"He is not dead, mistress. Did you ask me to kill him?" Padji enquired gravely. "No, you did not desire this."

Mrs. Gales threw him a baleful look.

"Then what's wrong with him?" Amanda asked, forcing steadiness into her voice. Her hands were shaking. "Why won't you let me see him?"

"He would not like it," said Padji. "The memsahib Gales speaks true. He would be ashamed to be seen, weak and ill, by the mistress."

"Drat you, I've already seen him weak and ill."

Padji shrugged. Amanda turned pleading eyes to Mrs. Gales.

The widow rose and crossed the room to release Amanda from Padji's custody. "If you wish," she said calmly, "we shall send James to check on Brentick. There is no need for you to go yourself." She dropped her voice to add, "My dear, you cannot go to the man's bedchamber."

Amanda did not care for "cannot" and "ought not." Over the past few weeks, Padji's cool distrust of her butler had swelled to black hostility. Tonight, Mr. Brentick, who was never ill, always by, was ill and absent. Meanwhile, Padji wore an ominously innocent expression. In these observations Amanda found quite enough to overcome any absurd notions of propriety.

On the other hand, Mrs. Gales's pitying expression gave Amanda pause. She flushed, and though she did agree to sending James, she insisted on a note from Mr. Brentick. If he was too ill to write, she'd go to him.

The footman went, and the note duly arrived a short while later. Mr. Brentick assured her he simply had a sore throat. He preferred to keep away from the rest of the household until he felt certain it was not a symptom of a contagious ailment.

Two hours after a dinner only the widow tasted, and following a frustrating conversation with Padji, Amanda joined Mrs. Gales in the drawing room.

"They did quarrel," Amanda said as she dropped wearily onto the sofa. "Padji admitted they both lost their tempers. He says he *may* have hurt Mr. Brentick a little, but only enough to calm him down. I can't believe Mr. Brentick would be so rash as to fight with Padji."

"I understand tempers have flared more than once belowstairs," said Mrs. Gales. "Bella says Padji has been teasing Brentick unmercifully from the start. Recently, he has taken to humiliation. Only yesterday, she says, Padji peered down at the man's head, and there before all the staff, very amiably offered to remove the *lice*."

"Lice?" Amanda echoed blankly. "But that is insane. You know how fastidious Mr. Brentick is."

"I'm afraid Padji knows as well. It is just the sort of comment to make Brentick quite wild."

Amanda nodded. She remembered how upset he'd become the day he'd arrived, when Padji had complained that Mr. Brentick stank like a pig.

"I collect your cook is bent on driving him away, Amanda. If, that is, he doesn't drive him mad, first." The widow hesitated briefly before adding, "I think you know why, my dear."

Amanda turned away. She knew why. Padji was convinced Mr. Brentick meant her ill. He claimed the butler flattered and bewitched her, day by day stealing her trust and affection, only to satisfy his base male appetite. When Amanda argued that her butler had been a thorough gentleman for more than four months, Padji only sneered. Brentick sahib was cunning. He wanted the mistress completely in his power. By the time he made himself her lover, his besotted victim would have given over all control to him. All her wealth would fall into his hands. Then, when he'd stripped her of reason, honour, and worldly goods, he'd abandon her. Padji declared he could no longer stand idly by, watching her make the same mistake his former mistress had made with Richard Whitestone.

"I know why," Amanda answered at last. "Padji has decided he must save me from myself."

"I daresay you could discharge him."

"How could I? He believes he's protecting me, which is his duty, his *dharma*. In any case, Padji chooses his employers. They don't choose him."

Amanda rose from the sofa to take a restless turn about the room, as though she'd find some other answer there. Yet she knew there was but one answer. Padji wouldn't kill Mr. Brentick outright, because that, for some inscrutable reason, required his mistress's command. He would, however, make the man's life hell.

"Padji wouldn't go, even if I discharged him," she said, pausing by Mrs. Gales's chair. "I owe him far too much to attempt that anyhow. Yet if he stays, he won't leave Mr. Brentick alone. It's my fault. The way I've behaved . . . because I wanted as much of Mr. Brentick's company as I could get. It was enough for me, truly it was—much more than I'd ever hoped for."

Mrs. Gales took her hand and patted it. "My dear," she said simply.

"I suppose this is what the rani meant when she spoke of

187

a love beyond reason," Amanda continued. "It had already taken hold of me, long before I realised, and so I was beyond thinking, even when I knew the truth. I wanted only to be with him. I would have done whatever he asked, I think. No wonder you were so worried, all of you. I gave you reason enough. Yet you've been so kind and patient, Leticia." She squeezed the widow's hand. "I wish I'd listened, if only to spare you anxiety."

"I'm afraid I've not been terribly helpful."

"Because you don't like to interfere or nag. In any case, I wouldn't have listened. But the madness is done now," Amanda said. Her voice shook as she added, "We'll go to London, and take Padji with us. That will be best. London will keep us busy enough. We'll go to parties, Leticia, and— and we'll drive in the Park. They shall have to endure me this time, because I have money. Not 'poor Miss Cavencourt' any longer, am I, thanks to Roderick. Even respectable now, after a fashion. You don't know about—about before, do you? That's all right. I'll tell you. Not tonight, but tomorrow, perhaps, and you will tell me how to go on. You always know, Leticia. I should have listened to you, long ago."

She bent and hugged her companion. "I wish I had listened," she whispered. "You said he was too handsome, didn't you?"

She gave an unsteady laugh, and hurried from the room.

By the following day Philip had recovered sufficiently to attend his employer in the library. His neckcloth concealed the bruises on his throat, and his hoarseness was easily explained as the aftereffects of a sore throat. If he staggered slightly when Miss Cavencourt outlined her plans to depart for London in early March, that, too, could be blamed on aftereffects.

"We shall probably return at the end of the Season," she said composedly, though she averted her gaze. "I daresay you'll manage with Mrs. Swanslow and Jane."

So, she did not intend to take him with her? This must be Padji's doing. What had the curst Indian told her? Gad, what the devil was he thinking? What did it matter? Philip would not have gone with her in any case. This was a pose, not a bloody career!

"Certainly, miss," he said meekly.

"I shall keep you apprised of our needs." She took up her pen. "That will be all," she added dismissively.

"I beg your pardon?"

She looked up, but still not directly at him.

"You aren't intending to work on your manuscript, miss?"

"Yes, I am, but I shan't trouble you today. You and Mrs. Swanslow will have enough to do, with preparations."

"We do have nearly a month," he said stubbornly.

"I wish to work alone today, Mr. Brentick," came the chilly reply.

Disagreeably chilly. The cold seemed to enter his bloodstream and trace frost patterns about his heart.

She was shutting him out. Small wonder, if Padji had been smearing his character. Very well. The Falcon was not about to beg for explanations.

Philip bowed and headed for the door. His fingers closed upon the handle, then froze there, his rage smothered in a flood of numbing desolation.

He swung round, saw her dark head bent over her work, and heard another man's voice—it could not be his—low, sharp, demanding—"For God's sake, what have I done?"

Her head shot up, and he saw her eyes glittering. Anger, he thought, as he returned to the worktable. When he neared, the glitter resolved to golden mist. Tears.

"What have I done?" he repeated. "What's wrong?"

"Nothing." She brushed hastily at her eyes. "I have a headache."

"I shall ask Padji to make up one of his herbal teas," he said.

"No! Oh, Mr. Brentick—" She flung the pen down. "Just keep away from him, will you? Stay out of the kitchen.

That is an order. Stay out of his way."

"I see," he said tightly. "Stay out of his way, stay out of your way. May I ask, miss, where you propose I take myself?"

She was staring at him now, her golden gaze wide and wondering as it darted from his face to his tightly clenched hands. He unclenched them.

"Gad, but you *do* have a temper," she said softly.

He swallowed. "I beg your pardon, Miss Cavencourt."

"You needn't apologise. I've heard Padji's kept you at boiling point. That's why I ordered you to keep out of his way. He told me you quarrelled yesterday, and he drove you to violence."

"We had a misunderstanding, miss," Philip said. "I was ill and out of sorts and—"

"And he might have killed you." She looked away, to the fire. "We'll be gone in less than a month. Surely you can keep away for that time."

"Yes, miss. Certainly, miss."

For the second time, Philip bowed himself out of the room, enlightened, yet no more satisfied than before.

A long day loomed ahead of him. He hadn't lied about not having enough to do. He'd trained his staff so well, they rarely needed his supervision. They had merely two ladies to tend, and no entertainments to clean up after. The scrubbing, dusting, and polishing was always done by early morning. He'd arranged all, in fact, to leave him free to keep his employer company most of the day.

Now she didn't want his company.

Now he discovered he wanted hers.

Philip returned to his room—carefully avoiding the kitchen en route—collected his coat and his cigar case, and headed for the garden.

Two cheroots later, Philip had left the garden and wandered out to the moors. The snow had melted and the air, though still cold, carried a faint promise of spring. He found the boulders where he and his employer had enjoyed their first picnic. There he sat, staring at the silver case she'd given him.

She was leaving, finally, and he was relieved, naturally. One long maddening year it had been, maddening even at the last. After all the Falcon's clever plans and manipulations, it was Padji who'd changed her mind, not the sensible widow. All those long walks, the sledding, the skating—all unnecessary.

Brentick had aroused Mrs. Gales's suspicions, as he'd intended, but in the end it was Padji who'd served him. Miss Cavencourt was returning to the world in order to keep her cook from killing her butler.

A waste of time, all those hours spent alone together, here in the brooding hills. A waste of time, fighting temptation, day after day. A dangerous waste of time. They'd grown too close, and he'd come to know her too well. She'd come to live within him, a part of him, just as her voice and scent formed some part of the air he breathed. Today the world about him was wrong somehow, dislocated, because she was missing.

It was the same wrongness and dislocation he'd felt when she dismissed him from the library. They were supposed to be together. *Together, Amanda. You need me to look after you. You're supposed to be with me. I made it so.*

He gazed about the bleak landscape and saw regret. He closed his eyes and tried to force the demoralising truth back into its dark closet, but it would not be stifled. The Falcon could lie to everyone but himself. He loved her . . . and in a month, he'd betray her.

# === 18 ===

Miss Cavencourt never locked up the receipt for the Laughing Princess because she didn't need to. The bank staff knew her. Only she could claim her statue. Thus, one week before her scheduled departure, Philip had merely to slip the receipt among the clutter of estate office documents he was organising into tidy piles. It was equally simple, a short while later, to pretend to find it for the first time.

"An item of value, it says, miss," he said, handing her the piece of paper. "Jewellery, I daresay. I presume you'll wish to take it to London."

She stared at it, then up at him. "Oh, I don't know. Do you think—" She caught herself and flushed.

"Yes, miss? May I be of assistance?"

Miss Cavencourt bit her lip, stared once more at the paper, then shook her head.

Unperturbed, Philip left the room. She'd call him back. She'd survived without him a mere three days before summoning him to assist with the book once more. Within a week, they'd fallen into old habits—or near enough. Their long afternoon activities had ended. When Miss Cavencourt wanted exercise, Padji accompanied her.

All the same, she was too accustomed to relying on her butler's judgement. She'd call him back. If not, he'd simply discard Plan A. Plan B or C would do as well.

An hour later, he was summoned to the library. Miss Cavencourt could not make out one of his notes.

When he'd done translating what was perfectly clear in

the first place, the lady asked with studied nonchalance whether he'd heard anything of Mr. Wringle. Bella had mentioned him just this morning. Bella, evidently, cherished hopes of meeting the fellow in London.

That, Philip knew, was a fabrication. Bella had nothing to do with it. He knew exactly what troubled his employer: she wanted to be sure it was safe to take the statue with her.

He affected astonishment. "In London? Doesn't she—" He stopped short. "Didn't I tell you?"

"Tell me what?" Her fingers gripped the table's edge.

"Good heavens," he said, shaking his head. "I believe I never *did* tell you. Though how it could have —"

"Tell me *what*, Mr. Brentick?" she demanded.

"I do beg your pardon, miss. I should have told you, but in the press of domestic crises, it must have slipped my mind. Later, no doubt, I assumed I *had* told you." He paused briefly. "Mr. Wringle was taken up."

Miss Cavencourt's golden eyes opened very wide. "Taken up?" she echoed. "By whom, for what?"

"By Bow Street officers. I had it from the employment agent, the first day I met with him. Evidently all York was buzzing about it. Mr. Forbish was most excited, having observed the arrest himself."

Miss Cavencourt appeared so utterly lost that her butler was strongly tempted to lift her out of her chair and carry her to safety. The trouble was, he couldn't take her anywhere she'd be safe from him.

"But that is very strange," she said after a moment. "What was Mr. Wringle doing in York? I thought he worked for a respectable London law firm."

"So it appeared, miss."

"But you said you'd been acquainted with him—and Randall Groves helped you get the position."

"I daresay Mr. Groves found no more reason to doubt the man than I did. I noticed nothing out of the way in Mr. Wringle's behaviour. That is, not until the regrettable incident in Portsmouth."

"I see." Her amber gaze dropped to the table. "Do you know what the charge was against him?"

In low tones her butler informed her that Mr. Wringle had been trafficking in stolen goods, among other felonies. Most shocking it was.

"Astonishing, to be sure," she answered slowly, as she digested the news and reached precisely the conclusion Philip intended. "Bella will be distressed." She looked up. "But we needn't tell her right away. I should hate to upset her now, when she has so much to do."

"Most considerate of you, miss. I only hope I haven't distressed *you*," he said, frowning in concern.

"Oh, no. I'm just . . . surprised. Well, not altogether, for this does explain his inexcusable behaviour to you, Mr. Brentick. The man is a hardened villain. Once he was home, safe and well," she said indignantly, "he had no more need for you. He must have feared you'd discover his true self. Certainly you would, because you are so clever and—and perceptive."

Philip had to drop his own gaze then. He wished she wouldn't look at him so. Her guileless golden eyes told him far too much. She not only believed every word, she believed in *him*.

It was a pity, really. So quick and capable her mind was, as she glided through the labyrinths of Hindu mythology and philosophy. So sadly inept, on the other hand, when it came to comprehending her faithless butler.

He heard her tell him she'd go to York the day after tomorrow to collect her "jewellery," just as he heard himself nod and answer calmly. This, after all, was precisely what he'd worked so hard to accomplish. Yet it seemed another man composedly acceded to her wishes, while Philip Astonley wanted to shake her and scream at her not to be such a beautiful, trusting little fool.

Padji rarely slept. He usually spent some part of the night prowling the house and another part roaming the countryside. As Philip had discovered the night he'd ended up in the closet, the Indian followed no predictable routine. Sometimes Padji never left the house at all. At other times he vanished before midnight and did not return until near daybreak. Twice he'd not turned up until after breakfast, leaving the meal to an irate Mrs. Swanslow. When he did go out, moreover, one could not be certain whether he lurked near the house or roamed miles away. The Falcon had therefore contrived several different schemes to accommodate all eventualities.

On the night before the planned trip to York, Padji chose to wander abroad. He returned shortly before dawn and headed for his sleeping quarters, a small room off the kitchen. Philip gave him time to settle in, then crept out to the kitchen.

"Hush," he said in a drunken whisper. He needn't raise his voice. Padji's ears were prodigious sharp. "We don't want to wake everyone."

He answered himself with a feminine giggle. Miss Cavencourt's giggle, to be precise.

A short, amorous conversation ensued, the Falcon playing both drunken servant and the tipsy mistress he enticed out of the kitchen and down the hall to his room.

He'd scarcely closed the door when he heard Padji in stealthy pursuit. Damp cloth in one hand and heavy saucepan in the other, Philip leapt upon the chair he'd previously placed by the door, and flattened himself against the wall.

The door flew open, Padji swung through, and Philip slammed the saucepan against the Indian's skull. The giant sank to his knees, and Philip swiftly pressed the cloth to his face. Padji collapsed.

Moments later, Philip was hauling the cook's inert body through the butler's pantry, then down the steps to the cellars.

He deposited Padji in the outermost wine cellar, tied him up, and gagged him. Then he locked the door, stuffed a few shards of metal into the lock, and began building a barricade of casks.

This labour done, he quickly put into place the dozen

booby traps he'd prepared days before. The Indian shouldn't come to for several hours, and he'd have a devil of a time untying himself, then breaking down the door, but it was best to create as many hindrances as possible. Every minute could count.

Philip returned upstairs, locked the cellar door, and speedily erased all signs of recent events. He checked his pocket watch and smiled grimly.

Knowing he could delay her if that proved necessary, he'd persuaded Miss Cavencourt to make a very early start. He'd already packed and stowed in the carriage his few belongings. He'd plenty of time to bathe and shave, time even to breakfast leisurely—if he'd had any appetite.

*A thief, a prince, a falcon. . . . A prophecy, perhaps.* Padji's words came back to Amanda as she sat, silently fretting, in the curricle beside her butler.

She'd felt uneasy all day because she hadn't told Padji her plans. He of all people was entitled to know she was retrieving the Laughing Princess. The trouble was, he'd want to guard her, and if Padji accompanied her to York, Mr. Brentick could not. She had not wanted to give up these last few precious hours.

Now, as they drove homeward, Amanda wished she hadn't been so stupidly sentimental. The disturbing dream had visited her again last night, leaving her anxious when she woke. She'd wanted to speak to Padji of that at least, but he'd gone wandering again. He was nowhere to be found this morning when she'd come down.

To compound these previous vexations, her butler had been behaving oddly all day. When she tried to make conversation, he answered absently, or with the polite detachment of the early days of his employment.

Their discourse en route to York had been desultory at best. Once there, he'd taken her briskly from shop to shop. He'd claimed business of his own when she stopped for refreshment, and left her to eat her meal alone. After that, she'd retrieved her statue from the bank, and they'd left. No, the day had not passed as she'd hoped.

She threw him a sidelong glance. He seemed very pale. Faint, grim lines at his eyes and mouth made his face taut and hard. This was not the laughing, boyish countenance of her teasing playfellow, or even the amused, ironic visage of her efficient secretary. He seemed another man, a chilling stranger.

Abruptly it occurred to her that they'd left York an hour ago, home waited nearly another hour's drive ahead, and they travelled at present upon a desolate stretch of a little-used country road.

What nonsense, she chided herself. She knew perfectly well this was the shorter route to Kirkby Glenham. Mr. Brentick's countenance was tired, that was all. She had no reason to be uneasy. She'd been alone with him countless times, in equally uninhabited locales.

It was the bundle at her feet that made her so irrationally anxious—that, the distressing dream, a poor night's sleep, and a devilish conscience. Not to mention a pathetic case of unrequited love which had long since robbed her of her reasoning power. *Idiot.*

She'd no sooner succeeded in talking herself round to sense, when the carriage stopped.

"Miss Cavencourt, I must speak to you," he said.

Her anxiety instantly resurged. "That's hardly reason to stop," she said. "It's growing late, and I promised Mrs. Gales I'd be home for tea. You *can* talk and drive at the same time, Mr. Brentick."

"Not this time."

She darted him a nervous glance. His expression had softened somewhat, and he did appear merely tired, or troubled. Lud, what a ninnyhammer she was!

She folded her hands in her lap. "What is it, then?"

He turned slightly toward her. "Miss Cavencourt, I'm afraid I can't continue working for you any longer."

Her heart chilled and sank within her, though she told

herself she'd expected this. She'd known a message would come one day while she languished in London. He'd grow bored. He'd want a more challenging and convivial position. He deserved better than the dull isolation of Kirkby Glenham. Still, she'd not expected the break so soon. She couldn't speak. She nodded stiffly.

A warm, gloved hand closed over hers.

"Look at me," he said. "Look at me, Amanda."

*Amanda.* Her head flew up. She looked square into blue, stormy eyes, and her heart wrenched painfully.

"I must leave. You'll know in a moment. Damn, I'm so sorry—yet I can't be. It's just not in my nature. *Bloody hell,*" he growled.

He pulled her into his arms and dragged her close against him, as though she'd try to run away, when of course she never would. He held her so a long moment while his hands moved over her back and shoulders in hard caresses. "I'm not a gentleman," he murmured into her hair, "and it's been hell pretending, Amanda. I've always wanted you."

Wanted her. Tentatively, her hand crept up his coat to rest over his heart, and she leaned back in his arms to gaze into his beautiful, troubled eyes.

"I want you, too," she whispered. "I—"

"*Don't.*"

"But I–"

His mouth crushed the rest, and the words she'd meant to utter melted in the first hot taste of him.

Her hand slid up the fine wool of his coat, past the starched linen neckcloth and up, to curl about his neck. She'd wanted him so long, waited so long for this. His mouth was bruising and his tongue impatiently seeking, yet she wasn't afraid. She loved him. She wanted all he'd give, and would gladly give all he wanted.

He plundered her mouth, an easy conquest, for the taste of him, wild and sweet, was a tantalising liquor racing through her veins. Happily she surrendered to the warm prison of his body, the hot, hard trap of his arms and the punishment of his restless hands. His mouth moved to her neck, to taste and tease until aching pleasure made her moan. Under his ravaging hands, her body strained eagerly for his. Her hands caught in his hair and pulled his face back to hers. More. She wanted more.

Time vanished, and all the world, leaving only endless yearning and heat. Black and glittering, it churned hotly about them, an eternal, fathomless sea. Only their two souls existed. They were prince and princess of the dark sea, as they had been in the dream. So like the dream. Even the Laughing Princess, lying at her feet . . .

Amanda's heart chilled, lurched wildly, and her eyes flew open. She jerked free of his mouth.

"Don't move," he said.

She became aware of something cold and hard pressed against her neck. Metal. A pistol.

She didn't move. Only her glance dropped . . . to the bundle at her feet. *A thief, a prince, a falcon. A prophecy, perhaps.* With a burst of glaring clarity, she understood. And then she realised she'd always known.

"You filthy bastard," she said softly as she looked up again into his clear blue eyes. Clear and blue and false.

"I see I was not an instant too soon." His voice was strained, hoarse. "You've a devilish way of piercing to the heart of an issue. The trouble is, you're devilish inconsistent about it."

"Bloody, thieving swine."

His mouth curled slightly. "You've called me that before, as I recollect. At the time, I wished I could see the expression on your face. Now I rather wish I couldn't. I wish a great many things, love, but it's no good." The cold gun barrel left her neck. "You'd better get down. I'll be needing the vehicle for a bit, I'm afraid."

"You'd better shoot me," she answered. "Go ahead. Murder me. For a piece of wood. I want to watch you do it. I want to carry that image with me into my next life."

He sighed. "In the first place, I'm a thief, not a murderer. In the second, you know I could never kill you. In any case, I don't have to. A tap with the handle will do well enough—but I'd rather not hurt you, Amanda."

"You already have."

"I know," he said quietly. "Please get down. I can't give you a hand, because I can't trust you now. Just get down."

She threw him one disdainful glance, then climbed down.

She'd left her reticule on the seat. He tossed it down to her. She let it fall into the road.

"Amanda."

She kept her face cool and rigid as she gazed up at him. Her throat was aching, but she would not cry. She would not give him one single tear.

"I imagine you'll be paid a great deal of money," she said. "You've certainly earned it. Risking your life that night in Calcutta was nothing to the hard labour of catering to me five long months. How you must hate me for the trouble I've given you. To think—I had the temerity to steal from the legendary Falcon."

"That was very well done, Amanda. I shall always admire you for it."

"You hated me for it, because I made a fool of you," she said. "That was unforgivable, wasn't it?"

"I did admire you, dear. All the same, one has a reputation to uphold."

"Oh, I understand," she said very softly. "The Falcon always gets the job done, regardless what it takes. You lied because you had to make me trust you completely. I understand that. But you accomplished that early on. You made a fool of me in a matter of days—weeks at most. Wasn't that enough? Did you have to make me love you, too?"

She turned her back to the carriage, to him, and stared blindly at the brooding pasture land beyond.

She heard his muttered oath, but she didn't move. If she moved now, or said another word, she'd break down. She wouldn't. She wouldn't cry and she wouldn't beg.

"Follow that path to your right," he said. "Once you

pass the rise, you'll see a cottage. It's inhabited. I've checked. Someone there will take you home." A short silence followed, while she remained rigid, unmoving.

"Good-bye, darling," came the last, choked words.

She closed her eyes tight. *Go, damn you.*

She heard the curt command to the horses, the light lash of the whip, hoofbeats, and the rattle of wheels. She waited until the sounds had faded far into the distance. Then she dragged her drained body to the nearest boulder, sank down, and burst into tears.

She was still sobbing hysterically when Padji rode up an hour later, leading a second horse. He dismounted, tethered the animals, and hurried to her.

As she took in his appearance, Amanda's sobs ebbed to astonished hiccups. He'd abandoned his traditional Indian attire for the garb of a groom. In stableman's dress, he appeared larger and more intimidating than ever. Or perhaps that was on account of the black scowl contorting his round face.

He dropped a bundle of clothing in her lap. "Go into the bushes, and dress quickly," he said. "We have no time to lose."

Dazed, she took up the garments. "These are boy's clothes," she said.

"Your mount bears a man's saddle, that we may travel more swiftly," he said impatiently. "Ah, mistress, do not delay with foolish questions. I might have pursued the fiend myself, for I know the way he will take. Yet I feared he had harmed you. My heart rejoices to find you safe. Now you must gather your courage and do, this once, as Padji commands, or the Princess is lost to us forever."

Though Amanda obediently rose, desolation had long since overcome her. She shook her head. "Let it be. The statue has done enough harm. I begin to believe it *is* cursed. It makes us all mad."

Padji folded his arms over his broad chest. "Is this the

daughter of the Great Lioness?" he asked reproachfully. "Does such a goddess speak so pitifully, content to remain weak and helpless like other women?"

"I'm not her daughter, and I'm certainly no goddess. I'm exactly like other women. I've let a man rule my mind and heart and—"

"Bah, he is but a pretty fellow who has betrayed you, just as his master betrayed the great rani. She wept, as you do now, yet she exacted her price. Will you abide quietly, O my golden one, when you might avenge her fully, and yourself as well?"

"Are you insane?" Amanda cried. "It's just a carved wooden figure, and vendettas are not considered good *ton*. I don't want revenge. I don't even want the Laughing Princess any more. I just want to go home."

"Very well, mistress. Padji will see to it himself." He turned and stalked towards his horse.

"No!"

"You cannot prevent me, mistress," he said stubbornly. "Padji has his own vengeance to seek. Twice the fiend—a man half my size—has tricked me, to my shame. Once he used my mistress's signal. This time, my beloved's own voice. My own mixture—a secret worth ten rajahs' treasures—he stole from me and used to make me sleep. For these offences, he will pay."

# =19=

To ACCOMPANY PADJI was madness, Amanda knew. The Laughing Princess was simply not that important, and an intelligent, mature woman would merely pity these misguided men. To seek revenge was beneath her.

On the other hand, the Falcon had used her unforgivably. From the start, she'd thrust aside the evidence against him, and blindly believed in Mr. Brentick. He'd known, and deliberately toyed with her feelings, callously exploited her trust. He'd spent five long months seducing her, led her to the brink of ruin—and he never even wanted her. Getting the statue wasn't enough. He'd wanted personal revenge, and so he'd humiliated her. How he must have laughed at his besotted employer.

Amanda took up the pile of clothes, stomped to the bushes, and quickly changed into the shabby smock and breeches. At least they fit relatively well, and she'd be far more comfortable travelling in this garb than in her narrow-skirted kerseymere frock.

Within hours she discovered the value not only of her attire but of a youth spent riding endlessly through the moorland. Roderick had made a sturdy horsewoman of her. Consequently, the pace Padji set, though wearying, was not beyond her endurance.

At every fork and crossroads, Padji stopped, dismounted, and studied the alternate routes, though he seemed sure of the way to go. Amanda guessed these pauses were more for her and the horses' benefit than his. In any case, when she questioned him, all she got was some incomprehensible piece of Oriental logic.

Dark had already fallen when they came within sight of a large inn. Padji reined in his horse.

"That is the place, mistress," he said in Hindustani, though there was no one to overhear. "Large and busy, with many people hurrying about. The man who employs the thief is noble and wealthy. He will not wish to make the exchange in a low place, where thieves and ruffians abound. This abode offers privacy and safety."

"I should think they'd feel safer a great deal farther from York," Amanda answered. "He must at least allow for the possibility you're after him."

"Nay, beloved. The Falcon will wish to be rid of the statue as quickly as possible."

"In that case, maybe he's already rid of it."

Padji shook his head. "I know the roads and the inns, mistress. Many times have I travelled these ways by night. Were I the thief, this site would I choose. But you do not understand. You know only the part of his mind he has shown you. Padji has used these many long weeks to study the part which is hidden."

She turned in the saddle to glare at him. "Many weeks? Do you mean to tell me you knew all along? You knew and never told me? A seducer, you called him. Why the devil couldn't you tell me he was the Falcon?"

"I adore you, my golden-eyed one, and your wisdom fills me with rapturous admiration. But you are a very bad liar. The instant you knew his secret, he must see it in your countenance. Too dangerous," Padji concluded.

"Too dangerous? More dangerous than this? You might have thrown him out on his ear the first day he arrived. Gad, you might have dispatched him while we were still on board ship. You knew then, didn't you?" Amanda accused. "You've known from the start."

"Mistress, this is not the time for lengthy converse. The villains are in our hands at last. Later we may talk."

"I'm not moving another damned inch," she snapped. "I knew there was more to it. I *knew* it. The whole curst lot of you have been using me. And here am I, like a fool, letting you use me again. What the devil is wrong with me?" She wheeled her mount round. "I'm going home, and if you don't come with me, I'll turn you over to the constables. I will. I swear it."

"Nay, mistress," Padji said quietly. He pulled his horse round to block her retreat. "The Falcon left you alone by the road to weep. Must that shape his last vision of you? How many scores of women do you think the fiend has abandoned to their tears? What reason has he to remember you among so many others? He's left his mark on you, beloved. Will you not mark him as well? Shall I merely kill him? Or shall *we two* make him pay, painfully, for his treachery?"

The large, richly furnished chamber was a place of luxurious repose. A fire blazed in the grate. A decanter of wine stood on the small table before it, between two sumptuous armchairs that invited weary travellers to bask in comfort and warmth.

Two weary travellers occupied the room at present, but neither seemed inclined to succumb to the beckoning languor of their surroundings.

Jessup paced the room, muttering crossly to himself. His master stood at the window, his hands tightly clasped behind him.

"Damn fool way to go about it," Jessup grumbled. "Half the day in York. The Indian could have caught up with you before she ever got to the bank, and then where'd we be?"

"He didn't and we're here, just as I promised. I had to give you time to get to Hedgrave, didn't I?"

"Aye, I got to him all right. He was at the tavern, waitin', and not likin' the waitin'—nor me much, when it come to that. And there I was, tellin' him you'd got it, when there was no knowin' for sure you had. He didn't like my harin' off ahead of him, neither, I'll tell you."

"From the moment she decided to go to the bank, the statue was as good as in my hands," Philip said tightly.

"As good ain't good enough. You was half an hour late."

"Our farewells took a bit longer than I'd planned." Philip closed his eyes.

*Did you have to make me love you, too?*

*Don't.*

*I want you, too.*

*Don't.*

He turned away from the window.

"You look like a bleedin' popinjay," said Jessup.

Philip glanced down at his costume: midnight-blue velvet coat and silver satin breeches. Relatively subdued attire for a pink of the ton. Still, the yellow satin waistcoat, upon which brilliant birds of paradise paraded, was all the most flamboyant fop could wish. Admiring oneself, unfortunately, proved hazardous. Even the slight bending of his head drove his shirt points into his jaw.

"Yes," he calmly agreed. "A precious peacock, am I not? I wanted to go out in a blaze of glory. After tonight, the Falcon retires."

"About bloomin' time. Your relations is drivin' me to drink. I swear that's near been the worst of this whole stinkin' business—runnin' back and forth 'twixt that addlepated ol' carcass in London and them vipers in Derbyshire. Five blessed months tryin' to keep 'em all quiet. You better keep a sharp eye out for that lot, guv. Now they've found out what a nabob you are, they're like to bleed you dry."

"I'm aware of your labours, soldier. Believe me, I do not underestimate the enormity of your sacrifice." Philip took up his eyeglass and inspected it. "That is why I've decided the entire reward will be yours."

Jessup stopped pacing so abruptly that he nearly toppled over backwards. "What? You gone clean mad?"

"The witch poisoned you, Jessup. No money on earth

can repay what you've endured on my account."

"Now, guv, we been over this a hundred times. You tole me time and again to be careful what I ate and where I got it from. It weren't—"

"This isn't a debate, soldier. I made up my mind long ago." Philip screwed the glass into his eye. "Now, only tell me what a pretty fellow I am, and we shall mince down to await his lordship."

"Oh, you're a pretty sight, all right," Jessup said grimly. " 'Cept I wouldn't look in the mirror if I was you. Might bust a gut, laughin'."

Philip felt no desire to gaze at his reflection. He knew what he'd see: a fool and a fraud. He'd discard the costume soon enough. Himself he could not discard so easily.

He took up the figure he'd so neatly wrapped after the last, careful inspection. She remained intact, this prodigious costly lady, smooth and beautiful as ever. How radiantly she'd smiled at him. How serene lay the tiny, perfect hands upon her swollen belly. And how the sight of her had sickened him.

He was sick of all of it—this curst piece of wood, Lord Hedgrave's obsession . . . but most of all, the Falcon was sick to death of himself.

*I want you, too.*

What could he have said?

*I love you, Amanda.*

Oh, aye. Then told her who he was, what he was?

He'd gone mad for a moment when, holding her, he'd thought he need not take the statue after all. He'd lie, tell Hedgrave it had been stolen again—better yet, claim it was all a mistake. The thing was still in India, he'd say. But Hedgrave would learn the truth, and set some other—even less scrupulous—after her. Or the marquess would hunt her down himself. In any case, it was too late. The time for honesty had come and gone a year ago on the ship, and the time since was all fraud and betrayal.

*She'd have forgiven you*, his conscience spoke.

*Perhaps*, the Falcon answered, *but I'd have despised her for it.*

Jessup stood by the door, his square, stolid face sunk in gloom as he gazed at his master. "You comin'?" he asked. "Or you goin' to stand there glowerin' all night?"

Philip flicked an imaginary speck of lint from his sleeve. "I'm coming," he said.

A short time later, an elegant equipage clattered into the inn's courtyard, and a host of obsequious minions hastened eagerly to tend to it.

No one noticed the two figures standing in the shadows.

"You see?" Padji whispered in Hindustani.

The carriage steps were let down, the door opened, and Amanda beheld a tall, lean, somberly attired figure emerge. As the man turned to speak to his coachman, the lamplight revealed a proud, handsome profile. The hair beneath the gleaming beaver was light.

"Are you sure it's he?" she asked softly.

Padji grinned, and pulled her towards the stables.

Lord Hedgrave had arrived with half a dozen outriders, and a public conveyance followed minutes later. Thus, most of the stablemen had hurried out to the inn yard. The two remaining within the stable made the mistake of objecting to Padji's entrance before they'd acquired reinforcements. He knocked one unconscious with a careless swipe of his hand. The other he threw against the wall. He quickly bound the unconscious men and dragged them into an empty stall.

"Guard the door," he ordered. "If anyone comes, divert them. I want but a moment. When you hear me cry out, run quickly, as I told you."

Amanda nodded. Clenching her teeth to stop their chattering, she moved to the doors. She had to strain to hear anything above her thundering heartbeats. To steady herself, she fixed her mind on counting out the passing seconds. She'd just reached two hundred when Padji's voice rang out, and she dashed through the door and round to the side of the stables.

The first startled whinny swelled into a cacaphony of shrieks and crashes. The stablemen rushed towards the noise, then swiftly scattered as a herd of terrified horses thundered down upon them. The crowded courtyard erupted into chaos. Cursing coachmen leapt to control their panicked teams. Screaming passengers ran every which way, tripping over baggage and each other. Grooms darted among the flailing hooves, some to drag guests to safety, others to capture the maddened animals.

The uproar without rapidly alerted those within, and in minutes the inn emptied most of its human contents into the courtyard's pandemonium.

Under cover of the tumult, Amanda and Padji easily slipped unheeded into the enormous hostelry.

The sprawling inn was a nightmarish maze of corridors, yet Padji never hesitated. He headed straight past the public dining room and down a passage to the left. There, to Amanda's consternation, stood a tall servant, wielding a pistol. He shouted a warning. Padji never paused. He caught the man by the shoulder and flung him against the wall. The servant subsided into a heap.

They turned into another hallway, where another armed guard waited. Padji flung him out of his path with a negligent motion that belied the strength of his arm. So it continued endlessly.

Time and again, Amanda watched one careless blow throw a man several feet, to crash into walls or timbers, and sink, unconscious, to the floor. As she skirted the bodies, she fervently hoped Padji had not broken their skulls. She had small time for pity or anxiety, however. She could only follow blindly, and pretend it wasn't happening. Always another turning, another guard, another hall beyond. Would it never end?

"It's a warren," she gasped as she sidestepped yet another sad heap of unconscious human. "How the devil do you expect to find—"

"Hist, mistress." Padji stopped short, and hauled her back round the corner they'd just turned.

She heard footsteps hurrying towards them.

"Who's there?" a voice called. "What the devil's up? What's all that racket?"

"Dear God," she whispered. "It's Mr. Wringle."

Padji nodded. "Quick, mistress. Go out to him, and draw him back this way."

She stared at her servant in horror.

"Do it." He pushed her forward.

Amanda crushed her hat down low over her forehead and, limbs shaking, rounded the corner once more.

"You there!" Wringle called. "Where you think you be goin'? This here area's private."

Amanda staggered back a pace. "Bloody hell," she croaked in a fair imitation of a drunken groom. "Where's the demmed privy?"

"Ain't no privy this way." Wringle stomped closer, his eyes narrowed. "How'd you get so far, anyhow? Didn't the others tell you—" He paused and peered suspiciously at her. "You ain't no lad," he growled as he reached for her arm.

Amanda jerked away and darted back the way she'd come. She rounded the corner, then jumped clear in the nick of time. Padji charged, caught Wringle, and with one graceful sweep of his hand, knocked him unconscious.

Within the cozy parlour, two men faced each other across a linen-draped table. If they were aware of the riot out of doors, they gave no sign. At any rate, a host of armed and well-trained men stood between them and external distractions. Lord Hedgrave had paid handsomely for both privacy and security. It was not his business to worry, but that of the men he'd paid. At the moment, only one concern appeared to possess him.

"It's a wooden statue," he said, gazing with displeasure at the Laughing Princess. "This is not what I requested."

"The Falcon had but one opportunity to study the rani's residence," Philip said. "He'd made a careful study of her character, though, previously. He knew she must have hidden it very cleverly, or she'd not have managed to keep it so long."

Lord Hedgrave glanced at the figure briefly, then at Philip, more consideringly.

"Many curious objects adorned her chambers," Philip continued. "This one the Falcon found most fascinating of all." He took up the statue and lightly caressed it. "He'd seen similar figures before, many times. Usually, however, such talismans are crudely carved and quite small, because they're meant to be worn. This I think you'd agree would make a most uncomfortable pendant."

"I see," said Lord Hedgrave.

Philip took out his knife.

"I presume the man already checked," the marquess said.

"That was neither necessary nor advisable."

The knife dug delicately into one of the drapery folds that lay beneath the figure's tiny hands. A curved sliver of wood broke away. Philip repeated the operation at the fold beneath the belly, and removed another narrow crescent of wood. Then he lifted away the curved piece representing the belly itself. Within the statue lay a mound of shimmering white.

"Good God," the marquess breathed.

Philip took out the great, tear-shaped pearl and held it up to the light. "The Tear of Joy," he said. "Perfect, isn't it? The faintest tinge of rose. Lovely colour, and quite flawless. Some would say this was a pearl beyond price. Certainly it has cost some of us dearly." He held the pearl out to the marquess. "I ought to warn you it's cursed," he added with a mocking smile.

A small smile of satisfaction began to curve Lord Hedgrave's stern mouth as he reached for the pearl. Then Philip felt a rush of air at his back and saw the marquess's countenance freeze, even as his hand did, while the colour swiftly drained from his face.

A familiar warning chill sliced down Philip's neck. He whirled round . . . to find himself staring down the barrel of a pistol.

At the other end, holding with two steady hands, stood Miss Cavencourt. Behind her, also pointing a pistol, stood a grinning Padji.

"The knife," said Miss Cavencourt.

Philip carefully set his knife upon the table.

"The pearl," she said.

His gaze locked with glittering gold. Hard. Merciless. In that moment, he knew she'd not hesitate to kill him.

She put out one hand. Without a word, without releasing his gaze, he dropped the pearl into it.

"No!" the marquess screamed. He shot round the table and lunged at Amanda, who quickly retreated. In the same instant, Philip caught a flash of metal, as Padji cracked his weapon against Lord Hedgrave's skull. The marquess sank to the floor.

It had all happened in a heartbeat, and even as she'd backed away, Miss Cavencourt's pistol remained trained on Philip. He'd not moved a muscle.

"He'd better not be dead," she warned Padji in a hard, quiet voice. "I told you not to kill him."

"He lives, mistress. It was but a little tap. In a short while, he wakes, and I give him something to drink. Then he will not wish to pursue the matter, I think. A little poison," he explained reassuringly to Philip. "It will not kill him, for my mistress tells me that would be unwise. He is a great prince, and his death would cause some annoying outcry." He paused briefly. "A mere thief, however, is another matter, is it not, mistress?"

Miss Cavencourt shrugged and lowered her pistol. She coolly stepped past Philip and collected the pieces of the mutilated Laughing Princess. The Indian's gun was pointed straight at Philip's head. The Falcon stood motionless. Only his eyes followed her. Despise her? How could he have dared? She was magnificent.

Miss Cavencourt did not spare him another glance. Statue and pearl cradled safely in her hands, she slipped from the room as quietly as she'd entered.

*Good-bye, darling.*

Philip turned his gaze to the Indian. Padji pushed the door closed with his foot.

"You must not trouble your heart, Falcon," he said. "You brought your master what he wanted. The object simply slipped from your hands. Such things happen."

"You're going to kill me," Philip said.

Padji nodded sadly. "It is my *dharma*."

"I pray you will not trouble your tender heart over that," Philip answered calmly. "I'm not afraid to die."

"Nay, only afraid to live, O Falcon. Such a fool you are. Like this one." Padji nudged the marquess's inert body with his foot. "He thinks the pearl is what he wants. A fool."

"I see we English are all fools, where you and the rani are concerned," Philip said. "This was all some sort of elaborate trap, wasn't it? Miss Cavencourt was simply the means to get you here, and you were to be the instrument of revenge. Yet you say you're not going to kill him."

"So it is. He must live. His fate is not yet unfolded."

"And what of Amanda? Or doesn't anyone care what becomes of her?" Philip scowled. "Evidently not. You and the rani left her to my tender mercies, didn't you?"

"Merely a painful education," said Padji amiably. "Her heart was too trusting. She is wiser now. Be at ease, Falcon. The rani will look after her daughter."

"She's no kin to that witch," Philip coldly returned.

Padji came away from the door. "You are clever, yet you are blind as well. It is the rani's own blood runs in the veins of the mistress you betrayed. Her mother's grandmother and the grandmother of the Rani Simhi were sisters."

"No," Philip said, aghast. "Amanda is not—"

"Her mother was weak, and so her heartless world destroyed her. They despised her for her tainted blood. It will not be the same with the daughter. The rani will see to it. Now, take up your blade," Padji politely invited. "I prefer not to kill you in cold blood."

Not the rani's kin. That was impossible. Yet what did it matter, after all?

Philip reached for his knife, though he knew the exercise was futile. He would die, of course. Without the element of surprise, he stood no chance against Padji.

As the Falcon's fingers closed about the handle, the room, and the moment, swept away in a rush of images. The ship . . . soft hands cool upon his burning face . . . a full moon gleaming above and the gentle splash of waves below . . . the stories . . . the scent . . . patchouli. Amanda, shrieking with laughter in the snow . . . careening crazily about the ice, her hands trustingly clasped in his. Amanda in his arms, her mouth ripe and soft, opening to his . . . her body, slim and sensuous, curving into his touch . . . gone . . . slipped through his hands.

He took up the knife and met Padji's enigmatic gaze.

"Please," the Falcon said, though there was no pleading in his cool, quiet voice. "Tell her I love her."

# =20=

LORD DANBRIDGE LOOKED up from his letter as the door opened and his caller entered.

"You took your time about it," said his lordship.

"Press of business," the visitor answered. The door closed silently behind him.

Lord Danbridge rose from his chair and crossed the room to shake his guest's hand. "Well, I'm glad to see you—though you have left me a pretty mess to untangle."

"Be thankful it wasn't the one I had to untangle for myself. Two grieving—or is it greedy?—widows, one hysterical solicitor, and one marquess promising to stick his spoon in the wall. Not to mention my loyal servant, who has spent the last month working endless variations on the theme of 'I told you so.' Bloody insolent devil he is. I ought to have packed him off years ago," Lord Felkoner complained.

"Hedgrave has recovered, I understand."

"Physically, yes. Padji treated him to one of his milder poisons. I rather wish the Indian had exercised less restraint. I've had all I can do to keep his lordship quiet in Derbyshire. Now he's well, he refuses to be quiet any longer. If I won't go after them—which I assured him I wouldn't—he'll do it himself, he says. I brought him with me because he wants watching, and because I'd hoped you might be able to reason with him."

Lord Danbridge shook his head sadly. "Ah, my lad, it's

a bad business. I never should have brought you into it."
He moved away and gestured to a chair. " 'My lad,' indeed," he muttered. "Still thinking of you as the wild young man I met all those years ago. It's 'my lord' now—and I don't mind saying I'm glad for you, Philip."

Viscount Felkoner accepted the offered chair. His host dropped into the seat opposite.

"How did you get out of it alive, by the way?" Danbridge asked.

"Simple enough. The Indian didn't kill me. Don't ask me why. He is as inscrutable as he is immense. I woke to a thundering headache and the melodious sounds of his lordship, Marquess of Hedgrave, retching into the carpet."

"Poor Dickie," Lord Danbridge murmured. "Dashed hothead, too, just like you, and just as stubborn. Never expected to inherit either, you know. Three older brothers in the way in his case. That's why he went to India. Got into scrapes, too, but earned his fortune, just as he'd planned. Hadn't planned for the woman, though. One never does. Of course, you couldn't understand. I daresay she's well past her prime now. Then . . . ah, Philip. A wildcat she was, the most beautiful wildcat I've ever laid eyes on."

He smiled nostalgically into the empty grate. "Too fiery and dangerous for my tastes. Even her husband was afraid of her. Not Dickie. She was just what he wanted. He never cared for safe women—safe anything, for that matter. I think he craved trouble the way some men crave drink, or opium."

Philip stirred restlessly in his chair.

"Well, you don't want to listen to me maundering on about the old days," his host said more briskly.

"I gathered you had a reason for sending for me."

"Yes." Lord Danbridge leaned forward slightly. "I'm aware Dickie's back on this hobby-horse of his. He's written to Miss Cavencourt, you see. She showed me the letter herself—"

Philip tensed. "You've seen her?"

"Oh, I've seen her," came the rueful answer. "Whirled in like all heaven's avenging angels, and gave me what for. Don't know how she tied me to the business."

"Padji," said Philip. "He knows everything."

"In any case, she told me to warn 'his deranged lordship'—those were her exact words—that if he or his hired villains came within five miles of her, she'd take her story to the papers."

Philip bit back a smile. "I imagine she'll express herself equally vividly to his lordship."

"No. She said she would not attempt to communicate with him because he was a prime candidate for Bedlam who ought to be kept under permanent restraint for the safety of the nation. She'd come to me, she said, because she assumed I had some modicum of sense. It is my delightful responsibility to inform Dickie that if he doesn't steer clear, she'll bring down a whopping scandal on his benighted head. I think she'll do it, too."

"She will."

"Which means, I'm afraid, that your illustrious name must be dragged in the mud as well. Not that she mentioned you by name," Lord Danbridge added. "I guessed she hadn't made the connexion."

"She rarely reads the papers," Philip answered. "Besides, we've kept the details quiet. Philip Astonley, very recently returned from the East, has succeeded to the title of Viscount Felkoner. Few would connect that fellow with the Falcon." He paused, his hands tightening on the chair arms. "She didn't mention the Falcon?"

" 'Hired criminals. The lowest sort of thieves and thugs.' The Falcon never came up by name, no."

"I see. Where is she now?"

Lord Danbridge looked at him. "You needn't worry Hedgrave will find her. She's—"

"Is she still in London?" Philip demanded.

"Heavens, no. She came to me because she was intending to return to India, she said, and didn't want to be pestered with any more of Dickie's 'minions.' "

Philip shot up from his chair. "No. She wouldn't. Dammit, man, when did you see her?"

"Near a fortnight ago. I wrote you immediately after." Danbridge struggled up from his chair. "What in blazes is this about?"

Lord Felkoner turned away from his mentor's sharp scrutiny and headed for the door. "A woman," he muttered. "A woman, devil take her." He slammed out.

Midafternoon found the new Lord Felkoner dashing wildly about the Gravesend docks, collaring sailors and dockworkers. In his wake trailed an exhausted and increasingly exasperated Jessup.

At length, the servant caught up with his master, and grabbed his aristocratic arm. "They ain't lyin' to you, guv," he shouted. "The bloody ship's gone. It's been gone near a week, and her with it. You're actin' like a bleedin' lunatic."

Philip shook him off. "There are other ships. She's only a few days' lead. We might catch up at Lisbon."

"*We*?" Jessup repeated. "You ain't gettin' me on no more ships. No thanks, your almighty lordship. I ain't packin' for you because it's a damn fool thing to do, and I ain't goin' with you, because that's crazier still. You set foot in India and you're a dead man, and I don't plan to watch you die or die alongside of you." He saluted smartly, then turned on his heel and stomped off.

Jessup's aching feet and empty stomach took him as far as the nearest chophouse.

He entered, fell into the first vacant chair, planted his elbows on the table, and bellowed for service.

A moment later, a shadow fell upon the table.

"Is that you, Mr. Wringle, making such a dreadful roar? Cross, are you? Well, that's what comes of not taking proper care of yourself, ain't it?"

Jessup lifted startled eyes to the vision standing by his shoulder. Then he blinked. Twice. "Bella, my lass, that ain't you?" he whispered incredulously.

"Who is it, then, I'd like to know?" she answered pertly.

"What're you doin' here?" he asked.

Bella pointed to a corner where an auburn-haired woman of middle age dined with a grey-haired fellow in captain's garb. "Cap'n Blayton wrote her he was coming, and she took me along to meet him. Weren't proper, she said, for a lady to come alone. I don't think she'll be a widow much longer," the maid confided in lower tones.

"But you here still, and your mistress gone? Why ain't you with her?"

"I had enough of them heathens," Bella said firmly. "Anyways, that little Jane was just begging to go, though what good she'll do my poor Miss Amanda, I couldn't say. That child don't know a comb from a coal scuttle. But she learns quick enough, and she'll do on the ship, I expect, and there'll be plenty of proper maids in Calcutta. Mr. Roderick—that is, his lordship—he'll see to it. And if he don't, why that wicked old woman—"

"Ah, my lass, never mind 'em," said Jessup as he took her hand and pressed it to his cheek. "Only come sit by me, do, and let me look in them snappin' black eyes o' yourn, sweetheart. I missed you somethin' fierce, I did."

Lord Felkoner was arguing heatedly with an exhausted sea captain when another gentleman noiselessly entered the shipping office.

"I'll pay you double. Triple," the viscount shouted. "I'll buy the damned ship."

"My lord, it isn't mine to sell," the captain said patiently. "Besides, we've only just come. The cargo's not unloaded.

If you please, there are several other—"

"They've *all* just come, dammit. Isn't there one curst vessel—"

"Felkoner," a quiet, firm voice interrupted.

Philip turned. "My lord," he said stiffly.

"Another voyage East, I take it? Calcutta perhaps?"

"It's none of your damned business, *my lord*."

"I'm afraid it is," his lordship answered. He nodded towards the door. "Come along, my boy."

Philip's eyes blazed and his posture grew rigid. "I'm not your damned boy, my lord. Furthermore—"

"Oh, be quiet, Felkoner. And do mind your language. You set a bad example for the seamen. Now come along."

"I'm not your hired help any longer. Find someone else—" A pistol flashed into view and Philip's sentence dangled unfinished.

"My lord," the alarmed captain began.

"Now you just look out the window, captain," Lord Hedgrave politely suggested. "You are an intelligent fellow. You've seen and heard nothing."

He gestured at the door with the pistol and Philip obediently moved in that direction.

"Don't try anything foolish, my lad," the marquess softly advised. "There's not a trick you know I didn't learn years ago, while you were still crawling about in skirts." He paused briefly before adding, "Though for the life of me I couldn't say which of us is the greater fool."

# =21=

TWO SARI-CLAD WOMEN stood at the carved vetiver entryway. In the moonlight, the garden was a wonderland of silver and shadow. The flowers' voluptuous fragrance drifted to them on a light, warm breeze.

"Anumati's night," said the rani. "The time is fitting to unfold my tale."

"You've kept me waiting long enough," Amanda said. Nearly a month I've been here."

"Nearly a month here, five months upon the ship, and still you weep." The rani turned away from the entry. "We must find a lover to dry your tears."

"I have had quite enough of love, thank you." Amanda followed the princess back into the chamber. "It offers precious little rapture to compensate for the madness."

"That is because you did not take him into your bed," the rani calmly returned. "But it is useless to speak to you of these matters. You have confused notions of sin."

As they sank onto the cushions, the princess signalled to a servant, who brought in the hookah. With another signal, all the servants vanished.

The two cousins smoked quietly for a while, the only sound in the room the bubble of the pipe.

"I lied to you," the rani said at last. "I am an excellent liar. The skill has many times saved my life. At other times, it brought me what I wanted. Tonight, however, I shall try not to lie very much."

Amanda laughed. "Why, thank you, *Mother*."

"Ah, I am a dreadful mother, but it cannot be helped," the princess said with a shrug. "Here is some truth: My husband gave Richard Whitestone the pearl in reward for taking me away. It is true the Englishman later abandoned me. I only failed to mention that I pursued him to Bombay. There, through means I will not tire you by describing, Padji and I tricked him and stole the pearl. My lover did not discover the theft until he was well upon the sea."

"You stole it for revenge. That's understandable."

The Indian woman nodded. "He loved me. He had not intended this, but it happened. This I know, just as I know he would have remained with me, but for an accident of Fate. He was the youngest of four sons. Shortly before he fulfilled his bargain with my husband, my English lover learned a fire had consumed his family home, and killed all his near kin at once. Thus he gained a great title he'd never dreamed would be his."

"Now I understand," Amanda said, her voice tinged with bitterness. "That's why he left you. He'd not want a pack of half-breeds to carry on his illustrious name."

"Certainly he would not. You saw how your mother was treated—and she merely a part Indian. I understood his reasons and saw his wisdom. Nonetheless, all his reasons and wisdom were blindness and folly. He married a noble English lady and they lived, loveless, as other noble couples do. I learned of it and rejoiced, just as I rejoiced when their union bore no fruit. No sons, no daughters. Richard Whitestone threw away a great love . . . and ended with nothing."

"That," said Amanda, "is just as he deserves."

"So I reminded him. I made the pearl the symbol of his folly. Each year, on the anniversary of the theft, he received a letter from me. I taunted him cruelly. He is stubborn, proud, and hot-tempered. To provoke him has never been difficult."

"No wonder he became so obsessed with the pearl."

Amanda gazed thoughtfully at the mouthpiece in her hand. "Yet it wasn't the pearl he wanted, was it?"

"No, but to believe so was far less humiliating to such a man than to admit the truth."

Amanda looked up to meet the rani's dark, liquid gaze. "Why did you give it to me?" she asked.

Her cousin sighed. "A complicated story. Lord Hedgrave has agents throughout India. For years, however, I found it easy enough to remain inaccessible. I waited until his wife was dead. Then I came to Calcutta, and awaited the approach of his pawns. Naturally, their clumsy attempts failed. To behold the Lioness is not to capture her. Eventually, I thought, the marquess must come himself, as I'd countless times dared him to do."

"But he didn't. He sent the—that thief."

"When I first came to Calcutta, the Falcon was unknown. Within a few short years, all India spoke of him. By that time, I had met you, and discovered a heart like mine beat in your breast. Like mine," the rani added with a smile, "were my heart not quite so black with sin. A lioness lives within you, nonetheless."

"I'm no lioness. I haven't a fraction of your wisdom or experience. Why give it to me?" Amanda demanded. "You knew how naive I was—and how unscrupulous *he* was. You were a match for him. I wasn't. Didn't you care what happened to me? Did you *want* Hedgrave to get the pearl?"

The princess reached out to take Amanda's hand. "I knew you would never let him have it," she said quietly. "Never. You know that as well, Amanda."

"I don't know anything like it, and I can't believe you could be so reckless as to rely on me. You didn't have to. You could have relied on yourself. Why did you have to make a perfectly simple matter so devilish complicated?" Amanda disengaged her hand and took up her neglected pipe. "This is no explanation at all," she grumbled. "I might have expected it." She inhaled deeply of the lightly scented smoke.

"There is more," said her cousin imperturbably. "I shall—" She stopped and listened. "Someone comes."

Amanda, too, heard footsteps in the hall beyond. She looked up.

Padji's immense form filled the doorway. "If you please, mistress," he said with every appearance of disgust. "Visitors."

Amanda tensed. "Roderick," she whispered. "He's found out I'm here."

The rani shook her head. "At this late hour?" she answered Padji reprovingly. "Send them away."

Amanda relaxed and brought the comforting pipe to her mouth again.

Padji did not move.

"If you please, mistress, they are mad," he said. "One holds a knife to my back. The other a pistol."

The smoke she'd just inhaled caught in Amanda's windpipe, choking her. Coughing and gasping, she watched through streaming eyes as Padji grudgingly moved aside and two men entered the room. Two tall, fair-haired men.

Amanda wiped her eyes, but that didn't help. She was hallucinating. What in blazes was in the pipe?

One of the men was hurrying towards her. No.

"Amanda," he said. "My love, I—" He halted midstride, his eyes riveted upon the rani.

Dazedly, Amanda looked at her cousin. The princess held a pistol, which was pointed straight at him.

"Back, Falcon," said the princess. "Your elderly friend will put away his weapon or I shall drive a bullet through your black heart."

She met Amanda's startled gaze and smiled. "Men," she said. "Just like children. They never think."

Lord Hedgrave—for that was the "elderly friend"—handed Padji his pistol. "Let him be, Nalini," the marquess said quietly. "Your quarrel is with me."

"Is it?" the princess answered haughtily without looking

at him. "I have no quarrels with feeble old men."

The marquess laughed. "Wicked girl."

"I am no longer a girl, Richard Whitestone."

"Perhaps not. Yet wicked you are."

The rani threw him a careless glance. She lay the pistol down.

The Falcon took a cautious step towards Amanda. She glared at him. "Go to the devil," she said.

"Ah, Miss Cavencourt," said the marquess. "I didn't know you at first. No wonder my travelling companion behaved so heedlessly." He turnèd to the rani. "When I first made the lady's acquaintance, she wore a smock and breeches," he explained. "The sari is a deal more becoming. Don't you agree, my lord?" he asked the Falcon.

Midnight-blue eyes bored into Amanda. "Yes," he answered hoarsely.

"Go to hell," she said. Her heart pounded so she thought the room must thunder with it. "You sicken me."

"If my beloved ones so wish it," Padji offered, "I shall cut out the dogs' hearts."

"Perhaps later," the rani said. "Go away, Padji."

Padji left.

"You as well, child," the princess continued. "Take your Falcon into the garden. I would speak privately with this pitiful old man."

"So you *will* speak to me, Nalini?" Lord Hedgrave asked as he crossed the room to her. "After all these years, and all my crimes?"

She shrugged. "Perhaps we shall speak. Perhaps I shall poison you. Who knows?"

Lord Hedgrave dropped gracefully onto the cushions beside her.

The Falcon held out his hand to Amanda. "Take me to the garden," he said softly.

The woman he followed outside was the goddess he'·

dreamed of for eighteen long months. She wore a sari of gold, but the moonlight transformed it to liquid silver, shimmering in sensuous curves about her slim form. Her long, dark hair fell in rippling waves upon her shoulders and back. The sari draped gracefully to conceal one arm. Her other lay bare and smooth, but for the small sleeve of her brocade *choli*. Thin gold bangles tinkled as she moved, and behind her trailed the faint scent of patchouli.

She led him down a path thick with flowers and shrubs, then on to the ornamental pool at the garden's heart. There she stood, her exotic countenance shut against him, her stance cool and straight. Unwelcoming. Unyielding.

He'd been mad to come. Where would he find the magic words to unlock the barrier his folly had built between them?

"Amanda," he began.

"I don't even know your name," she said with chilly politeness. "Your *real* name."

Remorse smote him in a swelling ache.

"It's Philip," he said. "Philip Andrew Astonley." He hesitated, then continued doggedly. "Viscount Felkoner. Of Felkonwood, Derbyshire."

"So that was you," she said, her tones expressionless. "Mrs. Gales showed me the piece in the *Gazette*. I should have realised. Felkoner—Falcon. I collect you chose that particular pseudonym to spite your father. The article said you lost two brothers. My condolences."

He didn't want polite condolences. He didn't want polite anything. He wanted to pull her into his arms and make her love him again, make her eyes fill with trust and tenderness once more. How had he thought he could live without that, without her?

"None of my predecessors will be greatly missed," he said stiffly. "A pity, because my father at least would have appreciated the irony. He was so certain I'd be the first to go. Not through natural causes, of course," he added, unable to keep the bitterness from his voice. "The gallows, perhaps, or some equally sordid conclusion."

"There's time yet to prove him right." She stared fixedly at the water. "You tempt Fate by coming here."

"I had no choice." He took a step nearer. She moved two paces back. His hands clenched at his sides.

"I wanted to come after you," he said miserably. "I wanted to come right away, but I didn't dare leave his confounded lordship out of my sight for an instant. How he found a chance to write you, I'll never know. If I'd caught him at it, I'd have broken both his arms myself."

She didn't respond.

"Dammit, why didn't you let Padji kill us both?" he demanded. "There were no witnesses, and—"

"Padji explained that," she said. "It is bad *ton* to murder a peer of the realm."

"Indeed? Well, it's perfectly good form to kill a thief. He meant to kill me. I saw it in his eyes. But he didn't. Why?" he asked. "Was that your doing?"

She shot him a brief, scornful glance. "You can thank yourself. It was your last maudlin speech changed his mind. Really, I had not imagined even you could sink so low. Not that it worked quite the way you intended. Oh, he believed you, amazingly enough, but he didn't spare you out of pity. He decided a lifetime burning in the fires of unrequited love was a more fitting punishment."

Hot shame swept his face. That was her opinion of him. She thought his dying words merely some pathetic attempt to save his own skin. As though he'd have begged for mercy, when all he'd wanted then was to be put out of his misery. She couldn't know how wisely Padji had judged.

"Padji knew exactly what he was doing," he admitted, his face flaming again. "He knew. *She* knew," he added, nodding towards the palace. "How, I can't say. She's not quite human, is she? But I've had time enough to reflect, and I could swear they knew I'd want you the moment I met you. You were meant to be my undoing, Amanda."

That earned him another disbelieving glance.

"You were," he went on determinedly. "You undid me utterly. I couldn't understand how I could be so careless. How I could misjudge, time and again. I, the Falcon. After you stole back the statue—the first time—I spent weeks in London trying to discover where you'd gone. Weeks. The Falcon should have solved that in a few hours."

"You'd never been on that end of a robbery before. I daresay the shock addled your wits." She moved several steps away.

He followed. "Do you really believe that was all? While I was in London, trying to track you down, I learned I'd inherited. All my life my father tried to crush me, as though I were some unspeakable vermin polluting his family. Suddenly, I found myself lord of all he'd denied me: his castle, his vast acres, his money—all mine. Yet the very day I got the happy news, I headed for Yorkshire."

Her face turned sharply to him, her eyes lit with incredulity. "You knew—before you came—and you travelled all the way to Kirkby Glenham—and worked as my *servant*? What the devil is wrong with you?"

"You," he said.

She refused to understand. "It was the damned pearl," she muttered. "It's definitely cursed. It makes men *insane*."

"It's nothing to do with the dratted pearl," he snapped. "The Tear of Joy was a convenient excuse, I admit. It made you a professional problem, and I thought I could solve you as easily as all the others. Yet the truth was always there. I locked it away in the dark, but couldn't stifle it. It never stopped trying to break out."

"There's no truth in you," she said coldly. "I stopped believing in you the instant I realised who you were. I don't know what your game is now, and I don't care. I won't play." She moved past him, and headed back the way they'd come.

Philip stood a moment while despair warred with need. He'd journeyed all this way, spent months on another curst ship. This time he'd travelled without her, and the way had been long and lonely indeed. He would *not* go back to his great, empty tomb of a house without her. If he could not return with her, he'd not return at all.

She'd walked away with cool dignity, unhurried. The Falcon darted after her, and caught her from behind. His hand covered her mouth before she could cry out, while his other arm dragged her back against him. Swiftly he pulled her into a narrow path sheltered by tall shrubs.

She fought him, just as she had that night so long ago, and her blows were no gentler now.

"Stop it," he growled. "Drat you, *stop* it."

She slammed her heel against his shin.

"Damnation," he muttered.

Her teeth caught at his hand. He yanked it away. She had scarcely an instant to draw breath for a scream before his knife was out and resting lightly upon her throat. She stilled.

"That's better," he said. "Now *listen* to me, damn you."

"Bastard," she breathed.

"I love you," he said. "I've loved you from the moment you jammed your elbow into my belly. I loved you that night in Calcutta and after, on the ship. I loved you after you stole back your sandalwood princess, even while I hated you and wanted to strangle you. I loved you the whole time in Yorkshire while I plotted to get it back. And I loved you when you held a gun to my heart and stole the pearl and your princess away again."

She made a slight movement. He pulled his arm more tightly against her waist, to mould the length of her back firmly to him. She gasped, but subsided against him.

"I have *always* loved you," he continued angrily. "I can't help that I've behaved like an unscrupulous, dishonourable, obstinate swine the whole time, because that's what I am. Damn it, Amanda, can't you understand? You understand *everything*."

"I understand," she answered breathlessly. "I just wasn't sure you did. Will you please put away the knife? It makes me nervous."

"If I put it away, *I'll* be nervous."

"You? The Falcon? You're not afraid of anything."

He sighed. "Except closets. And you. I'm scared to death of you, Amanda. I'm terrified you'll say No."

"To what?" He heard laughter in her voice.

His eyes narrowed. She was a deal too like her cousin, he decided as he took the blade away and let it fall to the ground. He turned her to face him, then gathered her close. She didn't struggle. Why should she? She knew he'd never hurt her. She knew why he'd come. She'd been waiting for him, waiting to get even. The little she-cat had tormented him . . . deliberately. Yet she'd forgiven him, and that was all that mattered.

"I want a wife," he said. "A Lady Falcon to come with me to Derbyshire to make the great, lonely aerie I've inherited a home. And fill it with disobedient, insolent, deceitful, thieving little brats."

"*My* children," she loftily informed him, "will not be bratty little thieves."

"Why not? Their father's a thief. Their mother as well."

She shook her head. "I refuse to live in a menagerie of wild beasts. I have books to write. I need order and peace. Quiet, angelic children. And a very good secretary."

"I'm an excellent secretary," he pointed out, "nearly as good as I am a thief."

Slowly she raised trusting golden eyes to him, and his heart ached with tenderness.

"The thief is a dreadful man," she said. "But the secretary is a superior being. I can't finish my book without him. I've tried, Mr. Brentick. It's no good."

"I'm not Mr. Brentick."

"You're everybody to me, Falcon. All the world. My tassel-gentle," she added softly. Her hand slid up his chest, then farther up, to stroke his cheek.

He turned his face to kiss her palm. He'd never been

gentle with her before, it seemed. He meant to, this time, but the scent of her skin sapped his reason. Silk rustled under his hands, and beneath it moved a warm, beckoning body. He pulled her closer and hungrily captured her mouth. He tasted sweet fruit and smoke. That was she. Light and shadow. Innocence and sin. Joy and madness.

The taste of her raced through his veins like sweet, hot honey. The more he drank of her, the more he burned with thirst. A long moment after, he broke away to rest his cheek against hers. "I want you," he said thickly. "*Now*. You can come willingly . . . or I'll steal you."

He heard her low, throaty chuckle. "The Falcon must do what he does best," she murmured.

He grinned. Then he swept her up in his arms, and carried her deep into the shadows.


In the carved vetiver doorway, a man and a woman stood. The man's arm circled the woman's shoulders. Her dark head rested serenely upon his breast.

"I'll have to put a stop to it," Lord Hedgrave said. "He can't ravish Lord Cavencourt's sister in the garden."

"Indeed, he cannot," the Lioness agreed composedly. "My cousin will not permit this. She will merely torment him and send him away. And he will return for more torment. Men," she said with a sigh. "Like children."

He smiled. "Women," he returned. "Like devils. Perhaps I was wrong to bring him with me."

"He would have come regardless."

"Yes, and I didn't trust him alone in his state. Not a vessel was to be had that day. If I hadn't taken him in hand and quieted him down, I daresay the poor devil would have *rowed* to Calcutta."

"He left it late enough," the princess said.

"What was he to do, with a half-dead peer on his hands? Though I rather suspect he remained with me primarily to keep me from dashing off after his darling," the marquess added with a chuckle.

"Perhaps his heart understood your fate was linked with his. In any case, he has found the jewel his heart sought. Her love will fill his life with joy."

"But a thief, Nalini?" he teased. "Don't you think you might have done better by her?"

"He was for her," came the confident answer. "It was meant to be. I saw it in his eyes, just as I saw through his false garb. Tall, strong, and passionate, as I had promised her." She glanced up at her long-lost lover. "Like you."

"Ah, yes, me. A feeble old man. I wonder why you bothered."

The rani shrugged. "Young lovers are tiresome. So hasty."

He laughed. "Well, you are in luck, my wicked love." He turned and drew her into his embrace. "This decrepit old fellow is devilish slow."

"Then we shall love but once," the princess softly answered. "Once, but very, very slowly . . . through all the time remaining until we die. And then . . . "

"And then?" he breathed against her lips.

"And then I shall find you in your next life and plague you again."

# === 1 ===

IT WAS LATE March 1814. On the Continent, Buonaparte's once-great Empire lay in smoking ruins about him, his Grand Army reduced to a handful of ragged, starved boys. Yet the Corsican clung stubbornly to his throne, even as the Allied net closed about him.

That was all far away, however. The stretch of English landscape through which Mrs. Charles Davenant travelled this day lay quiet. Yet snug and secure in her well-sprung carriage, the widow gazed into the grey distance as unhappily as if she too knew what it was to lose empires. She had, after all, been privileged to rule her own life these last five years. Now that precious sovereignty was slipping from her grasp, and in her sad fancy, she rode in a moving prison to her doom.

A small, wry smile tugged at the corners of her set mouth. Though her tiny kingdom seemed to be in ruins, remarriage was hardly Doom. Her predicament was a mere twist of Fortune, a hard tangle in the thread of one insignificant life.

Without, the darkening sky cast its chill shadow upon the spring countryside. The widow turned from the sombre scene to the more heartening one within the carriage: her niece, Cecily Glenwood. Here was the radiant sunshine of golden curls, the clear heaven of wide blue eyes, and the fair blossom of pink and cream complexion. Here was youth and promise, the endless possibilities of a life just beginning, for Cecily Glenwood was travelling to London for her first Season.

Like her sister and cousins before her, Cecily would succeed. She could scarcely help it. All the Davenants and their offspring, male and female, were blessed with abundant good looks. The majority were charming, as Mrs. Davenant's late husband had been. Some, also like Charles Davenant, had their failings. Selfishness, for instance, was a quality prominent among his siblings. Had these in-laws been otherwise—sensible and trustworthy parents, for example—neither Cecily nor her cousins (there were yet more approaching marriageable age) would have needed Mrs. Charles Davenant's help at all.

She had already guided three nieces through successful London Seasons and seen each happily wed. Though she loved this niece as dearly as the others, the widow could not help but wish, this once, Conscience would permit her to leave the responsibility where it belonged.

Fortunately, she was suited to her chosen responsibility. She was but eight and twenty and of remarkably unexcitable disposition. In physique and character she was built for endurance.

Lilith Davenant was tall, slim, and strong. Her classical features—a decided jaw, a straight, imperious nose, and high, prominent cheekbones—had been carved firmly and clearly upon cool alabaster. Her eyes were an uncompromising slate blue, their gaze direct, assured, and often, chilly. In fact, the only warmth about her was the tinge of red in her thick, shining hair. Still, even that rich, dark auburn mass was resolutely wound in rigid braided coils about her head.

Her character was as uncompromising as her appearance. According to some wags, Mrs. Davenant bore such a stunning resemblance to a marble statue that it was a wonder she had a pulse. Some doubted she had. No one of the masculine gender (excepting her husband, who was reputed to have died, not of consumption, but of slow freezing) dared approach near enough to find out.

This was precisely as Mrs. Davenant preferred, though

she'd hardly have said so, if anyone had been audacious enough to ask. Her manner did not invite personal questions. Her feelings were sealed and locked, as secure in her breast as were her funds in the Bank of England. More secure, actually, for Mrs. Davenant was running out of money.

Her former man of business had lost most of it in mad speculations during the last year. His replacement, in reorganising the widow's affairs, had come upon an enormous unpaid debt—Charles's debt—a small fortune lost in wagers to his erstwhile companion in debauchery, the Marquess of Brandon.

Once this last debt was paid, there would remain scarcely enough to keep Lilith. Seasons for her remaining nieces would be out of the question. This prospect was as unendurable as the alternative: to wed again.

The widow had spent the better part of the journey wrestling with Duty and Conscience, as well as a host of other demons she had rather not name. Yet not even her dearest confidante (if she'd had one) would have suspected Mrs. Davenant was troubled. She sat beside her niece, as cool, assured, and marblelike as ever.

"Oh, I do hope he'll be dark and devilish-looking," said Cecily.

Lilith slowly turned to examine her niece, who had remained uncharacteristically silent this past hour.

"To whom do you refer, my dear?" she asked.

"Him," said Cecily. "The husband I am supposed to catch in three months. That is a frightfully short time. There is one fox Papa has been after for seven years, and Papa is a brilliant huntsman. I don't see how I'm to catch anyone in just three months when I've had no experience at all."

In the seat opposite, Mrs. Davenant's plump companion suppressed a smile. Emma Wellwicke was older than her employer, and more tolerant—as perhaps a soldier's wife must be in these tumultuous times. While Mrs. Wellwicke might find Cecily's outspokenness amusing, the companion knew as well as anyone else that plain speaking would never serve in the Beau Monde. It had best be gently discouraged.

"My dear," said Lilith, "one does not speak of 'catching a man' as though it were a hunt."

"Oh, I would not say so to *them*, of course," Cecily answered. "But I cannot pretend to myself that catching a husband is not what I'm about—and I know I must do it quickly. Otherwise, Mama says she and Papa will be obliged to find me one at home. I know that is a deal more economical way to go about it, but it is not a pleasant prospect. None of the local bachelors is dark and devilish-looking—and I am so tired of blonds. We are all fair. It is so monotonous."

"Looks are not everything, Cecily," said Emma.

"Yes, I know. But I daresay you have never met Lord Evershot, whom Papa is so fond of. Such an ancient man—past forty, I think—and such a red, blotchy face. And you have never seen anything so absurd upon a horse. Meanwhile, Mama drops hints about The Honourable Alfred Crawbred, and he has the tiniest little black eyes and the most squashed-down nose. I am certain his nurse must have dropped him repeatedly upon his face. Yet he believes himself an Adonis and is forever waddling after the maid-servants."

Emma bit her lip.

"Cecily, please," the aunt warned.

"It is quite true. I once spied him chasing a housemaid—and he looked exactly like Papa's favorite sow, lurching to the trough at feeding time."

"That will do, Cecily," Lilith said quietly. "Though I cannot approve Mr. Crawbred's behaviour regarding the maidservants, neither can I countenance uncharitable observations upon his physical attributes. Nature is not so generous with everyone as she has been with my nieces and nephews."

Cecily gazed at her in surprise. "I did not mean to be

uncharitable, Aunt. I only meant I had much rather not become Mr. Crawbred's wife. Why, you know he will expect to kiss me—and that is not the half of it."

"Oh, my," said Emma.

Mrs. Davenant turned with an inward shudder to the window, in order to compose both herself and a suitably quelling yet tactful response. In an instant, all this was forgotten.

Hastily, she opened the coach window and called to her coachman to stop.

"What is it?" Cecily and Emma asked simultaneously.

"An accident."

The coach slowly came to a halt, and Lilith climbed out, adjuring the other two women to remain where they were.

Though somewhat in awe of her queenly aunt, Cecily remained where she was approximately seven seconds before clambering out. Emma followed, to urge the girl back. This was sensible on more than one count, for the rain which had threatened all afternoon had commenced, and the road dust was rapidly turning to mud.

In a ditch by the roadside lay what had once been a dashing black curricle. Cecily's practised eye told her the vehicle would never dash again; furthermore, neither would one of the horses. She clutched her aunt's sleeve.

"The poor animal," she cried. "Oh, do please have the coachman put it out of its misery."

"Yes, yes," was the impatient answer. "John will see to it, but I fear—"

"A man, missus," the coachman called out from behind the fallen curricle. "Not dead, I don't think."

Lilith ordered her niece back to the coach with Emma. As the girl reluctantly obeyed, the carriage which had been following with servants and luggage neared and halted. Summoning the stronger members of her staff, the widow led them down to the smashed vehicle. They stood patiently waiting in the rain as their mistress joined John.

The injured man lay partly under the curricle. Luckily for him, none of it lay upon him. He was bruised and filthy, and though not conscious, alive, as John had said.

Careless of the mud, Lilith knelt beside him. "Is anything broken?" she asked the coachman.

"Not as I could tell, missus."

"Try to be certain. I do not like to move him if it will cause damage."

Cold rain streamed from the coachman's hat down his neck. He glanced ruefully at the other servants, none of whom seemed any more pleased than he to be summoned to this scene.

"We could leave someone with him and go on to the next inn and send a party after him, missus," John offered hopefully.

He received an icy glance in answer. "Indeed," said his mistress. "I hope that was your intention originally. I noted you did not slacken your pace when we came upon this wreck—though it was not so dark then you could have missed it."

Returning her attention to the injured man, Mrs. Davenant took out her handkerchief and wiped the mud from his face. His eyes opened. They were a rare, arresting shade of green.

"Olympus," he muttered. "It must be. Hera, is it not? No—Athena. Death, where is thy sting? Athena, where is thy helmet?"

"He is delirious," said Lilith. "We had better risk it and carry him to the coach."

She began to rise, but the man grasped her hand with surprising strength.

"Have you appeared at last only to abandon me?" he asked weakly.

"Certainly not," she answered. "I would never abandon an injured fellow creature—but I cannot climb out of this ditch while you are clutching me."

He groaned softly and released her hand. Lilith gave him one brief, uneasy glance, then moved aside to let her servants do their work.

After some discussion and difficulty, the man was finally

placed in a half-sitting, half-falling position on the carriage seat. Since Mrs. Davenant was at this point nearly as dirty as he, she sat beside him and tried to prop him up as comfortably as possible in a carriage grown exceedingly cramped. He was a large, long-legged man who took up a deal of room.

Though he managed to keep from tumbling onto the carriage floor, he was too weak to remain fully upright. Eventually he subsided into a drowsing state, his head resting on the widow's shoulder—and once or twice slipping to her firm bosom, from which he was somewhat ungently ejected.

More than an hour later, he was carried into an inn. It took nearly another hour—and all Mrs. Davenant's imperious insistence—to obtain a room for him.

It happened that a mill was to take place the following day. The result was a hostelry overrun with noisy, demanding bucks, and a staff run off their feet attending to them.

After attempting in vain to receive further assistance, Mrs. Davenant sent one of her own servants in search of a doctor. Others she dispatched for hot water, clean towels and diverse other necessities. In between giving orders, Lilith became aware of the excessive attention the inn's male patrons were paying Cecily.

Once again, the widow cornered the innkeeper. Not long after, a pair of noble gentlemen were persuaded to chivalry. They gave up their chamber, and Cecily took refuge there with her maid from the chaos, while Lilith and Emma managed matters for the accident victim.

"Really, Susan," said Cecily as her maid poured tea, "I cannot understand why Papa says Aunt Lilith is cold and strange. What is cold and strange, I ask you, about giving a lot of silly girls a whole Season in London?"

"I'm sure I don't know, miss," said the maid wearily. "But I do wish we was in London now. I never heard such a din, and I can tell you I been pinched more than once—and John

7

says we'll never get there tonight, not in this weather. He says we should've left the man where he was, you know, and sent folks after him—"

"Which is just my point," Cecily interrupted. "If she were cold and strange, she would have done so, wouldn't she?"

"Yes, miss, and I don't like to be uncharitable, but I do wish she'd done just that."

"Well, then, I think *you* are cold and strange. He is dark and devilish-looking as they come." Cecily sighed. "But I believe he's rather old."

"His injuries are slight," the doctor told Mrs. Davenant as he left the patient's room. "His trouble is that he was ill to start and had no business out of bed. I would guess he hasn't had a proper meal or decent night's rest in days. One of those too stubborn to admit he's sick, though I think he might admit it now that he's made himself weak as a baby. Travelling alone, in his condition," the doctor muttered. "What are these chaps thinking of? Or do they think of anything, I wonder? Wyndhurst you said his name was?"

"That is what he told my coachman," said Lilith. "I have not spoken with Mr. Wyndhurst since we arrived. I trust my servants have tended to him adequately?"

"I daresay they did the best they could. I've had more cooperative patients, I can tell you." With that and a few instructions regarding medicine and nourishment, the doctor left.

A while later, Emma appeared with a steaming bowl of broth.

"I will see to that," said Lilith, recollecting the doctor's hints regarding the patient's uncooperativeness. She took the tray from her companion. "You need some sustenance yourself, Emma—and I have had more practice with invalids."

The patient, to Mrs. Davenant's surprise, was sitting up in bed. True, he was well propped up with pillows, but he did not appear near death, as she had expected. No dying man could have invested his green-eyed gaze with so much insolence. He boldly surveyed her head to toe, not once, but twice—quickly assessing the first time and lazily considering the second. Lilith's hands closed a bit more tightly upon the tray handles. This was the only outward manifestation of the acute tension which gripped her as she approached the sickbed.

Mr. Wyndhurst had begun as a muddy, injured mess requiring a great flurry of activity. Thus, beyond noting the rare colour of his eyes, she'd not had time to study him before. Now, washed and combed by her servants, he commanded attention.

His hair was black, curly, and luxuriant. The green eyes were fringed with thick black lashes. Their heavy-lidded look, the faint lines at the corners, and the sensual mouth intimated a depraved character. Mrs. Davenant was certain, moreover, that he had been looking down his long, straight nose at everyone his entire life. The strong cheekbones . . . the stubborn chin . . . everything about his hard, chiseled features bespoke arrogance. He was pale and ill, yet his entire frame exuded pure masculine power, utter self-assurance. He was devastatingly handsome. Regrettably, he seemed fully aware of this circumstance. He might have been the very model of a bored, dissolute scoundrel.

Lilith set the tray down on his lap and stepped back. "You can feed yourself, I trust?" she asked politely.

He eyed the steaming broth with a pained expression.

"If I could," he said, "I should also have the strength to hurl this mess out of window. Chicken broth? How could you?" he asked in aggrieved tones. "I thought Athena was wise and just, but she enters the room of a dying man only to poison him. Chicken broth," he repeated, shaking his head sadly. "Is it come to this? Then fall, Caesar!" He sank back against the pillows, his eyes closed.

"In your state, you will be unable to digest anything more substantial," said the widow, unmoved.

"Then bring me wine, oh wise and beautiful immortal,"

he murmured. He cocked one eye open and added, "Unless you've got some ambrosia about. Ambrosia will do as well."

"It will not do, Mr. Wyndhurst." Lilith drew a chair close to the bed, sat down, and took up spoon and bowl. "If you cannot feed yourself, I shall feed you—and you will swallow every last drop. You must do so sooner or later, or you will starve to death."

"A prospect too heartbreaking, I agree."

"If I had meant to let you die, I might have done so more easily by simply leaving you where you were, instead of inconveniencing myself or my servants." With the ease of long practice, she administered the first spoonful.

The submissive air Mr. Wyndhurst abruptly assumed was undermined by the gleam of amusement in his eyes.

"You see?" she said, ignoring the mockery she saw there. "It is not as nasty as you thought."

"It is every bit as nasty," he answered after swallowing another spoonful, "but I dare not combat the goddess of wisdom. If, on the other hand, you could contrive to be Aphrodite—and I'm sure you could, if you liked—"

"I do not like, sir. I did not come to flirt with you."

"Did you not?" He appeared astonished. "Are you quite certain?"

"Quite."

Mr. Wyndhurst spent some minutes mulling this over while Lilith continued feeding him.

"I understand," he said at last. "When you found me I must have been a most repellent sight. Naturally, you could not know what lay beneath the grime your servant so conscientiously—painfully so, I must add—removed."

He *was* vain, Lilith thought contemptuously. Aloud she said, "I am sorry if Harris was not gentle with you. He is more accustomed to grooming horses."

"No wonder my hide is raw. It is a miracle he did not try to brush my—"

"There are but a few spoonfuls left," Lilith hastily interjected. "You had best finish while it is still hot."

Though he accepted the remaining broth meekly enough, there was no meekness in his steady scrutiny of her face, nor in the occasional glances he dropped elsewhere. He was sizing her up, Lilith knew. Well, if he had any intelligence at all, he must realise he wasted his time. All the same, she was edgy. When at last the bowl was empty, she rose.

"Now I hope you will get some rest," she said as she took up the tray.

"I'm afraid that's not possible." He slumped back among the pillows once more. "Your company has been far too exciting for a sick man. You should not have agitated me so. I shall not sleep a wink."

"I fed you one small bowl of chicken broth," Lilith said with a touch of impatience.

"It was not what you did but how you looked when you did it. Such resolution in the face of ingratitude. Such militant charity." He smiled lazily. "And such eyes, Athena."

"Indeed. One on either side of my nose. A matching set, quite common in the human countenance."

"The Hellespont in a summer storm."

"Blue. A common colour among the English." She moved to the door.

"Really? They seem most uncommon to me. Perhaps you are right—but I cannot be certain unless you come closer."

"You are short-sighted, Mr. Wyndhurst?" she asked as she opened the door. "Then it is no wonder you drove your curricle into a ditch. Perhaps in future you will remember to don your spectacles."

She heard a low crack of laughter as the door closed behind her.

To Cecily's eager enquiries during dinner, her aunt offered depressingly unsatisfactory answers. Yes, Mr. Wyndhurst was well-looking enough, she noted without enthusiasm. He was also shockingly ill-behaved.

"Oh, Aunt, did he try to flirt with you? I was sure he would. He had that look about him."

11

"A look?" Emma asked with a smile. "You discerned a look under his impenetrable coating of mud?"

"He had the devil in his eyes," Cecily said. "I saw him open them when he thought no one was looking. He reminded me of Papa's prize stallion. The naughtiest, most deceitful, ill-mannered beast you ever saw. But when he moves, he is so graceful that one is persuaded he must have wings. Like a bad, beautiful angel."

Lilith put down her fork. "Whatever Mr. Wyndhurst may be, tending to him has been altogether wearing. I am not decided what to do tomorrow. We cannot leave him here, yet I cannot subject my servants to another night of sleeping in the tap-room—or wherever it is the poor creatures will lay their heads. I should have asked his destination. If it were near enough, we might have sent word."

"You've done all you can for one day," said Emma. "The decision can wait until tomorrow, when you're rested." She smiled ruefully. "At least I hope you'll be rested. I do think you should let me share a bed with Cecily. Having done by far the most work, you have earned the most comfort." She turned to Cecily. "I promise not to snore."

"Pray snore all you like, ma'am," Cecily answered with a grin. "I am a prodigious sound sleeper."

Though she was eventually persuaded—thanks to Cecily's threats to sleep on the floor—to accept Mrs. Wellwicke's offer, Lilith was wakeful long after her companions had fallen asleep.

She had no sooner thrust the obnoxious Mr. Wyndhurst from her mind than another gentleman pushed his way in: Sir Thomas Bexley, her erstwhile friend and, of late, patient suitor. His recent letters indicated he meant to repeat his offer of marriage in the very near future. Though her feelings had not changed since the last time, it seemed her answer must.

Poverty did not frighten Mrs. Davenant. She was disciplined enough to live frugally. She need not and would not in any case accept the charity of Charles's family. Unfortunately, poverty touched not only herself. Without funds, she could be of no help to her nieces.

She lay staring at the ceiling. The prospect of marriage was repugnant to her. There were reasons, but perhaps these were paltry. She would not be miserable with Thomas. He admired and respected her, and would exert himself to make her happy. Their tastes and personalities suited.

No, she could not be so self-centred as to reject marriage to a perfectly worthy gentleman—not when the consequence was a lifetime of wretchedness for those beautiful, fresh, innocent girls. Cecily, for instance, to be married to that repellent sot, Lord Evershot—or to that obese young lecher, Mr. Crawbred.

It was always the same: whatever wealthy and sufficiently well-born mate was handiest would do. Her in-laws took greater care in mating their precious horses. The children—whom they produced in such shocking abundance—they only wanted off their hands.

Well, it would not be, she told herself. Aunt Lilith would look after them: Cecily now, Diana next year . . . Emily next . . . and Barbara after . . . then it would not be long before Charlotte's girls came of age . . . and the eldest nephew, Edward, could do with some guidance—if he'd stand for it.

Thus, counting her beloved nieces and nephews instead of sheep, Mrs. Davenant finally fell asleep.

# = 2 =

DESPITE INADEQUATE REST, Mrs. Davenant was up and about early the following morning. She'd scarcely quit her room when Cecily's groom, Harris, who'd dutifully looked in on Mr. Wyndhurst, informed her the man had vanished.

The innkeeper expanded upon the news. "They came for him early," he told the widow. "Seems his lordship's relations were expecting him and sent someone to look when he didn't appear. Must have found the smashed rig and alerted the family because—"

"His lordship?" Lilith interrupted.

"His lordship the Marquess of Brandon, ma'am. On his way to his cousin's. Lord Belbridge, that is."

His patron's countenance grew stony.

The innkeeper went on quickly, "They came for him—the Earl of Belbridge himself and a pack of servants. As I said, it was early—maybe an hour or more before cock-crow—and Lord Brandon was very particular that we wasn't to disturb you about it. He said to thank you for your kindness and apologise for his hasty leave-taking. I think that was how he put it," the landlord said with a frown. "Anyhow, he paid your shot, ma'am. Said it was the least he could do in return for all the— What was it he said? He laid such a stress on it, the word—ah, the *inconvenience*."

After uttering a few cold words of acknowledgement, Mrs. Davenant turned away, her heart pounding with indignation. The Marquess of Brandon, of all people. Her servants had braved the cold, filthy storm and the muck of

14

the ditch, risking pneumonia. They had spent the night on floors—when they might have slept comfortably, warm and dry in their proper beds in her London town house. All this they had endured for the most foul libertine who had ever trod his polluted step upon the earth.

With her own hands she'd fed the man who had half killed her husband—for was it not Brandon who had mercilessly led Charles on an insatiable pursuit of the lowest sort of pleasure? Finally, when her husband was too ill for pleasure any more, this so-called friend had released what was left of him. Then Charles was hers at last—hers to watch nearly two years, while he crept slowly and painfully to his grave. Not once in all that long, weary time had this bosom bow deigned to visit him. A letter or two from abroad was all. Then, one curt, condescending note of condolence, two months after the funeral.

Now Brandon patronisingly threw a few pieces of gold her way—when she owed him thousands. She would pay him, Lilith vowed. She would sell the very clothes from her back if necessary. She would not be in his debt, not for so much as a farthing.

Mrs. Davenant stood staring at a small, poorly executed hunting print until she had collected herself. Then she returned to her travelling companions to break the news regarding their patient and urge them to a speedy departure.

She fumed inwardly the entire distance to London. Outwardly, she was as coolly poised and unapproachable as ever.

Even Cecily was eventually daunted in her efforts to penetrate her aunt's reserve. Questions about the Marquess of Brandon elicited only warnings: he was precisely the sort of man young ladies must scrupulously avoid; he had not been so near death as he pretended; if he could deceive an experienced physician, what hope was there for an innocent young girl—and so on. Cecily would have preferred to be told what she didn't already know.

As Mrs. Davenant's carriage was entering London, the

15

subject of her disapprobation was reclining upon a richly upholstered sofa in the cavernous drawing room of a massive country house many miles away. He was being wearied half to death listening—or trying not to listen—to his cousin's litany of woes.

Julian Vincent Wyndhurst St. Maur, Baron St. Maur, Viscount Benthame, Earl of Stryte, Marquess of Brandon, was a trifle tetchy this afternoon. He was affronted by the behaviour of the chill he'd contracted en route to Ostend. He had given it the cut direct. The ailment, instead of humbly taking itself off, had only fastened itself more firmly—and had apparently gathered equally boorish associates.

Though Lord Brandon was not so weak and ill as he had feigned for Mrs. Davenant's benefit, he was scarcely well. At the moment, he wished he had remained in bed. His inconsiderate cousin might have respected his peace then, instead of pacing agitatedly upon the thick Axminster carpet in a manner viciously calculated to bring on *mal de mer*.

"Do me the kindness, George, to sit down," Lord Brandon said at last. "That constant to and fro raises the very devil with my innards."

Lord Belbridge promptly flopped down upon the sofa by his cousin's feet. George was a rather stout fellow. The jolt of his heavy frame on the sofa cushions set off a wave of nausea.

"Damn," said Lord Brandon with a grimace.

"Sorry, Julian. Keep forgettin' you're ailin'. But I'm half out of my wits, what with Mother at me the livelong day—or goin' off in hysterics when she ain't. Even Ellen's overset—though it's the children she worries for, and how they're to hold up their heads—"

"Being attached in the customary way to their necks, I expect their heads will contrive to keep from tumbling off. Really, George, one would think no man had ever kept a mistress before."

"If he were only keepin' her, what should any of us care?

16

But he's been *livin'* with her—near two years now."

"Of course Robert is living with her. You keep him on a short allowance. He cannot afford two sets of lodgings, now, can he?"

George's jaw set obstinately. "Well, I ain't goin' to give him any more. He spends every farthin' on *her*."

"I see. You would prefer your brother spent his vast sums upon drink or hazard, I suppose. Come, George, you are a man of the world. As I recollect, there was a ballet dancer or two enlivening your salad days while she lightened your purse."

"That was different. I had my fun for a bit, then got another. I didn't talk of *marryin'* the tarts, Julian."

Lord Brandon's half-closed lids fluttered open. "My ailment appears to have affected my hearing. I was certain you mentioned marriage."

"He means to marry her," Lord Belbridge grimly confirmed. "He's only waitin' 'til he comes into his money, in less than four months. Can't touch his trust fund 'til he's five and twenty, you know. Then he's little need of his allowance. Not that it's any great fortune—but it's respectable. He wants to make an honest woman of her and set up his nursery." George groaned. "Expects we'll welcome her into the family. Can you see my sweet Ellen callin' a fancy piece 'sister'? And a damned Frenchie at that. Gad."

There was a moment or two of silence while George allowed his cousin to digest this piece of information. Lord Brandon pressed his fingers to his temples.

"Robert cannot possibly be so imbecilic as to marry his mistress," he said finally. "He must know you would seek an annulment if he did. Furthermore, I do not see what prevents your dealing with her yourself. Fill her purse and she will take her charms elsewhere."

"Tried," George answered sadly. "Again and again. She won't leave him. Why should she? She could get a wealthier lover, but not one fool enough to marry her. Not a lord, certainly." He uttered a heavy sigh. "That ain't the worst of it."

"Naturally not," his listener murmured.

"When she wouldn't listen to reason," George went on, "I took to threats. Told her we'd see the wedding never took place, whatever it took to do it. She only looked at me like I was somethin' pitiful. Then she told me about the letters."

"Letters," Lord Brandon repeated, his expression pained. "I might have known."

"Love letters," said his cousin. "She showed me one or two and told me there were a score more like 'em—all beggin' her to marry him. Callin' her his 'dear wife.' Sickenin', just sickenin'."

"Such epistles usually are, except perhaps to the recipient, for whom they undoubtedly must provide many hours of laughter."

"I went to my solicitor right after that. He hemmed and hawed for an hour before he broke the news. Which is, that if those letters end up in a court of law, they could be worth as much as twenty-five thousand quid in damages."

"Indeed," said Lord Brandon. "Robert quite astonishes me. He has fallen in love with his whore, proposed marriage to her, not once but many times, and all in writing, no less. If he marries her, there is a great scandal, his family is dishonoured, and he is ruined. If he doesn't marry her, she sues for breach of promise, there is a great scandal, his family is dishonoured, and he is ruined. How very neatly he has arranged matters. I must remember to congratulate him." Cautiously, he pulled himself upright. "I think I shall go to bed."

"Is that all you can say?" George cried, jumping up.

"I'm sure you will not wish to hear my feelings regarding being summoned from France—at Prinny's behest, no less—merely to be informed that my cousin is a besotted fool. This is the 'urgent family matter' so desperately requiring my assistance, now of all times? When, finally, Buonaparte is within our grasp, when all the wit and tact we possess will be required to return his obese Bourbon rival to his unloving subjects?"

18

"They wanted you home anyhow, Julian," was the defensive answer. "They said you was near collapse—and had done more than your share at any rate."

"As you say, I have done enough. As to Lord Robert Downs—my young cousin is so unspeakable an idiot that we were all best advised to cease recollecting his existence."

"But dammit, Julian, he is my brother—and think of the scandal. Think of Mary. Think of the children."

"I cannot think of anyone at the moment, George. My head is throbbing like the very deuce. Will you ring for a servant? One with a stout arm and broad shoulders, if you please. I shall require some assistance regaining the sanctity of my bedchamber, where I expect to expire gracefully within the hour. No mourning, I beg of you. Black is not Ellen's best colour."

"But, Julian—"

"Wash your hands of him, George. I assure you I do."

Not many days after her return to London, Mrs. Davenant met with her man of business. Mr. Higginbottom, possessed of the first good news he'd been able to offer his client in some six months, was buoyant. The debt, he told her, was cancelled. Lord Brandon had no wish to take bread from the mouths of widows.

The slate-blue gaze grew so icy that Mr. Higginbottom involuntarily shivered. Congealing within, he soon petrified, to sink into arctic waters as his client expressed not only profound displeasure that the marquess had been apprised in such detail of her private affairs, but also an adamant refusal to accept his lordship's charity.

It was futile to argue that gentlemen cancelled such debts every day for far more whimsical reasons. It was useless to point out that the Marquess of Brandon didn't want the money, most assuredly didn't need the money, and in fact cared so little about it that he had let the matter lie buried these last seven years. It was equally useless to point out that twenty-nine thousand pounds, sensibly invested, would earn such and such a return, that she need not sell both her remaining properties, that in a few years she might expect to see her income return to its previous level or very near.

Mrs. Davenant only coldly retorted that she was not on the brink of starvation.

"You will use the funds from the lease of my Derbyshire residence for the present," she said. "When the Season is done, we will discuss letting the town house. I wish the debt paid—with appropriate interest—as speedily as possible, though I hope your terms can accommodate certain matters of necessity. As you are aware, a family commitment requires my remaining in Town. Still, it will be as economical a stay as can reasonably be expected."

She paused a moment before adding—and this was her first and only hint of emotion—"I will not be beholden to *that man,* sir, not for any amount." She handed the businessman a slip of paper. "You will add this to the sum," she said. "There was a misunderstanding with an innkeeper."

"Yes, madam," said Mr. Higginbottom, and "Yes, madam" was all he said to everything else. Only that evening, to his wife, did he declaim upon the inscrutability of the ruling classes.


Sir Thomas called, as he had promised, at two o'clock. Mrs. Davenant, as she had promised, granted him a private interview.

The baronet knew his offer was expected. He was not, however, confident of an affirmative answer. Though he'd been granted the signal honour of her friendship, he could not be certain he had as yet awakened any softer feelings in the widow's breast. To be sure, he required only sufficient softening to produce the word "yes."

Sir Thomas was a widower of nearly forty. He topped his prospective bride by a mere inch or two; his square figure was not so fit as it had once been; and his light brown hair, to his grief, was thinning. Though he was well enough looking—his jaw firm, his brown eyes alert and clear—he had never been sufficiently handsome to break hearts, or even win them without effort. Thus, he had very sensibly concentrated on the winning of hands, and did so for practical reasons.

Though as ambitious as ever, he was no longer the nearly penniless youth he had been at the time of his first marriage. Then, as now, he was content to do without love, though for different reasons. Of his first wife he'd required only money. Of his second, he required strong character, irreproachable reputation, and superior breeding. He wanted, in short, the perfect political hostess.

There was nothing, certainly, of Love in her response. Lilith acknowledged she respected him and was honoured by his proposal. So far, so good.

"I should be pleased to be your wife, Thomas," she continued composedly. "But before we make an irrevocable commitment, I must deal frankly with certain circumstances of which you are at present unaware."

Sir Thomas's smile faded into a puzzled frown.

"As you may know, I had a considerable fortune in my own right," she went on. "As my grandparents' only living descendant, I inherited everything. The property was not entailed. My grandfather's title was recent—and the bulk of the property was my grandmother's."

"My dear," he quickly intervened, "I am aware of these matters. All the same, in like frankness I must remind you of my own situation, which is such, I flatter myself, that your finances are irrelevant. Certainly they are and always have been irrelevant to my wish to make you my wife."

She hesitated a fraction of a moment. Then, her chin just a bit higher, she answered, "Nonetheless, I prefer to be quite open with you. My income is sadly depleted. Mistakes have been made—certain investments my previous financial advisor—"

Once more Sir Thomas interrupted. "I am sorry you have been ill-advised," he said, "but there is no need to weary yourself reviewing the details. In future, I hope you will allow me to see to your comfort—the very near future, if you will excuse my impetuousness, my dear. That is to say, as soon, of course, as your niece is set up."

"I am telling you," she said patiently, "that I am no longer a woman of means."

He smiled and stepped towards her. "And I am telling you, Lilith Davenant, it matters not a whit to me. Will you become Lady Bexley, and make me the happiest man in Christendom?"

If the answering smile was tinged with resignation, Sir Thomas was unaware of it. He heard the quiet "Yes" he had wished for these eighteen months or more, and his heart soared. He did, truly, believe himself the happiest man in Christendom. He had achieved another great ambition and won the hand of the regal Lilith Davenant.

So great was his appreciation of and respect for her queenly reserve that, instead of embracing her as he was fully entitled, he only planted one fervent kiss upon the back of her hand. He did not perceive the way she had steeled herself for the obligatory embrace, nor did he remark the relief that swept her features when he only bent instead over her white hand.

"The good die early," Mr. Defoe once observed, "and the bad die late."

Thus it could come as no surprise to any reasonably intelligent person that, despite his relatives' unflagging efforts to plague him to death, Lord Brandon did not expire. On the contrary, he recovered surprisingly swiftly.

"Small wonder," his aunt remarked with a sniff. "Even the Old Harry is in no hurry to have *you*. A more selfish, insufferable, obstinate blackguard of a nephew there never was and never will be."

"Auntie, your tender affection will unman me," the nephew replied. "Really, you ought not dote upon me so extravagantly at mealtime. I cannot see my beef-steak for my tears." All the same, Lord Brandon cut into his beef-steak accurately enough.

He had just come down to breakfast. It was proof of his aunt's determination that she had risen from her bed before noon, only to be on hand first thing to nag at him.

The Marchioness of Fineholt was a small, fragile-looking woman with a will of iron and a tongue, her relative reflected silently, like a meat axe.

"I had always thought your sire the greatest villain who ever lived," she went on. "Yet worthless reprobate that he was, my brother Alec at least knew what was due his name and family. Though why I expect you to care about anyone's name when you don't trouble with your own—"

"My dearest Auntie, my name came to me when I was born and has remained with me ever since without my bothering about it at all."

"Thirty-five years old," she snapped, "and you haven't got a wife—not to speak of an heir."

"I can understand your wish not to speak of him," the marquess answered sadly. "His mama was so misguided as to have been born in Philadelphia—to a haberdasher. I cannot imagine what she was thinking of."

"I don't mean those dratted Yankee cousins, and you know it, Brandon. You haven't got a son—not on the right side of the blanket at any rate, though I don't doubt there's a score or more of the other sort peppering the countryside, here and abroad."

"Wicked girl," said the nephew between mouthfuls. "Will you not spare my blushes?"

"Spare you?" she echoed wrathfully. "There is your poor uncle—a sad invalid these last five years—and even he took pen in his poor, trembling hand to plead with that unspeakable woman. While you, strong and healthy as an ox, spend your days lolling about upon the sofa, refusing even to discuss this debacle."

Lord Belbridge entered the breakfast room at this juncture.

"Now, Mother," he placated as he sat down beside her. "You know Julian's not been lollin' about. He's been gravely ill."

"And bound to send me to an early grave in his place," she grumbled. "I should have expected it. Not a male in the lot with an ounce of ingenuity. Or if they've got any," she added with a darkling look at her nephew, "they'd rather spend it coaxing the next trollop into their bed."

"You mean to say there are trollops about this fair green countryside, Aunt?" Lord Brandon turned to his cousin in reproach. "You might have mentioned it, Georgy."

"Julian, please—"

"Don't beg him, George. It isn't dignified, and you've made a sorry enough spectacle of yourself as it is. There's the tart showing you her letters, and what do you do but politely give 'em back."

"Mother dearest, I couldn't well bind her hand and foot while I searched the premises. Besides, she's too dashed clever to keep 'em all with her. Stands to reason she'd have 'em locked up with a solicitor, or someplace safe."

"Reason," her ladyship repeated scornfully. "When were you and Reason ever acquainted, pray tell? Oh, that ever I should live to see this day." Her voice grew tremulous, and a very dainty lace handkerchief was applied to very dry eyes. "My baby, caught in the toils of a French drab, and no one will lift a finger to save him."

"Now, Mother—"

"You have no conscience, Brandon," she went on, ignoring her son. "No feeling for your kin."

"I am positively bubbling with feeling, ma'am. Unfortunately, the situation is beyond mending."

"Fiddlesticks! You have made a profession of bending women to your will. You will not persuade me you cannot wrap this baggage about your finger, clever though she may be. You are simply too lazy to trouble with any matter not pertaining to your own pleasure."

She rose to deliver her parting shot. "You are spoiled, vain, selfish, and far too clever and good-looking for your own good. I pray that one day—and may I be alive to see it—a woman will cut up your peace. Pleasure has taught

24

you nothing. Mayhap pain will." With that, her small, rigid figure swept out of the breakfast room.

Lord Belbridge threw his cousin a reproachful glance. "I wish you wouldn't tease her, Julian. She takes it out on me after."

"Have you considered sending her to Wellington, George? Perhaps she might be employed to browbeat Napoleon into submission. I wonder no one thought of that before." Having finished his breakfast during the marchioness's verbal bombardment, Lord Brandon took up the newspaper.

George sighed, went to the sideboard, and filled his plate. When he sat down again, his cousin asked from behind the newspaper in a very bored voice, "Are you acquainted with a fellow by the name of Bexley? Sir Thomas Bexley?"

"Not intimately acquainted. He's a deal too political for my tastes. Still, one can't help knowin' of him. One of Liverpool's protégés."

"I see. An ambitious young man."

"Ambitious, yes, but he's forty if he's a day. Looks older. Goin' bald," George explained. "Probably all those years in the West Indies did it. Bought plantations there, you know, with his wife's dowry. Made pots. Came back . . . well, I couldn't say when, exactly. Two or three years ago, maybe. After he lost his wife."

The marquess glanced over the paper. "Careless of him."

"She passed on, Julian," his cousin answered with a touch of vexation. "Dash it, you've got no respect, even for the dead. She passed on, and the poor fellow came back and I guess he buried his sorrow in politics. They say he's movin' on fast. Shouldn't be surprised to find him in the ministry one day."

George swallowed a few mouthfuls. After a moment or two, he asked, "If you don't know him, what makes you ask?"

"Boredom, I suppose."

"Somethin' in the paper?"

"Only that his engagement is announced."

George put down his silverware. "You don't say! He's

25

done it, then. Well, there's a few chaps stand to lose money on *that*. Mean to say—it's Davenant's widow he's marryin', ain't it?"

Lord Brandon nodded.

"Better him than me. Feel an east wind blowin' just thinkin' of her. Cold female, Julian. But you knew her, I expect. You and Davenant were together a good deal." George returned to his meal.

"I never met the lady then. She was in Derbyshire. Charles was in London. He took ill and returned to the country shortly after I was required to take residence out of England."

"I recollect. Annoyin' that. And not a bit fair. Stupid female. Burstin' out from the wood, shriekin'. If it wasn't for her, you'd have only winged him. A wonder we weren't all killed. Duel's no place for a woman."

"Perhaps, having provoked the situation, Lady Advers felt obliged to see it through to the conclusion. At any rate, she taught me a valuable lesson."

"Yes. Keep away from married women."

The marquess laughed. "Good heavens, no, George. What I learned was never to let my attention wander, on any account."

Two hours later, Lord Brandon threw his relatives into transports of joy and relief when he announced plans to proceed to London that very day. He was bored with rustication, he said, and from all reports, Castlereagh seemed to be muddling along well enough without his dubious assistance. Since he had nothing better to do elsewhere, Lord Brandon thought he might toddle off to look into this tiresome little matter of Robert's nuptials.

# === 3 ===

Lord Enders's opera box was rarely an object of interest to the audience. If he and his wife had company, it was bound to be the wife's brother, Sir Thomas Bexley, and he was sure to be escorting Mrs. Charles Davenant. Though Bexley was absent tonight, the widow was not, and her severely cut, sombrely coloured costumes had never aroused envy or even interest in her neighbours.

Lady Enders was equally unexciting. Hers were the same passable features as her brother's. Unlike him, however, she always appeared fussy, a veritable snowstorm of stiffly starched ruffles and furbelows heaped upon her gown, and the entire contents of her jewel-box mounded upon her throat and bosom.

Nonetheless, on this particular evening, the opera box received second, third—indeed countless—glances from a majority of the gentlemen present. This was because tonight a young lady broke the monotony. She was a jewel of a young lady, with her guinea-gold curls, her wide blue eyes, her dainty nose, and (here the sighs became audible) her pink, bee-stung lips. More than one masculine pulse accelerated at the sight of Miss Cecily Glenwood.

"I see we may expect a stampede at the intermission," said Lady Enders in an undertone. "I had not thought it possible, but the child is even prettier than her cousins."

One of her rare smiles softened Mrs. Davenant's features. "She is a dear, sweet girl as well," she said softly. "Those her beauty attracts will return on account of her nature."

"You have always been so fortunate in your girls, Lilith. Lady Shumway, on the other hand—Why, whatever are they gaping at?"

The enquiry was occasioned by a sudden stirring in the audience. The usual buzz of voices preceding the curtain's rise had swelled to a Babel, and every head was swivelling in the same direction.

Lilith followed the general gaze . . . and stifled a gasp. The Marquess of Brandon, in the company of one fair-haired gentleman and one brunette female—of obviously dubious character—had entered the box nearly opposite.

"Brandon!" Lady Enders whispered harshly. "I cannot believe my eyes. He has not been seen in Society in years. Why, he has scarcely been in England, to my knowledge—not since he killed Advers in that scandalous duel. Seven years ago that was, when Brandon had to flee the country. Wicked man! Do you see how brazenly he stares back at them, the insufferable scoundrel?"

Mrs. Davenant had looked away as soon as she recognised him. Like her companion, she had observed how more than one head turned away, abashed, upon meeting the marquess's haughty stare.

Cecily had not missed this phenomenon. "Why, Aunt," she said, "is that not the gentleman—" Then she fell silent.

Puzzled, Lilith slanted another quick glance at the box. She'd not regarded the other, younger, gentleman before. Now she perceived he was perfectly capable of attracting notice in his own right, for he was remarkably good-looking. Still, had not Cecily expressed an aversion to blonds?

Lilith was about to point out that staring was rude when she experienced a prickling sensation at the base of her skull. Almost reflexively, she looked away from Cecily and across the theater . . . and locked with Lord Brandon's mocking gaze.

The marquess smiled and made an elaborate bow.

Instantly, Lilith felt every eye in the audience upon her. Her poise held, however. She did not withdraw, in confusion or otherwise. Turning deliberately from the marquess, her own gaze swept coldly over the audience and finally came to rest upon the stage. To her relief, the orchestra started up.

Mrs. Davenant heard little of the performance. She could not have said afterwards whether it had been Gluck or Mozart. Lord Brandon's presence had spoiled it for her, tainted the very atmosphere of the hall. She was too conscious of him throughout, too tense with pretending he was not there. Nor did Rachel improve matters by relating in rasping whispers every outrage the marquess had ever committed.

By the interval, Lilith could not endure another word. She left Lady Enders to deal with any stampeding gentlemen, took Lord Enders as her own escort, and made for the box of an old friend of her grandmother.

Mrs. Davenant was careful to remain with the ancient dowager until the last minutes of the interval. There were several famous gossips in the audience. Thanks to Lord Brandon's attention-drawing gesture, they would be sure to seek her out.

She and Lord Enders had nearly reached the door of his box when Sally Jersey popped out of it.

"Why, my dear Lilith," the countess gushed, "whatever have you done with your betrothed?"

"Lord Liverpool had need of him," Lilith answered tightly. "Lord and Lady Enders were kind enough to invite my niece and me to join them this night."

"Oh, yes. Rachel made me acquainted with your niece. Charming girl. Naturally, you may expect vouchers for Almack's. We dare not deny them," she said with a silvery laugh. "The gentlemen would be sure to break out in violence."

"That is exceedingly kind of you." Lilith moved to let her pass, but before the widow could step through the door, Lady Jersey's gloved hand dropped lightly upon her arm.

"Speaking of gentlemen," the countess said too sweetly,

"I was not aware you were acquainted with Brandon."

"Nor was I," Lilith said with perfect composure. As soon as she spoke, she experienced once more the odd prickling in her neck.

"Not formally introduced, that is," came a low, resonant voice behind her. "May I suggest the oversight be corrected?"

Lilith turned slightly. The green eyes were lazily contemplating her shoulders—or rather, the prim few inches to be seen of them.

She threw him one frigid glance, then deliberately turned her back. Mercifully, Lord Enders was holding open the door to the opera box. As Lilith entered, she heard Sally say, "Why, Brandon, you rogue, I don't believe she wants to know you." The door closed, cutting off her ensuing tinkle of laughter.

Apprised by her husband of the confrontation, Lady Enders congratulated Lilith. "You did right," she declared. "One can only hope the others will follow your example and shun him as he deserves."

Cecily made no comment, and Lilith wondered whether the girl had heard a word. Though Cecily sat, her attention apparently fixed on the stage, a rapt expression glazed her eyes, and from time to time her glance stole across the hall.

The object of this devoted study knew nothing of it. Lord Robert Downs was, as usual, devotedly studying the countenance of his mistress.

As soon as Lord Brandon reentered the box, the mistress turned her amused attention to him.

"I wonder if I can make a guess, milord, what drove you from us the instant the curtain fell," she teased.

"There is no need to guess," he answered. "In twelve minutes, half the audience will know. In another twelve, the other half. By the end of the performance, the Watch will be announcing it."

"Ah, he bowed so beautifully, did he not, Robin? Still, the lady will not smile. She will not even look his way."

"Which lady is that, Julian?" Lord Robert asked. He was apparently the only person in the theatre who had not observed Society's latest sensation.

"It does not signify. It is certainly not worth interrupting your conversation with your beautiful friend." The marquess dropped carelessly into his seat.

"It is the widow, *mon cher*," Elise confided. "I have the suspicion your cousin takes a fancy to Madame Davenant."

"Madame who?"

Elise touched a finger to Lord Robert's lips. The music had recommenced.

Lord Brandon joined the couple for a late supper at the Piazza. As he'd predicted, word of the widow's snub had sped through the audience—thanks no doubt to the kind offices of Silence Jersey.

"She cut you, Julian?" Robert asked, aghast. "But no one has ever done that. No one would dare. Who the devil does she think she is?"

"She is the Widow Davenant," said his mistress. "Half the ladies are afraid of her, and all the gentlemen. She is a paragon. Everyone in the ton is naughty sometimes, no? But they are discreet, and so everyone knows, perhaps, yet they make believe they are all virtue. But Madame *is* all virtue. She has never stepped wrong, even the little step."

"Gad, she sounds awful. I must say, Julian, when Elise pointed her out, you could have knocked me over with a feather. She's not at all in your style."

Lord Brandon slowly turned his wineglass, apparently studying its colour with great care. "Thank you for calling that to my attention, Cousin," he said. "I was ill, you know. Evidently my vision suffered. My short-sightedness has been mentioned before."

Elise shrugged. "She is very handsome, I think. Not a great beauty, but very fine. It is her air, perhaps."

Something flickered in the green eyes. It was quickly hooded, but perhaps not quickly enough, for Elise continued, "She is strong and proud. I think she has great will. It is not easy for a widow—for any woman alone—even in the Beau Monde. Or perhaps it is more difficult there. Still, one hears never a whisper of scandal about her. She presents her nieces, and always they marry well."

"You seem to know a great deal about this lady," said the marquess.

"Ah, *je sais tout*. It amuses me. The shopgirls are always so willing to repeat what they hear. Everyone wonders about Madame, because she is a mystery. She has no intimate friends. Her companion knows as little what is in the widow's heart as do the horses of the fine carriage that brought us here."

By this time, Robert had had quite enough of the widow. He had much rather hear of doings in France and wherever else Julian had been.

Obligingly the marquess turned to Talleyrand and Castlereagh and Metternich and Czar Alexander and the rest. His anecdotes were, as one would expect, wickedly amusing. If the telling bored him even more than usual and his mind wandered elsewhere more than once, one of his listeners at least did not remark it.

The following Monday, Cecily's aunt accompanied her to the dressmaker's. As usual, Lilith's in-laws' notions of a proper Season's wardrobe had been sadly inadequate. Since this was usual, she was not taken unawares. She had carefully hoarded a sum for this express purpose. She would have probably done so in any case: treating her nieces to clothes and trinkets was one of her special pleasures.

She entered the shop . . . and stopped short, her pleasure abruptly extinguished.

Lounging in a chair, idly turning the pages of a fashion journal, was the Marquess of Brandon. He glanced up at their entrance, and his bored green eyes lit with amusement. Lazily he rose and made the ladies an extravagant bow.

Her lips compressed in a tight line, Lilith took her niece's arm and swept coldly past him, on to the dressing-room door. At that instant, the door flew open, narrowly missing Cecily, and a woman sailed heedlessly through. Lilith stepped hastily out of the way and stumbled against her niece. The woman made no apology, but headed straight for Lord Brandon. She was the one who'd been in his box the previous evening.

"Ah, *pauvre homme*," she cried. "Were you horribly bored, waiting?"

"Unspeakably so," he answered. "That is, until the very *last*."

Lilith hustled Cecily into the dressing room.

"I do not understand," the niece said. "Is it not impolite to ignore an acquaintance?"

"He is not an acquaintance," was the low answer. "We have not been properly introduced."

"But at the inn—"

Lilith turned to the eagerly listening modiste and asked for a moment's privacy. Reluctantly, Madame Suzette exited the room.

In still lower tones, the aunt explained that it was her Christian duty to help a fellow human being in trouble. Having fulfilled her duty, she was no longer under any obligation to converse with or even acknowledge Lord Brandon. Even if she were inclined—which she certainly was not—she would never do so without a formal introduction. "A lady," she pointed out, "does not respond to every person who seeks her attention."

Elise Fourgette was not only clever, but possessed of virtually infallible instincts. Though she teased Lord Brandon about the widow as soon as they were in his carriage, Elise knew this was merely a prelude.

The marquess had come to London with a purpose. All of Robert's relatives, it seemed, had come on the same business. This time, however, her adversary was more than worthy of her mettle. Even without hearing of his reputation, Elise would have sensed immediately that Lord Brandon was a force to be reckoned with.

He spent ten minutes fencing lightly with her about Mrs. Davenant. Then the duel began in earnest, and, figuratively speaking, the sword was at Elise's throat before she had time to say, *"En garde."*

"You have some letters in your possession," he said in deceptively easy tones. "I should like to have them."

"Ah, milord, that is what everyone would like, I think."

"But I am not everyone, *mademoiselle*." His voice was soft. His green eyes were pitiless. "You may give them up to me voluntarily today—or another day, quite soon, I promise, involuntarily. You see, the matter is excessively tiresome, and I should like to have done with it as quickly as possible. I hope you are not in a dilatory frame of mind. In that case, I should be obliged to ask certain more efficient persons to see to it."

His smile was utterly devastating. Were it not for his eyes, one would think he offered her *carte blanche*.

"That would be tedious and inconvenient for both of us, I believe," he added. "They are such uncomfortable fellows to have about."

Brandon, it was said, always got what he wanted, by fair means or foul. Since he was reputed to prefer the latter, Elise had no doubt his threat was genuine. Such persons as he spoke of existed, and he would not shrink at employing them. How she hated him at this moment, this devilishly handsome, rich and powerful English lord.

*"Je comprends,"* she said tightly. Then she set her brain to work.

No more was said until they reached the cramped lodgings Robert shared with his mistress. The younger man was still out, Lord Brandon having had the foresight to dispatch his cousin on an exceedingly time-consuming errand.

The marquess accepted the glass of wine Elise offered him, and leaned back, perfectly at ease, in his chair.

34

"I do not have all the letters with me," she said in French. "I can give you only some half-dozen this day."

He answered flawlessly in the same language. He had rather not be overheard by prying landladies.

"I did not suppose you were so careless as to keep them all in one place. Nor do I suppose," he added lightly as he turned the goblet in his hands, "you will be so impractical as to release them all. No one knows how many there are—least of all Robert."

"I am not so reckless of my health as to deceive you, milord."

"All the same, I shall not put temptation in your way. In addition to giving me Robert's letters, you will write one of your own to him. In it you will firmly and irrevocably, now and for all time, decline to be his wife."

Elise's dark eyes flashed. "That I will not do," she said quietly. "If you wish such a thing, you must hire assassins as well."

Lord Brandon covered a yawn. "I see you mean to be tiresome, after all. You are under some misapprehension that I cannot persuade you to write this letter. Let me assure you, dear lady, I can."

She laughed. "You will torture me, I suppose? I had not thought you so foolish. I have never told Robert how his relations bully and threaten me. He is so protective—and impetuous, you know. He would insist we be married at once."

"That is hardly to your advantage. His family will cut him off without a penny."

"We shall make do for a few months, I think. In July he is five and twenty, and no longer depends upon their charity."

"Yet you will always be outcasts. You will always be pinched for funds. His income is scarcely what a woman of your talents merits."

She smiled at him over the rim of her wineglass. "There is some compensation in wedding a nobleman. My mother is a whore, my father most likely a sailor. Mama never catered to the aristocracy, you see. How amazed she will be at my title! Perhaps she will come to live with us."

"I hope you have not built too many castles in the air, *mademoiselle*," he drawled, though it cost him something to suppress his revulsion at the prospect she painted for him. "Rest assured you will never marry my cousin. Or, in the unlikely event you do, please be quite certain the marriage will be dissolved—one way or another."

She must know she could not win, yet her features betrayed no hint of distress or alarm. In spite of himself, Lord Brandon had to admire her *sang-froid*, even as he acknowledged his own uneasiness. It was, after all, preferable that Robert know nothing of his family's machinations. The young man was stubborn and, as Elise had reminded, impetuous.

"It seems we are at *point non plus*," she said after a short, tense silence. "Yet how sordid we are, to goad and threaten each other. From you I had expected better. Of all I had heard, never once was it said Lord Brandon bullied women. What sport do you find in that?"

The marquess glanced at her calculating face.

"No sport at all, I agree," he said cautiously. "The matter is so absurdly simple it is a wonder I have kept awake throughout."

"Naturally. You are more accustomed to using guile. This requires neither wit nor daring. There is no difficulty, no challenge. I am an unworthy adversary. I cannot fight you on equal terms," she said. "I am not even your social equal."

Lord Brandon's expression softened slightly. "If you were, my dear, we should not be having this discussion."

"Thus I am left with no chance to better myself—not even to make my future secure. You will have these letters in the end, and I do not doubt you will soon drive Robert from me as well. You have not the courtesy," she added, her voice dropping, "to fight me fairly."

"You yourself admit the match is unequal. What would you have?" he asked. Though his tone was lazy, Lord Brandon was fully alert.

"A champion," she said. "I ask the right to choose a champion to fight on my behalf. Not Robert," she added quickly, before he could express his disappointment. "A woman. One who is your social equal. One strong enough to defy you, which I dare not."

"A champion, is it? You wish another woman—a lady, I take it—to wear your . . . er, favour? That bears at least the distinction of novelty. Pray elucidate." He raised the wine-glass to his lips.

"Madame Davenant," she said.

He put the glass down.

"It is simple enough. Seduce her and I set Robin free as you and all your noble family wish. Fail, and you set me free—absolutely. You and all of them must cease to trouble me."

Lord Brandon gazed consideringly at her for a long moment. Then he laughed and said, "Elise, you are a wicked woman."

"There are many wicked women," she answered with a shrug. "But I am intelligent."

"That I readily admit. I had suspected so before. Now I am assured of it. You must know the challenge is irresistible."

"I took care to make it so. I am not blind. I have watched how you change when you see her. The ennui leaves you. You are tense, like the hound when he scents the fox. You want her. That, any woman of my"—she paused briefly—"*profession* would know. But you will not have her, I think. Not this one, my handsome, powerful lord."

"Naturally you believe so. You would not have proposed this otherwise."

She smiled. "We understand each other, then. Do you accept the challenge?"

Lord Brandon's reflections consumed approximately thirty seconds. Since he had not particularly cared in the first place what absurdity Robert committed, Robert's future and his family's distress were a minor consideration. Besides, they would be distressed only if Brandon failed, which was inconceivable.

In the second place, the marquess had fully intended to seduce Mrs. Davenant. That, after all, was why he had come to Town instead of boarding the first sailing vessel bound for the Continent. Elise's challenge only added piquancy to the pursuit, made it a bit different—yes, more exciting, perhaps—than usual.

"I accept," he said.

Lord Brandon was granted eight weeks in which to effect Mrs. Davenant's fall from virtue. This was an absurdly generous amount of time. Elise, however, had laughingly maintained she might grant him an eternity and the result would be the same. Her patent belief in the task's impossibility only heightened Lord Brandon's zest for the chase.

By the following day, one of the marquess's most ingratiating servants had made the acquaintance of certain of Mrs. Davenant's staff. Within another few days, Lord Brandon began receiving regular reports regarding the widow's comings and goings.

These reports must have been accurate, for Lord Brandon and Lord Robert Downs were to be found strolling within sight of Hookham's Circulating Library when Mrs. Davenant's carriage stopped at the door, and aunt and niece disembarked.

"I believe I must step into Hookham's for a moment," said the marquess to his cousin.

Puzzled, Lord Robert glanced towards the building in time to see the widow enter it.

"Really, Julian, you aren't going to try again, are you?" he asked incredulously. "She doesn't want to know you, and I don't see why you want to know *her*."

The last words were spoken to air. Lord Brandon was already crossing the street. Curious, Lord Robert followed.

Since Mrs. Davenant had not seen either of the two men, she continued in an equable frame of mind. She even forbore commenting upon her niece's unfeminine tastes when that young lady went hunting for equestrian books.

Lilith took herself the other way, where the novels were. She picked up a copy of *Mansfield Park* and began to skim it, to ascertain whether this new effort by the author of *Pride and Prejudice* would be as rewarding as its predecessors.

The hour being early, the place was not crowded, and the aisle in which she stood was empty. Since she was not interrupted, she soon became engrossed in the novel.

She was halfway through the first chapter when she became disagreeably aware of being watched. She looked up.

Not five feet from her, the long, elegantly clothed form of the Marquess of Brandon lounged against the bookshelves. He played idly with his walking stick while his green eyes regarded her with amusement. Her muscles tensed.

Lilith turned to exit in the opposite direction. That way, she found, was now blocked by a set of steps. Upon it a hapless clerk stood, a stack of volumes in one hand. These he was with great deliberation returning one by one to their places. There were two more stacks of books on the steps.

Lilith steeled herself, turned once more, and marched up to the marquess. He did not move out of her way. On the contrary, he had set his walking stick across the narrow aisle.

She glanced at the walking stick, then up at him, her expression stony. He smiled. Her nerves prickled, but she had no intention of retreating. She took another step forward. He did not budge.

"Would you be kind enough to let me pass?" she asked coldly.

"It cannot be necessary. You have given me to understand I do not exist. In that case, you should not find it difficult to walk right through me."

In one carelessly graceful movement, he came away from the bookshelf and planted himself directly in her path.

Lilith was a tall woman, and he was not a heavy-set man,

yet that lean, athletic form with its broad shoulders shut out everything else from her sight. She was acutely conscious of a faint scent of sandalwood.

"I do hope you will make the experiment," he went on, his voice dropping. "Surely you cannot expect a collision—though I should not object if there were."

"Your remarks are not amusing, sir. Let me pass."

"I am too tired. I am but recently—and not fully, I'm afraid—recovered from an illness. You had better scream for help. I haven't the strength."

"I see," she said. "You wish to create a scene."

"And you do not." The green eyes glittered with mischief. "The question is, which of us has more to lose?"

The goading words and his oppressive physical presence turned her hot and cold simultaneously. "I have no wish to bandy words with you," she said icily. "The aisle has two ends."

"But it is bad luck to walk under ladders. I shall be obliged to warn you, very loudly, not to try it."

"You just said you hadn't the strength to raise your voice."

"Did I? My senses must have been disordered. I am struck all of a heap to find you so . . . very . . . near."

Though he had not moved, the space between them seemed to vibrate.

"You are silent," he said. "Dare I hope the feeling is mutual?"

"I will not be the butt of your crude humour, sir." With a strength born of anger and desperation, she pushed her way past him.

Her shoulder struck a muscular arm, her hip an equally hard limb. The shock of contact, brief though it was, caused Lilith to drop her book. She did not pause to retrieve it, but, palms perspiring and heart thumping, marched off in search of Cecily.

He did not follow her.

# === 4 ===

ON THE DAY Lord Brandon had reached Town, the Grand Duchess of Oldenburg had arrived as well. She put up at the Pulteney Hotel; or rather, was put up, for it was the Lievens who paid the two hundred ten guineas a week; or rather, was put up with, for the Czar's sister was a difficult guest, having promptly declared her own private war upon the Prince Regent.

On this same day, Czar Alexander ánd the King of Prussia had entered the French capital at the head of their triumphant troops. Immediately thereafter, the Czar and Talleyrand met to settle Buonaparte's fate. Within five days, the news had burst upon London, to drive the populace into a frenzy of celebration.

Nonetheless, these and other international sensations took second place one evening in early April to weightier issues: that is, the appearance—at an informal gathering of two or three hundred of the Countess Lieven's dearest friends—of the Marquess of Brandon and his cousin, Lord Robert Downs.

Lord Brandon's notoriety had not at all dimmed in the seven years of his self-imposed exile. True, he had returned from time to time, but only briefly, and rarely to good company. He had become a shadowy figure, occasionally glimpsed among the more infamous of the *demimonde*, like a dark Lucifer among a host of lesser fiends.

One might wonder then, on this particular evening, why the virtuous did not shrink from him in fear and revulsion.

Instead, they crowded about his tall, athletic, black-coated figure as though he were Baal and they the idol worshippers. Perhaps virtue was a commodity in short supply in the ton, as Elise had hinted, or perhaps virtue was no match for an unimpeachable bloodline, a strikingly handsome face, a powerful masculine figure, a devastating charm, and an obscenely large income. In any case, there was scarce an individual at the gathering who did not talk either to or about the Marquess of Brandon.

Lord Robert was a lesser light. Still, he had some claim on the company's attention, for he had not been seen at a Society affair since he'd commenced one of his own with a French-born courtesan.

Even the most jaded of the countess's guests could not resist speculating what had brought these two elusive prizes back into the Great World.

Lord Robert, at the moment, was equally perplexed.

In the blaze of thousands of candles, the glitter and flash of jewels was nearly blinding. Dashing silks and satins of every tint mingled with fragile white muslins, like a bouquet of vivid summer blooms set off by delicate sprays of baby's breath, amid the darker foliage of expertly tailored superfine and velvet. The affair, in short, was as insipid as every other.

Lord Robert had rarely been in polite company in nearly two years, yet the faces were depressingly familiar. The few new ones belonged mainly to the latest crop of misses, who were, naturally, exact replicas of the previous crop. Lord Robert had arrived very late, scarcely half an hour ago, and already he was bored nearly frantic.

He had agreed to accompany his cousin because he was curious what it was Julian said and did that drove women of every station and every shade of virtue to lose their hearts, minds, and—if they had them to lose—their morals.

What Lord Robert had observed at Hookham's only whetted his curiosity: the quiet conversation with the clerk, the glint of coins changing hands, the discreet positioning of both the steps and Julian himself. Robert had not been near enough to hear the exchange, unfortunately, or even to observe the widow's expression, until, to his very great surprise, she had thrust his cousin out of her way. Even then, her face had appeared carved from stone.

Julian, naturally, had not mentioned a word of the matter afterwards. He could be irritatingly inscrutable when he liked. Now, for instance, he conversed with Sidmouth and Eldon as though dreary politics were all he lived for.

Since there was nothing at present of interest there, Robert looked about him for an acquaintance whose conversation would not put him to sleep.

He spied two of his friends, Lord Maddock and Mr. Reginald Ventcoeur, forming part of a court around the species of china doll who appeared every Season under different names. Lord Robert sighed and made for his friends.

He was not sure afterwards how it had happened. He remembered being introduced to a pair of eyes the colour of a bright summer sky and a voice as clear and musical as the rippling of a country stream . . . and the next he knew, they were dancing.

Miss Cecily Glenwood was fresh from the schoolroom and country-bred, as she was quick to confess.

"Now, you must keep a sharp lookout," she warned as the music commenced. "I have had ever so many lessons, but I haven't yet danced in fine company very often, let alone with a sophisticated gentleman. It would be too mortifying for me to trample on your slippers—but even more painful for you, I promise. Rodger reminds me constantly I'm no featherweight."

"Two feathers," said Robert, amused. "You can't be more. Who is Rodger?"

"My brother."

"That explains it. Only a sibling would tell such outrageous fibs."

"That sounds like the voice of experience," said Miss Glenwood.

43

"I'm the youngest of four. I have two elder sisters who tormented me—and still do, even though they have handier victims these days in their husbands."

"I'm fourth as well. I have a younger sister, but she can be just as provoking as the others. Are you *all* fair?"

He nodded.

"Is it not monotonous?" She coloured. "Oh, dear. I did not mean *you* were monotonous. You are not at all. At least your eyes are not blue—well, not very. They are more grey than blue."

Her earnest scrutiny nearly put him out of countenance, but she must have recollected herself, for in a moment her long lashes had lowered demurely over her own brilliant eyes.

"I suppose you think me dreadfully forward," she said after a moment. "Really, I am not. It is just ignorance. The hay yet sticks to my shoes, I daresay."

"Not at all, Miss Glenwood," he answered smoothly. "You appear as elegant and sophisticated as any other young lady making her debut."

She laughed. "Which is to say, not very. But you say it so convincingly I must pretend to be reassured."

"You can't possibly want reassurance," he said, smiling in return. "When I approached, I thought you'd be smothered in the crowd of gentlemen pressing about you."

"Yes, and the whole time I was terrified of blurting out The Wrong Thing. My aunt," she explained, "has warned me more than once about my alarming tendency to say precisely what is in my mind."

"Good heavens! You must never do that in Society. Not unless you mean to throw down civilisation as we know it."

"I know," she said with a sigh. "Really, I begin to think a Season wasted on me." She glanced quickly about her, then added in an undertone, "You must promise to tell no one, because they will think me ridiculous, but the truth is I am very, very bored."

"At the start of your first Season? Miss Glenwood, you

44

are more sophisticated than you pretend."

"Not at all. I am still a child, I'm afraid. I want to go to Astley's," she confided, as though this were a heinous depravity, "and to the Tower, and Madame Tussaud's—oh, a hundred places. There is so much to see in London, but all I do is shop and dance and talk and dance and talk and shop."

She appeared so wistful that Lord Robert might have patted her on the head and promised her a sweetmeat if he had not had to mind his steps. As it was, he found himself soberly expressing sympathy and wondering what he could do to relieve the poor child's boredom.

Being occupied elsewhere, Lord Robert did not observe how his cousin closed in on his prey.

Lord Brandon remained at a distance, seemingly engaged in renewing old acquaintance. Nevertheless, there was not a moment he did not know precisely where one staid taupe gown was located.

Thus, the instant Mrs. Davenant and the Countess Lieven moved apart from their neighbours to talk, Lord Brandon began making his roundabout yet speedy way across the room. Bexley, he had noted, had wandered out of the ballroom talking earnestly with Count Lieven a quarter hour before. Lady Enders was gossiping with Lady Shumway and a gawky girl with spots.

Lord Brandon was careful to come up on the widow from behind, allowing her no opportunity to withdraw gracefully. Then he greeted the countess and asked for an introduction.

Mrs. Davenant's slate-blue eyes turned to ice, but she could not, he knew, decline the honour without insulting the haughty Madame de Lieven. Given Bexley's political aspirations, this would be most unwise.

The widow did not decline. She even managed not to appear outraged, which he knew she must be. Lord Brandon pressed his advantage.

"Now that we have proper leave to know each other, I wonder if we might dance together," he said, his tones studiously polite. "Will you favour me with the waltz about to begin, Mrs. Davenant—if only to honour the delightful lady who first introduced it to Society at Almack's?"

The Countess Lieven acknowledged the compliment with a gracious nod. Mrs. Davenant's lips tightened.

"Thank you," she said stiffly, "but—"

"Ah, now we are in for a treat," said the countess. "We have never yet seen Lord Brandon waltz. I am afraid only our allies—perhaps our foes as well—have had that privilege. We shall at last see for ourselves whether he is as accomplished in this as in so much else."

The marquess raised an eyebrow.

"I referred to your skill in dancing, you teasing creature," she said with a faint smile. "But go. The music begins and my own partner approaches."

Followed by many curious eyes, Lord Brandon led his unwilling partner out. Not that Mrs. Davenant appeared unwilling. Her face was perfectly composed. He felt her tense, though, the instant his hand clasped her waist. He suspected she would have wriggled away if she might have done so with dignity. His grip was quite firm, however.

"You are displeased with me," he said. "I placed you in a difficult position. I am very sorry for it, but you left me no choice. I could hardly continue invisible forever. It is undignified."

"And to make a nuisance of yourself is not?" Her tones were cold, but the gloved hand in his was very warm.

"Once, perhaps, it might have been. But I have been a nuisance so many years now, it has become a part of my character. You may have noted that perseverance forms another part."

She did not respond.

"I believe it is accounted a virtue," he prodded.

"When properly applied," was the unencouraging reply. "Children are known to persevere in naughtiness. One wishes they applied the same industry to their lessons."

"If you were my tutor, I should listen very attentively. What would you teach me, Mrs. Davenant?" he asked, his tones softening.

"How absurd. You are long past teaching."

"No one is past teaching. Not if the lessons are pleasant ones."

"Mine should bore you to extinction. You must have heard them a hundred times in your boyhood. Given the results, I collect you had been asleep most of the time."

"Which is to say you mean to read me sermons."

"Yes, I am very dull."

"If you think so, it is you who want a lesson." He pressed her closer and drew her into a turn. In the process, his thigh brushed hers and he felt her recoil.

"You are an excellent partner," he said after a few moments' throbbing silence. "You follow my lead instinctively. I feel as though we had been waltzing together all our lives. But then, I was certain it would be so. I have remarked more than once how graceful you are, even when you are furiously storming away. It is amazing how well acquainted I have become with your back."

"In that case, there should be no need to conduct a physical examination, my lord. You will please to keep your hand in one place."

"I beg your pardon," he said. "My hands are unsteady. I seem to be nervous."

"I should say impudent, rather."

"Perhaps you're right." As though to prove it, he drew her into another perilous turn. He would have liked to keep whirling her until she grew too giddy to stand, and collapsed against him, but that was too crass. He had rather weaken her defences little by little.

A barely perceptible film of moisture was forming on her smooth white brow.

"You are breathless," he said. "Ladies *will* fasten their stays so tightly."

"I do not—" She bit her lip.

"No, I know you do not. I am acutely observant."

A faint colour singed her slender neck.

"You do not require such artificial moulding," he persisted. "Your waist is as slim and supple as a young girl's."

The colour heightened. "You please to mock me, my lord. I should not be surprised. Your manner from the first has been nothing but mockery."

"You are hopelessly confused," he said pityingly. "From the first I have admired everything about you, yet you insist upon being deaf, dumb, and blind to all my touching confessions." He glanced down at her in sudden concern. "You aren't deaf, are you? You were blind for a time, I realise, though assuredly not dumb—"

"I do not understand," she said, "how you can chatter incessantly while you waltz. Your lungs must be prodigious strong."

"When I am flirting, I have the strength of ten men. You will not flirt back, but that cannot stop me. The habit is too deeply ingrained. I find a stunning woman in my arms, and I must flirt with her."

"You have obviously confused me with some Incomparable. It is your lamentable eyesight, I daresay."

"I hope not. You have no idea the *inconvenience* I was put to in order to get you in my arms so that I should be compelled to flirt with you."

He saw the shadow of uneasiness flit across otherwise immobile features.

"You must not be alarmed for my health, Mrs. Davenant," he said comfortingly. "I promise to make up for the exertion by lying abed very late tomorrow."

Had Lilith suspected just how much the marquess learned about her during their one waltz, she would have been considerably more shaken than she was—and that was already too much.

She had wanted every iota of her rigid training to maintain a semblance of composure. A semblance only. Good grief—she had practically announced she did not wear stays! Not, she reflected bitterly as she sought a quiet corner of the ballroom, that there had been any need to inform him.

Before she could even begin to regain her equanimity, Lady Enders pounced upon her, canary ruffles jerking in agitation.

"Everyone is talking," Rachel said.

"It is a social event. People are obliged to converse."

"They are talking about you and Brandon. If I had been you, I should have been put completely out of countenance, with everyone staring so. To dance with the man—and of all dances, a waltz. I really do not understand, Lilith."

What she meant was that she did not approve, though Rachel had not the audacity to tell her future sister-in-law *that*.

"I am not a green girl, Rachel. I do not require the sanction of Almack's patronesses to waltz. In any event, it was one of them obliged me to. I suppose you would prefer I had offended Dorothea?"

"In your place, I should have pleaded a turned ankle."

"In that case, I should not have been able to dance with Thomas later."

"I am sure my brother would have been happy to support a necessary falsehood. A man in his position cannot wish his intended bride to be an object of speculation."

"If that is so, perhaps he might spare a moment to his intended, instead of hiding away in the library talking politics with his colleagues," Lilith snapped. "I was left to deal with an awkward situation quite on my own, and chose *not* to insult the Russian ambassador's wife."

This was so unlike her cool, immovable self that Rachel stepped back a pace. "My dear Lilith," she said placatingly, "I did not mean to question your judgement."

There was a brief pause.

"I am sure you did not," Lilith answered with something

more like her customary chilly politeness. "Our friends' eagerness to make gossip of the most trivial matters distresses you, as it does me. All the same, I think we were wisest to disregard it."

Though a large circle of masculine admirers had already begun to make great demands upon Cecily's attention, she had sufficient of that article remaining to cultivate several feminine friends as well. Among these, the most agreeable was Anne Cleveson, whose mama, Lady Rockridge, happened to be Lord Robert's first cousin on his papa's side.

Lady Rockridge was a sensible, good-natured woman who presented daughters almost as continuously as Mrs. Davenant presented nieces. The two women were well-acquainted. They both respected and liked each other and had more than once traded chaperon duty. This was what Lady Rockridge was proposing on the day following Countess Lieven's informal gathering, for Cecily was invited to join a small group of young people Lord and Lady Rockridge planned to escort to Astley's.

In any other case, Lilith would have instantly agreed. This time, however, there were problems. For one, she was out of sorts, having slept poorly. For another, Lord Robert was to be one of the party, and Lilith much doubted he was suitable company for Cecily.

His connexion with Lady Rockridge was a point in his favour. His mistress and his connexion with Lord Brandon were points against. Cecily's behaviour the night of the opera must be considered as well—though Lilith was not entirely certain in what light to consider it, because the girl had offered no indication of infatuation since.

While Lilith did not list aloud these points for and against, Lady Rockridge must have guessed some of them, because she promptly ordered Cecily and Anne to take a turn in the garden.

"My dear Lilith," she said when the girls were safely out of the way, "I know exactly what is in your mind, and of course I cannot blame you for thinking ill of him."

Lilith gave the tiniest start—so minute as to appear a flicker of shadow upon marble.

"You are too well-bred to mention it," her guest went on, "but we both know Robin has made an utter fool of himself over that French demi-rep."

"I am sure, Glenda, I should never disparage your relations."

"And I am sure you may do so all you like. You cannot abuse him—or his immediate family—any more heartily than I have myself. What a great lot of fools they are! When a spoiled child demands bon-bons, which will make him sick, does it serve to tell him, No, he must not? Indeed, it does *not* serve," said her ladyship, shaking her head vigourously. "As a child, Robin was wont to hold his breath until he turned blue in the face. At present, I believe he is doing precisely that."

"I am not certain I take your meaning," said Lilith, though a vision of the rakish Lord Robert Downs in a childish tantrum drew a hint of a smile.

"Everyone has been ranting at him to leave her. If they had simply ignored the entire matter, I'm sure he would have tired of her very soon, but every new 'No' only makes him dig in his heels the more."

"That scarcely recommends his maturity, Glenda."

"But don't you see? He is not so worldly and jaded as he likes to think. I only wish you could have heard him urging Astley's as a treat for the girls. Rather like an older brother who wants the treat for himself as well. I should like him to have it. I believe the experience will be good for him. At any rate, it is innocent entertainment for a change."

"I hope it may be," said Lilith slowly. "The question is whether it would be good for Cecily. She is inexperienced, young, and impressionable, and he is exceedingly handsome—and, as you said, worldly."

"Yes, of course, but we are going to the circus, my dear, not the Cyprians' Ball," was the brisk reply. "Rockridge and

I will be there, and I daresay we may keep a handful of lively young people in order."

This Lilith could not deny. Glenda's common sense was always to be relied upon. Furthermore, for all her open warmth, Lady Rockridge was a thoroughly reliable dragon.

The following Tuesday was quickly agreed upon, Lilith being engaged to dine that evening with Lord Liverpool. The invitees were mainly of political persuasion, and Cecily had already expressed a disinclination to accompany her aunt.

"She told me she would feel like the village idiot in such company," Lilith said with a smile.

"Meaning, I take it, she expected to be bored to pieces. Well, we shall spare her that, shall we?"

# === 5 ===

THE TUESDAY EVENING found the eminently sophisticated man of the world, Lord Robert Downs, at Astley's. He had dextrously managed matters so that he sat next Miss Glenwood—only, he told himself, for the amusement of watching her childlike excitement. This infantile enthusiasm manifesting itself in sparkling blue eyes, half-parted moist, pink lips, and a propensity to clutch at his sleeve during moments of high suspense, he might have been accounted tolerably amused.

From time to time the lips came disconcertingly close to his ear, as Miss Glenwood was inclined to whisper eager comments on the proceedings.

"How do they do it?" she asked during a display of equestrian feats. "It takes forever to learn how to keep your seat without a saddle—but to stand—and turn—and leap in the air—I could never do that. The last time I tried to stand—"

Lord Robert's head whipped towards her. "You what?"

Captivated once more by the performance, she did not appear to hear him.

"They make it seem so easy," she said after a moment. "Yet it wants tremendous concentration."

"Miss Glenwood, did you just say you have tried to stand upon a horse?" Lord Robert asked, appalled.

"Once only. I can ride without a saddle, but no more. I shall never be an acrobat," was the modest reply.

"You do not ride saddleless," he insisted.

"But of course I do. Why, I have done it several times already in Hyde Park." She must have remarked his look of horror finally, because she hastened to explain that she had done so very early in the morning, and naturally she had her own groom from home with her, and of course she wore her brother's old clothes. One could scarcely ride bareback in a woman's riding habit, she pointed out patiently.

"Miss Glenwood—"

He got no further. Lady Rockridge's dragon eye having noted the two golden heads bent close together, she promptly ordered her husband to change places with Robert.

While the innocent Cecily was throwing Lord Robert into a dither, her aunt was experiencing her own brand of disquiet.

Sir Thomas had as usual forgotten her existence in his absorption with a political issue, but this was habitual with him. At any rate, Lilith had never expected or wished him to live in her pocket, even after their betrothal.

Tonight's issue was again the Grand Duchess Catherine's blatant hostility towards Prinny, her efforts to humiliate him at every turn, and her skill in making everyone detest her. The Czar's sister seemed to devote all her waking hours to making mischief. Since she had considerable influence over her brother, and wrote him constantly, it was feared Alexander's proposed visit to England would not be an auspicious one.

Thomas, who had any number of ideas regarding what might be done to appease the harridan, took every opportunity to express these views. He would not be averse to a diplomatic post, and this was a good way to start. Consequently, he devoted all his energy this night to business— and therefore, the most powerful men in the group.

The disquiet of the nation must, after all, take precedence over the disquiet of one woman, Lilith well knew. Her problem was not with Thomas.

The source of her uneasiness sat the length of the dinner

table away. Amid the buzz of dinner conversation, one low, drawling murmur—inevitably followed by peals of feminine laughter—pierced her concentration as loudly as if there had been no other sound.

In the same way, she saw Lord Brandon without looking directly at him, because he was always there, in the periphery of her vision when she turned to respond to her dining companion. The black coat moulded to broad shoulders . . . the immaculately arranged neck-cloth in whose snowy depths an emerald winked from time to time, a counterpoint to the flickering green glance which lit here and there with equal lack of interest. Once, Lilith had felt that glance settle hard upon her, but she would not raise her eyes to acknowledge it, and the sensation soon vanished.

Her discomfort did not. He had done no more than greet her and Thomas politely at the start of the evening. At least, the words had been unexceptionable. But as they were moving past him, Lord Brandon had shifted his balance slightly, and his coat sleeve had brushed her gloved forearm. She had felt a tiny shock, and ever since, she had been unable to shake off her awareness of him, even when he stood a crowded room's length away.

Lilith ate dinner with her customary marblelike composure and could not have said later what she had put into her mouth. When she withdrew with the other ladies, she conversed in her usual coolly courteous manner and could not remember after a single word. When the gentlemen rejoined them, she talked and drank her tea and might have been talking Hindoo and drinking ditch-water for all she knew of it.

Once more the marquess spoke only a few unexceptionable words to her. Then he drifted away to a group of gentlemen in a corner, where he remained the rest of the evening. Yet he might have been breathing down her neck the whole time, so relentlessly did his presence grip her.

Thomas was among those with whom the marquess conversed. The night wore on, and Thomas showed no signs of wearing out. Instead, the conversation seemed to grow into an intense debate with Sidmouth and their host. So engrossed were the three men that they never noted the other guests taking their leave.

Rachel approached her future sister-in-law.

"Enders says they are like to keep on all night and into the morning," she said, nodding towards her brother. "Can I persuade you to leave with us? Thomas will find his own way home. Heaven knows he has done this a hundred times if he has done it once, and we shall be asleep on our feet waiting for him."

Lilith was only too willing to leave, even if it meant abandoning her betrothed.

"It is about time," said Rachel when the carriage finally arrived. "Nathan has been prodigious slow in coming."

"They are all behindhand, it seems," said Lord Brandon from somewhere behind Lilith's shoulder. "My own carriage was ordered at the same time, and even Ezra—usually a miracle of celerity—has dawdled. Perhaps they too have been debating affairs of state. Mrs. Davenant, you are losing your shawl. May I assist you?"

"No, th—"

He scooped up the end dragging on the carpet and draped it artistically upon her shoulder without touching her.

Lilith murmured polite thanks and quickly moved away, but she found him at her shoulder again as she stepped out onto the walkway.

"Perhaps you didn't require your wrap, after all," he said. "The night is unseasonably warm. You must beware growing overwarm yourself. That is an excellent way to take a chill. Shall I—Well, that is odd."

He stepped away from her towards Lord and Lady Enders, and stopped the latter as she was about to enter the carriage.

Lilith saw him whisper something to Matthew and gesture towards the coachman. At that moment, to her very great surprise, the coachman toppled sideways onto the seat.

"What the devil is wrong with the fellow?" Matthew cried.

Lord Brandon inspected the head dangling over the coach seat. "Drunk, it looks like," he said coolly.

"Drunk?" the others chorused.

"I am sorry to say the man reeks of gin." The marquess retreated a few steps from the head, and turned back to Matthew. "He will not recover for many hours, I'm afraid. May I offer my own carriage as substitute? Ezra has taken a vow of abstinence from strong spirits, and the vehicle is commodious. What good fortune," he added, with the barest flicker of a glance at Lilith. "My curricle is in pieces, or else I should have taken it and been unable to accommodate you."

After making the obligatory objections to inconveniencing his lordship and receiving the obligatory chivalrous responses, the three climbed into his carriage and were quickly on their way.

Lord and Lady Enders promptly began to quarrel regarding Nathan's future. The lady insisted he be turned off at once without a character. The lord, being more forbearing, was all for a sound scold, a signed oath of abstinence, and a second chance.

Lord Brandon pointing out the merit of both sides of the debate, it continued at full spate during the entire journey.

Lilith was too painfully conscious of a dove-grey wool-encased knee three inches from her own to formulate any opinions, let alone give voice to them. The knee was giving her a headache.

Thus it happened that Lord and Lady Enders were deposited at their front door before they knew it, and Lord Brandon's carriage had travelled merrily down the street and was turning the corner before Rachel realised what had happened.

"Good heavens!" she cried, interrupting her spouse mid-harangue. "He is alone with Lilith—in a closed carriage!"

It was a curious circumstance that the loss of two passengers rendered the vehicle more confined than it had been, as though the masculine presence opposite Lilith possessed the power to expand to fill all available space.

She quickly thrust this fancy aside and tried to quell her rising anxiety. There was nothing in taking Rachel and Matthew home first, she told herself. The coachman had merely taken the shortest route, and certainly he seemed in a hurry, for they'd arrived at Enders House precipitately. Which was just as well. Lilith was eager to be home, to lay her throbbing head upon her pillow. She would travel in greater comfort and doubtless arrive more swiftly than she would have in the Enderses' coach.

She had scarcely formulated the thought when the carriage began to abate its spanking pace. Lilith glanced out the window.

"I do not believe this is the correct turning," she said. "This is South Audley Street."

"And you are alarmed. Perhaps I mean to abduct you and hold you for ransom."

She suppressed a gasp, and instantly took refuge from anxiety in anger. "You would get precious little, as you well know, my lord," she snapped. "While we are on the subject—"

"Of abduction?"

"Of money—"

"I did not know that was our topic. I hope not. It is exceedingly dull."

"I am a dull person, as I have mentioned before. My man of business tells me your representative refuses to discuss terms of repayment."

"Yes, and I wish you would stop plaguing them both, Mrs. Davenant. It hints of a disordered mind, not to mention a woeful want of consideration for poor Mr. Higginbottom."

"He is well paid to engage in such work."

"Another lamentable waste of your resources. Really, your affairs are in such a muddle it is a wonder the man hasn't hanged himself—or that you haven't been deposited in the King's Bench already. Did your previous agent not do sufficient damage? Or was his disease contagious?"

"I freely admit I ought to have kept a closer watch on him," she said frigidly, "but that is hardly to the point. The fact is, I owe you—"

"Davenant owed me. You do not."

"I will not accept your charity, my lord."

He studied the top of her head. "Now I wonder why not," he said meditatively. "It cannot be a greater blow to your pride than accepting Bexley. *That* decision carries a lifetime of consequences."

Without heeding her gasp of outrage, he went on. "Not that I blame you. Women have so few economic alternatives. Still, I cannot but wonder at your choice."

"How dare you," she said, her voice choked. "You have no right to refer to matters—to personal matters—or to speak slightingly of a worthy gentleman."

"I did not say Bexley was unworthy. I was referring to his hairline, which is receding at an alarming rate. I can only hope your offspring will not suffer premature baldness," he said charitably.

"I find your conversation in the worst possible taste, my lord."

"I beg your pardon. Perhaps baldness does not distress you. I have noted your preference for a coiffure designed, apparently, to pull your hair out slowly by the roots," he said, his eyes once more upon the tight coil of dark auburn braid. "I cannot look at your head without wincing in sympathy—which is a great pity, because I have very recently acquired a partiality for redheads."

Lilith decided not to dignify this with a reply. She turned her gaze to the window, and immediately discovered, with a return of alarm, that they were circling the darkest square of London.

"This is Berkeley Square," she said, forcing her voice to be steady. "Is your coachman drunk as well?"

"No, he has infallible instincts, which have apparently informed him of my wish to kiss you. Naturally, the locale must be poorly lit. I realise you are shy, Mrs. Davenant."

She had her hand on the door handle before he'd finished speaking.

"Ah, you wish to alight," he said calmly.

The coachman, to Lilith's confusion, was ordered to halt. To her further confusion, the marquess assisted her in disembarking, and in the next minute, his carriage was clattering away, leaving her alone, on foot, with its owner.

He offered a bland smile, took possession of her arm, and proceeded to stroll in the most leisurely way down the street with her.

Lilith's wish to escape the carriage had been reflexive, and for perhaps two whole minutes she had actually believed she would walk home. Now, in the shadowy square, reason returned. A lady did not walk anywhere without escort, and most certainly not at night.

"You see what comes of permitting me to provoke you," he said, voicing her thoughts. "Though how you could have helped it, I cannot imagine, considering the pains I took."

"You upset me deliberately," she said, half disbelieving, half accusing.

"Yes. I hoped you would fly at me and do me some violence. But you are far too well bred for that. Your composure is extraordinary. What a dragon of a governess you must have had."

"She wasn't—" She paused and looked at him, but there was too little light. She could read nothing in the arrogant profile. "Why did you wish to provoke me?"

"Because I find it disconcerting to converse with a stone monument. You do it very well, I admit. One is tempted to hold a glass to your lips to ascertain whether respiration has ceased."

She was both angry and frightened, and his remarks could not be construed as complimentary. All the same, the long-suffering note in his voice made her want to laugh.

"Stones do not scold," she said, moving on again.

"That is the trouble. Virtually the only words I can prise from you are scolding ones, yet I know you can converse quite amiably. Your suggestions to Lord Velgrace regarding the draining of his fields, for instance." He glanced at her baffled countenance. "My hearing is very acute—despite my illness."

"If you wanted my views on agriculture, you had only to ask."

"Had I? I think not. The evening cools," he went on, gazing upwards, "and the heavens make a mighty struggle to clear. I discern one courageous star striving feverishly against the London smoke."

Lilith looked up at the faint twinkle in the heavens.

"I recommend you make your wish now, Mrs. Davenant, before the haze crushes it altogether. You will doubtless use the occasion to wish me to the Devil."

"I hope," she said quietly, "I have wishes more worthy of a Christian than that."

"Then what will it be? A cabinet post for Bexley? No, that is not altogether worthy, either. Too mercenary and selfish. Something for your niece, perhaps—but I will not press for details, or the wish is spoiled."

They walked on for a while in silence. The air had cooled, as he'd said, but not uncomfortably so. Lilith felt warm enough. Her shawl was cashmere, after all, and exercise was known to aid circulation. The tall figure beside her could not be a source of warmth, unless it were the warmth of security. He was trim and strong, and he moved with the grace of complete assurance. She doubted any ruffian would have the temerity to attempt Lord Brandon. With him, she was safe from others.

She wished she could feel as certain she was safe from him. She could not comprehend what he was about. Worse, she could not comprehend what *she* was about, to be ambling through the West End with an infamous libertine. But he had somehow goaded her into it, and now there was nothing she could do about it, except hope no one she knew saw her behaving so improperly.

For a moment, Lilith almost resented the impropriety.

She had never before walked about Town at night. Only gentlemen might wander as they pleased. Men had, perhaps, more freedom than was good for them—did not the living proof walk beside her? Nonetheless, she had always rather envied them . . . when she permitted herself such reflections. Thus, for the present moment at least, she revelled in this mild liberation.

His low, lazy tones jerked her back to Reality.

"You are exceedingly quiet," he said. "Are you tired? I am aware ladies are accustomed to traverse no distance greater than that between front door and carriage."

"I am country-bred, my lord. Walking is not new to me."

"That is a pity. I had hoped you would ask me to carry you."

"A while ago, you hoped I would fly at you. You are either a poor judge of character or in the habit of absurdly fanciful thinking."

"If you think I could not realise either of these hopes—if I truly set my mind to it—then *you* are a poor judge of character."

"You need not war—remind me you are accustomed to do precisely as you please."

"Yes, I am every bit as willful as yourself. I cannot deny that you have the greater self-restraint, but I have superior physical strength—which makes us even, you see."

"You will please refrain from placing me in the same category as yourself," she said frigidly.

"But you *are* willful, Mrs. Davenant. Your carriage alone proclaims it. That haughty lift of your chin, for instance—and one might use your spine as a scientifically exact measure of the perpendicular. It is in your voice as well, and in your terrifying eyes. I should be thoroughly cowed, of course, if I did not find the combined effect so utterly adorable."

Some long-stifled feeling fluttered within her at the last words, but she quickly suffocated it, and iced over for good measure.

"Yes, I am a great joke to you," she answered. "Do you mean to mock at me the entire way home? I ask only to be prepared. I know it is futile to hope you will stop."

"Now I have hurt your feelings," he said, all contriteness. "Upon my honour, that is never what I meant. It was a compliment, Mrs. Davenant. I was flirting with you—albeit in my own clumsy, perverse way."

"I do not wish to flirt with you, or be flirted with in any sort of way, my lord. I cannot think how I allowed myself to be goaded into this predicament. No more can I comprehend how any gentleman could stoop to provoking a lady with whom he is scarcely acquainted—one, moreover, who has done him no injury she knows of."

"Your thinking is lamentably muddled. You saved my life. That is the exact opposite of doing me an injury. Now my life is yours, you see. I am your slave *forever*."

She glanced up at him in alarm, then quickly looked away. "You most certainly are not," she responded, a bit short of breath. "I never heard such nonsense."

"Ah, you have some old-fashioned notion of slaves grovelling at the feet of their master . . . or mistress. Perhaps there are such humble beings yet in existence, but I'm afraid I can't grovel. Faulty education, no doubt. Or perhaps I can. I'm not certain. I have never tried it, but I shall, if you like. Shall I kiss the hem of your gown while I'm about it? That I should be most eager to do, inasmuch as it may afford me a view of your ank—"

"You will do no such thing!"

"No, I will not," he said, so gently that she feared his sharp ears had detected the edge of panic in her voice. "I was only teasing. I can't help it, you know. There is some fiend takes hold of my tongue at times and—"

He stopped as they turned the corner. Lilith looked up to find his lordship's carriage heading towards them.

"You are spared," he said. "Ezra has a low opinion of his betters' locomotive powers, I'm afraid, and though I had rather walk with you until dawn, I dare not disappoint him.

It might result in a fever of the brain."

For the first time in many months, Lord Robert Downs did not spend the night at his love nest. Instead, he availed himself of a bed at his cousin's town house. Julian had said he might stay whenever he liked, so long as Robert did not attempt to usurp the marquess's valet or use the chandeliers for target practice.

The house was large, luxurious, and impeccably managed. The servants glided about, noiseless and efficient, magically producing whatever one needed before one had even thought of needing it.

Still, Lord Robert had not deserted his mistress this night because he missed luxury and the attention of fawning menials. He only wanted to be sure of a decent night's rest before getting up at an ungodly hour of the morning.

# = 6 =

LORD ROBERT AROSE as he'd intended, at a perfectly inhuman hour, and managed to wash and dress more or less efficiently, despite his eyes' stubborn refusal to remain open during the process.

Nonetheless, they opened wide enough when he arrived at Hyde Park in time to see Miss Cecily Glenwood, attired exactly as she had described, dismount from a saddleless horse. Her groom threw him one anguished look, then turned his back and began to resaddle the beast.

As the young lady met Lord Robert's stupefied grey gaze, she coloured, as well she might.

His focus jerked from the top of her cap—from which one golden strand escaped—to stumble at the worn jacket, before colliding with the snug-fitting breeches. Heat stung his neck, and he barely skimmed the scuffed boots before returning to her rosy countenance.

"You are about early, my lord," she said brightly.

"Miss Glenwood."

"Oh, you're going to scold," she said. "As though Harris hasn't been doing it half the morning already."

Lord Robert yanked his brain back from wherever it had gone, shook it to attention, and got very little for his pains. "I—I can't scold," he said. "I hate it when people are always lecturing at me. But Miss Glenwood." He stopped dead, again at a loss.

She moved closer to stroke his mount's nose. The horse nuzzled her, and she giggled. Lord Robert dismounted.

"Miss Glenwood," he tried again.

"I suppose you are very much shocked," she said, more to the horse than to the gentleman.

"Well, you know it is not every day that one—one sees a young lady in—in, well, not in a frock, you know. It isn't the usual thing, actually, and so I suppose it is a sh—a surprise."

"You should not be surprised. I did tell you, after all."

"Yes, Miss Glenwood, and I do hope you've told nobody else."

"Oh, no. I shouldn't have told even you, because now you'll— No, you won't, because I warned you, didn't I, that I have no hope of being a fashionable young lady? Maybe I should not have told you that, either, but you are so *understanding*." The wide blue eyes opened full upon him then, a cloudless, innocent sky, and his heart gave such a thump that he started.

"Well, I do know what it is to be chafing under rules and ordered this way and that, but . . . but— Oh, really, I can't think what to say," complained the sophisticated man of the world.

"Maybe you'll think of it later." She glanced at her now-saddled mare and long-suffering groom. "You can tell me then. I had better not stay, in any case. Good morning, Lord Robert."

He watched her wave away Harris's helping hand and climb lightly into the saddle. Lord Robert should not have watched, because the rear view was even more disconcerting than the front, and the image of one small, round bottom burned into his brain as though it had been applied with a branding iron.

As Lord Robert dragged his gaze from Miss Glenwood's retreating figure, he discovered another figure advancing— if so staggering and crablike a motion could be calling an advance—towards him. It was attired in a bottle-green coat and canary-yellow trousers, and its hat was balanced precariously over one ear.

"Downs!" the figure called out. "What ho, Downs!" It gave a lurch, sending the hat flying, and hurled itself at Lord Robert, who stepped out of the way in time to avoid being knocked over. The figure tottered dangerously towards the horizontal, then clumsily righted itself.

"You're abroad early, Beldon," said Lord Robert.

"Jus' goin' home. But I say, d'you see that?"

"What?"

"That." Mr. Beldon flung his arm in the general direction of the vanishing figure of Cecily Glenwood. "A girl, don't you know? A girl in chap's clothes."

"You've had a long night of it, Beldon," said Lord Robert calmly as he retrieved the hat. Equally composedly, he handed it to his acquaintance. "Those were my cousin's stable lads, exercising his cattle. You had better get yourself to bed before you begin seeing pink elephants and purple tigers as well."

"Good heavens, Robin," said Lord Brandon when his cousin—after going back to bed and making a futile attempt to sleep—came in to breakfast. "You are as pale as a ghost. Was there a pea in the mattress?"

"No," said Lord Robert. "I was perfectly comfortable, thank you—that is to say—well, I was not comfortable in my mind."

"I wish I could sympathise, but I am always quite comfortable in that way. I have a very well-regulated conscience. It never troubles me, and I return the favour, and so we get on famously."

"It isn't conscience—at least—no. But I can't think what to do."

"Why, nothing easier. There is the sideboard. Fill your plate, or summon someone to fill it for you. Personally, I prefer to do without my staff's assiduous attentions at breakfast. A dollop of austerity in the morning gives me a properly balanced view, I find."

Lord Robert rubbed his forehead and walked with a

vacant air to the sideboard. He stood there for several minutes, staring helplessly at the array of covered dishes.

"It doesn't matter what you take, Robin. The affairs of state will continue grinding, even if you choose a rasher of bacon over a sausage."

His words proving ineffective, Lord Brandon rose, filled a plate for his cousin, and guided the young man to a seat.

"Take up your fork," said the marquess. "It is a scientifically verified mode of beginning."

"Thank you," said Robert absently, and absently he swallowed a few mouthfuls before putting his silver down. "I am confused," he said.

"Indeed you must be. You have just emptied the saltcellar upon your bacon."

"Regarding a young lady," said Robert. "That is to say, I feel I ought to do something, but I can't for the life of me think what it is."

"Perhaps you will think of it later," said Lord Brandon, betraying not a glimmer of curiosity.

"That's what *she* said. Yet I've been churning at it for hours now, and nothing I contrive will do. No, it won't do at all," he said, shaking his head.

Lord Brandon calmly stirred his coffee. "I never pry, Robin. Still, if you wish to unburden yourself—and would not violate a trust in doing so—I shall give an excellent appearance of attending."

The younger man threw him a look of gratitude. "Yes, please, if you will—that is—well, it *is* a secret, so I must ask—"

Lord Brandon solemnly swearing himself to eternal silence, his cousin proceeded to relate the morning's experience.

"Ah, yes," said the marquess when the tale was done. "I recollect her. Miss Glenwood struck me as a young lady of uncommon energy."

"She's very high-spirited, Julian, and really she's practically a child—so how could I read her horrid sermons about propriety? But you know it won't do. Beldon saw her, and if he hadn't been utterly cast away at the time, I'd never have convinced him it—she—was one of your grooms, and the news would be all over London by now. So she must be got to stop, of course, and I suppose her ogre aunt could stop her—but then, I should be carrying tales, you know."

"No, you had better not upset her aunt." Lord Brandon might have added that Mrs. Davenant was sufficiently upset for the present, thanks to him, but he did not, for he was not, generally, a boastful man.

"Then what's to be done?"

Lord Brandon reflected for a few minutes as he sipped his coffee, while Lord Robert strove for patience.

"Well?" the young man prodded, when his short supply of that article ran out.

"Being very young and country-bred, Miss Glenwood is likely accustomed to far more freedom than she has in Town. Her family is horse-mad, I understand. Undoubtedly, she has been riding since her infancy. In that case, sedate trots along bridle paths cannot be satisfying. If she had a riding companion equally skilled and daring, and if she rode out sufficiently early with proper chaperonage, I daresay she might have a decent gallop, even in London, without causing a stir. Perhaps that would obviate the necessity for dawn rides in breeches."

Lord Robert considered. "You think I ought to go with her, Julian?"

"Oh, any skilled horseman—or -woman—will do, I suppose," said the marquess, covering a yawn. "So long as the individual is not objectionable to the aunt. She—or her companion at least—will be a tiresome but necessary adjunct."

"Gad," said Robert. "Now I must turn the aunt up sweet, and I don't think it can be done."

"Perhaps not. That is a great deal of exertion on account of one high-spirited miss."

"But if I don't, she'll be found out, and everyone will say she is a hoyden—or worse—and really, she's a very good sort of girl. A child, actually, though—" He stopped short, flushed, and cleared his throat, then hastily rose and excused himself.

As early as was decent, Lord Robert Downs presented himself at Davenant House. He could do no more, unfortunately, than leave his card.

The family were not at home to visitors today, the butler informed him, though naturally they would look forward to seeing his lordship on the following evening.

When Lord Robert's face went blank, Cawble unbent sufficiently to say, "Miss Glenwood's comeout ball, my lord. I was given to understand you had accepted the invitation. It was sent to Lord Brandon's domicile, along with his own, inasmuch as the family had not your direction."

Lord Robert showing no signs of moving, and appearing, if possible, further at sea than ever, Cawble unbent a bit more.

"Perhaps," he invented, "the notice being so short, his lordship accepted on your behalf and neglected to mention it in the press of his numerous obligations."

Lord Robert's face cleared then. "Yes, he must have done. Yes. Quite so. Thank you. Good day."

"I do not understand," said Lilith. "How can they accept invitations I never sent?"

She, Emma, and Cecily were in what would be the supper room, revising arrangements. Following the Countess Lieven's ball, some score or more invitees had discovered they did not have previous engagements after all.

They were coming, Lilith knew, to obtain tidbits about her imagined relationship with Lord Brandon. Until this morning, she had enjoyed the prospect of disappointing them, for she had not and had never intended to invite the marquess. Now the vexatious man was coming anyhow.

"Oh, my," said Emma. "It was I sent them."

Lilith looked at her. "But they were not on my list."

"No."

Cecily came to Mrs. Wellwicke's rescue. "I asked her," she said. "The other day, I asked if she had sent Lord Brandon and Lord Robert invitations yet, because Lord Robert never mentioned coming, though all the other gentlemen have— and so I thought his might have gone astray, you see. You did invite all the others I've met, so naturally I thought—" She studied her aunt's stony countenance. "You did not mean to invite him at all, Aunt?" she asked, evidently baffled.

"Oh, dear," said Emma. "I simply assumed she had discussed it with you beforehand. Meanwhile, obviously Cecily assumed I would know who might be invited and who might not. Well, this is a muddle."

Lilith's mouth tightened a bit, and her shoulders straightened a bit, and she said in her usual cool way, "Not at all." And that was the end of it.

The matter was ended, that is, until Lady Enders arrived to help.

She worried that the flowers would not be delivered on time, and if they were, they would be the wrong ones and the colours would clash and the lobster patties would upset Lord Enders's digestion, and the Prince Regent would come after all, which meant the windows must be kept tight shut and everyone would faint, and other like catastrophes. Then, done with "helping," she set upon the real object of her visit, the satisfaction of raging curiosity regarding Lilith's ride home the previous evening.

Rachel would not dare question her directly, Lilith knew. Regardless how she was questioned, the widow had no intention of confiding any of her troubles to anybody—and most especially not her future sister-in-law.

Still, Lilith had to endure a set of apologies: Rachel and Matthew should never have consented to being taken home first, and if that could not be helped, they should have taken Lilith with them and sent her on in a hired vehicle, if

71

necessary, with Matthew as escort, and they would never forgive themselves, especially if Lord Brandon had been disagreeable in any way, which Rachel hoped he had not been?

When Rachel wished to pry, her idea of subtlety was to end declaratory statements on an interrogatory note.

"A libertine is by definition disagreeable to me," Lilith answered. "All the same, there is nothing to pardon in you. I am not a green girl, and I imagine one brief unchaperoned ride will not sink me beneath reproach."

"Of course, my dear. Naturally, he saw you home speedily, as he ought, and it was foolish of me to be concerned for your safety? Even Brandon must know better than to behave improperly with an affianced lady?"

"Yes, I am sure he must."

"I do hope you had not to wait up for Cecily. I recollect you were feeling poorly, and I worried you would not have sufficient rest. But I daresay she was home before you were?"

"She returned quite early, according to Mrs. Wellwicke."

Lady Enders scrutinised her face. "I fear, all the same, you did not sleep sufficiently. You seem pale, Lilith. Doubtless it is the comeout ball on your mind? Arranging a young lady's debut can be so stressful, perhaps even more so for her family than for herself?"

"Perhaps."

"Well, at least you will be spared one distressing guest. You did say Brandon was not invited. I remember distinctly, because I thought at the time it reflected so much to your credit. Many hostesses will invite some of the most unsavoury characters, merely because they are attractive and amusing— as though these men were no more than decorations."

"It appears we shall have such decoration," Lilith said, folding her hands very calmly before her. "There has been a misunderstanding, and both Lord Brandon and his cousin, Lord Robert Downs, plan to attend, I am informed."

Several stiff green ribbons jerked to attention. "A misunderstanding? You do not mean to say he had the effrontery to invite himself?"

Lilith briefly explained the situation, accompanied by her guest's expressions of disbelief and dismay.

"Indeed. Well, I am very sorry," Lady Enders said, shaking her head. "Though I see it cannot be mended now. One can only hope he will not again subject you to the sort of attentions which gave rise to so much distressing talk scarcely a week ago. One is, unfortunately, judged by the company one keeps."

"I trust you do not mean to imply I am *keeping company* with such a person," came the chilling reply.

Lady Enders spluttered and fussed and declared this was not what she meant at all. The trouble was, Lord Brandon had singled Lilith out at the Lievens' ball, had danced once with her, and left almost immediately thereafter—

"Perhaps," Lilith interrupted, "because I bored him to distraction."

"My dear, it is not I who say this, but others. You know how it is. No one has ever been able to breathe scandal about you, and lesser persons are always too eager to bring others down to their level. There are some who say he pursues you for precisely that reason—because you are so far above his touch."

"Then I must congratulate their acuteness of vision. It is far superior to my own, for I perceive no signs of being pursued and therefore need contrive no fanciful reasons. In any case, I feel we have this day expended far more breath upon the topic than it merits."

The afternoon had advanced considerably when Lord Robert's conscience finally awoke and agitatedly reminded him of his mistress. Filled with self-reproach, he sped to Henrietta Street, and within a quarter hour had thrown this same conscience into twelve fits by telling a series of bouncers.

"Drunk?" Elise repeated. She sat at her dressing table,

staring at his reflection in the glass. "I cannot comprehend. You are always so moderate—in that, at least," she added with a naughty smile.

He did not observe the smile, being preoccupied with sniffing in a baffled way at the air.

"Robin?"

"What? Oh, sorry. Did that clumsy maid spill your perfume again? The room fairly reek—that is to say," he hastily corrected, "everything smells odd today, don't you know. I expect it's the aftereffects. Really, you should be thankful I kept away. I wasn't a pretty sight, according to Julian—and this morning I was cross as a bear."

"Poor boy," she said, turning slightly. She reached up to tousle his fair hair affectionately. "You had not your little Lise by to nurse you."

"Well, I didn't want to subject you. That's hardly fair, when it was my own dratted fault. But really," he went on hurriedly, "it was one of those curst dull parties, and there was no other way to amuse myself, so I made free with the wine. I should have thought. I'm so sorry I worried you. You look as though you haven't slept a wink. What a selfish beast I am!"

"But, *mon cher* . . ." She paused. Her looking glass reflected a beautiful young woman, well-rested, her skin smoothed with exotic emollients, the paint subtle, virtually invisible. She was five and twenty, yet might easily have passed this day for five years younger.

"Ah, I slept," she said after a moment. "But my dreams were bad."

In touching proof of his remorse, Lord Robert promised not to stir from his mistress's side until late the following day. He didn't want to leave her even then, he assured her, but if he appeared occasionally in Society, his relatives' ruffled feathers might be smoothed a bit. It would be pleasant, wouldn't it, to spend the next few months free of harassing visits and letters? After that, of course, the family must stop pestering him, mustn't they? Because then he and his darling Lise would truly commence their life together.

The noble self-sacrifice he proposed, along with his expressions of affection and loyalty, ought to have touched his future bride's heart. Regrettably, that was about the only way she was touched. Today there were no passionate embraces, and the few caresses he bestowed were perfunctory. Mainly Elise was showered with words—from a young man whose verbal gifts were not of the highest order.

Furthermore, Lord Robert seemed to be in the throes of very long-enduring drink aftereffects, for Elise caught him more than once sniffing the air in the same vaguely disturbed way. That night, he fell asleep as soon as he climbed into bed.

Lying beside him, the wise Elise found in these and other small matters much to reflect upon. Being wise, she put them together logically enough, and was troubled all the more.

# = 7 =

THEY WERE SMALL white orchids, tinged with the exact shade of pale mauve as her gown.

With Sir Thomas's spray of white rosebuds and baby's breath had come a note, properly worded and lightly touched—but only lightly—with sentiment, as became a man of maturity and sense.

The orchids bore no card, no note, yet Lilith knew who had sent them. Perhaps the marquess thought it high irony to send such exotic flowers to a dowd. The sprays lay before her on the dressing table, where her maid had placed them a few minutes before.

Lilith now looked enquiringly up at Mary.

"I thought perhaps you'd wish to wear the orchids in your hair," the abigail said. She had served her mistress nearly fifteen years, and was therefore less easily intimidated than the rest of the staff. "I wouldn't have suggested it, but they might have been dyed to match your gown, and it seemed a shame—"

"I cannot wear these," her mistress cut in. "Furthermore, I am not a young girl, to wear flowers in my hair."

"Well, I don't know many young girls who could wear orchids, for that matter. It would take a precious sophisticated one, I'm sure."

Mary took up one mauve-tinged blossom and set it against her mistress's ear. "I'd like to know who picked it out," she said. "Creamy white, as though it had been made from your skin. There's not another lady has your complexion, madam—as smooth and white as a flower petal. As to young girls—why, what are little rosebuds for, then?"

"Mary, Sir Thomas sent me the rosebuds. That is what I shall wear. Or, if you object to them as too young for me, I shall do very well without any flowers at all."

"*He* won't notice," Mary muttered. "He never notices anything. But the other gentleman must. That I'd swear to."

"You are very talkative this evening."

"I do beg your pardon, madam." The abigail promptly set down the orchids, took up the comb, and proceeded to plait her mistress's hair. She pulled the strands so firmly that Lilith thought her eyes would pop out of her head.

"Not quite so tight, if you please," she said, wincing. "My hair feels as though it is coming out by . . . the roots. . . ." She trailed off, gazing into the mirror. After a slight pause, she added, "I feel a headache coming on, at any rate. Perhaps not . . . not so tight a coil. Perhaps—"

"You're quite right, madam. I'll pull it up behind instead, with a knot, and leave it softer at the top, shall I?"

Her employer nodded.

"Now you've mentioned it," Mary went on, though Lilith had not opened her mouth, "we might do both. One or two small orchids and two rosebuds, twined in the knot, so. Practically hidden, your hair is so thick and full. Just peeping out a bit. This way, neither gentleman can complain—or think too much of himself, either," she added with a small, self-satisfied smile.

More than a dozen bouquets had been placed upon Miss Cecily Glenwood's altar by her admirers. Nonetheless, she had no difficulty in declining all these lesser sacrifices in favour of the greater one: a spray of pink roses delivered personally by her brother Rodger.

Overcome by some fit of fraternal obligation, he had for the night abandoned his horses and horsy friends to support poor Cecily in her hour of trial. This he did, when the ball commenced, by being rather a trial himself. He announced

77

loudly and repeatedly that he didn't know her without the odour of the stables about her. Then he proceeded to disconcert her eager beaux with malevolent stares when they dared venture near his little sister.

Luckily, Lord Robert soon took the younger man in hand, introduced him to several sporting acquaintances, and left the rustic fellow contentedly debating the merits of Tattersall's versus Aldridge's in the art of equine auctioneering.

"You are exceedingly considerate," Cecily told Lord Robert when he returned to claim his dance. "I know Rodger only means to be protective, but he does choose awkward moments, doesn't he? The way he glared when Lord Maddock asked me to dance—I'm sure his lordship was convinced he'd be murdered. But you weren't a bit afraid of Rodger, were you? Not that I can wonder at that," she said with an admiring look at his broad shoulders. "I imagine you could knock him down with one blow, if you had even half a mind to. Naturally, you must be confident when you're so fit."

"A great many of us appear fit—thanks to our tailors," her partner answered modestly, though his chest expanded and his shoulders grew even broader and straighter. "We London fellows are an idle lot, I'm afraid."

"All the same, your shoulders are not padded, nor your—" She quickly withdrew her glance from his muscular calves and went on smoothly, "At any rate, you sit your horse exceedingly well. One would think you'd been born in the saddle."

"That compliment I must return, Miss Glenwood. Though I must say—" It was his turn to change direction abruptly. "I should very much like to ride with you one day. Not at dawn," he added hastily, "but in the morning."

"I should like that, my lord."

"Then I shall persuade your aunt to accompany us. Otherwise, I'm afraid, it wouldn't be the thing, you know."

Persuasion of the aunt, Lord Robert soon decided, could wait until the morrow. At the moment, Mrs. Davenant's demeanour had all the welcoming attributes of an iceberg.

The widow was dancing with her fiancé, who gave the lie to Mary's earlier mutterings by taking note of the flowers. He told Lilith they suited her new coiffure, the effect was altogether elegant, and she was undoubtedly the handsomest woman in the room, the guest of honour notwithstanding.

"I'm not a foreign power," she answered. "There is no need to turn me up sweet, Thomas."

"I never flatter you, my dear, because I know you don't like it. But to say you are handsome is a simple statement of fact," he said judiciously. "Nor can you convince me any other lady in this room can match your elegance of manner. I know I'm a lucky man. I never wanted Alvanley's pointing it out, I promise you."

She stiffened. "What had Alvanley to say to you? I am sure he scarcely speaks two words to me."

"He is a lazy, ramshackle fellow. But he tells me to keep a sharp eye, for there are some gentlemen excessively envious of my good fortune. 'While you are courting the goodwill of the Grand Duchess,' he warned me, 'others may be wooing your bride-to-be.' "

"What nonsense."

"Not at all. I have seen Brandon cast more than one glance in your direction this evening, and now I dare not leave your side. They say he has a devilish way with the ladies, not to mention most of us would give a right arm to have one half his good looks."

"Minus an arm, you should not have all your own, Thomas."

He smiled. "Well, he might keep his handsome face, I suppose—so long as I keep my handsome lady."

Lilith did not cast any glances of her own at the marquess. Numerous other ladies had undertaken that duty for her. Besides, she had no need to study him. She had seen enough when she'd greeted him earlier, in the reception line.

His midnight-blue coat and dove-grey inexpressibles,

impeccably cut, seemed knit to his powerful, lean frame. Tonight, one diamond winked in his cravat and another on his right hand. As he'd bent over her hand, she'd breathed the scent of sandalwood, and could almost feel how crisp were the black curls that glistened in the candlelight. The serpentine green eyes he'd raised briefly to hers gleamed with humour. His low voice caressed her ears, and though he uttered the merest civilities, her heart had beat a devil's tatoo in answer.

Contemptuous of superstition and magic, Lilith Davenant had never believed such a thing as fatal charm existed. Nevertheless, she could not deny the pull the marquess exerted upon her, which seemed to grow stronger each time she saw him.

With him, she was so tense she could scarcely think. Away from him, her mind churned with recollections of every word, every gesture, every expression and nuance of his too-handsome countenance. This was how thoroughly he had insinuated himself into her thoughts, after a mere handful of interactions in the three weeks since she'd found him half dead by the roadside.

Though Thomas made a creditable effort to keep by his lady, another siren call beckoned more irresistibly. In less than an hour, he was planted in a corner arguing with his Parliamentary colleagues.

Past experience told Lilith he would not be uprooted until supper, if then. Had one lady joined the group, she might have found an excuse to join as well, but few ladies would endure the somber debate above half a minute.

Cecily did not require her, being occupied with one partner after another. In the intervals between sets, the girl was speedily surrounded by young people—of both genders, Lilith was pleased to note. Her niece was lovely enough to inspire the most malicious sort of envy, yet her open, warm, unspoiled manner won feminine hearts instead of alienating them. There was no question of Cecily's success—on every count.

Since she had no need to hover by her niece, Lilith walked with apparent ease among her many guests, chatting briefly before moving on. She found she needed to move on frequently. She would no sooner begin to relax with one cluster of guests than she would hear a familiar low-pitched voice somewhere in the vicinity. Lazy, insinuating, it would rise and fall amid the buzz and laughter of other voices. Though she moved from one group to the next, his voice seemed always nearby, until she began to feel—it was absurd, she knew—like a hunted creature, never allowed to rest.

She was trying to find a partner for Lady Shumway's unfortunate granddaughter when Lilith saw Rachel try to draw Sir Thomas away from his discussion. Thomas only smiled absently and waved her away.

Lady Shumway's charge was safely deposited with a freckle-faced baronet in the nick of time, for in the next minute Rachel, all angry ruffles and ribbons, was charging at Lilith.

"It is no good telling Thomas," Lady Enders said, vexed and red-faced. "Half the company speaks of nothing else, and no wonder. I have never seen anything so brazen as the way that wicked man looks at you. When Sally Jersey finally asked what made him stare so, he only laughed—I heard him myself—and claimed he was trying to devise a name for your new coiffure."

It was only years of rigid discipline prevented Lilith from reaching up and ripping the orchids from her hair. Her grandmother's lectures rang in her ears: "A lady *never* indulges in displays of emotion, regardless how great the provocation."

She did not wring her hands, as Rachel was doing, or flush with embarrassment. "There are some persons," Lilith answered coldly, "whose every word and action attracts notice. Lord Brandon is Society's latest circus animal. When the novelty of his return wears off, everyone will leave off watching and commenting."

This was uttered with such regal disdain that Rachel very nearly dropped a curtsy. "All the same, he ought have more consideration," she said, hastily recovering. "He knows he's the centre of attention, and therefore draws attention to you."

"I have never heard it remarked Lord Brandon was a considerate man. Will you excuse me, please? I believe Cawble is having trouble with one of the footmen."

Mrs. Davenant's servants were far too greatly awed by their mistress to dare experience difficulties of any sort. She had simply told a falsehood in order to escape the company. She did not hurry from the ballroom, or along the hallway, yet she was short of breath when she reached the safety of the supper room.

Everything, of course, was as it should be. Cawble had made the punch himself from his own carefully guarded receipt, a copy of which any hostess in the ton would have given a vital organ to possess. There was an excellent nonalcoholic version and a sublime spirit-laden one. The cold dishes were artistically laid out. The warm ones would be served at the last possible moment. The china and plate, the table linens, the decorations—all was in perfect order, as Lilith ought to know, having reviewed the situation some fifty times already.

She was examining every detail for the fifty-first time when a chill tickled her neck. She knew the marquess stood behind her, even before he spoke, though she had not heard him enter. Her body stiffened.

"The centre-piece wants to move a bit to the right," he said.

She turned slowly to face him. "It is precisely where it belongs."

"Unlike certain parties you could mention?" He moved a few steps closer.

"Now you have mentioned it, I would prefer you returned to the company, my lord. Your disappearance will be remarked, and I do think you have caused enough talk as it is."

"But my hostess will not talk—to me, at any rate. I wonder why that is."

Another step brought him a few inches from her, and Lilith, retreating, found herself backed up against the table.

"Now I wonder whether you mean to clamber over it," he said gravely. "You cannot be comfortable as you are."

"Will you please—"

She heard footsteps approaching. In the same instant, his hand clasped her arm, and in one smooth series of motions he'd drawn her away from the table and guided her through the opposite door into a small room adjoining.

The well-oiled door closed soundlessly behind them. Beyond it she heard two servants talking softly, then the sounds of chairs being moved. After two or three endless minutes, the footsteps and voices faded away.

"They are quiet and efficient," said Lord Brandon as he folded his arms and lazily leaned back against the door. "Yet all servants are bound by some unwritten code to convey every tidbit they discover to every other servant with whom they are remotely acquainted. Thence the tidbit, enlarged to prodigious size, is conveyed for the delectation of their masters. Speaking of delectable, Mrs. Davenant—"

"I must insist you return to the company, my lord," she said unsteadily.

"Your new coiffure," he went on, "is a delicious concoction. Is that an orchid—no, two—nestled among the curls? I rather fancy orchids. I have a gardener who works magic in a damp, dark hothouse. Still, I have never seen the species displayed to such advantage."

"It appears they came to me by mistake. Since there was no card, it was impossible to return them. My abigail believed they looked well enough with the rosebuds."

"They suit you better than rosebuds. You are not a common rose sort of beauty, but a rare and dangerous exotic. Dangerous to my peace of mind, at any rate," he added, his voice very low. "You don't want me, but I cannot keep away, you see."

"I see that you are standing in my way. Still, there is another exit," she said, clasping her hands to stop their trembling.

His glance caught the movement, then the green eyes were piercing hers. "You are always wanting to run from me," he said. "Do I frighten you?"

"Certainly not," she answered, nearly choking on the words. "I simply do not care to be made an object of speculation. I cannot believe you are so insensitive as to be unaware of that. Yet you seem—it seems at times as though you go out of your way—as though you have some game with me. I do not know what it is or why you should wish to distress me and annoy my fiancé. We have neither of us done you any ill."

"It," he said calmly, "is attraction, and the game is the oldest one in the world."

Her face grew very warm. "I see. You are not done mocking me."

"No, I am trying to court you."

She barely suppressed the gasp. "This offensive joke has gone far enough, my lord. Court, indeed. I, engaged to be wed—even if I were not the very last woman in England a man of your sort would be attracted to. Your idea of humour is distasteful."

He sighed. "I knew how it would be," he said, coming away from the door. "Your brain has not yet recovered from years of being tortured by those cruel coils. I shall have to provide scientific proof."

He crossed the small room. Panicked, Lilith retreated to the opposite door. Just as her shaking fingers touched the handle, his hand closed over them. His touch was an electric shock, succeeded by a wave of shocks as he gathered her into his arms and kissed her.

She had been married. She had been embraced before, and always her body had stiffened at Charles's impatient intimacies. Always she had felt awkward and inadequate. Thus, she had simply frozen, praying he would be done and her mortification ended quickly. She froze now, tense and anxious within, rigidly unresponsive without, and endured, waiting for Lord Brandon to give up.

Or tried to wait. Because he seemed to have no inkling he was kissing a glacier.

His mouth moved slowly over hers, lazily tasting, while his fingers idly stroked the back of her neck. Under that light, almost negligible touch, the stiff muscles warmed and relaxed, and warmth trickled down her spine. She caught her breath in surprise, and his tongue flicked over her parted lips lightly, teasingly, before his mouth closed fully over hers once more. Tingling heat washed through her then, weakening muscles, swamping will, melting everything in its path, so that she scarcely knew she was answering his kiss until it stopped.

She opened shocked eyes to a heavy-lidded green gaze. His face was still very near.

"You appear skeptical yet," he whispered. "I had better provide more evidence."

"No!"

He did not move. She could discern the faint lines at the corners of his eyes and a minute scar over his left cheekbone. His breath lightly caressed her face, and the scent of sandalwood teased her nostrils. Her heart skittered wildly.

She looked the other way, and wished frantically he would move away, because she could not. His face was so cool and assured, while her own was hot—with shame, no doubt, because he had so bewitched her that she'd very nearly brought her lips closer again . . . for more. But there was no magic and therefore could be no bewitchery, and so she made her voice cold and steady as she spoke.

"I certainly need no further proof," she said, "that you are despicable."

"I was much goaded, Mrs. Davenant. Your perfume made me desperate."

She was desperate in any event, because he still had not moved, and in the narrow space between them was a treacherous current. She had been drawn in once, all unwitting. She would not be so again.

She pushed him away and, on unsteady legs, quitted the room.

Lord Brandon discovered that the other door opened onto a hall that would take him out of the house unseen by any but a few servants. One of these, upon retrieving his lordship's hat and stick and whispering a few words, received a generous vail.

It wanted two hours until the marquess's appointment with an actress. He might have spent these at the theatre, but her onstage performance was not what entertained him. Therefore, he returned to his town house to change into less formal attire.

As he was unwrapping his neck-cloth, his glance fell upon his left shirt cuff. He frowned.

"Hillard," he called.

His valet hastened into the dressing room.

"M'lud."

"Bring me a pistol."

Mr. Hillard had been with his master twenty years.

"Yes, m'lud. What sort of pistol did you have in mind? Mr. Manton has made you several."

"You cannot ask me to make such a decision at a time like this. I am a broken man. There is a thread," Lord Brandon said in sepulchral tones, "hanging from my cuff."

"M'lud, that is impossible. I beg your pardon for contradicting, but it is completely impossible."

His lordship put out his hand and pointed to the offending cuff. "What do you call that?" he asked in the same hollow voice.

Hillard stepped closer and peered at the object. "M'lud, I call it a hair. A long, reddish one," he added, his face immobile, "with a curl to it. I can't think how it got there, but it isn't a thread. Shall I remove it?"

"No, Hillard. You have suffered enough. I have grievously offended you. I hope you will come to forgive me one day, for there were extenuating circumstances. The light is dim and my eyesight is failing me. That has been pointed out to me on more than one occasion."

"I am sorry to hear it, m'lud."

"Now I have depressed your spirits. You had better step round to the butler's pantry and restore yourself with some beverage appropriate to the circumstances."

"But you meant to go out, m'lud, did you not?"

"Later. Perhaps I had better rest first."

When the valet had left, Lord Brandon carefully removed the gleaming strand from the stud on which it had caught—when he had caught her, he reflected with a small smile. Cornered and caught her, trembling, in his arms.

That had been a novel experience. He had never before embraced a frightened woman. Angry women, yes, and those who feigned shyness, and those who were eager—but never one genuinely afraid. Never before, either, had he encountered so powerful an effort to resist.

Yet she could not, and he'd known she could not. Which was no conceit in him, only statement of fact. Elise notwithstanding, he would not have pursued the widow if he had not believed there was an attraction from the start.

His instincts never failed him in such cases. Even so, he had toyed with her first, to be certain, and all his artful teasing since had had one clear object: to make her inescapably aware of him.

Lord Brandon's smile twisted slightly. He had teased himself as well. That could not be denied. Wooing her he'd known would require patience. Nevertheless, though he was not an impatient man, tonight . . .

He drew the strand of hair out between his fingers.

For that endless time when she'd refused to succumb—when she stood, rigid as a marble column in his arms—he had wanted to shake her. The silken alabaster skin, the rich mass of curling hair, the surprisingly lush perfume wafting languorously to his nostrils . . . yes, the haughty countenance as well, and the strong, lithe body recoiling from his own. It had been, for a moment, maddening. But only for a moment, because she had weakened at last.

"At last," he murmured. "What was it then, madam?" he asked the fragile trophy of his night's work.

Then, he answered silently, he had tasted a young girl's kiss, tentative and inexperienced. Though she had been married six years and widowed five, one might have believed it was a virgin prisoned in his arms. All the same, her response had moved him. Even now, reflecting upon it made him . . . uneasy.

He glanced at the fresh linen, coat, waistcoat, and pantaloons Hillard had set out for him. It was time to dress. Brandon never kept his paramours waiting.

He could not repress a sigh. He had done it all a thousand times before. He had known them all, drab to duchess, and they were all, apart from details of packaging, the same. There was no challenge in the pursuit—no pursuit required, actually. No need for guile, as Elise had said. No danger and certainly no consequences of failure.

Small wonder the widow excited him.


"Thank heaven *that's* done," said Cecily when the door had closed behind the last of their guests.

"My dear, I hope you don't mean your comeout ball was an ordeal," said Emma. "You seemed to be enjoying yourself well enough."

"Oh, I did," Cecily said with a quick glance at her aunt. "How could I help it, when Aunt Lilith made all so splendid—so perfect?"

The widow was staring at a centre-piece one of the footmen was carrying out of the supper room. She did not respond.

"Aunt Lilith?" Cecily moved to her aunt's side and took her hand.

Lilith looked at her blankly.

"Thank you so much, Aunt. It was the most beautiful party, and I cannot think when I've had a better time—away from my mare, that is," she added with a grin. "I was only relieved I managed to survive the evening without committing any outrageous *faux-pas*."

"Oh, Cecily." To the girl's astonishment, her aunt threw her arms around her and hugged her—almost desperately, it seemed.

Then, just as abruptly, she drew away. "You are a great success," she said with her usual composure. "Equally important, you have deserved it. I am very proud of you, my dear."

"Well, I'm glad to hear it, Aunt. I shall have to tell you every compliment I received, naturally, and every silly thing the gentlemen contrived to say, and draw up a lengthy list of the men in London who'd do better for a dancing master. But not tonight—or this morning, rather. It's nearly dawn, isn't it? You must be exhausted, because the hostess has the most laborious job of all. Indeed, my aunt had better go to bed right away, don't you think, Emma?"

Emma bent a troubled glance upon the widow. "You have one of your headaches," she said. "Why don't you go up, as Cecily advises? I shall make you a nice herbal tea, shall I?"

"Thank you, but I am only a bit weary. This has been altogether a long day . . . and evening . . . and . . ." Lilith turned back to her niece. "Of course I shall want to hear every detail of your triumph," she said with a forced smile. "But we will all do better for some sleep."

As soon as she had attained the safety of her dressing room, Lilith tore the flowers and pins from her head, took up her brush, and savagely attacked her hair. Tears had started to her eyes when she heard her abigail's light footstep. "Go to bed, Mary. I told you not to wait up."

The brush was taken from her hand. "But it's as well I did, isn't it? You being run off your feet, and your head probably ringing from all the noise. I'm sure this was twice the crowd we had for Miss Georgiana. And, naturally, twice the number of biddies needing to be attended to. I could hear them squawking all the way downstairs, pesky old hens," Mary grumbled, all the while plying the dark auburn tresses with slow, soothing strokes. "And here I am, bad as any of them, jabbering at you when you must be tired to death of talk."

Lilith was more than tired to death. Her guests had pricked and stung her at every turn, in chorus to the pricking and stinging of her own conscience.

Every female in the company, it seemed, had remarked her brief disappearance and felt compelled to point out the odd coincidence of Lord Brandon's vanishing at the same time.

Their hostess had her answer ready, the same answer for them all. Had Lord Brandon left? She had not noticed, yet she was scarcely surprised. A young girl's comeout must seem to him a very tame affair. One could not be amazed at his leaving to seek livelier entertainment.

Thus she had endured, and told herself she had endured worse—her marriage, for instance. Still, she prayed for great news from abroad to distract the Beau Monde from its obsessive attention to herself. Such news would not be forthcoming this evening, but tomorrow, perhaps. Tomorrow, perhaps, Lord Brandon's odd whims would be forgotten . . . by others, at least.

# === 8 ===

UNFORTUNATELY FOR MRS. Davenant, rumours of Buonaparte's attempted suicide the previous day could not possibly reach London in time to distract her gossip-hungry acquaintances. The afternoon following the comeout saw her drawing room packed with visitors, not all of them Cecily's dancing partners.

Lady Enders did her best, making a great piece of work of minor matters, such as Hobhouse's obstinate determination to procure passports to Paris for himself and Lord Byron, despite the Government's equally firm resolve not to issue any. She even went so far as to describe in tedious detail the illuminations at Carlton House celebrating the triumph of the Bourbons, though everyone had seen them and raved sufficiently days before.

Neither illuminations, Louis XVIII, nor even the capricious Lord Byron could be half so sensational a subject as the lavish bouquet of lilies that arrived just as Lady Jersey did, and five minutes before Lord Robert Downs made his appearance.

"I have never heard such a fuss about a lot of posies," he whispered to Cecily when he had elbowed several other fellows out of the way and had her, for the moment, to himself.

"I know. You'd think Napoleon himself had been delivered. But Lady Jersey recognised your cousin's servant, it seems, and so she must peep at the card, and then declare it is Lord Brandon's hand, for she'd know it anywhere, and then she must tease my poor aunt to read the note to the company."

Robert looked at the flowers, which had been exiled to the darkest corner of the room in a futile attempt to subdue curiosity. Then he looked at Cecily. "*Julian* sent them?" he asked. "What did the note say?"

"Good heavens, you don't suppose Aunt Lilith actually read it out, do you? She never even looked at it, but crumpled it up and thrust it into her pocket." Cecily grinned. "Lady Jersey is ever so vexed. She's bursting to know what it said. If she dared, I imagine she'd wrestle my aunt to the floor to get it from her. But even she is a little afraid of Aunt Lilith—though she hasn't left off teasing altogether."

Lord Robert certainly would not have had the audacity to tease Mrs. Davenant. She had never looked more glacier-like than now, her face frozen in politeness, her chin high, her gaze at its most imperiously icy. He would as soon take a dip in the northernmost depths of the North Sea.

"I suppose," he said, "this is not the best time to ask permission to ride with you."

"Actually, it's the perfect time," said Cecily. "Just don't mention flowers or your cousin. Since you'll be the only one to refrain from those topics, she'll be touched by your delicacy."

His expression must have been very doubtful, because Cecily added, "Shall I ask her, then—or would that be excessively forward of me?"

If the widow's own eighteen-year-old niece was not intimidated at the prospect, then a man of the world certainly could not be.

When Mrs. Davenant had seen off a frustrated Lady Jersey, Lord Robert approached his hostess.

"Riding?" she echoed blankly, as though he had been speaking Egyptian.

He was not sure after exactly what he'd said to that frosty figure, though it must have been some garbled paraphrasing of Julian's comments the other day. Whatever it was, it worked—or else the widow was too much preoccupied with other matters to interrogate him closely, for she gave her consent rather abstractedly, and agreed to accompany the two young people the following morning.

"Well, my dear," said Sir Thomas after the remaining visitors had left, "what is this I hear about a rival?"

"What is it you hear?" his betrothed responded stiffly.

"I met up with Sally Jersey—not long after she'd left here, I take it, and she tells me Brandon is sending you love notes and lilies."

He stood by the table that bore the infamous bouquet. His hands folded behind him, he appeared to be weighing the flowers as Parliamentary evidence.

"I have been hearing a great deal of Brandon lately," he went on. "In fact, in the last twenty-four hours, I have heard his name linked with yours more often than my own. I know better than to credit every piece of idle gossip I hear, and I know better of your character than to credit what has been hinted to me. All the same, I do not take my treasure for granted." He turned to her. "Have I any reason to speak to him regarding the matter?"

Lilith removed the crumpled note from her pocket and handed it to him. "Judge for yourself," she said frostily. "I have not read it. I have no wish to read it." Her chin was high.

He scanned the note quickly, then threw her a puzzled glance. "He thanks you, according to this, for your 'exceedingly wise counsel.' He says your advice was invaluable. What advice was that, my dear?"

"Drains."

"I beg your pardon?"

"Drainage. Of his fields. It is . . . it is one of my hobby-horses, you know."

Sir Thomas chuckled. "Poor Sally. All a-fever to know of midnight assignations and stolen kisses, and we can offer her nothing but agriculture. How I wish you had read her the note."

"I had no desire to read it, as I said. In any case, whatever was written, she would have put some base construction upon it—and certainly it is none of her affair."

"No, my dear, and none of mine, I am sure. I am done with farming, thank heavens. All the same, I wish Brandon would take himself off to tend those fields of his. Even innocent, he is a troublesome fellow to have about, I think."

Lilith watched the two young people tear off at a frightening pace, Cecily's groom trailing doggedly behind them. Cecily was a countrywoman, happiest in the saddle and—judging by her speed—galloping neck or nothing. Fortunately, her companion was a match for her.

As Glenda had said, there was an eager boy under the veneer of jaded sophistication. Lilith had not observed Lord Robert very closely before. She'd had too many distractions—or one too great a one. But en route to the meadow, she had found much to meet with her approval. He was not sly or insinuating. He was good-natured, and behaved towards Cecily as though she were his sister.

Equally important, Cecily was her usual level-headed self. The elegant gentleman did not seem to throw her into any sort of confusion. He might have been her brother.

Such fraternal behaviour scarcely promised a match, yet so long as Cecily's heart was not affected, one could not object to the friendship.

All the same, one could not help wishing the Season done already, with Cecily wed or soon to be. Lilith had never been overly fond of Town, though she made the best of it for her nieces' sakes. At present . . . oh, London seemed a den of fiends. One, certainly, plagued her mind and heart.

The hoofbeats seemed to come in response to the thought. She glanced over her shoulder at what might have been an apparition, for in the shadowed path man and beast appeared one. As she recognised the rider, her heart began to thud ominously. In a moment, Lord Brandon was beside her, his restless dark stallion pawing impatiently at the ground, agitating her mare.

"She is like her mistress," he said, subduing his mount. "She wants to bolt—though we mean them no harm, do we, Abbadon?"

The beast snorted, and Lilith's mare backed away.

"We have only come for our scold," he went on. "I trust you've had sufficient time to compose a thundering one."

"That would be a waste of intellect and energy. You are beyond sermons. You are beyond any civilised rules of behaviour."

"I object to having my life ordered by prigs, if that is what you mean by civilised rules. It was but a kiss, after all."

She winced.

"I shall never be sorry I did it," he added, his smile as unrepentant as his words, "though you threaten me with all the fire and brimstone of all eternity. You, on the other hand, *are* sorry, and therefore obliged to take it out on me. Well, do your worst. I shall gaze at your lips the whole time and not comprehend a syllable."

A breeze ruffled the boughs above them. The shifting beams of sunlight played over the clear planes of his face and softened it, gentled even the mocking smile and insolent green gaze. Or perhaps it was the low, beckoning sound of his voice that weakened something within her. Her own glance lingered on his mouth longer than it ought, and then upon his eyes, and within her grew a yearning that shamed and enraged her as soon as she recognised it.

"I *am* sorry," she said tightly. "To you it is nothing—a whim to amuse yourself. It is no joke to me, my lord. It does not amuse me that I have betrayed my affianced husband, dishonoured myself, earned the censure of my peers—oh, yes, and earned your contempt as well."

"Good heavens, one would think you had committed patricide. It was not even adultery—though I'm hardly the man to discourage you from *that*."

Lilith tried to hold her temper, but it was already ripping

95

loose. She was sick at heart at the sin she'd committed, while to him it was nothing. *She* was nothing—her feelings were a joke to him.

"No, you would not," she said. "You delight in wrecking marriages. A betrothal must be a mere bagatelle."

"Not at all. *Your* betrothal is an atrocity. A woman of your spirit—to be shackled to that stale speechmaker. No wonder you are so short-tempered."

"Your opinion is of no consequence, my lord. Whatever you think of him, Sir Thomas is my own choice. I will not permit you to sully my reputation and make a laughing-stock of him. I will not permit you to taint my existence any longer. You have already killed one husband," she went on in low, furious tones. "Was that not sufficient? Must you make a shambles of my life once again?"

There was a heartbeat's pause. The teasing light went out of his eyes, and his voice was cold as he answered, "As I recollect, madam, your first was consumptive."

"Consumptive, yes—though I know it was his so-called friends hastened him to an early grave. If you can call it friendship to encourage a sick man to exhausting follies—drinking, gambling, dissipating—when he should have rested. Perhaps you call it friendship to lead such a man to the stewpots of a filthy city, when he needed to breathe fresh air." She blinked back angry tears. "He might have had a few more precious years—even one—were it not for *friends* such as you. But with you it is always an endless pursuit of pleasure. You have no care for anyone but yourself. Now you have a whim to amuse yourself at my expense. You shall not," she said, her voice choked. "I despise you and all you stand for."

It seemed as though every sound had been stifled about them, so potent was the silence when she finished. Even his restless mount stood still as a statue.

"I am not omnipotent," he answered at last. "My mere presence is not sufficient to befoul your lily-white reputation and cuckold your fiancé. As to your late husband, I doubt even the Almighty Himself had the power to sway Davenant from his chosen courses. He was a wastrel and debauchee long before I met him. If marriage to a wealthy, eager-to-please, generous-hearted girl was not enough for him, then his case was hopeless."

The pain wrenched her so suddenly that the tears spilled over before she could recall them. She turned her head, though she knew he'd seen her weakness.

"I beg your pardon," she heard him say more gently. "My presence distresses you. It will do so no longer."

Then he was gone.

"Idiot!" Lord Brandon muttered as he rode away. "Clumsy idiot!"

Abbadon uttered a derisive snort.

"You needn't rub it in," his master grumbled. "It was clumsy, yes—and craven—to stoop to defend myself. Still, I was much goaded. You must admit that, at least."

The unsympathetic animal tossed its head.

"Ah, you had your mind—or some part—fixed on the mare. You were not attending. You did not hear her contempt. You could not read the loathing in her eyes. Until, that is, your crude bully of a master reduced her to tears. That is a fine way to win a mistress, don't you think? Damn."

Abbadon pricked up his ears at the oath.

"Away, then, you devil," Brandon growled, nudging the impatient animal's flanks with his heels. The horse surged into a gallop, and man and beast thundered recklessly along the bridle path. Had anyone observed their headlong fury, that witness must have been convinced it was the devil and his familiar, plunging to the fiery place.

While the furious ride eventually pacified his horse, it did little for Lord Brandon except make him hot and dirty. A bath and change of clothes improved his appearance but not his temper.

Later, he stood in his dressing room, glaring at his

reflection in the glass. He was not, he thought, vain—or not excessively so—yet he could not understand how a rational woman could look upon him with such utter revulsion. His crisply curling hair had not turned white suddenly. It was as black and thick as ever. His face was not yet mottled with age and dissipation. His green eyes were clear, his posture straight. He had not turned into a troll overnight.

His appearance was not the trouble.

Lilith Davenant hated him for what he was, and what she believed he had done, and though he had done a great many things deserving of her prim displeasure, he had not done what she accused him of. Yet it was not the injustice that had angered him—and perhaps the feeling wasn't precisely anger. Maddened for a moment, yes . . .

He turned away from the mirror.

There was no denying. Her slate-blue eyes had turned to ice, and she had raised her stubborn chin and opened her mouth, and—while the accusation was unjust, or only partly just—her words had pricked him. Very well, *wounded* him. He was not one to shy away from facts, however lowering they might be.

To be wounded by a woman was a novelty—not an agreeable one, certainly. Still, it was a fact: Lilith Davenant had stabbed him, and he was still smarting.

As he formulated the thought, he smiled wryly. He must remember to congratulate Elise on her choice of champion. Meanwhile, he had better set his mind to repairing the damage. Nearly a fortnight had passed since he had made his wager—and all he had to show for it was one absurdly chaste kiss!

Elise had not attended Eton, Harrow, Winchester, or any other ancient educational institution. All the same, she could count. Since the night he'd spent at his cousin's, Robert had made love to her exactly once, with a conspicuous want of enthusiasm. Once in nine days. Last night, again, he had not come home.

Being wise, Elise had immediately sensed a woman in the case. Being well-informed, she had not required the entire nine days to ascertain who the woman was. Being practical, she turned her intelligence to determining the simplest, most direct way of eliminating her rival. Accordingly, she paid a visit to her dressmaker, and a bribe to Madame Suzette's assistant.

On the Sabbath, Mrs. Davenant took herself to church. She prayed for forgiveness and strength. She came away feeling unshriven and weaker than before. She'd found no comfort in the minister's words, though he, accustomed to preach to the nobility, wisely forbore mentioning such vulgarities as hellfire and eternal damnation.

Lilith had looked up at him and seen herself, standing all those years ago before another minister: The shy girl, barely seventeen, who'd wondered at the powers that had given her as husband so golden and godlike a creature.

The young bridegroom at her side must have wondered as well, for he'd got the worst of the bargain. Even now, at eight and twenty, Lilith was no beauty. As a bride, she'd been a carrot-haired, freckle-faced, skinny adolescent, inwardly awkward and unsure. Outwardly, she had been poised, of course, cool and perfectly mannered, because manners, poise, and self-control had been drummed into her from the day her grandparents had taken in the orphaned child of their only son.

They had not, however, taught her how to make her husband love her. That, perhaps, was too much to ask. His family had wanted the match because their youngest son was too expensive to keep any longer. Her grandparents, their own title spanking new, had wanted the connexion with ancient nobility.

Love in such a case was not to be expected—even if there had been anything remotely lovable or attractive about her. Yet she had wished. She had wished at least that Charles

Davenant would teach her how to please him. She could never express such a wish aloud, though.

Thus his rare visits to her bed were impatient and hurried, and his distaste only made the intimacy the more humiliating. When he was done, he left her hating her own body because it could never please him. Charles's gawky child bride could not compete with his London beauties. She could not even inspire affection. She bored and embarrassed him, and even drunk—as he inevitably was—he could not wait to be gone from her.

Lilith had not wept for her husband in years. Even at his death, her tears had been for the waste of the man he might have been. So young, strong, handsome . . . to dwindle to a frail shadow, weak, fretful, and afraid. She had wept as well because he'd left her no golden children to whom she might give the love he'd never sought or wanted.

Now she wept silently in the church after the others had gone, because Charles's friend had pierced the cold tomb of her heart, and revived the pain so long sealed within.

EARLY MONDAY MORNING, the much-harassed Mr. Higgin-bottom met with both Lord Brandon's man of business and the marquess himself. Two hours later, Mr. Higginbottom was able to inform Mrs. Davenant that terms had been arranged at last, and to remind her, with gloomy satisfaction, that she would now be obliged to practice the strictest possible economy.

The greatest of her expenses having been incurred already, Lilith had few qualms about her ability to last the Season. Shortly after, she would be wed, and money would no longer be an issue. All she would lose was her independence. She persuaded herself she'd already more of that article than most ladies.

For five years she had been free to manage her own affairs, without having to accommodate a husband's whims. She had not to chase him down when major decisions were required. She had done it all herself, without interference—and in the end she had made a bad job of it, had she not?

Furthermore, there must be some gratification in having at last won this particular war of wills with Lord Brandon.

To Mr. Higginbottom she expressed her satisfaction. Inwardly Lilith felt as though she were now a bill marked "Paid," filed away and forgotten, and her victory was tinged with regret she despised herself for feeling.

By early afternoon, this matter took second place to a more urgent one.

Lilith was in her sitting room with Emma and Cecily, the

two older women plying their needles while Cecily read aloud from *The Corsair*. That was when the box arrived from the dressmaker for Cecily.

"I declare I'd forgotten completely about the walking dresses," the girl said as she untied the string. "No wonder. I'm sure I have dozens already, though I never seem to *walk* anywhere lately. It is always— Oh, my."

She giggled as she pushed away the tissue paper. "Not a walking dress, I don't think."

Emma, sitting by her, turned pink. Lilith promptly rose from her chair to investigate.

Even the widow's marble features became tinged with colour as Cecily withdrew from the box two intriguing garments.

They were negligees. One was a maidenly pink. That was its sole connexion with maidenhood. It was of gossamer silk, its plunging neckline caught with cherry-coloured ribbons. The other was a froth of black lace, equally transparent.

"Not walking dresses, to be sure," said Cecily with a smile as she held the black one against her and modeled it for her two stunned companions.

Lilith, who had stood numb with shock, hastily recovered. She snatched the two garments from her niece and threw them back into the box.

"Obviously there has been a mistake," she said.

"I should say," Cecily answered, grinning over the note she held in her hand. "I cannot be anybody's 'Dearest Lise,' and who, I wonder, is my 'adoring Robin'?" She giggled again. "I have never seen such naughty night-rails."

"I should hope not," said her aunt. "This box will be returned immediately, and I shall certainly have something to say to Madame regarding her carelessness. The idea—to send such—such wicked things to this house."

"Of course it was a mistake," Emma soothed. "There must have been another package, and another lady has Cecily's frocks, I daresay."

"A *lady*, indeed," Lilith said half to herself. "That *her* lewd belongings should pollute this house, and *he*—" She broke off, recollecting her niece.

Cecily, however, was still studying the note. "But of course," she said. "It's Lord Robert's *chere amie,* is it not? Anne told me her name was Elise, and that she's French, and the family's in an uproar because he's been living with her for years and years."

Lilith tore the note from her hand.

"Anne should have told you no such thing. Ladies know nothing of—of these matters."

"Well, they pretend they don't, but they must be blind and deaf to be unaware, I should think. It's not as though he hides her away. Why, he was with her that night at the opera. I recall distinctly. She was very lovely and elegant. Frenchwomen are so stylish, are they not?"

"I most certainly did not regard her," the aunt answered quellingly.

Unquelled, Cecily continued, "I was much amazed. I'd always thought trollops looked like the tavern maid at Squeebles. Molly's rather stout, but I daresay she's the best the gentlemen can find in the vicinity when they're of a mind for that sort of thing."

"Cecily—"

"I wonder if Lord Robert's friend is witty and clever," the girl said meditatively. "They say that's why Harriette Wilson is so popular. Certainly she's no great beauty. Still, she has a very generous figure, so perhaps it's not all conversation. When the horses are bred, you know, the stallions—"

"Cecily!"

"Well, they do go directly to it," the girl said, turning her innocent blue gaze to her aunt.

Mrs. Wellwicke covered her twitching mouth.

"It looks rather uncomfortable for the mares," the niece added. "No wonder the gentlemen must pay—"

"Cecily, pray hold your tongue," Lilith snapped. "It is bad enough these disagreeable objects are among us. Worse still that they should elicit such unladylike, immodest speculations. You see how depravity taints whatever is near it. I shall have a servant return this package immediately. Furthermore, as of this moment you are to have nothing to do with Lord Robert Downs. He is obviously not a fit person for an innocent girl to know."

She marched from the room, bearing the box well in front of her as though it were a chamber pot.

Cecily chased after her. "But Aunt, you can't mean it," she said. "It isn't his fault."

"We shall not discuss this before the entire household."

Cecily followed her aunt in silence down the stairs and into the study. She waited patiently while Lilith wrote a short note, sanded and sealed it, summoned a servant, and dispatched box and note to the modiste.

When they were alone, the girl tried again. "Dear Aunt, you know it isn't Lord Robert's fault the package was misdirected. It hardly seems fair to blame him—to cut him—because of an innocent mistake."

"Innocent?" Lilith echoed coldly. "Innocence does not purchase such immodest costumes for—for such persons. Innocence is not acquainted with such persons. And so you shall not be."

"Well, what on earth else is a gentleman to do? He must get his pleasure somewhere. That's how men are. I think it's far more sensible to keep a mistress than to take his chances in the streets and alleys."

"Gracious heavens, child, I cannot believe what I am hearing. Where on earth did you learn of these—these matters?"

"From Rodger." Cecily shrugged. "Though living in the country in a horse-breeding family isn't likely to keep me in ignorance, is it? Though I've never understood why I should be. How is a girl to protect herself when she doesn't know what to protect herself from?"

"She leaves her protection to her elders," her aunt said in awful tones. "Which is precisely the case at present. You will have nothing further to do with that man."

Further argument, as Cecily later informed her maid, was obviously futile.

"Still, I tried," she said with a sigh. "But I'm afraid Aunt Lilith is a bit irrational on the subject. It isn't logical at all. I'm sure half the gentlemen I know do far worse than Lord Robert does. Why, he's been with the same woman two whole years, Anne says. Other men are not so faithful to their wives."

"Mebbe when you've been a wife, you'll think different, miss."

"But I'm not a wife now, am I? At any rate, I certainly can't cut him without explanation. That would be monstrous rude, as well as unfair."

Accordingly, Cecily found her writing materials and immediately composed a note to the ill-used young man. When she attempted to hand the note to her maid, Susan demurred.

"Your aunt won't like it," the abigail said.

"Then obviously she'd better not know about it, had she?"

"But Miss Cecily—"

"Don't be tiresome, Susan. You know perfectly well how to get this note to him. You and Hobbs have passed along other pieces of news easily enough to his cousin."

The maid's mouth dropped open.

"I suppose you mean to marry one day, and wish to set something aside. I know Papa does not pay you very generously, so really, I can't blame you, can I?"

The maid stammered and protested, but her mistress only looking reproachful, Susan ended by muttering that Miss Cecily had always been a deal too *quick*.

"Well, I shall not pry into your private affairs," Cecily said magnanimously. "Everyone says Lord Brandon is irresistible, and of course he is dark and devilish-looking, so I collect you couldn't help yourself. Still, if you're not very discreet, my aunt will find out what you've been about, and

I daresay she won't be best pleased."

She thrust the note into her mortified abigail's hand. "So you'd better be discreet, hadn't you?"

The note reached Lord Robert some hours later, when he and his cousin had returned to dress for the evening. Dressing being a wearying business, they had elected to fortify themselves first in the library with a glass of Madeira.

The note was presented on a silver salver.

Lord Robert took it, stared at it a moment, then opened it.

The butler glanced enquiringly at Lord Brandon, who shook his head and gestured the servant away.

Betraying not a smidgeon of interest, the marquess poured the wine and handed a glass to his cousin. The young man absently took it while he perused the note a second time. Finally he looked up.

"I have been cut off," Robert said in disbelief. "I am banned, banished, and outlawed." He handed the sheet of paper to his cousin. "Did you ever hear the like?"

The older man quickly skimmed the round schoolgirl script. "I have never *seen* the like," he answered. "She has not mis-spelt a single word. Moreover, she states the case so plainly and simply, it might be a receipt for a poultice. Most extraordinary."

"I told you she was level-headed. I only wish her aunt were. You'd think I'd tried to ravish the girl."

"You did not order up lingerie for Elise?"

"How should I know? We're always at the dressmaker's or the milliner's or somebody's. That is to say, of course I must have—but what's that to do with anything?"

Lord Brandon dropped gracefully into a chair. "It has everything to do with everything, Robin. Miss Glenwood is fresh from the schoolroom. She is not supposed to know of mistresses and their intimate attire. Now the girl is no longer ignorant, and, unluckily for you, Mrs. Davenant knows precisely where to pin the blame. This is what comes of excessive letter-writing."

"It's completely irrational. I'm banned because some fool servant delivered the wrong package to the wrong house. Banned—and I'm not even *courting* her niece, drat it. Does she mean to investigate the private affairs of every fellow who talks to the girl? Ventcoeur isn't banned, and he spends half his nights in the Covent Garden alleys. Even that loose fish, Beldon, who has the bailiff camped on his doorstep—"

"Their indiscretions have not been waved under Mrs. Davenant's nose as yours has been by this unfortunate accident. An accident of fate, Robin. Drink your wine and put the matter from your mind. We shall dine with Scrope Davies tonight and bury our disappointments in wine and laughter. He is a very amusing fellow, an intimate of Byron's. Perhaps the poet will join us. I understand he's decided not to accompany Hobhouse to Paris after all."

"He's a moody, pretentious bore," was the sulky answer.

"I admit he has not Miss Glenwood's immense blue eyes and guinea-gold curls, and being some years older and lame as well, he cannot be as lively—"

"It's nothing to do with her looks, Julian. It's the—the principle of the thing, dash it! Here I've been dutifully going about in company to pacify the family. I meet one girl who doesn't bore me out of my wits. At last there's someone sensible to talk to, so the evening isn't an endless punishment—and now I'm not to talk to her, not to go near her. I feel like a damned leper. Confound her aunt. Mrs. Drummond-Burrell isn't half such a prude."

Robert stomped to the tray and refilled his glass. "It's all the more astonishing to me now how you ever got such a stiff-necked prig to even speak to you—let alone dance with you."

"Perhaps I took advantage of a fit of temporary insanity," said the marquess. He rose. "I believe I shall dress now. You, of course, may amuse yourself as you wish. Freers will bring you another bottle when you have done soaking up that one. I expect he'll also provide a litter to carry you to bed when you have completed your liquid meditations."

Lord Robert had not meant to drink himself unconscious. Still, he was exceedingly put out, and in the course of execrating Mrs. Davenant at length, grew thirsty. Since he continued grumbling to himself for hours, he had frequent need to soothe his parched throat, with the result his cousin had predicted.

The young man awoke very late the following day and, suffering the usual consequences, was more out of sorts than ever. He spent that night in a fit of the sullens with his mistress.

Elise's forbearance only compounded Lord Robert's unhappy state, for she added a generous dollop of guilt to the already indigestible compound of indignation and frustration. Consequently, Robert spent the greater part of the following week in his cousin's company.

The constant companionship of a young man behaving like a petulant little boy must eventually irritate even the most serene of natures. Otherwise, Lord Brandon would have been his normal unruffled self. Certainly he could not be chafing yet over the mere pin-prick of one lady's displeasure.

Lord Brandon had known he'd be unwise to seek the widow out immediately. He'd told himself she wanted time. She was not a stupid woman. Given time to reflect, she must surely come to see the injustice of her accusations. Being the soul of rectitude, she must therefore repent of them.

He was confident of this. The waiting was tiresome only because Robert was tiresome. This, clearly, was the sole reason Lord Brandon rounded upon his cousin on the seventh night of Lord Robert's banishment, as they were leaving Watier's.

"What the devil is the matter with you?" the marquess snapped as they reached the street. "You've been growling and sulking without cease for a week. I do wish you'd entertain your mistress with your megrims. She's paid to endure you. I merely have the misfortune to be related to you."

"Why should I talk when there's nothing to say? Everyone says the same things and makes the same jokes over and over. Why can't a man hold his tongue if he wants? He might as well, when he's a damned *leper*. An outcast. A—a—"

"A bloody bore is more like it. I see we are about to play once again the monotonous tune of your persecution."

"She danced twice tonight with Ventcoeur," muttered his unheeding cousin. "And twice with Maddock. And once with that lout, Beldon. And once with Melbrook. And she went in to supper with—"

"You've already been through the catalogue with me three times this night. Confound you, Robert. You might try to understand the aunt's position."

"She's a stiff-necked old cow. Aargh."

This last remark was occasioned by Lord Brandon's taking his cousin roughly by the neck-cloth and lifting him several inches off the ground.

As he put the young man down again and released the mangled cravat, the marquess said in low, dangerous tones, "Mind your manners, boy."

He was answered by a series of croaks as Lord Robert strove to recover from near strangulation. When he'd regained his wind, he apologised.

"That sounds more like reason," said Lord Brandon. "A reasonable man would understand that Mrs. Davenant was obliged to take the steps she did. A reasonable man would also clearly perceive her to be neither ancient nor in any way bovine. That her posture is stiff may be blamed upon the board strapped to her spine at a tender age. Your mama was once so accoutred. Ask her if you don't believe me."

Subdued, Robert withheld further comments until they were at the marquess's town house.

Never one to hold a grudge, Lord Brandon invited his cousin into the library for a brandy.

"I suppose," said Robert after sipping quietly for a time, "I have been rather disagreeable."

"I will not debate that."

"Still, you must admit the situation is provoking, fair or not."

"The situation is provoking," said Lord Brandon, gazing at the amber liquid in his glass, "though probably fair enough."

"Gad, I wish I had your cleverness. If it were you in my place, you'd have her talked round in no time."

"Would I? I wonder."

"What would you do in my place, Julian?"

"Whatever it is, I suppose I had better do it," came the bored reply. "Since you are not philosophical by nature, you'll go on worrying the thing forever. Even as a child, a word of denial would send you into fits for hours. Now you are a man, you have graduated to weeks."

"You mean you'll talk to her aunt?" Robert eagerly asked, disregarding the aspersions on his maturity.

"I shall try. But be warned, my impetuous cousin. I am not at present in Mrs. Davenant's good graces myself. My interference may do you more ill than good."

# === 10 ===

THOUGH IT WAS a nearly two-hour journey to Redley Park, no one who received an invitation thought of declining. The elderly Earl of Redley and his young countess were reclusive, rarely seen in Town. Once a year, however, they invited half the Beau Monde to a lavish entertainment on their sprawling estate.

There, champagne flowed like a mighty river, delicacies of every kind beckoned from the great table under its ornate canopy, while jugglers, magicians, and fortune-tellers practised their amusing arts. The atmosphere was that of a street fair, but untainted by the vulgar rabble that usually mobbed such events. For those of higher sensibilities, a string quartet performed in a shady arbor of the vast garden. Perhaps most delightful of all, the half who had been invited enjoyed the sweet prospect of lording it over the half who were not.

The house itself was a small, rather shabby relic of Tudor times, to which little except basic maintenance had been done in centuries. The Earls of Redley preferred to devote their energies and incomes to improving upon Nature.

For the previous earl, Lancelot "Capability" Brown had built gently rolling slopes where before had lain a generally flat expanse of meadow and woodland. A lake, replete with swans, now glistened where once had been a narrow stream and minuscule duck pond. Even the village had been relocated another mile distant, because the present Lord Redley's mama had complained of its cluttering the landscape.

Redley Park, in short, was a kingdom unto itself. It was also an excellent place in which to become lost, as amorous couples knew. Twisted, mazelike paths and shady, private nooks abounded, and so long as the heavens did not loose a downpour, one could always declare an urgent need to find shelter from the sun's fierce rays.

Following a luncheon best described as wretched excess, one after another lady made such complaints of the heat and glaring sun to Lord Brandon. He sympathised, he spoke charmingly, and then—to the bafflement of each lady in turn—he vanished.

It happened that, just as he eluded these others, one lady eluded him. Certainly, he always knew where to find her. The trouble was, she had constantly someone clinging to her like a leech—her companion, her fiancé, her future sister-in-law—and she and the leech of the moment would be found amid a group. One bodyguard Lord Brandon might detach her from; a host of them was too much even for his ingenuity.

He waited with mounting impatience until his opportunity arrived at last. His gaze lit upon Miss Glenwood just as she was slipping away from a crowd of young people watching a juggler. He glanced at Mrs. Davenant. She, excellent chaperon she was, had her eye upon her niece.

Lord Brandon promptly made for the niece.

He'd scarcely uttered two sentences before the aunt was upon them.

"Ah, Mrs. Davenant," he said. "I was about to recommend Miss Glenwood not allow herself to become separated from her friends. Redley Park is a veritable maze of paths and byways, and on her own, she might be lost for weeks."

"I know," said Miss Glenwood. "That's why I was looking for Anne. I can't think where she's got to."

Though she appeared not at all flustered, Lord Brandon was certain the girl was lying. The particular lie, however, was a gift from Heaven. He decided he approved of Miss Glenwood.

"Your aunt and I shall find her, Miss Glenwood, never fear," said he. "You may watch the juggler with an easy mind."

The girl left, and he turned to Mrs. Davenant.

"Perhaps I was presumptuous," he said. "Perhaps you would prefer I sought Miss Cleveson on my own?"

"Thank you, my lord, but I'm sure Sir Thomas will be happy to assist me," she said stiffly.

"He is well-acquainted with Redley Park, I take it? If not, I must accompany you both, or we shall have three lost sheep instead of one."

He saw her glance towards Bexley. The baronet, true to form, had promptly got himself entangled with Clancarty.

She turned back to Lord Brandon, her cheeks tinged a faint pink. "He has never visited here before today, my lord, and—"

"And at present he is occupied with more momentous matters."

They soon spied Anne Cleveson, for she had hauled her brother only far enough from the others to quarrel without being overheard. From what Lilith caught of the debate— she and Brandon were several yards from the two—Freddie had hurt Lady Shumway's granddaughter's feelings, and Anne, in her own way, had decided to call him out.

"Shall we leave them to their squabble, Mrs. Davenant?" said the marquess, moving towards an alternate path. "Miss Cleveson has the right of it, and he wants his ears blistered, I think."

Lilith was surprised, though perhaps she shouldn't be. The marquess was not, she knew to her shame, entirely without compassion.

"Indeed he does," she said. "Miss Twillworthy can't help her spots—not when her foolish grandmother overindulges her in sweets and keeps her trapped in that oppressive, musty house all the day. The girl scarcely ever goes out, but at night, like a little mole."

While she spoke, Lilith debated what to do. To go with him was asking for trouble. On the other hand, she had something to say that could not be said before others. The matter on her conscience proving powerful enough to squeeze out other anxieties, she walked on with him.

She had kept clear of Lord Brandon all the past week. Now they were alone, she knew she could no longer—and should not—shrink from the apology she owed him. Had he appeared as coldly hostile as he had that morning in the park, her task would have been easier. She might simply make her speech and, her duty done, exit quickly.

His amiability made her far more uncomfortable. Either he was a remarkably forbearing man or too careless and unfeeling to be affected by—to even recollect—the harsh, unjust accusations she'd flung at him.

It didn't matter what he was, she chided herself. She had made a grievous error and must apologise. She swallowed, lifted her chin, and spoke.

"My lord, a few minutes ago you referred to—to ears being blistered. I believe—I know—that is—some days ago, we had words."

He stopped and looked at her. "We did. Mrs. Davenant, I do humbly beg your pardon for that. I was a beast. I was just this moment trying to compose my apology. Yet what expressions of regret could excuse me? I am still appalled by my behaviour. I never knew I had a temper, but I must have, because I lost it. And for what? Because you spoke some unpleasant truths."

"Unpleasant, yes, but the truth—"

"Oh, it was that."

"It was not," she blurted out guiltily. "It was not the truth you hastened my husband's death. He did that himself. It was not the truth you destroyed my marriage. It was wreck from the start. There was no repairing it, no matter how I—"

She hesitated, but that was foolish, when he knew already. His words the other day—as though he had known

114

her intimately all those years ago, or had somehow looked into her heart. A generous heart, he had said. He must be generous, certainly, to forgive her and regret his own remarks.

"No matter how I tried," she said softly. Though tears pricked her eyes, there was relief, she found, in saying it aloud, finally, after all these years, and so she went on. "If I had been older and wiser, perhaps I would have seen the futility." Willing back the tears, she mustered up a smile. "Or perhaps not. I am supposedly older and wiser now, yet I needed you to point out my mistake."

"You are far more generous than I deserve. No more on this topic, I beg, or I shall commence sobbing uncontrollably."

A small titter escaped her, and she had to admire how deftly he'd drawn her back from perilous emotional waters.

He threw her an admiring glance. "What a remarkable girl you are," he said.

"Hardly a girl," she answered as she resumed walking.

"You are eight and twenty. I am seven years your senior. What do your calculations make me, I wonder? Shall I order a Bath chair at once?"

Her smile broadened at the image. "Now, there's an intriguing picture. My Lord Brandon—a pair of spectacles upon his nose, a horn at his ear, shawls wound round him—being trundled about in a Bath chair."

"A fitting end. I know that's what you're thinking. You can't deny it."

"I should not presume to say what would be fitting in your case. Recollect I have but recently been tumbled from my throne of judgement."

"Then you must be in need of support."

He offered his arm and she, reluctant to spoil their truce, took it.

"If you continue in a penitential frame of mind," he said, "I had better hasten to take advantage. I have a case to plead with you. Not my own," he added before her newfound ease in his company could dwindle. "You may assume your wig once more, My Lady Judge. Take out your black cap if you will—though I hope you will not have occasion to don it."

"A cardinal offence, is it? Not murder, I hope."

"Not precisely, though a life is at stake, in a manner of speaking. A man's life or—in the interests of accuracy—a fool's. My cousin, Robin."

His handsome face was serious now, or appeared so. Lilith thought she had better not study it too closely.

"I do not see how any judgement of mine could in any way affect Lord Robert's life," she said carefully. "If you refer, as I assume you do, to this business with Cecily—"

"I do, and I beg you to reconsider. I do not believe you acted wrongly. I have told him so myself, repeatedly, but he refuses to listen. In consequence, I've had to endure a week of his incessant complaints and gripes and sulks and sullens. If you will not take pity on him, I wish you would take pity on me. Another day of it and I shall shoot him."

His face was still grave, but his aggrieved tones made her grin. "I am to be responsible for your cousin's murder and your own hanging, my lord? Is that not excessive?"

"You would not say so if he were moping and grumbling the livelong day in *your* house, or if you had the hauling of his morose carcass about."

"You cannot be hinting he is serious about Cecily. He cannot have serious intentions towards two women simultaneously. I need not, I hope, remind you of the moral character of one of these women."

"Miss Glenwood is the only human being who has managed to draw Robert from the *demimonde*. I cannot say what his feelings are. I know only that since he met her, he has neglected his mistress. He has taken up quarters in my house—he who would scarcely leave his paramour's side for an hour, is gone from her days at a time."

"Yet he continues to send her gifts."

"When passion dwindles, one often finds presents easier to give than time and attention. In any event, the less time he devotes to his mistress and the more among his social equals, the better his chances of finding a more suitable object—in the family's eyes, at least."

"I do not prevent his enjoying good society," she said.

"Miss Glenwood's is the only society that interests him at present. Banished from her, he is bored and fretful. Worse, with each passing day, the risk increases he'll return to his mistress." He paused briefly, as though to allow the implications to sink in. "I'm convinced Robert means your niece no harm. Still, I shall promise to keep a close watch on him, if you will be so compassionate as to end his exile."

She did not answer immediately, though she knew what her reply must be. She who had accused Brandon of leading her husband astray could not refuse to help lead another man aright.

"You are an eloquent solicitor, my lord," she said at last. "I seem to be hoist by my own petard."

"Not at all. I counted on your generous heart." His gaze was warm.

Lilith looked away. "The heart that concerns me is Cecily's. If I discern any signs of infatuation—unreturned, that is—"

"Then I shall knock the lad unconscious and drop him onto the first vessel bound for New South Wales."

"I do not demand so extreme a remedy. Paris will do," she said magnanimously. "Or Rome. With the end of hostilities, I expect half the Beau Monde will be flocking abroad."

"With the hostilities ended, the Continent is not so interesting to me," he said, a shade of meaning in his voice. Then, more briskly, he went on, "At any rate, Redley and his ancestors have transported half the Continent here. What works of art they could not buy or steal outright, I understand, they copied. There was once and I expect may still be an excellent reproduction of Bernini's 'Apollo and Daphne' round the next turning. Will you permit me to expound upon its aesthetic qualities?"

The path, shaded by enormous rhododendrons, opened

into a large clearing, in the centre of which the statue stood. The shrubbery all around was tall and dense. A narrow opening through the leaves indicated yet another path, leading heaven knew where. The foliage was too thick to permit more than a glimpse of the way beyond. The place was quiet, except for the occasional ruffling of leaves in the light breeze.

"I was mistaken," said Lord Brandon as they approached the sculpture. "This, as I recall, is the work of Lord Redley's artistic great-grandfather. He called it 'The Abduction of Helen.' The pose obviously owes something to Bernini's "Pluto and Persephone"—though I never considered the two ladies' cases quite the same. I prefer to believe Helen went with Paris of her own free will."

He had already treated Lilith to several amusing theories regarding the expected Bernini. He was surprisingly well-read. Lilith wondered wryly when he'd found time for books. She had known he could be charming, but she'd expected a more shallow, social charm. She had not expected to find his conversation quite so . . . stimulating.

She smiled up at his sun-dappled face. "You think Helen willingly abandoned the throne of Sparta? Were Greek women so impractical, then?"

"I have decided she was very young, in an alien land, the husband chosen for her an old, insensitive lout. Paris appeared, and the two young beauties were instantly smitten. They tried to be discreet, but their affair was betrayed to Menelaus. Helen fled with her lover to escape a horrible death."

Lilith laughed. "Leave it to you to devise extenuating circumstances."

"I can't help it. I am a hopeless romantic." There was a pause—two heartbeats, maybe more.

Then, in lower tones, he went on. "I can guess, at least, what the Trojan must have felt when he met Sparta's queen. In my vision she is tall, proud, and spirited, with eyes like Poseidon's storms and hair tinged with Hephaistos' fire."

Lilith's smile faded, along with her quiet pleasure in his company.

He was no longer looking at the statue, she knew, though she dared not meet his gaze. She must not listen, she told herself. He was too perceptive, too clever, and honeyed speeches came too easily to him. With forced calm, she disengaged her arm from his and walked to the entwined marble figures.

"Have you seen the Bernini?" she asked, keeping her voice light. "Is this very like, do you think?"

"I'm afraid at the moment I can't think." He moved up behind her. "I should not have brought you here. I should never be alone with you. Every good resolution I've made is smashed to pieces."

His breath was warm on her neck.

"My lord—"

"Lilith." It was a whisper, and his lips touched her neck, light as a whisper, yet the touch seared her.

He is the Devil, she told herself. It is all practised wickedness. But his lips had touched her neck again, and the hand gently clasping her arm burned too. A dangerous yearning incandesced within her. He turned her unresisting, betraying body towards him.

"I meant to be good," he said softly, sadly, it seemed, as his face lowered to hers. "I cannot."

"No—"

His mouth silenced her and her lips answered his kiss, just as her body answered the light pressure of his hands urging her closer. Light, yes, and gentle, yes, but she was helpless against the current drawing her to him. There was too much tenderness in its beckoning. She, who had never known tenderness of any kind, who had never heard sweet words of longing, could not resist what he offered, but hungered only for more.

She knew nothing of moments passing, nothing of the world about her. There was one world only, in his arms, a world that smouldered, then glowed, then crackled into flame against a growing darkness. There she was lost, utterly.

Lord Robert, emerging from the other path, immediately turned and pushed Cecily back.

"That wasn't at all necessary," she reproached when they were out of range. "You can't think I would burst upon my aunt without warning. I hope I'm not such a clodpole."

"Your eyes are a deal too sharp, Miss Glenwood," he complained. "We'd better go back—or I shall be in your aunt's black books *forever*."

"We can't leave them like this."

"We most certainly can. They're adults. It's none of our business."

"What if someone else comes? My aunt will be ruined."

Lord Robert forbore rejoining that Mrs. Davenant was as good as ruined already, if that passionate embrace was any indication. "I am not going to stand guard until they're done," he said. Then, as he recollected what getting done would inevitably entail, he added primly, "And you certainly will not."

"Don't be silly. We must simply give them a moment to recover themselves. Lord Robert," she said, so loudly that he winced, "you must go away. You should not have followed me. My aunt will be most displeased."

"Miss Glenwood—"

"Louder," she whispered. "Don't be such a slow-top. Argue with me—or plead—or something—but so they can hear you."

The feminine voice pierced Lord Brandon's consciousness like a gunshot, though it took another moment for the message to be relayed elsewhere. Then, cursing inwardly, he reluctantly raised his lips from the widow's right earlobe. Her eyes fluttered open.

"Someone is coming," he said, his voice thick.

Instantly, Lilith jerked away from him, leaving chill

emptiness where her warm, supple body had just been. Forgetting other voices, he reached out instinctively to draw her back, but she had moved apart. With trembling hands, she was trying to smooth her frock and her hair simultaneously.

He heard Robert then, complaining loudly. Lord Brandon bestowed another silent though heartfelt malediction upon his cousin. "I shall *kill* him," he muttered. "Was ever a man so cursed in his relations?"

He looked to her again, and felt a stab within. She was still flushed and utterly discomposed. Unlike many of her noble sisters, she was unaccustomed to coolly erasing evidence of an indiscretion. Her eyes appealed to him for help.

He moved to her, quickly smoothed a few curls from her face, and twitched the waist of her dowdy grey frock aright.

"It's only the children," he said. "Appear enraptured with the sculpture."

The children came into view minutes later, stopped abruptly as they caught sight of their elders, and showed every evidence of surprise and confusion.

Cecily hastened to her aunt. "Please do not be angry, Aunt. We came upon each other quite by accident. I was just telling Lord Robert that I am not to speak to him, because I might say that at least, mightn't I?"

"Mrs. Davenant, I do apologise," said Lord Robert. "It's all my fault—"

"Certainly," Lord Brandon interjected. "It is always your fault. Here I have been trying to explain the misunderstanding, and this lady has not only kindly heard me out, but graciously allowed you a second chance. Now you blunder in like the confounded, clumsy idiot I have just been telling her you are not," he finished with some heat.

The widow found her voice, though he detected a slight quaver as she spoke.

"We shall not compound one misunderstanding with another. Naturally, your meeting with Cecily was an accident." Her gaze fell upon Cecily. "I know my niece would never deliberately disobey me. Therefore I cannot entertain for a moment the notion she arranged, behind my back, to meet with you."

"Oh, never," said Lord Robert chivalrously.

He reddened, though, and the marquess had no doubt why.

"Lord Brandon tells me you are the . . . the victim of a hoax," the widow went on.

Brandon gazed at her in surprise. That was inventive of her. A hoax would serve admirably.

"Did he? Yes, well, I am—was—that is to say—"

"Then we shall consider the matter closed, Lord Robert. Though I should advise you in future to choose friends with less distasteful notions of humour. I will not have my niece suffer further shocks to her sensibilities."

"No ma'am. You're quite right. Thank you, ma'am. You're exceedingly kind. Really, I—"

"As to you, Cecily," Mrs. Davenant said, disregarding Lord Robert's protestations, "I thought you had already been advised against wandering off by yourself."

As she spoke, she put her arm protectively about her niece's shoulders and took the girl away, so that Lord Brandon heard nothing of the ensuing lecture.

He heard as little of his cousin's expressions of gratitude and wonder, although Robert walked beside him. They had taken the other path. While it was a more circuitous route to the party proper, Lord Brandon was in no hurry to be back. His rage with his cousin had subsided, yet the marquess was not quite as easy within as he appeared without.

He was still irritated, which was foolish, when naturally matters could not have proceeded to any satisfactory conclusion. He'd no intention of ravishing Lilith Davenant in broad day in somebody's garden. The problem was, he'd no intention of allowing matters to go even as far as they had done.

He knew by now that her conjugal experiences with Charles had not been happy ones. That was why she was so skittish. Accordingly, Brandon had taken care not to lead her too far too soon.

The trouble was, he'd found himself drawn too far, from pleasure . . . to hunger, and long after she'd broken from him, the feeling remained, like an ache. It lingered yet, not so strong as at first, but uncomfortable nonetheless. It should not have existed at all. Lovemaking was an art, not the mere release of some base animal need.

Impatience, he reassured himself. He'd never had to woo so long or face so many obstacles. What aroused him was the difficulty and challenge of this pursuit. The seduction of Lilith Davenant was proving a more exhilarating and novel experience than he could have predicted. Since it *was* novel, one must expect the occasional aberration.

These reflections eased his mind considerably, and he began at last to respond to his chattering cousin. Occupied in devising ironic sallies to Lord Robert's effusions, the marquess neglected to explain satisfactorily to himself the other, altogether different twinge he experienced from time to time, at the recollection of one pleading pair of smoky blue eyes.

# === 11 ===

MEMBERS OF THE company who'd noticed Lilith's departure with Lord Brandon held their collective breath while counting the minutes until her return. They would have all been asphyxiated if Lady Fevis hadn't decided to have her fortune told.

The Future was no sooner revealed than the heretofore sweet and gentle Lady Fevis burst from the gypsy's tent, flew at her husband, and began thumping his head with her parasol. When the weapon was wrenched away by her mama, and her husband dragged away to safety, the enraged wife fell back momentarily. She collected herself, then made another mad rush—this time at Lady Violet Porter, whose hazel eyes Lady Fevis showed every inclination to tear from their sockets.

Mr. Porter tried to pull Lady Fevis away from his wife. Lady Fevis's brother, Mr. Reginald Ventcoeur, ordered him to remove his filthy hands. Mr. Porter made an uncomplimentary observation. Mr. Ventcoeur rushed forward, spun Mr. Porter round, and knocked him down. Mr. Porter jumped up and rushed at Mr. Ventcoeur and brought *him* down. The two young men commenced to savagely pummelling each other.

Lady Violet screamed. Lady Fevis fainted. Friends rushed forward to help. Two gentlemen, trying to separate the foes, knocked their own heads together. Instantly, they gave up pacifism and began flailing at each other. One of Mr. Ventcoeur's friends was heard to make a remark regarding "horns."

Two of Mr. Porter's friends immediately fell upon him.

In short order, thanks to the enlivening effects of large quantities of champagne, nearly all the younger gentlemen had thrown themselves into the battle. Of their elders, the greater part busily made wagers, while an unheeded minority called for order.

It was during the melee that Cecily slipped off to her forbidden rendezvous with Lord Robert. He, having retired to a distance to await her, was unaware of the excitement until it was well over.

In fact, the battle itself lasted scarcely five minutes. The confusion it engendered, however, continued long after. Though the ladies of the company had been led away to safety, a score felt duty bound to fall into swoons or strong hysterics. Between tending to these and the male wounded, considerable time and effort was expended in restoring tranquillity to Redley Park.

Thus, except for those directly concerned, not one person of the several hundred realised Mrs. Davenant had been gone with Lord Brandon nearly an hour. She rejoined her battle-weary fellows to find her reputation safe. Of her virtue, Lilith was not so certain.

The first time Lord Brandon had kissed her, at Cecily's comeout, he'd taken Lilith by surprise. Though this scarcely made it right, it was an excuse of sorts. Unfortunately, such a frail excuse works but once. What she'd done this time didn't bear thinking of.

Had her schooling in deportment been less mercilessly thorough, Lilith could never have faced her fiancé. As it was, the strain soon told in the usual way, with a headache. Fortunately, she never needed to plead illness. Thomas was eager to be gone from a party that had turned into a thoroughly barbaric spectacle.

Though Lilith said little during the ride home, her silence went unremarked. Cecily was too busy trying to extricate details about the contretemps from a tight-lipped Sir Thomas. He refused to discuss the cause, except to speak vaguely of silly misunderstandings and a lot of ill-mannered youths drinking more than was good for them.

On the subject of manners, he grew more talkative. Striking one another with fists and rolling upon the ground like a lot of Cockney ruffians was not Sir Thomas's idea of gentlemanly behaviour.

One of the combatants had been thrown against a servant who carried a tray of champagne glasses. The tray, sent spinning into the air, had struck the back of Sir Thomas's head. He was lucky, he told the ladies, not to have been cut to shreds by broken glass. It was the sort of episode one might expect in a gin shop—not at a great society affair.

"Young men nowadays," he intoned, "have no notion of self-restraint. I can only blame this obnoxious fad for boxing. In my day, the gentry set the example. They did not imitate their inferiors. But what can one expect of fellows who consider it the height of fashion to adopt the costume and manners—or lack thereof—of common coachmen?"

"Well, I'm sure it was very disagreeable for you," said Cecily. "All the same, I do think fists preferable to pistols and swords. I'm glad duelling is illegal. It may be more elegant, but it's also far more deadly. I do wish I knew what had started it," she added with a sigh. "I should like to have something exciting to write Rodger."


Lilith was not altogether surprised to see Lord Brandon at Almack's the following night, though the assembly hall's staid exclusivity, unappetizing refreshments, and inept orchestra could scarcely appeal to a man of his cosmopolitan tastes. He *would* come, of course, because he was the last person on earth she wished to see. She had but to glimpse his gleaming black hair and broad shoulders, and every mortifying detail of the previous afternoon came back to flog her conscience.

When he approached, her heart raced. But the marquess stopped only long enough to exchange a few civilities with her and Thomas.

Brandon danced with several ladies, including two of the patronesses and, to Lilith's astonishment, Lady Enders, who blushed and giggled throughout. He also danced twice with a very pale Lady Fevis. The second was a waltz, during which the lady's colour and spirits revived remarkably. Lord Fevis's colour was observed to heighten about the same time. When the next set commenced, he gratified the company by stalking up to his wife to announce it was time to go *home*.

Eventually, Lilith realised she was studying Lord Brandon's movements more intently than was seemly. Her gaze went immediately in search of her niece.

Lilith's eye lit upon Cecily just as Lord Robert was taking the girl's hand. The widow did a rapid calculation and began to move even more rapidly across the hall. Before she could reach them, she saw Lord Brandon approach, say something to Robert, then lead Cecily out.

The marquess brought Cecily back to her aunt at the dance's end.

"You needn't scold her," he said. "I've just rung a peal over them both. Robert apparently experiences difficulties with higher mathematics."

"I'm so sorry, Aunt," said Cecily. "I had my mind on something Anne said and forgot completely I wasn't to dance with any gentleman more than twice."

"There are some matters one has not the luxury of forgetting," Lilith said repressively. "In future, Cecily— "

She was interrupted by the arrival of Mr. Ventcoeur, who, sporting a swollen upper lip and bruised jaw, had come to claim his dance.

When the younger man had swept Cecily to safety, Lord Brandon turned to Lilith. "Will you do me the honour, Mrs. Davenant?"

"No, thank you." She managed a polite smile for the benefit of any interested onlookers.

"I knew you would refuse. I kept away so I would not be tempted to ask. It's no good, you know. There's no substitute for dancing with you—a matter *I* have not the luxury of forgetting." He turned his gaze to the dancers.

Though she wished he would go away, Lilith was obliged to acknowledge the service he'd performed.

"Thank you for rescuing Cecily from her mistake," she said, her eyes, too, upon the dance floor.

"I promised to keep watch on Robert. At any rate, it was the least I could do. Miss Glenwood's timely appearance stopped me in the midst of a greater error yesterday. I should have had more care for your reputation, regardless the heat of the moment," he added gently. "I was abominably selfish and thoughtless."

Her chin went up. "My reputation is not in your keeping, my lord," she answered. "You will please refrain from making me out to be a helpless victim of your irresistible charm. I resent your implying I do not know right from wrong. I am not a backward child." With another polite smile, she left him.

The next morning, Lilith chaperoned Lord Robert and Cecily on yet another attempt to break their own and the horses' necks simultaneously.

The black stallion and its master arrived moments after the young pair had dashed across the meadow.

"Is this not devotion?" his lordship asked. "To arise at such an hour, merely to speak with you?"

"I wish," she said tautly, "Lord Robert did not make a habit of revealing his plans to everybody."

"He had no need to tell me. I had but to observe his retiring betimes and hear him at daybreak clomping down the stairs. Not that I wouldn't have stretched him on a rack for the information, had that been necessary. You cannot tease me with provocative statements, madam, and expect to be left in peace."

She stared blindly ahead, trying to recall exactly what she'd said the night before, when the marquess had so infuriated her.

"You set me down for taking the blame all to myself for our . . . indiscretion," he reminded. "Now I'm on pins and needles to know whether or not you've concluded it was entirely your fault. Was it you led *me* astray, Mrs. Davenant?"

Her face grew warm. "You know that is not what I meant."

"What did you mean, then?"

"I wish you would not affect stupidity. It is another insult to my intelligence."

"I want to know exactly what you meant," he said stubbornly. "Your remarks might be construed in several ways. Shall I conclude you came with me knowingly and willingly? I should very much like to believe that."

"Though I'm engaged to be married, my lord? I know you have little regard for such commonplaces as vows—but have you so much contempt for me as to believe I deliberately—Why do I ask?" Lilith said bitterly. "I've earned your contempt. You were selfish and thoughtless, you said. Does that excuse *me*?" she asked, pressing her hand to her thumping heart. "I'm no cypher. I have a mind—and a will—and morals—or so I thought. But now I scarce know what to think myself."

He dismounted, threw the reins over a bush, and approached her. "Come down," he said, holding up his hands.

"No."

"Don't make me pull you from the saddle, Lilith."

His hands grasped her waist, and she, seeing no alternative, cooperated. She caught her breath as her body brushed his in the process, but in an instant she was on solid ground and he'd let go of her waist to take her hand instead. Even through the leather glove, she felt pulse beating against pulse.

"More than once," he said, "you've spoken of my contempt for you. As if that weren't bad enough, you persist in claiming you've earned it. Because of a few kisses, a few caresses? Be sensible, Lilith. If my disdain is so easily earned, what must I think"—he paused and smiled—"well, of the other women, you know."

She would not be weakened by that slow, affectionate smile. "I've never believed you could have a high opinion of women," she said. "If you had, you wouldn't make a habit of using and discarding them."

"Such habits reflect the frailty of my own character. Therefore, I should be the object of contempt."

"It's always the women despised in these cases for their weakness."

"That's what Society says, and Society is composed merely of human beings, as fallible as ourselves."

"It's hardly necessary for Society to point out my error. No one need remind me I've been false to my betrothed—twice—or that I ought—" She stopped herself.

Too late.

"I see," he said. "You're in torments because conscience tells you to break off your engagement, while self-preservation warns you'd better not."

"I have no intention of sacrificing my entire future because of a few foolish moments," she answered frigidly, drawing her hand away. That sounded mercenary, she knew. Very well, then. Let him think her so. She had rather that than his pity.

He was silent a moment, studying her flushed face.

"Odd," he said. "I persist in seeing your betrothal as the sacrifice. Why did you accept him, Lilith?"

"I know you have a low opinion of Thomas. Try to understand that others may not share it."

"I'm trying to understand *you*," he answered gently. "Your conscience demands you pay a debt you don't owe me. The same conscience insists you marry a man you believe you've played false. The one I may ascribe to pride. The other? The better I know you, the more difficult it is to explain satisfactorily."

She turned a bit away from him. "You don't know me."

"Not well, perhaps. I know what all the world does—that you're a model of breeding and deportment. But I know also that you're astonishingly well-informed. Also, you have an eye for the ridiculous and thus a proper appreciation of my wit." He paused, then added more somberly, "And I know you're in pain. I can't be the cause of all your trouble. You were suffering before you met me."

He touched her shoulder lightly, to turn her back to him again. "You don't want me for a lover . . . and I suppose I must accept that."

"Yes, I wish you would."

"May I be a friend, then?"

"A friend?" she echoed, incredulous.

"Yes. To tell your troubles to. Why should you not, when I know so many already? By now you must be aware I don't repeat all I know."

"I know you can be inscrutable when it pleases you."

"Also sympathetic. However, we must draw the line at your crying upon my shoulder or into my neck-cloth. No matter how great the emotion, there is no excuse for wrinkling fabric. Not to mention the proximity of . . . well, we won't mention it." All the same, his eye fell upon her somber riding hat.

She remembered how, a few days before, his fingers had lovingly stroked her hair. Though at the moment she wanted solace, she was wary of that species of comforting.

"I don't think we can be friends," she said. "Not, at least, the confiding sort."

He seemed to be studying her face still, though he answered lightly enough. "Very well. Let us be the gossiping sort, then. What do you make of Lady Fevis's extraordinary behaviour?"

Lady Fevis's rout was that evening.

Routs are intended to be crushes. Always there must be more people than square feet to accommodate them. This one was a suffocation.

Cecily had elected to go with Anne Cleveson and her mama to a small card party. Cecily, her aunt reflected as yet another person trod upon her toes, had better sense than to go to a gathering the sole purpose of which was to make everybody hot, tired, bruised, and—since refreshments were rarely provided—hungry and thirsty as well.

Lilith stood next her betrothed. He was reviewing with Lord Gaines the Grand Duchess's latest machinations on behalf of Princess Caroline. The two men had been talking nearly half an hour, and Thomas was just getting his steam up.

Lilith was very weary with standing in one place listening to the same opinions she'd heard two dozen times before. The air was stale and heavy with clashing perfumes. She would have liked to step away, to try to find a cooler, less crowded spot, if such was to be found. Around her on all sides was an impenetrable mass of bodies—some, she noted, in grievous want of soap and water.

She interrupted Thomas to remind him they hadn't yet greeted their hostess.

"Yes, my dear," he said. "Certainly. In a moment." Then he turned back to Lord Gaines.

Lilith gazed about her in despair. She was looking longingly down at the staircase they'd scaled with such difficulty when her gaze fell upon a head of crisply curling hair, black as midnight. Lord Brandon looked up at that moment. The boredom left his green eyes, and he smiled.

It had taken Lilith and Thomas twenty minutes to move from the first landing to the first floor. Lord Brandon covered the distance in one tenth the time. In another minute, he was at her side.

"Mrs. Davenant looks ready to faint, Bexley," said the marquess. "Shall I hew a path for her to an open window?"

"Oh, yes—That is . . . are you ill, my dear? Only too happy, of course, if my lord Gaines would—"

Lord Brandon assured the baronet there was no need to interrupt government business. "I must seek out our hostess in any case," he said. "I daresay she's chosen an airier position for herself."

The preoccupied Thomas managed a nod before plunging back into his debate.

They found Lady Fevis by a window embrasure at the far end of the corridor.

She appeared very embarrassed, and very young, as they came upon her. "I did not mean to hide from the company," she explained, "but I needed a breath of air, and this is the only place where any is to be found."

"If you will share it with Mrs. Davenant, she will be much obliged," said Lord Brandon.

"Oh, of course. I do beg your pardon, Mrs. Davenant. I know these affairs are supposed to be shocking squeezes, but this is altogether unbearable—and all because I was—"

At which point, she swooned.

Brandon caught her, lifted her easily in his arms, and carried her to the nearest room. Lilith meanwhile got the attention of a servant and, adjuring him to complete discretion—lest the entire crowd bear down upon his mistress at once—ordered water and *sal volatile*.

Lady Fevis came to before the remedies arrived, but Lilith made her sip the water and lie still while Lord Brandon went in search of her husband.

They returned a few minutes later. Lord Fevis rushed to his wife, fell to his knees before her, clasped her hands, and cried, "My poor darling! Oh, such an idiot I've been. The woman was nothing to me, I promise, nothing. Oh, but Clarissa, my dearest, why did you not tell me?"

The marquess was already escorting Lilith from the room. He closed the door upon the reunited couple.

"She ought to have told him, you know," he said as he led her back to the secluded embrasure. "A man has a right to know he's going to be a papa."

"How did *you* know?" Lilith asked, astonished. "She could not have told you such a thing when you danced with her."

"When I danced with her? When was that?"

Lilith looked up at him. His green eyes glittered wickedly.

"I had no idea my actions were under such close scrutiny," he said. "I must exercise more caution in future."

"You are a coxcomb," she said.

"If I were, I should not have been surprised at your knowledge of my dance partners. Yet I'm altogether amazed . . . and flattered. This is a far cry from invisibility."

She returned his gaze, her face expressionless. "When I cross the street," she said, "I look up to make certain no vehicles are bearing recklessly down upon me. I also look down, to make sure no noisome object lies in my path. I have found it necessary in recent weeks to observe similar precautions at social events."

He laughed. "A reckless vehicle is apt enough—but the other? I am put in my place, just goddess. Your hair curls naturally, doesn't it?"

"Yes," she said, uncomfortable to find the talk redirected so speedily to her person.

"I thought so. You've never had to suffer the indignities of curl papers or scorching tongs."

"Not those, no."

"But others? What were they? Steel corsets when you were but a babe?"

"We will not speak of such garments, if you please," she said in her best *grande dame* manner. "I meant applications of lemon juice, three times a day, day after day, week in and week out."

"Ah, *freckles*," he said. "Ghastly things."

"Well, they were."

"Don't be silly. I'm sure you were adorable with your freckles."

"I was not remotely adorable. I was too tall and too skinny, and my hair was too red, and I had forty-seven freckles upon my nose alone."

"Then I wonder they never stood you in a field to frighten away the birds. You might have made yourself useful," he said in tones of reproof. "Still, it is a relief to know you, too, had a misspent youth."

She bit her lip, but the vision of a gawky, adolescent Lilith standing haplessly in a field of newly seeded corn was too much for her, and what began as a titter swelled into laughter.

"Mrs. Davenant," he said sternly, "a misspent youth is nothing to be giggling about."

"A scarecrow," she said, still smiling. "Isn't it odd that I'm one now? Flapping my arms to frighten off any wicked gentlemen birds from my nieces."

"Protecting the tender young crop."

"Yes."

"Someone must, I suppose."

"Yes." Her smile faded. The mischief was gone from his eyes, and compassion had taken its place.

"That is why," he said almost inaudibly.

She pretended not to hear, though she knew what he meant and what she had, unwittingly, revealed to his too-keen perceptions.

"Thomas will be wondering what's become of me," she said coolly enough, though her voice sounded shrill to her ears.

Lord Brandon returned Mrs. Davenant to her intended, then, more perturbed than he'd ever expected to be, left the Fevis house.

He'd known about the nieces and their Seasons with their widowed aunt. He hadn't suspected she financed these ventures single-handedly, though now he recollected that there had been some oblique reference to the matter in his conversation with Higginbottom.

He should have realised. If Mrs. Davenant was too proud to let him cancel Charles's debt, she must be too proud to accept Bexley merely for her own financial security. She must have more compelling reasons for so ludicrous a match.

Still, this information changed nothing, Lord Brandon

reminded himself. He'd never intended to break up her engagement. There was no reason Bexley should not marry her . . . after. No reason she should not continue presenting nieces until she had daughters of her own to bring out. A dozen daughters if she liked. A dozen fiery-haired, tall, passionate creatures like their mama.

He frowned. Or bland, tiresome, priggish, prating creatures like Bexley.

Gad, what did it matter? She would dote upon them even if they all looked like Lady Shumway's unfortunate granddaughter.

"You will *not*," he told himself firmly as he headed for the Cocoa Tree, "contemplate the *getting* of these grotesqueries."

"THE BLUE SILK?" Sally said, aghast. "But Mrs. Davenant don't wear blue. Brown, grey—"

"If you know what Suzette makes for her, then you must know as well why she doesn't give Suzette her custom any more," said Madame Germaine as she nudged her assistant towards the rack in the sewing room.

"That was because Suzette sent some tart's negligees, and Mrs. Davenant is very prim and proper," Sally answered stubbornly. "She'll take a fit if you show her the blue, mark my words."

"Seeing you're so wise, I wonder you don't open your own shop."

Thus silencing her assistant, Madame Germaine drew out the slate-blue gown she'd made for Lady Diana Stockmore before her ladyship had discovered she was increasing. "They're nearly a size," she went on thoughtfully. "We can do the alterations in a minute."

Sally groaned. "But, missus, we're over our ears as it is."

"The others can wait. Everyone knows Mrs. Davenant pays her bills as soon as she gets them."

"Oh, no," said Mrs. Davenant when the slate-blue silk was displayed. "Nothing for me. My niece only."

"And Sally's measuring her at this moment, isn't she? Such a lovely girl Miss Glenwood is. I'm sure anything we put on her will do us credit. Still, it takes time to measure properly. There's no careless haste in *my* shop, Mrs. Davenant."

"I shall be content to look at your pattern books," said Lilith, though her glance lingered upon the tempting silk.

"Madam," said the modiste. "I scorn flattery. I will *not* say this gown was made for you. It was made for another lady. But just once I'd like to see it on a proper figure before I have to cut it to pieces for some dab of a creature and trick it out with ruffles to make it look *dainty*." She spoke disparagingly, though she had a score of petite customers whom she happily garbed.

"I suppose we giantesses are few and far between," said Lilith wryly.

"Giantess, indeed. And you so slender and well-proportioned—and with such posture." She led Lilith to the dressing room. "I'll assist you myself," she said as though she were bestowing the Order of the Bath.

The slate-blue silk appeared at Lady Gaines's ball that evening.

"I was sure my eyes were playing tricks on me," said Lord Robert, glancing past Cecily towards a corner of the room. "I couldn't believe that woman was your aunt, even when I heard her speak."

"You did stare, rather," said Cecily.

"Everyone's staring—not that you can see her for the crowd about her. Why, she looks ten years younger. What a difference a frock makes!"

"And to think we have your naughty friends to thank for it," said Cecily. "If they hadn't played their joke, Aunt Lilith wouldn't have changed dressmakers. Madame Germaine must have a gift for managing her customers. She managed my aunt beautifully. Still, I'll take some credit, because I did persuade Aunt Lilith to let Mary cut her hair a bit."

"Well, I never thought I'd say so, Miss Glenwood, but your aunt is a stunner. No wonder Julian—" Scarcely missing a beat, he went on, "Is that a new scent? You remind me of a garden after a spring shower."

"Damp and mouldy, you mean. What a pleasant compliment."

"That isn't what I meant at all. Clean and sweet and fresh."

"I'm glad you think so. Your cologne is much more agreeable than Mr. Ventcoeur's, so I'm sure your judgement must be sound."

Lord Brandon stood by the French doors leading onto the terrace. The doors were open now. Prinny having come and gone, the company might at last inhale fresh air. The marquess might have stood nearer Lilith Davenant half the night without calling undue attention to himself, since there was a respectable crowd of gentlemen about her. He'd tried that already, and didn't like it.

Unlike the others, Lord Brandon had not needed to see Mrs. Davenant costumed in a becoming gown to know she was desirable. Nonetheless, he could not have guessed the impact such a gown would have upon him.

At first, it was her hair he'd noticed. The tightly braided coils had disappeared the night of her niece's comeout. Even so, the widow's style remained far too severe for a young woman of eight and twenty. Tonight, however, gleaming auburn curls danced wantonly about her face. The rest was caught up loosely behind, so that she looked tumbled, as though she'd just risen from her pillows.

Then he'd bent over her hand, and a creamy, silken expanse of bosom swam into his vision in swelling curves. He'd caught his breath . . . and remained breathless as his gaze slid discreetly over the smoky blue fabric that gleamed softly against alabaster skin and clung lovingly to her long-legged, supple figure. A wave of hot impatience had washed over him then, and he told himself he'd waited long enough.

Yet the marquess waited now, standing idly by the terrace doors, his habitual expression of lazy boredom masking the discontent within.

He'd grown wary of this restiveness. More than once it had led him to rush his fences, which had meant time wasted repairing the damage. He knew himself better now. He must not seek her out when he was chafing. If she wouldn't come to him, he'd let it go this evening and entertain himself elsewhere. All the same, knowing he wanted no elsewhere, no other, he *willed* her to come to him.

An hour passed while he watched his friends gravitate to her. In that time he saw a dozen expressions cross her face. They were unreadable to others, perhaps—the faintest trails of expression crossing her cool countenance.

All the same, Lord Brandon comprehended her confusion and surprise, and every phase leading her gradually to understand that the gentlemen suddenly found her very attractive. He read the widow's feelings as easily as if they'd been writ out in bold letters above her head. Then, as he perceived the faint flush of pleasure and slow, beguiling curve of her mouth, he found himself smiling as well. Whatever else he'd wanted of her, it was not her unhappiness. Her own kin first, then Davenant, had given her enough of that. Yet it never ceased to amaze the marquess that so desirable a woman should have so low an opinion of herself.

Before the hour elapsed, Brandon watched her stand up with her betrothed and be taken from him in the next set by Lord Worcester, who relinquished her in the next to Brummell.

It was Brummell brought her to the marquess when the dance had ended. This was to settle a dispute.

"Mrs. Davenant insists it is *not* milk baths," the Beau announced, "but the consumption of vegetables and exercise in the open air accounts for her flawless complexion. Bexley will not tell me whether this is cruel teasing, for he is blasting Hamilton about some tiresome political triviality. You are better acquainted with this lady than I, Brandon. Is this irony or fact?"

"I certainly have no notion of her bathing habits," his lordship said wickedly.

A rosy tint glowed upon the widow's high cheekbones.

"I beg your pardon, Mrs. Davenant," said the Beau. "This was my fault. An injudicious choice of phrasing." He returned to Brandon. "I only wished to ascertain whether you had ever seen Mrs. Davenant eat vegetables."

"Indeed I have. Moreover, I am informed by reliable witnesses that she rides, several times a week, in the early-morning air."

Brummell's face fell. "I have an open mind," he said bravely. "I shall take a turn about the terrace. But *vegetables*. Good heavens!" He sauntered through the French doors.

"Does he never eat vegetables?" Lilith asked.

"He claims he once ate a pea. You're very beautiful tonight, Mrs. Davenant."

Slowly, her mouth curled into a delicious smile.

"Thank you," she said. "I've been terrified into it, you know."

"Have you indeed?" he asked, intrigued, charmed. "I've never heard of anybody's being terrified into beauty."

"Then obviously you're not acquainted with Madame Germaine. I've never been so scolded and threatened—not since I was in the nursery, I'm sure."

"Good grief! What had this dread female to say?"

"You are not to repeat it," said Lilith, lowering her voice.

He bent his head to listen and caught a whiff of jasmine.

"She said Cecily's beaux will wonder whether she'll take after me."

"But you're not her mama. You're not even a blood relation."

"Her mama wears nothing but ancient riding habits, which is worse, I daresay, and I'm on the spot to be taken as model."

"You did not tell this upstart shopkeeper you've already riveted several nieces successfully?"

"I did," said Lilith, her blue eyes dancing with an amusement as enchanting as it was rare. "In my best set-down

141

manner. She only shook her head pityingly and sighed and answered, 'But only think how much better the dear creatures *might* have done.' "

"If you will excuse me," said Lord Brandon. "I believe I must depart now—to set fire to her shop."

"You don't approve my transformation, then, despite the compliment."

"No, I do not. All these weeks I've feasted upon your beauty in solitary dignity. Now I must dine with a mob," he complained. "I shall be forced to listen to Brummell rhapsodise about your complexion. I must endure Byron's odes to your eyes and Davies' puns upon your lips. No doubt there will be violent quarrels whether your hair is Bordeaux or sienna, copper-tinted or russet, and one numskull will call another out on the issue." He paused. "Now, there's a thought," he said. "Perhaps they'll all kill one another."

"So long as a duke or two remains standing to marry Cecily, I can't object," she said. "Madame Germaine won't be satisfied with any lesser rank, I'm afraid."

"I wonder, if you dance with a marquess, whether that will send one peltering after Miss Glenwood. Then, seeing the marquess give chase, perhaps a duke will join the pursuit. All of which is to say I wish you'd dance this waltz with me."

There was a heartbeat's pause, enough to send a shiver of anger through him, but she consented, and the only vestige of rage remaining was with himself, for being so shaken at the prospect of refusal.

His hand clasped her waist—and encountered something altogether unexpected. "I shall burn down her shop," he muttered, "*and* throttle her with my own neck-cloth."

"What on earth—" Her eyes must have caught the mischief in his, because she became flustered. "You will not—"

"Stays," he said grimly. "That wretched female has persuaded you to crush your rib cage in one of those fiendish instruments of torture."

"My lord, you have an annoying habit of referring to exceedingly intimate matters," she said with a touch of asperity.

"I am appalled to find you have acquired an even more distressing habit."

"I had to wear it," she said, vexed. "The gown was indecent otherwise. Oh, stop looking at me in that aggravating manner. Why did I ever agree to dance with you?"

"An attack of conscience. You haven't danced with me in an age. I daresay you finally decided I'd been punished long enough."

"I was not punishing you."

"It felt exactly like punishment."

Her face became shuttered, and he cursed himself silently. "You needn't poker up," he said. "It's simply that you've found me in bad temper."

After a moment, she asked what had put him out of temper.

"Who knows?" he said. "Talk to me and make me forget. Quiet my mind with some tranquil image. Tell me of your place in Derbyshire."

"It isn't very interesting," she said. "In Derbyshire, I'm a farmer."

"Very well. I shall give up Athena for the moment and transform you in my mind to Demeter. Tell me of sheep and cows and corn and—oh, above all, tell me of *drainage*."

He watched her face soften and her eyes light up with enthusiasm as she described the vast, ill-maintained estate her grandparents had given her as a wedding gift, and of the years spent making it productive again. She could not suppress her pride in her accomplishment. Not that she should, he thought. She deserved a great deal of credit. She'd educated herself about modern agricultural methods, single-handedly set about persuading her tenants from their old-fashioned ways, and managed the whole herself.

She'd had time enough on her hands, hadn't she? No social life until after her husband died. No children, except those she adopted temporarily for some three or four months of the year.

The estate, his lordship knew from conversations with

Higginbottom, was at present let to a retired military officer, who would very likely make a purchase offer at the summer's end. That, Brandon realised as he studied her animated countenance, would probably break her heart.

The waltz ended and Mrs. Davenant went on talking, like an eager girl. He continued to ask questions, and she answered happily, even after he led her back to Bexley.

This would do no harm in Bexley's view—if he were paying attention, which was not altogether certain. Still, the spirited discussion of agriculture must silence the gossips, at least temporarily. Moreover, it was not a topic to excite her new admirers. Those who owned property preferred to leave the business of maintaining it to others. They knew less of modern agriculture than their sheep did.

Fortunately, the marquess knew something—more than something, actually. Thus he enjoyed the added pleasure of watching surprise, then growing respect, brighten her beautiful eyes.

The following day, Mrs. Davenant met in her study with her butler.

"Certainly, madam," said Cawble when she'd done explaining. "It can be managed discreetly. I shall send Jacob with the centre-piece, the two larger candelabra, the great coffee-urn, and the other items you suggested. They will not be required, unless you plan a large entertainment in the near future."

"I am sure we shall redeem them long before I plan such an affair," said his mistress.

"Yes, madam. This is a regrettable necessity, yet one cannot plan for every emergency, I am sure."

All the same, the loyal butler could not help reflecting disapprovingly upon his employer's man of business. Mrs. Davenant should not be placed in the mortifying position of pawning her silver, simply because men who were supposed to sign pieces of paper chose to dawdle over the matter. They had no business dawdling, Cawble reflected indignantly. They had little enough to do. That a lady of her means should not be able to put her hands upon ready money the instant she required it was an affront to the British Constitution.

Shortly thereafter, Mrs. Davenant reappeared at the dressmaker's. Instead of her niece, she brought a footman, who carried several large packages. Mrs. Davenant explained she'd lost some weight. Perhaps Madame would be so kind as to make a few alterations?

Madame contemplated the dismal colours, then her client, then shook her head sadly. "I never speak ill of a colleague," she said, "but sometimes I do *not* understand what they're thinking of."

"These were made precisely as I ordered," was the defensive answer.

"Yes, madam, and the question I ask is 'Why?' Meaning no offence, because I'd never question your taste. But this taupe . . ." She took up the offending garment and pursed her lips. "Enough fabric here for two gowns. Such a *waste*." She shook her head again. "It wouldn't trouble me if you had flaws to conceal, but with *your* figure . . . well, I can't understand why the gown had to be made like an overcoat."

So saying, and without appearing to hear any of her customer's stammering negatives or observe the crimson repeatedly suffusing the lady's face, Madame proceeded to measure and pin and snip and slash.

What she proposed might be an outrage to her client's sensibilities, but the client was no match for the evangelical fervour that possessed Madame Germaine. It was in vain to protest that one felt half naked, when one's dressmaker only cried, "Precisely!" and flourished her scissors like a sword.

# === 13 ===

MRS. DAVENANT'S ALTERED garments began making their appearance the following week.

Tonight, at Almack's, she was dressed in the same taupe gown she'd worn to the Countess Lieven's party. Well, not quite the same. At least a yard of fabric was gone from the skirt, causing it to hug her hips as it had never done before. Madame had insisted "only an inch" was taken from the bodice. This was the grossest of understatements.

Though such renovated costumes did not trigger quite the sensation the blue silk had, they continued to win admiring glances, and not a little flattery. Even Cecily's beaux seemed less intimidated. Sir Matthew Melbrook had begged a dance of the heretofore terrifying dragon aunt, and Mr. Ventcoeur, Lilith was told, had startled his friends by boldly asserting that Mrs. Davenant had a sense of *humour*.

Lilith bit her lip. She'd heard that from Lord Brandon.

Determined, apparently, to be the gossiping sort of friend, he'd begun sharing with her every *on dit* that came to his ears. What he didn't hear, he invented, leaving her laughing helplessly at outrageous stories of Lady Shumway's passionate affairs with a series of fictitious Cossacks, or the ancient Lord Hubbing's adventures at Vauxhall, or any of a host of other imaginative atrocities.

Yet, ever since Lady Gaines's ball, he'd become the confiding sort of friend as well, because he had a knack for getting past Lilith's guard. Once launched upon the topic of

Derbyshire, she was easily led to more personal subjects: her grandparents, her childhood, the young parents she scarcely remembered, her nurse, her governess, her studies. Somehow, too, she'd revealed something of her own girlish dreams and hopes, even as she thought she spoke of Cecily and Georgiana and the rest.

But a few weeks ago, uttering one sentence to him had been an effort, because his presence disturbed her so. Of late, the struggle was to keep from telling him every thought and feeling.

It was a struggle now to keep her eye on Cecily, dancing with Mr. Ventcoeur, rather than on the tall, dark form that moved so gracefully through Almack's throng.

Lilith never knew when she'd find Brandon at her side. She knew only that he always came, and they would dance once and talk a great deal. Strangely enough, no one else seemed to regard this new camaraderie.

Perhaps the Great World was preoccupied, as Thomas was, with Louis XVIII's arrival in France and its consequences. More likely, Society wasn't remotely interested in so dull a matter as mere friendship between a man and a woman.

After all, Lord Brandon's compliments were light and civil, no more. He scarcely flirted with her lately, though other gentlemen did.

This quieted Lilith's conscience somewhat, but not altogether. She had no defence against his amiability, no excuse for shunning him, yet she wished she had.

She could no longer deny she'd been drawn to him from the start, attracted in spite of herself by his compelling physical beauty and charm. Now the pull was stronger. She'd discovered kindness, sense, compassion, intelligence—oh, and too many common interests.

Or so it seemed. She frowned.

"Your brows are knit," came a low voice behind her. "Brummell will be cross with you for wrinkling the flawless surface of your complexion." The marquess moved to her side, brushing her arm in the process.

"I can live with his disapproval," Lilith answered coolly enough. "Until a week ago, the only notice I got was a singularly pained expression whenever he happened to glance my way."

"Which only shows he's not so discerning as he appears. Why do you linger in this dismal corner? Are you hiding from your beaux? Or waiting for one? If so, he's unforgivably dilatory. I'd better take his place and teach him a lesson."

Lilith caught the edge of impatience in his voice. Wondering at it, she threw him a puzzled glance. He stood with his usual careless grace, but the tension in that stance was not usual. He seemed . . . angry?

"What is it?" he asked. "Have you discovered a crease in my lapel?"

"If I had, I should never dare tell you, for fear your valet would be found murdered in the morning. You seem a trifle out of sorts this evening, my lord," she said frankly.

Surprise flickered in his green eyes, only to be hooded in the next instant. "Hardly. I've been dead bored, as usual—until now, of course."

"You were with Thomas. If he bores you so much, I wonder you bother to speak with him at all."

"I'm obliged to appear as friendly with the gentleman as I am with his fiancée. If I'm not, my motives become suspect, and the fiancée suffers for it. Society punishes the victim, while the alleged criminal goes scot- free. A curious kind of justice, is it not?"

"Society is hardly a court of law," she answered uneasily. "One might well be blamed for not avoiding dangerous company."

"You think so? Why shouldn't my alleged victim decide for herself whether I'm a menace? You believe we must none of us think for ourselves, but always adhere to the general opinion?"

More disquieted still, she glanced away. "I used to wonder how Eve could have been so foolish as to listen to the serpent. But whenever you and I debate morality, I can only conclude he must have had your gift for turning right and wrong inside out, plain black and white to shades of grey."

"It isn't morality we discuss, but the appearance of it. My wish to enjoy your company is a crime for which you'll be punished, unless I dress it up as a general wish to enjoy every damn fool's company as well."

"Sir Thomas is not a fool," Lilith reproved, as she must. "Because he isn't as witty and entertaining as you, you find him boring. All the same, he doesn't want intelligence."

"He wants something in his upper story—or in his heart—to neglect you so shamefully. If you were my affianced bride, I'd exploit the privilege. I'd talk with you the whole day and dance with you all the night."

She made herself smile and pretend he'd spoken lightly, though the intensity burning in his eyes told her otherwise. "That is mere theory. When you get a fiancée, we shall discover whether or not you live in her pocket."

"I don't speak of imaginary females. It's your company I want, your voice I want to hear," he said, his tones dropping lower. "It infuriates me—he can have all I want so easily, incurring no one's displeasure, and he doesn't care. I meanwhile must make do with five minutes snatched here, ten stolen there. I must amiably accept every interruption, all the while anxious lest your reputation be sullied by my contaminating presence. God knows," he went on with suppressed fury, "I don't dare touch you."

Thus he shattered all the fragile tranquillity she'd achieved in the last few days.

She'd wanted his company too. She'd needed to look at him, hear his voice, find him near. No wonder her conscience would not be quieted. Under the veneer of friendship, her shameful longing had only grown. Why else should he make her heart ache when he spoke so?

"You will not disparage Sir Thomas to me," Lilith made herself say. "Our relationship is our own affair."

"What of *ours*, Lilith?" he demanded. "Is this all there is for us? Are we to share nothing but what can be found in a few minutes, with all the world watching and listening?"

She remembered where she was then, and made herself glance easily about her. Lady Jersey was smiling at her. Lilith smiled back, before turning again to the marquess.

"Perhaps," she said, "we'd better not share even that." And with the same civil smile pinned to her face, she walked away.

"How kind of you to take so much trouble for me," Miss Glenwood told Lord Robert as he swept her into the waltz. "I was sure it would be months before the patronesses let me waltz."

"It wasn't any trouble at all," he said. "Why shouldn't they let you? They've all had plenty of time to approve your behaviour, the tiresome prudes."

"Still, I was much amazed when the Countess Lieven presented you."

"Because she's so haughty? Or did you think I wasn't a respectable enough partner?"

"Good heavens, why should I think that? If you weren't respectable, they wouldn't let you in, would they? But you're right. I shouldn't have been amazed at your gallantry. You always know what to say and do to put a girl at her ease. I never feel clumsy when I dance with you."

He smiled. "You're never the least awkward, Miss Glenwood, and you waltz exceedingly well. Not at all like a beginner. You've been practicing in secret."

She did not appear to hear the compliment. Her attention had fallen upon something—or someone—past his shoulder. Lord Robert experienced a twinge of irritation. "What is it?" he asked. "Has someone fallen into a fit?"

Her gaze came back to him. It was troubled. "I rather think someone has," she said softly. "Only look at Lord Brandon."

Robert drew her into a turn in order to observe his cousin. The marquess's countenance was black as a thundercloud.

"He looks like murder," said Robert, taken aback. "He's a devil of a temper, you know. Usually he doesn't show it—not in public, I mean. What's set him off, I wonder."

"I think he's quarreled with my aunt," said Cecily. She sighed. "Oh, dear, how tiresome of them."

"Quarreled with— Well, it's none of our business, of course."

"Of course it is. He can't go on glaring at her all night. People will notice."

"I wouldn't have noticed if you hadn't called my attention."

"That's because you're not a prying busybody. But Lady Enders is, and half a dozen other ladies as well. Now everyone will begin buzzing again. I'm sure I'm not the only one saw how they were arguing. And then my aunt marched off in that horrid outraged Empress of the World way of hers, and he hasn't taken his eyes off her since. Lord Robert, you must do something."

"I?"

"You must make him stop."

"I? Make Julian stop?" he said, aghast. "What do you expect me to do, drag him from the premises?"

Miss Glenwood's small gloved hand squeezed his, and her enormous eyes opened wider yet. "I know you can think of something," she said confidently. "You're so clever. Probably you'll find some tactful way to let him know he's wearing his heart on his sleeve—though of course you'd never say anything so silly as *that*."

Although the pressure of her hand sent a surge of strength through him, it was not quite enough to conquer all Lord Robert's sense of self-preservation.

"Egad, I should hope not, Miss Glenwood. Not if I mean to keep all my teeth in my head," he said, feeling beleaguered as her gaze grew reproachful. "I shouldn't say so, but Julian's hideously touchy about any references to your aunt. When he's in a good humour, he only delivers a set-down, but when he's moody he . . . well, he doesn't know his own strength."

"Then you must be sure to step out of the way quickly, mustn't you?" the pitiless girl responded.

The waltz ended far too soon, in Lord Robert's opinion. He dutifully returned Miss Glenwood to her aunt and saw the girl promptly swallowed up in a crowd of admirers. Then, reluctantly, he made for his cousin's gloomy figure. Julian's gaze was not welcoming.

"I've had enough of Almack's," said Lord Robert. "I think I'll be going now."

"I am not your nurse. Do what you like."

"Still, a man can't always do what he likes, you know. Most of the time, he can't even show what he's thinking, which is even harder . . . well, for me at least . . ."

"Robert, I hope you're not about to honour me with boyish confidences. I'm not in a humour for confidences."

Not open to hints, either, apparently. Nothing for it, then, but to state the facts . . . and step quickly out of the way.

"You've been staring daggers at her for half an hour now," Lord Robert said, moving back a pace. "If even I noticed, don't you think half the world is going to?"

Instantly, the familiar mask of boredom was back in place.

"If this is half the world," said Lord Brandon languidly, "we're best advised to seek out the other half tonight, I think."

Lilith was badly shaken, yet she chatted with her normal composure and danced with her betrothed without stumbling. Tonight of all nights, Thomas danced with her several times, as though Lord Brandon's vexation had somehow communicated itself to his rival.

Not a rival, Lilith hastily amended. She'd already made her choice—not that there had been or could be any choice. It was a husband she needed, not a lover.

Thus she behaved as she always did, and when Thomas had taken her and Cecily home, Lilith invited him, as she often did, to stop for a glass of wine.

Brandon thought her betrothed took her for granted. This wasn't just. To Thomas, socializing was business, and she'd never expected or wished him to neglect his chosen business on her account. During these quiet times at the end of an evening, Thomas would share with her his thoughts and wishes, reporting on what he'd said and learned. He even solicited her opinion from time to time.

He did not take her for granted, she argued with the sardonic masculine voice in her head. He simply chose an appropriate time and place for private conversation.

Tonight he was occupied with Norway, and vexed at the prospect of a blockade of that nation, for it was Sir Thomas's firm belief that Norway was the King of Denmark's problem, as Earl Grey maintained.

Lilith did not remind her fiancé that Lord Liverpool had already taken measures towards a blockade. For one, Thomas was already troubled by his mentor's actions. For another, she had no wish to prolong the monologue. She had rather hear of the Corn Laws or even the Catholic Question. The technicalities of peace treaties made her head spin.

Her confusion must have shown, because Thomas stopped mid-speech to give her a rueful smile. "Ah, the matter shall be debated all the coming week, and a word or two on my part would have sufficed. Yet every issue these days seems to go against me," he said, shaking his head. "I am concerned that sufficient precautions have not been taken regarding Buonaparte's move to Elba. I wish I might have spoken to Castlereagh myself. If only I had been on the spot as Hobhouse was, to carry those dispatches."

"One day you'll have a direct voice in such matters," Lilith said loyally. "I'm certain of it. I wish for your sake you had it now, Thomas."

"Well, I cannot altogether regret it. Had I gone with the dispatches, I must be away from you, and that I should be sorry for."

He set his empty wineglass upon the tray and stepped

towards her. "It seems to me you become more elegant every day, my dear. Is that a new frock?"

"You've seen it before."

"It appears different somehow. *You* have appeared different."

"A few alterations." She made herself smile. "A great man ought not be shackled to a dowd."

He took her hand. "I have never approved of slavishness to every fashion, as you know. Yet you wear the change with dignity, and it becomes you."

"You hadn't mentioned it before. I thought perhaps you disapproved this . . . this frivolousness."

"You are never frivolous, my dear. We two are past frivolity, I hope. Still, I am not so aged a fellow as to be unmoved by grace and elegance, though I do not shower you with flattery every minute."

He brought the hand he held to his lips. The kiss he placed there was a lingering one, as was the glance that fell upon her bodice. Thus, Lilith was not altogether taken aback when her heretofore decorous suitor enfolded her in his arms.

Nonetheless, she stiffened when his mouth touched hers. The warm, moist kiss did nothing to warm her inwardly. On the contrary, her muscles grew more icily rigid, and within was the familiar rush of anxiety . . . and distaste. In seconds, it seemed, he grew more heated, while she grew frantic to break free. She endured it as long as she could, which was not very long, though it seemed an eternity. Then she made a slight struggle, and he released her.

He appeared not at all happy about it. A few strands of hair stuck damply to his forehead, and his brown eyes were clouded.

"My dear, we are betrothed," he said, a shade of irritation in his voice, "and you are not a green girl."

"We're not yet wed," she said, flushing at her hypocrisy. Even as she was trying to contrive a better excuse, Thomas was collecting himself.

"We are not—yet," he said stiffly. "All the same, it is not improper to embrace the woman one has solemnly pledged to wed."

"That is so, and I do not mean to be missish, Thomas. Yet I cannot be comfortable—that is, do recollect it has been many years since . . . since I was a wife."

He seemed to understand then, because he apologised for his haste. Still, the edge of vexation in his voice warned this was not the end of the matter.

Lilith could not blame him. Neither, however, could she bear his touch—not now, not so soon. She'd endure it once they were wed, as she was obliged, but not before. She hadn't misled him, she told herself. She'd never pretended passion, never even mentioned love. She'd never been given to displays even of affection . . . with one appalling exception.

"Modesty, naturally, is always becoming in a lady," he was saying in his considering, Parliamentary tones. "You are quite right. We are not yet wed—though I assure you I had no intention of anticipating our conjugal vows. In all fairness, I must admit I have not been loverlike. I suppose I have shocked you this night. Let us hope you will not be shocked in future when your husband-to-be wishes to embrace you. I have been preoccupied of late. Nevertheless, I trust you understand our life together will not be entirely taken up with matters of state."

Lilith nodded and forced a smile.

"Believe me, my dear, I look forward to the peace and intimacy of domestic life," he went on sonorously, "and to the growth of mutual affection which provides man his greatest happiness. Mutual affection and, of course, such tokens of that esteem as Providence sees fit to bless us with."

He had no need to say more. Lilith understood him well enough. For all his decorousness, he was a man, with a man's needs. This man also wanted children.

He left soon after. She bid him a polite farewell, then returned to the library to pour herself another glass of wine.

Wine perhaps would deaden the vile clamour in her brain.

*What of us, Lilith?* Angry, pleading. Against that voice, which made her heart pound even now, the tones of her intended husband, judicious, yet annoyed. Disappointed, impatient—as he had a right to be.

Perhaps it was wrong to marry Thomas. Perhaps he wanted more than she could give, and she'd make him unhappy.

No, of course she wouldn't. She'd chosen for herself this time. No one had coerced her. She'd known exactly what she was choosing and why, and she'd make the best of it. Thomas would never know a devil possessed her heart.

The devil was not abroad this night. He watched the play at Watier's for an hour or so and drank a glass or so, and was in his own bed by two o'clock in the morning. At three o'clock, Lord Brandon woke from a disagreeable dream and found himself in process of throttling the pillow—not, as he'd thought, Sir Thomas Bexley.

"By God, woman," he muttered as he jammed the pillow back into place, "you shall pay for this, and dearly. To keep a man from his proper repose—"

He fell back upon the pillow, his green eyes wide, staring at the canopy above. "Believe me, I'll return the favour, Lilith Davenant. Before the week is out, I vow."

Having vowed so, Lord Brandon ought to have been easy in his mind, but his gaze remained fixed upon the canopy.

He hadn't meant to speak as he had. It was a tactical error to press her when he'd only begun to win her trust. He'd promised himself he'd keep away from her this night, to make her wonder . . . and worry. But he'd watched her move, so proud and graceful, through the crowd, talking with her friends. He'd observed the other men as well. He was aware how their eyes lingered upon her imperious face, and dwelt longer still upon her slim, supple form. He'd recognised the instinctive masculine drive to conquer and possess. He'd not very much enjoyed seeing his own feelings reflected in a dozen other men's faces.

Unbearably restless, he'd gone to her. Then the words, wholly unprepared, had spilled from him, and once begun, he couldn't stop himself. Some fiend indeed must have taken hold of his tongue. It could not have been his own heart produced that lovesick speech.

Well, he'd never been a saint. Why should he have the patience of one?

Frustration, then. Nothing to be alarmed about. As to the speech itself—there was no harm in *seeming* lovesick.

She'd left him, true, with a rebuff. Nonetheless, she'd not heard him unmoved. He'd read her inner struggle—a painful one—in her eyes. Even as he raged at her, he'd known she was weakening. Which made him rage all the more within. She wanted what he wanted. Why not yield and be happy? Why should not two adults find pleasure in each other's arms? And why must those troubled eyes haunt him? No, he corrected, that was only his frustration with her.

It would end soon. The serpent in the garden, she'd called him, unwittingly revealing that she, like Eve, was tempted. Would she fall? She must.

All the same, for all his confidence, Lord Brandon's eyes did not close again that night.

# === 14 ===

ON THE FOLLOWING day at breakfast, Lord Brandon made a remark regarding what Hell hath no fury like. Though several more specific comments were needed, Lord Robert eventually recollected the long-suffering Elise.

Before noon, Robert was with his mistress. He brought her a bouquet, a box of chocolates, and an exquisite midnight-blue silk shawl.

Elise gazed at these sadly and told him he was too extravagant.

"Not at all," he said, neglecting to add that Julian had provided the money. "I should shower you with diamonds, you've been so patient and understanding."

"Yes, but I must be. I know you make the sacrifice for me. I never see you now, but for a few hours at a time. Every night you must go about with your friends and be so bored and lonely—and all for me," said Elise, smiling bravely.

"Yes, hideously bored. But I do bear it for your sake—for ours, I mean."

She took up the shawl and draped it over her shoulders. "So beautiful, Robin. How lovely it will be with my gown— the wine-coloured one, you remember?"

Lord Robert nodded enthusiastically, just as though he did remember, which he didn't. His mind was taken up lately with pastel muslins.

"Of course you remember. It is your favourite," she said, stroking the shawl. "You are so good to me. I think tonight you must have some reward for all your sacrifices. Why do we not go to the theatre? I shall wear the gown and this beautiful gift."

Panic shot through Lord Robert. Miss Glenwood would attend the theatre this evening, and he'd promised to be there. She was a remarkably open-minded girl. Her aunt, unfortunately, was not. To be seen tonight with Elise was to invite permanent exile.

"I can't," he said, thinking rapidly. "Promised to dine at Holland House, don't you know? Julian begged off at the last minute, and Lady Holland pounced on me so quick I couldn't think." This was not actually a lie, Robert told himself. Lady Holland had invited him.

Elise sighed. "Well, it is unfortunate, but I know you cannot be rude to the lady. Still, it is wearying to remain always at home."

"Perhaps you could visit some of your friends," Robert suggested. "I think Julian mentioned Bella Martin was having one of her soirees tonight. You like Bella."

"No, there will be too many gentlemen, and it is so tedious always to be saying no, no. They do not understand I am not the Elise I was. My heart is not free now." Her smile was tender, but the sparks in her dark eyes made Robert nervous.

"I think I shall go all the same," she went on. "I shall take my maid. It is better that way. The play will distract me, and I shall not feel sorry for myself."

His heart sank. If she couldn't be got to change her mind, it must be Holland House for him after all. Ahead, instead of Miss Glenwood's lively company, lay a stuffy, stupid evening—not to mention being forced to jump up and down a dozen times, because Lady Holland was inclined to revise seating arrangements straight through dinner.

Although Robert did not leave his love nest for several hours, nothing he said or did could sway his mistress. As he made his lachrymose way down the street, he wondered why he hadn't noticed before how obstinate Elise was. Furthermore, something must be done about her taste in perfume. A man ought to be able to breathe in his own lodgings.

The marquess arrived at the theatre earlier than was his custom, and headed immediately for the Enders box. He found Lady Enders, Bexley, Cecily, and Mrs. Wellwicke, but no Lilith. Assuming she must have stepped out with Lord Enders, Brandon lingered. Consequently, he had to endure Bexley's opinions of the King of Denmark at numbing length. He listened, the time passed, and neither Enders nor the widow appeared.

Finally, minutes before the curtain was due to rise, Bexley paused to catch his breath, and Cecily spoke up.

"Was there a great crowd in the corridor as you arrived, my lord?" she asked. "Lord Enders very kindly offered to fetch me a glass of lemonade, though I would have been happy to wait until the interval. I do hope he won't miss the opening scene on my account."

"In such a service, Miss Glenwood, any gentleman would gladly forgo the entire drama," Brandon said gallantly. "Still, if I spy him, I shall convey your anxiety."

"There is no need for alarm," Lady Enders told the girl sharply. "Enders will be along any minute."

"Yes, how silly of me. I am just uneasy in general, I daresay, on account of my poor aunt. Perhaps I should have stayed home with her after all. It isn't good for her to be all alone, whatever she says."

Lord Brandon shot the girl a glance, but she had turned her attention to the stage.

Moments later, having expressed appropriate sentiments regarding Mrs. Davenant's ill health and feigned fascination with Bexley's imbecilic explanations for her headaches, Lord Brandon was striding rapidly down the corridor. So intent was he upon his plans that he did not observe Elise's approach until it was too late.

"A moment, milord," she said, taking hold of his arm.

He was about to shake her off, but a glance at her face stopped him. Her dark eyes glittered an angry warning.

Fortunately, the corridor was empty. Leading her to one side, so that he could keep watch on the stairs for late arrivals, he politely asked how he might serve her.

"You might serve by keeping to our agreement," she snapped. "It was simple enough. But you play another game as well, I think."

"There is only one game I am aware of, *mademoiselle*."

"I am not blind, milord. Little passes in your Great World that does not reach me. I comprehend what you have done. Our bargain, you find, is not so simple as you thought, so you arrange to win another way. You keep Robert from me, and use as bait that pretty child with her golden curls and so-blue eyes."

"I see you have been spending too much time alone, brooding," said his lordship. "Otherwise you would not have persuaded yourself that a mere girl—pretty or no—gives you any reason for alarm, or that I have any need to hedge my bets."

"Do you not? How long is it now? Nearly five weeks, I think."

"You were so generous as to give me eight. I see no reason for haste."

"But reason for other precautions, no? Is this your honour? I trusted your word as a gentleman. Why did you tease me with a bargain you never meant to keep?"

"I fully intend to keep it," he said, controlling his swelling anger. "Do you call me a liar, *mademoiselle*?"

Though he'd kept his voice level, the tart must have sensed she was treading on thin ice. "I only wish to be assured," she said in lighter tones. "Can you blame me? To win our wager, you need only seduce Madame Davenant. Why do I see Robert kept from me meanwhile? That was no part of it."

"I have done nothing to keep him from you," he said as patiently as he could. "If you believe he's playing you false, you must deal with that between yourselves. Now, if you will excuse me, I must be going."

For all her assurances to Cecily, Lady Enders was not at all easy in her mind about Matthew's tardiness.

It was Matthew who'd hastened to Lady Violet Porter's assistance during the battle at Redley Park, and Rachel had not at all approved the assiduousness of his attentions.

Forced to relinquish Lord Fevis to his wife, Lady Violet was free to pursue other game. This evening, Lady Enders had perceived the smile the woman threw Matthew when she arrived. Consequently, Rachel little doubted it was Lady Violet her husband was reconnoitering, not lemonade.

This was why, as the curtain was rising, Lady Enders left her box and stepped into the corridor.

Thus she saw Lord Brandon lead the demi-rep round the corner by the staircase. Judging by the woman's tones, she was in a temper.

Rachel told herself she had no interest in their discussion. This was a public corridor, and she had as much right as anyone to walk there. She needed to drop a hint to Mr. Porter, didn't she? And wasn't his box that way?

Just before the corner, however, she stopped dead. The tart's words rang perfectly clear now. Perfectly, monstrously clear.

Lady Enders did not wait to learn more. Trembling with shock and indignation, she turned and hurried back.

Lilith, who had every sort of trouble but the headache she'd claimed, was bent over her desk, reviewing accounts, when she heard the tap at her study door. Expecting Cawble with the tea she'd ordered, she didn't bother to look up when she bade him enter.

"Is this a new cure for the headache?" a low, familiar voice asked.

She jumped from her chair, knocking over a stack of papers. "How did you get in?" she gasped.

"Bribed the footman. Your butler was otherwise occupied, thank heaven. He is lamentably incorruptible."

This evening, a deep-blue coat made Lord Brandon's hair glint blue-black. His linen was blinding white, nearly as dazzling as the diamond that shot sparks from the folds of his neck-cloth.

His tall, broad-shouldered figure made the small, cluttered room seem a narrow cell. Lilith herself felt like a peasant. She wore an old grey muslin day dress whose right sleeve bore a spattering of ink stains. It was her working costume.

Stunned at his entrance and embarrassed by both the room's and her own appearance, she could only watch helplessly as he gathered up the papers. To her dismay, he did not return them to the desk, but commenced perusing them.

"These are scarcely two days old," he said reproachfully. "It is bad ton to pay one's creditors before one has been dunned twenty-five times at least. I must warn you against the practice. The upper orders are obliged to set proper examples for their inferiors."

"I see no merit in driving to bankruptcy tradespeople who serve me in good faith," she said. "Nor do I see how this is any business of yours. You will please to give them back—and leave this house." She put out a shaking hand for the papers.

He turned away from her and continued to thumb through the stack. "Ye gods," he said. "This is only the past month's? Thank heavens I leave all that to my secretary. I should never have time for anything else. Why don't you leave it to Bexley? What's the point of marrying a rich man if you don't let him pay your creditors?"

"I have no intention of presenting my betrothed with a pile of debts. May I also repeat, this is none of your concern. Nor have you any right to invade my privacy—particularly at this unseemly hour."

He did not even look up as he answered. "I know you're

angry with me, my pet, but I wish you wouldn't make stuffy speeches. It spoils my concentration and— Aha!" He spun round, holding aloft the pawnbroker's ticket. "What is this? Have you played too deep at piquet, wicked girl?"

Heat tingled in her cheeks. "Even the most well-regulated households at times have need of ready cash."

"Ah, yes. An unplanned expense. What was it? That ghastly corset? Or perhaps a provocative negligee—black lace, I hope—for your wedding night?"

It was scarcely a cry, more a painful catch of her breath, but he heard it, for he dropped the papers on the desk and moved to her. Placing his hands on her shoulders, he asked gently, "What is it?"

"Let go of me. It is no great matter. The blue silk . . . some alterations . . . Madame—well, she did it all practically overnight. I wished to pay at once, in thanks for her trouble."

"So you pawned your silver? Higginbottom didn't tell me matters had reached such a pass."

"I will have something at the end of the month. I have enough now—or nearly—but I'd rather keep it in reserve. Cecily may need stockings or ribbons—or her fan may break, or some catastrophe."

If he did not take his hands away soon, she would be stuttering. As it was, she had to stare hard at the diamond stick pin to maintain any composure.

He released her. "I see." He stepped back to the desk, picked up the stack of papers, and thrust them into his coat. "This is utterly absurd," he said. "You should not be tormenting yourself with creditors. Why should you not have new gowns if you want them? Why should you not have whatever takes your fancy? What have you done to deserve penury?"

"I am not tormented. I don't want any new gowns. And I most certainly will not permit you to pay my debts. If I would not permit my betrothed—"

"Don't preach at me, Lilith. It's bad enough I must see you shackle yourself to that staid Parliamentarian. I will not watch you pinch and scrape in the meantime."

There was again the barely contained anger she'd heard the night before.

"Don't," she said. "Don't speak this way."

He moved to her again. "What does it matter what I say? Who's to hear it? Is it so villainous that I don't wish to see you suffer? Come, my love," he said, lightly touching her cheek. "I have so few real amusements. This is amusing, truly it is. To keep a woman for my rival will be a novelty. I've never attempted such a thing before, you know, and we are told love makes men do the oddest things."

The distance between them had closed to mere inches. He was so near he must hear her heart pounding. There were many sensible things to say, any number of proper speeches, all of them dismissals.

All she could say was, "Don't."

"Lilith."

Slowly, she raised her head. In his green eyes burned the same compelling ardour she'd tried to ignore last evening.

"I love you," he whispered. "Is there to be no happiness for us?"

"My lord, I beg you—"

"Julian. Not your lord, but yours."

He raised her trembling hand to his lips, then turned it over and kissed the palm.

Lilith had battled with her treacherous self all night, and believed she'd conquered at last. She'd thought Reason and Right had won. Her will must be stronger than her need. More potent even than physical desire, that need encompassed the happiness he spoke of. He'd given her joy she'd never before dreamt of, just as the guilty misery he'd brought her was beyond even her long experience of pain. Into her life as well he'd driven passion, which she'd never known at all until he'd touched her.

But her will had conquered all this madness, she reminded herself as his lips pressed her wrist and her limbs grew weak. She pulled her hand away.

At that moment came a soft tap at the door. Lilith

retreated from the marquess.

The door opened, and Cawble entered with the tea tray. Apparently unmoved by the presence of a gentleman in his mistress's private study, the butler calmly set the tray upon a table by the small, well-worn settee.

Lord Brandon bit his lip and strode to the fireplace.

The butler had brought but one teacup. Politely, he enquired whether madam required another.

"No," she said. "His lordship is leaving."

His lordship threw her a reproachful look.

"Leaving shortly," she added weakly.

Cawble exited.

"You *are* leaving," she said more firmly when the door had closed. "You will return those papers to me, my lord. I am not at the workhouse door yet, and even if I were, I should not accept your *carte blanche*. That is what you mean, though you put it so prettily. I am not a fool, though at times I seem to behave like one. Still, having no experience with men of your ilk, I cannot be as well-armed as I could wish."

A shadow crossed his features, leaving his eyes dark and uneasy. "You can't believe that," he said. "After all this time, you can't believe my feelings aren't genuine. You must believe I love you."

Too tender. Too sincere. It was a dangerously beguiling voice, uttering those melting words.

"I can scarcely believe you have so little conscience as to give your desire for mere pleasure the name *love*," she said. "Mere pleasure, or the sport of ruining me—I don't know which. I shall never understand you," she added wearily, unhappily. "But if there is any pity in your heart, I beg you to leave me in peace."

He hesitated, his face stiffening. Perhaps, at last, she'd touched whatever he had of a conscience. She waited, praying he'd go quickly, because the sorrow in his countenance was weakening her with every passing second.

He moved at last, but not to the door, and by the time his arms folded round her, all her resolve was crumbling.

"I can't leave you," he breathed against her hair. "Don't talk to me of pleasure, when I haven't known a moment's peace since I've met you. Oh, yes, this is fine sport—to scheme and wait, just for a word or two—to want to touch you, hold you, care for you—and know all the while that what I want can only hurt you. You drive me mad, Lilith. What am I to do?"

All the same, he knew what to do. His fingers raked her hair and drew her head back, and his mouth was claiming hers before she could answer. Then it was her body answered, as it always did.

His mouth was hungry and seeking this time, and the hands tearing the pins from her hair moved urgently, impatiently, until the whole heavy mass fell loose upon her back.

She knew heat, and the wild rhythms of her quickening senses. The scent of sandalwood . . . the throb of muscles tensing under her fingertips . . . cool, crisp curls brushing her face and throat . . . a trail of kisses like sparks leaping into flames. Strong hands moulded her to the lean, powerful length of him in a hungry meeting that burned up all her will and left Reason in ashes. He was the Devil, consuming her, body and soul. She could not withstand him. She only craved.

Her hands moved to his neck, to pull his teasing, tormenting mouth harder against her own. In the growing turbulence, she never knew how they came to the settee. In his arms, where she had to be, she was lost to all the world. Only his world existed: his mouth and hands, caressing, inflaming . . . his heart, pounding its fury against hers . . . and his voice, low, and ragged with longing as fierce as her own.

Somewhere, miles away in the storm, a bell tolled.

Julian was about to tear off his neck-cloth when he heard the sound again. A chime. Coming from somewhere. A hall . . . in a house.

His hand paused at the knot of his cravat. *Her* house. He groaned as reality thumped down upon him. A house, filled with servants—and a niece and companion like to return any minute. What time was it?

He had not counted the chimes, and he could not reach for his pocket watch, because a lady was in the way.

Her eyes, dark with passion, opened, and a shaft of pain shot through him. Gad, those eyes. Oh, and that mouth, swollen now, ripe and so inviting. He bent and kissed her lingeringly, then groaned again, because it must stop. Now. *Now,* he commanded himself as her hand crept to his hair.

He took the hand away and kissed it. "My love," he said hoarsely. "I must go."

She blinked once, twice, uncomprehendingly. Then the world must have come back to her as well, for the colour rose in her cheeks even as the smoky passion ebbed from her eyes . . . and left them troubled.

That, he thought, would not do. He kissed her again, then wished he hadn't, because there could be no surcease for him this night, and holding her in his arms with no hope of consummation was only torment. He'd been tormented enough, all this long while. Was it an hour, two? Or only minutes?

He couldn't think, not with her warm body pressed against him. But the body began to struggle, and a hand was pushing at his chest.

He drew back slightly.

"You said you were going," she said, panting. "Then *go.*"

He looked at her. Her hair was a riotous tumble of gleaming, fire-tinted curls. At her throat, a mere three of the long parade of tiny buttons were undone. That had been accomplished with so much difficulty, he thought a lifetime needed to undo the rest.

"You might at least contrive to appear sorry," he complained as he helped her sit upright. "Obviously, you have no notion the agonies I suffer at having to stop."

The teasing note was in his voice only, not in his heart.

He should never have been so incautious. What might have happened had he not chanced to hear the clock chime?

"You would have had no difficulties if you hadn't begun." She pushed her heavy hair back from her face.

"Don't say that, Lilith," he said quickly, appalled at the ominous glistening in her eyes. "Don't make me feel like a criminal for loving you." He took both her hands in his. "Look at me," he commanded softly.

The smoky blue gaze swept his face.

"I can never hurt you," he said. "I only wanted to hold you for a little while. No, that isn't true. You know I want more—but I can be content with what you're willing to give." He smiled wryly. "If not, I should have ravished you by now."

"Indeed. In my own house, filled with servants—in my study, no less. And my niece—Good heavens! What time is it?" She jerked her hands free and jumped up so quickly she nearly knocked him off the settee.

He recovered his balance and drew her back down beside him. "Not so late," he said. "But I shall not go without a promise."

"No promises. Oh, Julian, please leave, do." She tried to pull her hand free again, but his grip was firm this time.

"In a moment. But I must see you again—and not in a crowd of Argus-eyed friends. Drive with me tomorrow."

"Oh, certainly. In Hyde Park, I expect, at five o'clock."

"There's no reason we may not take a turn in the park. My new curricle is ready. Surely you can ride in an open vehicle, with my tiger to lend us countenance?"

"No."

"My love," he coaxed. "Only a short drive. Can I not have you to myself now and then?"

"You've had me to yourself half the night—and see what comes of it. Oh, heaven help me, what is to be done with you?" Her searching scrutiny of his countenance made him uncomfortable. "You've the Devil's own tongue, and all his arts, I'm sure. You're like the bad angel, whispering in my ear—and I always *listen*."

All of which was to say she'd consented. His heart should have soared, because she'd listen, too, when he coaxed her to a small but luxuriously appointed house in Kensington that had been awaiting her some time now.

Lord Brandon's heart did not quite soar, though he wanted her more than ever, if that were possible. He could not recollect when any woman had so stirred him with mere kisses, or when the lightest caresses had ever aroused such maddening desire. It had been enough, certainly, to make him forget where he was—aye, and who he was, if it came to that.

He was happy, and relieved, naturally, because his trials would soon be over. Still, her words troubled him. Though he'd used all his arts upon her, he did wish she wouldn't remind him.

As soon as Julian had gone, Lilith ran up to her bedchamber. Having firmly declined Mary's services, Lilith doggedly prepared herself for bed, though she was in such a tumult she could scarcely see straight.

She was not, as she'd reminded her would-be lover, a fool. Besotted though she was, she possessed sense enough to understand tomorrow's ride would be no mere turn about the park. He would not be content to sit beside her, talking about draining fields or breeding cattle. Nor, she admitted to her shame, would she.

She had sufficient sense as well to comprehend that "love" was Julian's euphemism for physical pleasure. Why he should want Lilith Davenant she would never understand. That hardly mattered any more. She wanted him, craved his company, longed for the sound of his teasing voice, yes, and ached for his touch. He was, just as everyone had claimed, irresistible. Thus, yet another infatuated woman would succumb to him.

She sat at the dressing table and brushed out her tangled hair. He'd pulled out every single pin in seconds, it seemed. Tonight he was not the teasing, lazy lover she'd first known.

This night, passion had come in a thundering fury. He might have ravished her easily enough in that tempest.

Yet a sweet tempest it was, sending joy surging through her . . . and that was why.

She put down the brush and began to braid her hair, the steady motion a counterpoint to the quivering ache within.

She'd never known such furious joy. She never would with any other. She would have it once, with him. She would not deny him, though she knew he'd leave her soon after. That was his nature. All the same, she would not deny him, because she would not deny herself. She must have his passionate lovemaking once—though she be damned for it. She must have that . . . because she would go on loving him all the rest of her life.

# === 15 ===

RACHEL'S FIRST INSTINCT was to tell her brother what she'd
overheard. In any case, had he bothered to glance at her
shocked face when she entered the box, he would have
questioned her immediately. Luckily, the box was dark, and
he was too busy explaining the moral of the play to Cecily.

Thus the first wave of outrage passed, leaving more
sensible second thoughts in its wake: if Thomas learned of
the wager, he'd have to challenge Brandon to a duel, and
the marquess would kill him. Even if Thomas survived the
duel, his career would never survive the scandal.

Consequently, Rachel kept her news to herself, and took
out her frustration on her husband when he appeared some
ten minutes later.

At eleven o'clock the next morning, Lady Enders was
closeted with Lilith in the latter's sitting room.

Though her husband was an active MP, Rachel was
scarcely a politic woman, and her terse revelations fell plain
as bludgeon blows. All the same, except for a momentary
loss of colour and the rigid set of her features, Lilith
appeared to digest the news with her usual impassivity.

"A wager," she repeated expressionlessly when Rachel
had done ranting about perfidious males and the punishment they'd suffer if ever *she* had a hand in the nation's
management.

"Yes—as though a defenseless woman were a pack of
cards or a set of dice. Oh, I knew he was a villain, but this

172

is beyond mere villainy. It is beyond anything! How can a man appear so pleasing, with his heart so black and vile inside him? 'Whited sepulchres,' " Rachel quoted, " 'Which indeed appear beautiful outward.' And so he did, my dear. Even I was taken in, so amusing he was, and such an agreeable smile. I should have known better. The leopard doesn't change his spots. I shall never forgive myself."

"For what?" Lilith asked coldly. "It is merely a wager—a foolish one, since he cannot but lose, and I'm sure it's nothing to him to lose a few thousand pounds. Or a horse. Or whatever the . . . the stake was."

"But to wager on such a thing—a lady's honour—"

"I have my honour still, Rachel. Or perhaps you had doubts?"

There was a flurry of ruffles, and Lady Enders's face turned puce to match them. "Good heavens! How can you say such a thing? The thought never crossed my mind. I should never have mentioned the matter, I am sure, but that you . . . well . . ." She hesitated.

Lilith lifted her chin. "Yes?"

"My dear, it is only that you have been quite friendly with him of late."

Lilith made no answer, and Lady Enders plunged on. "I thought it my duty to let you know what sort of *friendship* he had in mind. Knowing of this matter, naturally you will not wish to continue the acquaintance? We do not know how many others are part of this infamous speculation, or in what manner he is to demonstrate—that is—"

"I understand what it is, Rachel. You need not be anxious. I hope I know how to conduct myself in these—or in any— circumstances."

Lord Brandon arrived, as he'd promised, promptly at a quarter to four o'clock.

He'd scarcely contained his impatience the whole long day, though he found enough to do in ordering up champagne and every sort of delicacy, in seeing the small house in Kensington filled with flowers, in checking the gowns hung in the wardrobe and the lingerie tucked with sachets into drawers. Today, for a few precious, uninterrupted hours, Lilith Davenant would be entirely his, at last.

And at last he was shown into the drawing room. He was not surprised to find her alone. He was surprised to discover she was not dressed to go out. She wore a plain brown frock, and her hair was braided tight about her head. Deep shadows ringed her eyes. As he moved eagerly across the room to her, he saw as well that she'd been weeping. A chill of anxiety ran through him.

"My love," he said, holding out his hands.

She retreated a step. Her white face set into taut lines and her posture stiffened.

"You will not touch me," she said. "You will not say another word. I meet you this once only to tell you our acquaintance is at an end. Henceforth, I do not know you."

The chill clawed at his heart now. "Lilith."

She turned and pulled the bell-rope. "Cawble will show you out. Good day, my lord."

"Lilith! What is this?" He reached for her hands, but she moved back another step and folded them tightly before her.

"This is how you lose a wager, my lord," she said.

He felt the blood rushing to his face.

"Good God," he breathed. "You must . . ."

The door opened, and Cawble appeared. "Madam?"

"His lordship is leaving, Cawble."

Lord Brandon left quietly enough.

Dismissed.

In a few cold sentences.

So cold, so certain, they'd crushed argument before it could begin, or when he might have begun, came the death-blow. He'd not mistaken the words: "This is how you lose a wager."

Numb, he climbed into his curricle. He stared blankly at

the house a moment, then set the horses in motion.

He'd driven on blindly, he knew not how far—a street, a turning, another street—when Sims, his tiger, spoke up.

"My lord, it's that Hobbs. He wants you to stop."

Only then did Lord Brandon take note of the figure running after the curricle, shouting something. The marquess drew the horses to a standstill, threw the ribbons to Sims, and jumped down.

"Beggin' your pardon, my lord, but Susan told me I was to stop you no matter what."

"So you have," said his lordship. "I am at your disposal."

"She told me to tell you Lady Enders was by this morning. Her and my mistress was locked up private most of an hour, and when the missus come out she was—she was—What was it?"

Lord Brandon waited.

"In a taking, I think. What did Susan say? Up in the boughs. That was what Miss Glenwood told her. Up in the boughs like no one ever seen before." He looked up at Lord Brandon's still, hard countenance. "I 'spect she was warning you, my lord, or trying to. But I was down in the kitchen and no way to step out before you come. But Susan said I was to tell you anyhow."

Lord Brandon gazed blankly about him. Lady Enders. That was how Lilith had found out. Lady Enders must have overheard . . . last night. His fault. He'd been so impatient to get away, he'd scarcely watched the stairs, let alone the corridor. Anyone might have overheard.

He dropped a few pieces of silver into Hobbs's hand, thanked him, climbed back into the curricle, and headed for the village of Kensington.

When they reached the house, the marquess sent Sims and the curricle away. Neither would be required this evening. He'd already dispatched the other servants, because strangers would have made Lilith uncomfortable.

Julian entered the small, tastefully furnished room where

a cold meal had been laid out. The door to the adjoining bedchamber was partly open. He closed it.

He pulled a bottle of champagne from the silver ice bucket, opened it, and filled one crystal goblet.

Lilies had been cut into the crystal. Lilies bloomed everywhere, in one form or another—upon the wall coverings and draperies and carpets. There were orchids, as well, because he'd once compared her beauty to orchids, and because she'd worn them in her hair—his gift. The first of many gifts, he'd thought. He would shower his imperious mistress with tributes.

He took his wineglass and walked to the window, where he stood a long while. Evening was hours away, yet black night seemed to be falling already. The heavy clouds had darkened, and rain tapped steadily upon the windowpanes.

She might have been with him now. They might have stood together, watching the rain draw hurried, swirling patterns upon the glass.

He would have appeared to watch the rain, but his glance would steal to her face, to study her proud profile. He would not have heard the pattering beat against the windowpanes, only her quiet, cool voice, its cadences rich and smooth, even when animated, when she talked of Derbyshire and her land. Or wistful, as she sometimes was, caught by some bittersweet memory.

He would have made her laugh, perhaps. But he would not have been quite content until he had taken all the pins from her hair. He would not have been altogether easy until she was in his arms. Then he would sweep her into the storm with him, because hers was a passionate spirit, demanding and willful as his own. Not to be broken or bent. Still, he might have possessed it. Even now, all that was Lilith Davenant might have been his.

*This is how you lose a wager.*

He turned and hurled his wineglass across the room. It struck the mantel and shattered into sparkling shards.

Lost—aye, lost *her*—and all his own doing.

What had he told Elise? Something about the challenge being irresistible, wasn't it? A challenge merely. The tart had known him better than he knew himself. She'd comprehended quickly enough the extent of his overweening vanity.

That was it. Vanity and one thoughtless moment—and his was a lifetime of such moments—had cost him this one woman he wanted above all others. Wanted, he discovered now, as some blade seemed to twist in his chest, more than anything else in this world.

A few minutes after Mrs. Davenant had left her niece's room, Susan appeared to dress the girl for the evening. She found Miss Glenwood curled up in a chair, her chin resting on her hand and her brow puckered. She looked up at the maid's entrance.

"Oh, Susan, how I wish you and Hobbs had been quicker— though I much doubt it would have helped. It is worse than I thought."

"I was as quick as I could be, Miss Cecily," said the maid. "But Hobbs couldn't get away in time, and if the missus was to get wind—"

"She's got wind of something, and I wish I knew what it was. It must have been dreadful, because she is so miserable, and terribly, terribly confused. Why, she just now said she'd been *neglecting* me. Have you ever heard the like? And such a long lecture about my gentlemen friends. She said it all so kindly and sadly, I didn't have the heart to remind her I already knew all *that*."

"All what, miss?"

Cecily stood up and walked to the wardrobe. "I should like to wear the pink muslin, but tonight we'd better do without the lace."

"Do without? Your aunt'll have my head. You know how she feels about young girls showing their bosoms."

"Yes, and I should not wish to upset her, so I must be late

going down, and you must be certain to arrange my wrap very carefully."

The widow's party was unusually late arriving at Lady Violet Porter's rout.

Lord Robert, who'd been elbowed, backed into, and trod on this last hour, was beginning to wonder how he could have been so mad as to come. He had no one to talk to, and he couldn't breathe. He'd have done better to spend the evening pacifying his mistress. Julian had warned that an emotional woman like Elise might so far forget herself as to create scenes at the most inconvenient times.

Then Lord Robert spied Miss Glenwood proceeding slowly up the stairs, her aunt on one side, Sir Thomas on the other. Miss Glenwood met his glance and smiled. Lord Robert promptly began shoving his way through the crowd. He reached the top of the stairs just as the trio did, greeted the widow and the baronet politely, greeted Cecily—took a second look at Cecily—then hastily excused himself.

He was about to plunge back the way he'd come, when he happened to glance back. He saw Mr. Ventcoeur bend over Miss Glenwood's small hand. In the next moment, that hand was tucked into Mr. Ventcoeur's arm.

Lord Robert left the rout.

Indecent was what it was.

What on earth could her aunt have been thinking of, to allow the girl to go about half naked, so that every lout in London could ogle her? And of all the louts to give her arm to, that crude imbecile, Ventcoeur.

Well, if the aunt didn't know better, Lord Robert Downs certainly did. He would give Miss Glenwood a serious talking-to. Tomorrow.

Tomorrow came and went and there was no talking-to, because Lord Robert found no opportunity. The one country dance Miss Glenwood allotted him was hardly conducive to serious conversation. She was winded at the end of it—as was all too evident in the rapid rise and fall of—

At any rate, by the time they'd both caught their breath, her next partner had stepped in to claim her.

The following night was exactly the same.

Consequently, early Monday afternoon, Lord Robert borrowed his cousin's curricle without permission, called at the house, and invited Miss Glenwood to drive with him.

She was very quiet until they reached the Park gates. Then she sighed and said she had something to tell him.

"Yes, well, I have something to tell *you*, Miss Glenwood," he answered. Before he could lose his courage, he plunged into the sermon he'd rehearsed.

She listened very attentively, then looked at him in a puzzled way. "I don't understand," she said. "When Papa wants to sell a mare, he doesn't cover the poor animal with blankets, but displays her to best advantage. I'm on the market, you know."

"On the what?" he cried.

"To be married. That's why I'm in London, isn't it? That's why all the girls come. And I don't at all understand what's so immodest. Lady Rockridge is quite strict, yet Anne's frocks are much more daring than mine, and no one's shocked. Even my aunt had to admit *that*, though she blushed the whole time. But poor Aunt is so confused."

Lord Robert made no answer. Miss Glenwood was a levelheaded girl, and it was quite true about Anne's frocks—indeed, about most of the gowns to be seen in any Season. All the same, it seemed very wrong for Miss Glenwood to go about in such revealing costumes. She was a child, still. Well, not exactly, but—

There burst into his mind at this moment a vision of a feminine form in breeches, and he grew dizzy.

"It's because they've quarrelled, you know," Cecily continued. "I know it was something dreadful because I heard Aunt Lilith tell Cawble that Lord Brandon was not to be admitted to the house. And your cousin must be just as angry, because he keeps away."

Lord Robert shook himself to attention. His cousin he could talk about articulately.

"Miss Glenwood, I must tell you, Julian would never keep away from anything on account of a woman."

"He was not at Lady Violet's rout Friday, or at Lady Shumway's Saturday, or Lady Greenaway's last night."

"Saturday was Kean's first appearance as Othello," Robert argued. "Naturally, Julian would go."

"For weeks and weeks he's always appeared wherever my aunt is. Yet ever since they quarrelled, we haven't seen him. I expect he's just as miserable as she is, and they're both too proud and stubborn to admit it."

"In that case, they're better off apart, don't you think?"

"How can you say such a thing?" Her blue eyes flashed a reproach. "You know they must marry. Fortunately," she added reassuringly, "I have a plan."

He was so startled he nearly dropped the reins.

"Marry? Each other? Your aunt is *engaged* already."

"Well, she can't marry that tiresome, preaching man, can she?"

"Miss Glenwood—"

"You're confusing the horses, Lord Robert. Do call the one on the left to order before takes us into that tree."

Lord Robert drew the carriage to a halt.

"Miss Glenwood—"

"You needn't be anxious. It's a very good plan, and really, quite simple."

At this moment, an enormous grey cloud swallowed up the sun. The heavens darkened, and Lord Robert felt a chill at the base of his skull. "Drat," he said. "It's going to rain."

Miss Glenwood glanced up. "Not for hours," she said.

Sure enough, the cloud moved on and the sun shone brightly again. Nonetheless, Lord Robert felt as though the cloud had settled within him. "Miss Glenwood," he said gently, "you really oughtn't be contriving any plans. It's none of our affair, and even if it were, it wouldn't do any good, because Julian's a hardened bachelor. If they've had a row, maybe it's for the best."

Miss Glenwood appeared to consider. "Perhaps you're right," she said after a moment. "It must be the strain telling on me. Aunt won't let me stir a step without her any more. I assumed that was because she didn't know what else to do with herself. And, naturally, when I heard all that long lecture about you, I was bound to think she must be a bit irrational. How could she imagine I didn't know all that already?"

The cloud within seemed to grow heavier and darker then.

"About me?" Lord Robert said uneasily. "I hope she wasn't repeating a lot of idle gossip."

"Not at all. But such obvious facts, I'd be utterly feather-brained not to be aware of them. Really, there was no need to tell me you couldn't possibly be a serious suitor. Even if you weren't desperately in love with that beautiful Frenchwoman, what on earth would you want with an ignorant country girl? Certainly I'm not grand enough for you, and naturally your family must object. I couldn't blame them, could I? After all, my portion would hardly keep you in neck-cloths."

The sophisticated man of the world blushed hotly, which must have vexed him, because he grew altogether unreasonably irate at the perfectly reasonable way in which Miss Glenwood had just discounted him.

He did not see, he told her, why there was any need for her aunt to warn her against him. Had he behaved improperly? He hadn't even attempted to kiss her—though he had no doubt Ventcoeur had, such an unprincipled, crude character he was. Her aunt didn't warn Miss Glenwood against any other fellows, though Lord Robert had seen them all ogling and gawking in the most *obscene* way. As to portions, he had far less need of a huge dowry than Beldon had.

"I may be a younger son," he raged, "but I'm certainly not so pinched for funds that I have to dodge the bailiff. I'm very shocked, Miss Glenwood, indeed I am, that you'd for a minute think I'd ever marry for money, or be looking out for some duke's spoiled, stuck-up daughter just to please my stiff-necked family."

"Of course not," she answered calmly. "That would be so silly, when you practically have a wife already—and very beautiful she is, too. Also clever, I expect, or you'd be excessively bored, being so very clever yourself."

"Miss Glenwood," he said, acutely uncomfortable, "this is not a proper subject to discuss."

"Very well. What would you rather talk about?"

While he was desperately seeking a topic, his cousin's spirited cattle began snorting and prancing with impatience. Experienced horsewoman that she was, Miss Glenwood's gesture must have been instinctive. She only reached for the ribbons, and her small gloved hand touched his.

Then she blushed . . . and bit her lip . . . and hastily folded her hands in her lap.

Lord Robert looked at her pink, downcast profile and at the soft, full lip caught between her perfect white teeth, then at the dainty gloved hands.

While he was looking, the ribbons somehow transferred to one hand while the other took hers.

Her long lashes swept up slowly.

"Oh, Lord," he said.

"You should not be holding my hand," she said softly.

"I know," he said. "I can't help it. Miss Glenwood."

"Yes?" Her face was lifted to his, her lips slightly parted. There was an odd ringing in his ears, and Lord Robert had a curious sensation of falling—which, in a manner of speaking, he *was,* because his own face lowered to meet hers . . . and before he knew what he'd done, he'd kissed her.

Being a level-headed miss, the young lady ought to have boxed his ears. She did not. Thus the kiss continued a deal longer than it should have done. Long enough so that, when he finally remembered to stop, he could not possibly pretend it had been a mere friendly token of goodwill.

"Oh, my," she said.

"Miss Glenwood, I do beg your pardon. I don't know—"

She gazed at him in admiration. "Oh, but I think you *do.* That was ever so lovely. Really, it was a revelation. Rodger has never kissed me like that. All I ever get from him or James is a peck on the cheek, and only when they're in exceedingly good humour."

"Yes, Miss Glenwood, but I'm not your brother. I wouldn't be your brother," he added vehemently, "for anything in this world."

"Wouldn't you? What would you like to be?"

Lord Robert took a deep breath, tore his gaze from her blue, unwinking one, and stared fixedly at the horses.

"I don't mean to be forward, but I do wish you'd settle it in your mind," she said. "You can't be in love with two women at the same time, you know, and if you're not in love with me, it would be most unkind to confuse me with such agreeable kisses. I can't afford to be muddled at present. I have too many responsibilities."

With the matter thus set so plainly before him, Lord Robert could hardly fail to grasp it. In fact, he was mortified. He could not understand how he could have been so obtuse.

"I'm afraid I'm very much in love with you, Miss Glen—Cecily," he said, his face scarlet.

"I'm glad to hear it," she said. "I was beginning to feel quite ridiculous. I've been in love with you ever so long."

Relief quickly succeeded astonishment. He opened his mouth to speak, then changed his mind. There could be no other response to such a sweet, frank avowal but another fervent kiss. But as he drew away, the reality of his situation hurtled upon Lord Robert like a runaway carriage. Her disapproving aunt, bound to throw obstacles in their way . . . as though his own family wouldn't be quick enough to do that, though she was hardly in the same category as Elise— Good God! Elise!

"Egad!" he blurted out. "Now I'm in a devil of a fix."

"Not at all," came the confident response. "So long as we've got matters straight between us, we can mend everything else—because two heads are ever so much better than one, aren't they?"

# == 16 ==

WHATEVER OTHER PROBLEMS two heads might solve, that of Elise was Lord Robert's alone. No gentleman could possibly expect a gently bred innocent to advise him how to be rid of his mistress, especially when he'd solemnly pledged to marry that mistress in two months' time.

Accordingly, feeling like the lowest species of cur, Lord Robert drove to his lodgings.

As he opened the door, the scented atmosphere nearly turned a stomach that was already in knots. His mistress's affectionate greeting sent his conscience into screaming fits. He thought perhaps his confession could wait until tomorrow, but he'd no sooner thought it than he remembered Cecily's sweet, innocent mouth. He backed away as Elise moved to embrace him.

"What is this?" she cried. "You cannot be angry with me. What has your poor Lise done to make you so cold?" She retreated as well. "Ah, but you are often so, I find. I think so much time in grand company makes you despise me."

He swallowed. "I don't despise you. Not at all. You've been—you've been wonderful to me. Better than I deserve. That is to say, I don't know why you've stuck it out so long."

She turned glistening eyes upon him. "So long? But I told you *forever*. Have I not promised? Have I not pledged myself to you?"

"Yes, well, maybe you shouldn't have." Lord Robert took another deep breath, made himself look her in the eye, and said, "I'm afraid I've fallen in love with someone else."

Her dark eyes opened wide in shock. He turned away and moved to the mantel.

"I didn't mean to," he said, picking up one of the framed silhouettes that stood there. "It just happened. I think it happened weeks ago, but it never occurred to me. I never dreamed I could love anyone else. But I do, and—and so I came to ask you to let me go. You can't want to marry a man who's in love with another woman."

He replaced the picture and waited.

There was a long silence. Then she said, her voice hurt but gentle, "Ah, my poor Robin. You have some infatuation, I comprehend. Well, I must be patient. It will fade, and you will find me still waiting."

"Elise, I'm sorry, but it's not like that," he answered, vexed at her humouring him. "I'm going to marry her—as soon as I can."

Mademoiselle Fourgette promptly swooned.

An hour later, Robert drove away, in worse case than when he'd arrived. He'd talked until he was blue in the face, and Elise—usually so perceptive—had been utterly unable to understand him. She was thoroughly convinced his new passion was but a whim.

At length, torn with guilt and not a little frustrated, he'd tried to buy his mistress off. Half his trust fund he'd promised. It would be hers forever. He'd have papers drawn up immediately.

Then she'd fainted again, and when she revived, there was no talking to her at all, because she was hysterical. She could not think, she told him. Her head was spinning. It was too much to take in at once. He must give her time to recover from the shock. He could not be so cruel as to press her now—and to speak of money!

Still, Robert told himself as he brought the carriage to the mews, he would press, because she must be got to go away peaceably. Good God—what if she took to haunting him, as Lady Caroline had haunted Byron all last year?

What if they met up in public and Elise created a scene?

She very well might. Julian had warned about that only the other day. Cecily might understand, but her aunt— Gad, if Elise enacted any scenes in front of the widow, he and Cecily would be done for.

Julian. Of course. Julian always knew what to do. First, unfortunately, there'd be hell to pay about borrowing the curricle. Still, he'd only rip up fierce for a while, and after, he'd order brandy. Then Robert would ask his advice.

Accordingly, when Julian had returned to the house to change for the evening, Lord Robert squared his shoulders, marched up the stairs, and knocked at the door.

He found the marquess standing by the window, staring out. "What do you want now?" Julian asked.

Stammering a good deal, Robert made his confession to his cousin's back.

"Sims would not have let you take the curricle if he did not trust your skill," was the dispassionate response. "Feel free to drive yourself to perdition."

"Yes, well, that's very kind of you," Robert said nervously.

"Indeed, I am a model of every Christian virtue."

Julian turned round. His face was its usual mask of boredom. Obviously, then, he could not be miserable, regardless what Cecily believed. Tired, perhaps.

"I hate to bother you," Robert said, trying for airiness, "but I'm in a devil of a fix, don't you know? You see, I borrowed the curricle so I could take Miss Glenwood driving— "

The black eyebrows rose slightly. "Her aunt permitted the girl to drive with you?"

"Well, not exactly—though I don't see why she shouldn't. Anyhow, she'd gone to Lady Enders's. Still, Mrs. Wellwicke didn't raise any sort of fuss. Don't see why she should. No harm in a fellow taking a girl out for a drive in an open— "

"Good God."

"I beg your pardon?"

The marquess turned back to the window. "Get out," he said.

"But, Julian, I have to speak with you. It's very important. Elise—"

"Go to hell."

Man of honour or no, Lord Robert saw no alternative but to confide these latest developments to Cecily. Julian clearly was not going to be any help. He was apparently in a perfectly hideous fit of the blue devils. Even Hillard had quietly advised Robert to keep out of his cousin's way.

If Julian wouldn't help pacify Elise, the poor distracted woman might very well do something rash. It was only fair to prepare Cecily for that eventuality.

The information was relayed that night in short bursts while they danced.

Cecily accepted the news with her usual imperturbability, and told him not to worry about *that*. The major problem at present was Aunt Lilith.

"She was terribly disappointed in me because I went driving with you," said Cecily. "And so we had another heart-to-heart talk, and now you and I must be exceedingly cautious."

Caution, it turned out, meant that Lord Robert was not to attend every single affair she did. Cecily had promised her aunt she'd not spend so much time with him.

Cecily had not promised anything else, which must have made her conscience perfectly easy regarding the notes which thereafter travelled surreptitiously between the marquess's and the widow's town houses.

While these letters were being exchanged, the owner of a few dozen far more torrid ones was weighing her prospects.

Elise suspected within three days of the event that the widow had given Lord Brandon his *congé*. Elise heard of his reappearances at several of his old haunts, and saw him herself at the performance of *Othello*.

Therefore, she put off Lord Robert, visited with her friends, and listened to the shop girls' talk. Before a week had passed, her suspicions were confirmed: Society noted with disappointment that Lord Brandon had once again vanished into the depths of the *demimonde*.

Little more than a fortnight remained of the stipulated seduction period. He would lose, as Elise had been certain he would. She was equally certain his pride would not permit him to revert to his previous threats.

Perhaps he no longer cared what became of the letters or of Robert. On the other hand, what of the girl Robert was so eager to marry? Surely the marquess would wish to forward this oh-so-suitable match. In that case, he was bound to offer more than a mere half of Robert's paltry trust fund—and more likely to pay. Once wed, Robert might conveniently forget what he owed his mistress for two years' fidelity. Besides, Robert could not legally promise any portion of his trust fund until he was twenty-five. He might be wed before then.

Mlle. Fourgette concluded that, of her two options, the marquess was the lesser risk. She would gamble on him.

When, at the end of her week's recovery, Lord Robert called to renew his pleas, Elise was adamant: she would *never* give him up. He'd made a terrible mistake, but she'd forgive him, and would wait until he came to his senses. She did not, however, promise to wait quietly.

My Darling Cecily,

I've done my best but it's just as you feared and I know we're bound to raise the very Devvil of a Dust but there's no Choice. Julian and your Aunt are too wrappt up in their own Troubbles. Do forgive me Dearest Darling Cecily because I should of known better and been Patiant, you are always so Level-Headed. Now I only wait for you to give the Word only please let it be Soon as possibble, we can't wait much longer and don't dare. I know I can't wait much longer to make you Mine.

Your Adoring

Robert

Miss Glenwood did not, as was her custom, tear this missive to tiny pieces and burn it. She only smiled and murmured to herself, "Dear Robert. How sweetly you write—and so cleverly to the purpose."

Susan entered a while later, looking for the reply she knew must be forthcoming. "You'd better make haste, miss," she warned. "Hobbs can't be lingering about much longer."

"There's no need for him to linger," said Miss Glenwood. "Tell him the answer is *Tuesday*."

On Tuesday evening, Lord Brandon stood before his glass and stabbed an emerald pin into his cravat. The pin set off admirably the green embroidery of his satin waistcoat, and the combined effect drew riveting attention to his eyes.

This effect might not have been altogether desirable, considering his eyes were edged with deep shadows, the lines at the corners clearly evident, even in the flattering candlelight of his dressing room. In a few years, the lines would set deeply, and the furrow between his dark eyebrows would harden and deepen too. His face, like those of his older acquaintances, would reflect the empty, corrupt life he lived. In another few years, he'd look like every other aging roué.

Still, so long as he had money, he'd never lack for company. Even a troll could find some trollop to warm his bed, so long as he had the gold to persuade her.

Not that this night's harlot would require any great expenditure, he reflected. He was not decrepit yet, and though he'd not troubled to exert his notorious charm, the woman was willing. Another actress—but then, weren't they all?

He turned from the glass as Hillard entered.

"I've conquered the thing at last," his lordship said, with a brief glance at the heap of discarded neck-cloths he'd flung onto a chair. "Still, even Brummell has his share of failures."

"So he does, m'lud," said the valet, taking up his master's black evening coat. As the marquess thrust his arm into the left sleeve, a folded piece of thick stationery fell out. Hillard picked it up and handed it to him.

Five minutes later, Lord Brandon was running down the stairs, shouting for his curricle.

"The bloody fool!" he raged as he stomped to the vestibule. "I'll hang him myself! Where the devil is my curricle?"

A trembling footman wrenched open the front door. His lordship thundered through, and stormed round the corner to the stables.

"He's taken it?" Lord Brandon repeated, glaring at his tiger.

"I was just comin' to tell you, my lord. I was out, enjoyin' a pint with Hobbs and Jem, and these others," Sims said indignantly, glaring at two much-abashed stable lads, "didn't know any better."

"Never mind. I'll take the other carriage. Only, be quick, will you?"

While he waited for the carriage to be readied, Lord Brandon considered his options. He could go after them himself—now. They could not have more than an hour's start of him, more likely less. But Lilith—did she know yet? He hoped not. That idiot Bexley would be no help. His plodding nags would be better employed behind a plough.

"Had Hobbs any word for me?" he asked his tiger.

"He only said his mistress was going to Lady Jersey's, and the young lady—Miss Glenwood, that is—was sick at home. The other lady was staying with her. I meant to tell you, my lord, but I come back and these *numskulls*—"

"It doesn't matter. Where's Ezra?"

"You gave him the night off, my lord."

"Damn." The marquess briefly considered taking his horse, but quickly discarded that idea. The closed carriage was best. More discreet.

"Cover the crest," he told Sims. "And I'm sorry to offend your dignity, but you must serve as coachman this night."

When they reached the Jerseys', Lord Brandon remained within the vehicle and sent Sims round to the servants' entrance with a few gold coins and a message.

A quarter hour later, Mrs. Davenant was hurrying out the door and up the carriage steps.

She stopped short when she saw who was within.

Quickly he yanked her inside, and the carriage rumbled into motion.

"You—you —"

He put his hand over her mouth. "It's not a trick, and I'm not abducting you. Your niece is in trouble." Then he took his hand away and gave her Robert's note.

"What is this?" she cried. "How am I to read it in the dark?"

"I'll tell you what it says, but you may read it later if you don't believe me. They've eloped—my blasted fool of a cousin and your niece. That's why you were strongly advised to come alone. How did you keep your loyal fiancé from following, by the way?"

"He was talking with the Prince of Orange. I only repeated the message: that Cecily had taken a bad turn and Emma had sent Mary in a carriage for me. He offered to come, but I could not see what use he would be."

"Quite right. Men are useless when it comes to illness. I shall take you home, so that we can make certain Miss Glenwood is gone, and then—"

"She can't be," Lilith insisted. "I can't believe Cecily would do such a thing."

"Judging by Robert's purple prose, they consider themselves in desperate case."

She stared blindly at him a moment. "Oh, no," she said faintly, dropping back against the thick squabs. "It's my fault. I had no idea there was any—any serious feeling between them. I warned her repeatedly against him—but it was only to prevent her discouraging her other suitors. Oh, she couldn't have run away with him. She couldn't have misunderstood me so. I'm sure I never expressed any dislike of him."

"I'm sure you didn't," he said while inwardly cursing his cousin and Miss Glenwood. Desperate or no, couldn't they have considered how this woman would suffer?

"Still, I lectured. Too much, I see now. To think how the poor child must have wanted to confide the true state of her feelings—and didn't dare. She must have suffered terribly, or she would never, never do such a shocking thing."

Lord Brandon decided to keep his own counsel on the subject of Cecily's sufferings. His cousin, he was convinced, had neither the forethought nor the intelligence to plan an elopement. This had obviously been planned. Had he known sooner about Miss Glenwood's "illness," the marquess would have smelled a rat. Cecily Glenwood was the type of girl who never took ill. Left naked in a monsoon, she'd come away without so much as a sniffle. Furthermore, unless he was very much mistaken in her character, Miss Glenwood had planned everything, down to the last detail.

Except perhaps the note. The girl would not have been so careless as to leave clues. The note must have been Robert's own fevered piece of work. Quite the correspondent that boy was.

Miss Glenwood, as the marquess had predicted, was not in her room, or anywhere in the house.

All that turned up after a frantic search was one crumpled note—again Lord Robert's. Emma found it by the wardrobe door, where Cecily must have accidentally dropped it.

Lilith read it, then handed it to Lord Brandon.

His lip curled as he glanced over it. "It only confirms the obvious. They've been planning this some time," he said, thrusting the note into his pocket. "I'd better be off. They've nearly two hours' start by now, and a speedier vehicle. Still, I have no doubt Sims will make up the time. With any luck, I'll have them back before morning."

"*We* shall have them back," Lilith corrected. "You can't believe I'd stay behind. My niece will need me."

He paused at the doorway and turned around.

Lilith had been too overwrought to spare him more than a glance. Now, she was taken aback by the grim set of his countenance and the deep shadows round his eyes. He looked ill—as he had when she'd first met him. Or more ill, perhaps. His face was thinner, older, and his green eyes were dull with fatigue.

"You can't come," he said. "You'll be jolted to pieces for hours on end. Besides, there's always the chance I *won't* be in luck, and you must be here to keep off the scandal-mongers."

Lilith turned to Emma. "You'll see to that, won't you?"

The plump lady nodded. "Certainly. I've only to mention the ailment is contagious, and everyone will keep away." She threw Lilith a reassuring smile. "I'll see to everything here. Naturally, you must go. If nothing else, Cecily must come back chaperoned."

As she spoke, Emma was opening drawers. "I'll put together a few things for Cecily—and you must take some necessaries yourself. You don't know how long you'll be upon the road."

The marquess glanced from one woman to the other. "I'll wait downstairs," he said.

# === 17 ===

THEY SAT IN opposite corners of the coach, staring out the windows. Not until they were well out of London did Lord Brandon break the silence.

"I'm sorry," he said.

"It's hardly your fault," Lilith made herself answer. "If anyone's to blame in this, it's I—"

"That's not what I meant. Or at least, it's not all. My aunt—Robert's mother—has no high opinion of the men in our family. A lot of contemptible rogues, she thinks us. Some weeks ago she told me . . . well, it doesn't matter—but I do wish it hadn't been my own cousin, of all men, to bring you such trouble. You've been injured enough. By God, Lilith, I'm sorry."

Her throat ached. She waited until she could control her voice, then said, "They will have to stop to change horses. Cecily will not let him abuse your cattle. I shall pray the ostlers are very slow."

"Lilith."

"She packed very little. Perhaps they'll have to stop to purchase—"

"Lilith, please. I'm not asking you to forgive me—but there's something you must know."

She returned her gaze to the window. "We shall likely be journeying together many hours, my lord. You had meant to travel alone. Perhaps it would be best to behave as though you were doing so."

There was a moment's heavy silence in the dark carriage.

Then he said wearily, "Yes, perhaps, as always, I am."

Though the carriage stopped frequently so that Lord Brandon could make enquiries, he had by sunrise still no word of Cecily and Robert.

"I don't understand it," the marquess said as he climbed back in for what seemed the hundredth time. "How is it possible no toll-gate keeper, no innkeeper, has seen them? Robert could not possibly have had sufficient funds to bribe every human being en route."

The widow's hand was pressed to her temples. Her head must be aching horribly.

"I begin to think they may not be headed for Gretna after all," she said. "Perhaps the note was written to mislead."

"But where else would they go? I doubt my cousin could have obtained a special license. It's not as though the bishops hand them out to every hot-headed young idiot who comes along."

"You're right. Very likely they've merely made a few detours. But they must return to the Great North Road at some point, mustn't they?"

Her voice, as always, was evenly modulated, low and controlled. Another woman would have spent the journey in complaints or hysterics. Not Lilith Davenant. For hours she'd sat mute, staring into the darkness. This was the longest conversation they'd had since his abortive attempt to . . . to what? Apologise? Explain? As though there could be any apology, or explanation.

He'd had ample time to reflect, and thus to wonder why he'd believed it could signify in any way that he'd wanted her from the first, and wanted her yet. Regardless the motive, his aim had always been seduction. He'd never had her best interests at heart. All that had moved him was Desire.

He'd struggled, all these hours, to keep from looking at her. He'd been trying, all these last endless days, to banish her image from his mind. Now he must begin all over again.

All the same, in spite of his resolutions, his glance stole to her white, still face. She had not wept—not once. But her fine, slate-blue eyes were red-rimmed, her proud countenance tired and drawn. She'd seemed exhausted even before they started out, yet she refused to rest, and she'd scarcely touched a morsel when they stopped. She remained calm and upright by sheer force of will.

"You're tired," he said. "We'll make a longer stop next time."

"There will be time enough to rest when we've found them," she murmured. "If you traveled alone, you would not wish any delays."

"Don't be obstinate, Lilith," he answered briskly. "You won't be of any use to your niece if you collapse at her feet. In any case, we must endeavour to spare Sims. To enact the role of coachman is beneath his dignity, you know. In his view, coachmen are common servants. A tiger, on the other hand, is a professional—an artist, if you will."

This elicited a weak smile, and Julian felt a queer tugging at his heart as he recollected warmer smiles, and the rich, haunting sound of her laughter. He slumped back into his corner.

Emma Wellwicke was at the breakfast table, perusing a letter. Her husband had written it while in Spain, four months before, but it had arrived only this morning. While the letter was old, the sentiments Colonel Wellwicke expressed were eternal, and sufficiently heartening to take the lady's mind off present domestic anxieties.

Emma looked up at the sound of light footsteps. Then her mouth dropped open. "Cecily!" she gasped.

"Good morning," said Cecily. She dropped a light kiss upon the thunderstruck Emma's forehead. "Aunt is not down yet? How odd. Normally, she is up with the servants. Was she very late at Lady Jersey's?"

"Cecily!"

Miss Glenwood, who'd immediately headed for the sideboard, paused and peered at the companion's round face. "Good heavens, Emma, you look as though you've seen a ghost. I do hope you've not had bad news in that letter."

"Cecily Glenwood, where have you been?" Mrs. Well-wicke demanded.

"In my bed, of course," was the puzzled response. "Where else should I be?"

"Where else? Where else? On the Great North Road, I should think. Where your poor aunt is at this moment, searching for you, and worried half to death."

Cecily pulled out the chair next to Emma and sat down. "Oh, dear," she said.

"Cecily Glenwood—"

"Oh, dear."

"Where were you last night? And don't say 'in my bed' because you weren't. Your aunt and I turned the house upside down. Now the poor woman is racing off to Scotland after you."

"Good gracious! You don't mean to say my aunt went alone?"

"She left with Lord Brandon. To prevent an elopement." In a few curt sentences, Mrs. Wellwicke described the previous night's excitement, closing with the demand, "Where *were* you?"

"Oh, dear. I shall explain everything, Emma. What a dreadful muddle! But first, don't you think we'd better send someone to bring them back?"

Half an hour later, Harris was tearing his way out of London, and Mrs. Wellwicke and Cecily had retired to the latter's sitting room.

"Yes, I did promise to go away with Lord Robert," Cecily was confessing calmly. "But when it came to the point, I couldn't do it. I only crept out to tell him so, but he was ever so stubborn. We argued—oh, for hours, I think. I expect he's still very cross with me. He said he was going to get drunk. I expect he's at his cousin's, sleeping off the aftereffects, poor man. Still, I'd rather have him on my conscience than Aunt Lilith, as I told him. I just couldn't pay her back so cruelly, after all she's done for me, even if she doesn't understand—"

"She *might* have understood," Emma reproved, "if you'd done her the courtesy of telling the truth, instead of sneaking about behind her back."

"Yes, of course you're right. But you see, I'm so dreadfully fond of Lord Robert, and she seemed to take him in such dislike. Well, I'm lamentably ignorant. If I weren't, I wouldn't have been so confused. But it's very confusing to be in love. Everyone says so." Cecily sighed. "Poor Aunt. Even *she's* confused, and she's so much older and more sophisticated. Still, we mustn't be overanxious. I'm certain Lord Brandon is taking very good care of her."

Mrs. Wellwicke studied the innocent, blue-eyed countenance in silence for a moment. Then she rose and left the room, wondering why she felt so very certain that Cecily had not quite explained everything.

Julian had at length persuaded his companion to take some refreshment when they stopped, but he could not persuade her to rest. So long as Sims declared himself perfectly satisfied with a quarter hour's nap snatched here and there, Lilith refused to admit she wanted any naps at all.

It was not until late morning, when the clouds began mounding into black thunderheads, that either of these two would consent to be reasonable. Sims had no taste for driving through thunderstorms, and Lilith, at this point, could scarce sit upright.

They reached a large inn just as the first heavy drops began to fall. As soon as the coach had rattled to a stop, Lord Brandon sprang out.

Lilith had declined his hand every other time. This time, when he saw her stumble to the carriage door, he ignored her protests and swung her down.

Her feet had no sooner touched the ground than her knees gave way.

"I knew it," he muttered as he lifted her in his arms. "Obstinate, pigheaded—"

"Put me down."

"Be quiet, or I shall drop you into the trough."

He carried her into the inn, shouted for a room, and began trudging up the stairs, the landlord scurrying after.

The latter had discerned no recognisable marking on the carriage, and this imperious guest had not deigned to mention his name. Nonetheless, Mine Host knew nobility when he saw it and the voice of authority when he heard it. In minutes, Mrs. Davenant was tucked into the hostelry's most luxurious chamber, surrounded by servants whose sole aim in life, apparently, was to make the lady comfortable.

While Lilith rested, Julian made the rounds of the inn, questioning everybody everywhere, from tap-room to stables. Though he dropped coins wherever he went, he could obtain no word of the eloping couple.

The storm exploded into a fury of fiery flashes and deafening thunder. The inn quickly filled with soaked travellers, all of whom the marquess questioned. No one had noticed the distinctive black curricle. No one had glimpsed the young pair. It was as though they'd vanished.

Lord Brandon sat alone in a corner of the public dining room, nursing a mug of ale and thinking. More than ever, he was convinced he was on the wrong trail. The trouble was, he had no idea what the right one might be. At length, he decided to leave it to Lilith. If she wished to continue to Scotland, they would do so. If not—well, he would do as she wished. After all, the elopement promised only minor problems for Robert. It was the girl who'd most to lose. As always.

The women always paid dearly, he reflected. He should not have allowed Lilith to come. She would pay as well, to have been gone overnight with neither maid nor companion—and with him, of all men.

Yet how his heart had leapt when she'd insisted on accompanying him. How he'd wanted her company, even despising him as she did. Even cold and silent, shut off to him as irrevocably as if she'd been sealed in the vault beside her husband.

Lord Brandon pushed the mug away and stood up. He might as well take advantage of the bed he'd procured for himself, since the storm offered no sign of slackening. While sleep was the furthest thing from his mind, he could at least lie down. He had not slept in days. The strain would tell eventually if he was not careful.

His chamber was at the opposite end of the hall from Lilith's. As he reached her door, he paused. Even as he was telling himself to keep on to his room, his hand covered the doorknob.

It opened easily. Julian frowned. She should have locked it. He'd better wake her and tell her.

Noiselessly, he moved to the bed. She lay, fully dressed but shoeless, on top of the bed-clothes. She slept soundly, her breathing slow and even. Better to let her sleep, he thought. He would have the door locked from outside.

Yet he stood, watching her. The thick, curling hair streamed over the pillow in fire-tinted waves. One tangled strand had fallen over her eye. He reached out and gently brushed it away.

She seemed so young and vulnerable, curled up on her side, one hand tucked under the pillow, the other across her breast. "My beautiful girl," he murmured. He kissed her forehead.

It was only a feather touch, but the long, sooty lashes swept up, and he found himself gazing into dazed, blue-grey eyes.

"Julian," she breathed sleepily. Then she blinked. "Oh. What is it? What time is it? Did I sleep?" She pulled herself upright, her eyes wary now.

"It doesn't matter what time it is," he answered unsteadily. "We can't leave until the storm abates."

A resounding boom shook the window.

"As you can hear," he went on, "it's raging like all the furies of Hades."

"Then they must have stopped as well."

"No doubt. Only . . . " He hesitated.

"What is it? Have you heard anything?

"No—and that's the trouble." He turned away from her worried gaze. "Lilith, I think that note of Robert's was meant to put me on the wrong track. Not a hint of them, after all these hours. It doesn't make sense. Robert wouldn't have taken detours and back roads. He doesn't know the countryside well enough, and he's too impatient. I can only conclude your suspicions were correct, and Gretna wasn't their destination. The problem is—"

"I know," she said. "The problem is, we have no idea where they *have* gone." She glanced up at him. "Do you wish to return to London?"

"Only if that's *your* wish. Your niece is the main concern. My cousin may go to the devil who spawned him. Confounded, rattle-brained moron that he is," he went on heatedly. "Damn him! Oh, damn me as well. It was my fault his path crossed your niece's in the first place. If I'd left him to his tart—if I'd never met the scheming— Well, it scarcely matters, does it? What's done is done."

"Yes."

He saw her face close against him then, and scarcely thinking what he did, he clasped her hands in his. "Lilith, please believe me, I never meant what you think. No, that isn't right. I meant it at the start, perhaps—and to my shame—but not at the last."

She snatched her hands away. "Always *you*," she said. "What do I care what you meant, at first or at last? Whatever your game—your wager—whatever you intended—it was *I* let you play it. You have only behaved according to your nature, while I—I," she repeated, pressing her fist to her breast, "have behaved in every way contrary to mine. That you cannot explain. That you cannot excuse. I am not your— your damned puppet or pet, you conceited, selfish man! How dare you apologise to me!"

A moment passed, while he took in the furious beauty of

her countenance and all the imperious passion blazing in her eyes, and in that moment he was lost.

"Because I want you," he said helplessly. "I want you still. I miss you. I've thought of nothing but you all these days and nights, all the while I willed myself to think of anything else. I've never wanted anyone, anything, so much in my whole life as I want you, Lilith Davenant. How I wish I'd never met you."

"And how I wish," she retorted fiercely, "I'd left you in the ditch that day."

"Lilith—"

"Don't. Not another word. I made up my mind I would not stoop to question you. There is nothing you can say I wish to hear. It's all lies—always lies, and easy speeches." She scrambled to the other side of the high bed and pushed herself off.

He watched her ransack the contents of the small bag Emma had packed for her, and disentangle a hairbrush from a chemise. He ought to leave, but he could not. He'd never felt so lonely, so utterly shut out, yet somehow it seemed worse, far worse, to leave the room.

The brush tore into her scalp, and Julian winced.

He crossed the room to her. "Let me," he said as he tried to pry the brush from her rigid fingers. "There's no need to rip your hair out just because I'm a conceited, selfish beast."

She pushed him away. "Leave me alone."

"Lilith."

She hurled the brush across the room. It flew past him, narrowly missing his shoulder, and struck the bed-post.

"I hate you! I hate you!" she cried. "How could you say those things to me? How could you be so unfair, so unkind, Julian? What had I ever done to be used so? How could you talk of love to me, and then laugh with that woman—at me, at the fool I was? How could you?"

He caught her in his arms and pressed her tense, stiff body close. "Not a fool, my love," he said. "Never that. Ah, if you only knew how that woman has laughed at me. But never you, my beautiful girl. She knew you'd break my heart."

"You haven't got a heart," she returned in a watery voice. "Or a conscience . . . or morals—"

"Then it was only indigestion," he said gently. "That's why I can't sleep or eat. That's why I can't bear to speak to anyone. That's why my staff is half terrified to death."

"It was only your pride was hurt. Because you lost your wager."

"That was all? My pride?"

"Yes." She stirred a bit. "And indigestion."

He glanced down at her bent head. A tumble of copper-tinted curls hid her face. She didn't try to break free, but her body remained taut, unyielding.

His fingers moved to her hair, to stroke it tenderly, as one would soothe a troubled child. He'd never meant to hurt her, but how could he have helped it? She was not like his other women.

Her head dropped a little lower to lay wearily against his chest. His heart ricocheted against his ribs. He bent to kiss the top of her head. "I've missed you," he whispered. "God, how I've missed you."

His hands slid to her back and tightened about her. He felt the slight shudder that ran through her. "Lilith."

She raised her head at last. The anger and hurt was gone from her eyes, and something sadder and gentler there called to him, making his thrashing heart ache.

He breathed her name once more. Then his mouth closed over hers, and the storm without was nothing to the tempest unleashed within.

Lightning seared the room in blinding white. The heavens roared and rattled the windowpanes, but it was a mere zephyr to what raged between them as they clung to each other.

In minutes, he'd swept her to the bed and torn off his coat, neck-cloth, waistcoat. Frantic, hurried, desperate, wild to press her close again, to taste and touch . . . and above all, to *possess*. *His*. His at last, he thought, as she pulled him down to her and her lips sought his again.

He felt her hands upon his chest, and the touch scorched and chilled at the same time. He heard his own voice, murmuring urgently, but it was unintelligible, lost in the crash of thunder and the blood pounding in his ears.

His shaking fingers finally found the row of tiny buttons at her back. He nearly screamed with frustration.

Merely buttons, he pacified himself. There was no need for haste. Brandon was never hasty. Yet his fingers seemed to thicken to thrice their normal size, while the buttons simultaneously shrank to tiny, obstinate nails imbedded in armour.

*I'll rip the damned thing open,* he raged silently. *I'll buy her a hundred frocks—what does one matter?*

He raised his head from her neck and looked at her.

"What is it?" she whispered. Her eyes slowly widened, searching his. That was when he saw it.

Or perhaps he'd seen it before, but refused to recognise it. He recognised it now.

He caught his breath and looked away . . . and was ashamed.

# === 18 ===

"WE'LL BE BACK before midnight," Julian said as he turned away from the carriage window, "even if we stop for dinner."

They were returning to London.

Lilith was not hungry, but she agreed to the dinner. It would give Sims time for rest and nourishment. He ought to be considered, regardless how desperate she was to be home again. These last few hours had been torture.

Oh, Julian had apologised. He could not have been kinder, and, as usual, he must take all the blame. He had cursed himself a hundred times for his thoughtlessness and selfishness. He'd injured her enough, he said. He would never forgive himself for so abusing her trust. Angry and hurt, anxious for her niece, she'd been worried to death, utterly distracted. He'd behaved abominably, to take advantage of her confusion, her need for comforting. He'd very nearly ravished her. Thank heaven she'd brought him to his senses.

Indeed, it would have been a sweet apology, if Lilith hadn't known better. It was he who'd stopped it. He'd come to his senses all on his own.

He'd only wanted what he couldn't have. Once it was offered— She stifled a shudder of embarrassment. Still, there was no hiding from the truth. She'd heard the tenderness and sorrow in his voice, seen the regret in his eyes, and believed, because she could not do otherwise. She'd offered herself shamelessly. Yet for all his coaxing words, he'd found her wanting, just as Charles had. She'd bored him—or disgusted him, perhaps.

Very well. She'd made a fool of herself. Contemplating her stupidity served nothing. She had far graver matters to consider: her niece, first and foremost. Scandal was unavoidable. Good society would be closed to Cecily for years, if not forever. Nonetheless, the families could and must be appeased.

Julian had promised to help. Lord Brandon, Lilith amended. He would deal with his aunt, uncle, and cousins, while she dealt with her in-laws. The young couple must at least be accepted by their families.

Thomas would have to be dealt with as well, but that would be simple enough. Naturally, given the scandal, he'd wish to cry off. That scarcely mattered now, since her nieces would never be trusted to her again.

In a short while, the vehicle slowed and turned into the courtyard of yet another in the endless succession of inns.

Lilith allowed Lord Brandon to assist her from the carriage, though she wished he wouldn't press her hand so tightly, or hold it so long after she'd alighted. The warm, firm clasp made her want to weep. She was trying to swallow the lump in her throat when she heard the shout.

Lilith turned towards the sound. A small, thin man was running at them. She blinked. Harris? But this filthy, wet creature, his cap a sodden lump upon his head, could not be Cecily's groom. He stumbled to a stop before her.

"Oh, missus," he gasped. "Thank God I found you—"

There was a buzzing in her ears, and an odd, numb feeling in her spine. Lilith clutched Julian's arm for support as the world about her glared yellow, then faded to black.

Lilith opened her eyes to anxious green ones. A warm, strong hand held hers.

"Do you mean to remain with us this time?" Julian asked.

"I—I fainted, didn't I?"

"Repeatedly. We've had a confounded time bringing you round."

A pillow supported her head, but the settle she lay upon was narrow and hard. Gingerly, Lilith began to pull herself up to a sitting position. He released her hand to help her. Then he did not take it again.

"I should give your groom a sound thrashing," he said. "I can't imagine what he was thinking of, to spring at you in that outrageous way. I've never beheld so hideous a spectacle—and stinking to high heaven as well. No wonder you swooned."

"It *was* Harris," she gasped. "Is it about Cecily? Is she hurt?"

"Cecily is perfectly well. You may be quite easy. We've been off on a precious wild-goose chase. The girl never left London."

"Never left?" she echoed weakly.

"Never left, never eloped. It was all a hum." Julian rose from his chair. "I mean to say, it was a misunderstanding. From what Harris babbled, I gather Robert intended to run away with her, but your niece must have developed qualms at the last minute. She must have sneaked back after we'd gone."

He'd not much else to tell her. Harris was exhausted, having ridden hard since early morning. In any case, the groom had not been given many details.

"It doesn't matter," Lilith said as the news truly penetrated and relief washed over her. "So long as she's safe at home. I should have known. I should have trusted her. She has far too much sense to do such a thing. I wish I'd been more confident at the start. I might have spared you—"

"Not at all. I told you I'd keep an eye on Robert, and I failed you. Naturally, I must have gone after him, regardless your confidence in your niece. I only regret that several hours must pass before I can wring his neck." He moved to the door. "I shall order a large dinner, which we may consume at our leisure. Then, we have but to return you discreetly in the dead of night, bribe Harris to hold his tongue, and all is well with the world."

"Yes," she said. No, she thought. Nothing would ever be altogether well again.

Considering he'd expected to be murdered, Lord Robert ought to have been grateful his cousin merely threw him against the library wall and half throttled him before turning away in disgust.

Lord Robert was relieved to escape with so negligible a physical punishment. He was not, however, sufficiently appreciative to keep silent.

"Go home?" he bleated, rubbing his aching throat. "You can't send me home. You haven't any authority over me, Julian."

"Don't test my patience, Cousin. That commodity is in short supply at present."

"I'm not going home. Cecily needs me. I'm not going anywhere without her. We're going to be married—I don't care what anyone says. She doesn't care, either."

Julian poured himself a glass of wine.

"In that you are sadly mistaken," he answered. "Or lamentably ignorant. I'm afraid you don't understand precisely the sort of predicament you've gotten yourself into."

He dropped his weary body into a large overstuffed chair, sipped his wine, leaned back, and proceeded to explain Robert's predicament in numbing detail.

When the marquess was done, Robert stumbled to the chair opposite and fell into it.

"Twenty-five thousand pounds," he said dazedly. "Breach of promise. She couldn't. She wouldn't." He turned a pleading countenance to his cousin. "She can't, Julian. She'll ruin everything. I could never marry Cecily. I couldn't do that to her."

"Naturally not. Her family wouldn't let you. In fact, if you have any feeling for her, you'll not venture into Miss Glenwood's general vicinity. I warned you the sort of scenes you might expect from your discarded mistress."

"But Julian, there has to be some way. Surely if *you* talked to Elise. Gad, give her what she wants—the whole trust fund."

"She wants a title or revenge, the latter in the form of a scandalous, expensive, interminable, but eventually highly profitable lawsuit."

"I won't marry her. I can't believe I ever thought I loved her, when all this time she's only been planning how to ruin me."

"Yes, you were a great help to her in that."

Robert groaned. "How could I have been so stupid—stupid, stupid, stupid, and blind? Gad, I wish you *had* killed me. What am I going to do?"

The marquess stared into his wineglass. After a moment, he asked, "Are you quite certain you wish to marry Miss Glenwood? Are you *positive* you're truly in love with the girl?"

Robert's sinking head shot up. "How can you ask?" he demanded indignantly. "I adore her. I've been crazy about her since the moment I met her."

"You never mentioned it."

The younger man squirmed. "I didn't realise at first. I only thought of her as a . . . well, a friend, I suppose. Then, when I finally figured it out, I did come to you. Don't you remember? That day when I told you about the curricle?"

Julian only stared at him.

"I tried after that, but you were never home. Or when you were, you stayed locked in your room, or in the library, or somewhere. And you just ignored me, even when I pounded on the door. Or you told me to go to blazes. Well, it was obvious enough what your—" He caught himself up short. "That is to say, a man has to deal with his own problems. You're not my nurse, as you've told me a hundred times."

"Indeed. You've dealt with your problem marvelously, I see."

"I never pretended to be as clever as you," Robert shot back angrily. "You can sneer if you like. You don't know what it is to be half crazy about a girl—while everyone else makes it completely hopeless for you. It's all right if *you* go into the ugliest sulk there ever was and treat me like a pesky infant. But I'm not. I'm a grown man. I'm sorry I'm not as wise and blasé as you—but I couldn't just sit down to a card game and brandy and forget. I had to do *something*."

"So you did," was the dispassionate answer. "What amazes me is Miss Glenwood's consenting to such a hare-brained plan."

"Well, it was her—that is to say, I had a devil of a time persuading her."

Julian eyed him consideringly. "Why, I wonder, do I suspect it was the other way round?"

Robert squirmed again. "What nonsense."

"Naturally, you will not betray your beloved," said the other with a sardonic smile. "I know you're lying to me. Still, she *is* your beloved, evidently." He stood up. "I'm going out for a while."

"Now?" Robert shrieked.

"There's no need to agitate yourself, Cousin. You and Miss Glenwood have made your point. Attention has been called to your plight—though I'm not certain what you think Nurse can do with this unmitigated disaster. Really, Robin, you have quite the knack. Thank heaven you never went for the military. England could not possibly have withstood the blow."

With that, he left the room.

The sun shone brightly in the neat, tiny parlour. Its beams shot through the sparkling decanter, turning the wine to a glowing garnet. Elise handed her guest his glass.

"A toast," Lord Brandon said, touching his goblet lightly to hers, "to your victory, *mademoiselle*."

Her fine, dark eyebrows rose a fraction.

"Our wager," he explained. "You've won. I congratulate you."

"You are precipitate, milord. More than a week remains

210

to you," she answered cautiously.

"By that time, I shall be gone," he said. He moved to the plain, shabby mantel to examine the two small silhouettes displayed there. The profiles—one of Robert, one of Elise—faced opposite directions. "To Paris," he added after a moment.

"Ah, the pursuit palls. You are bored."

"No, I've failed. You chose your champion well."

"I had no doubt of that."

He turned back to her. "I agreed to cease troubling you on Robert's account, and honour demands I abide by our terms. On the other hand, honour demands I do no injury to innocent persons. If I keep silent, I do such an injury."

"English honour," she said. "Such difficulties it makes."

"I think you are aware of this particular difficulty," he said quietly. "You know Robert wishes to marry a certain young lady. You know, then, you can't keep him. That you can make trouble for him I won't deny. His future is in your hands. Perhaps that's no more than he deserves. All the same, the young lady—"

"Yes, the young lady who has destroyed my future, milord. Do you come to plead on her behalf? Do you think to soften my heart towards my rival?"

All this time his face had been its customary bored, impassive mask, his voice cool, expressionless. Nonetheless, there was a shadow upon him. Elise perceived it in his eyes and in the set of his mouth. She had suspected. Now she was almost certain. She waited while he turned the wineglass slowly in his hand.

"You have no more heart, my dear, than I do," he answered. "We are two of a kind, untroubled by heart or conscience. I will speak to your intellect." He met her gaze. "Lawsuits are time-consuming, expensive, and often exceedingly unpleasant matters. I can spare you the ordeal. I am prepared to settle an annuity upon you. In addition, I have a comfortable house in Kensington. You are welcome to inhabit it until such time as you find a replacement for my cousin. The annuity, naturally, would continue regardless. One thousand a year is not twenty-five thousand in a lump, but you know as well as I what will remain of a court's award . . . if, that is, you win."

She had expected an offer. She had not dared imagine one so generous. She said, "Two thousand."

A pause. "Two thousand, then."

"I begin to think you have a conscience after all," she said smiling.

The green eyes flickered. "I have a responsibility," he corrected.

"Oh, *certainement*. To your family. To your honour."

"To the girl. I should be happy to let Robert pay for his mistakes. I cannot permit an innocent young lady to pay for mine. Had it not been for our wager, I doubt she would have met my cousin, let alone fallen in love with him."

"Ah, *love*. The English are so romantic—and the men worse than the women." She shook her head. "*Pauvre homme*, I think she has dealt you the death-blow, the proud widow. I was wiser than I guessed."

His face had frozen, but he made no answer.

"A moment, milord, if you please."

She stepped out of the room briefly. When she returned, she carried a small enameled box. She handed it to him.

"Robert's letters," she said. "All of them. On top, you will find the letter you so much desired from me. It suits the purpose, I believe. One does not require many words to refuse one's hand."

He opened the box and read the topmost letter. Then he refolded it and tucked it into his pocket. "Thank you," he said. "You are most gracious, *mademoiselle*."

She laughed. "I am merely a common slut, not gracious at all. I have but lost a lover. I will find another—and better. When one has money, one may be more selective. Your generous recompense will ease my little pride's ache."

"I am gratified to hear it."

"But there will be no ease for you, I think," she went on,

not troubling to conceal the triumph she felt. "You say you have no heart. But my champion, she has found yours—and cut it to pieces—has she not?"

He smiled faintly. "Now it is *you* who wax romantic."

"I see what I see."

"Do you? What is it you see, I wonder? Is my neck-cloth askew? Perhaps a dust mote upon my boots leads to the conclusion I am in romantic extremity?" He placed his wineglass upon a small table. "Naturally, one cannot be altogether pleased with failure. That is a new experience, but not so amusing that I plan to make a habit of it."

"Of course. To lose is not agreeable. Still, you will go to Paris, and you will forget."

"Yes." He took up his hat and gloves and walked to the door. Then he paused. "We *are* two of a kind, you know—a pair of precious knaves."

"So we are," she said. "*Âmes damnées.* Fortunately, we are beautiful, and still young enough."

"I leave for Dover on Sunday," he said as he drew on his gloves. "Perhaps you would join me. It has been many years since you visited the land of your birth, I believe."

Elise eyed him with critical appreciation. He was a beautiful man. Not golden, like Robert, but far more striking was the marquess, with his dark, arrogant looks. Tall and strong, his hair thick and black, and his eyes—ah, they were calculated to make a woman's heart drum to wild music. But not hers.

"*Merci,* milord, but I think not."

"As you wish. If you change your mind, feel free to send me word."

When he'd gone, Elise walked to the table and picked up the glass he'd left there. He'd scarcely touched it. She shook her head. "I will not pity you," she said softly. "The revenge is too sweet, my great and powerful lord. You would have crushed me if you could. No, it is just as you deserve."

At four o'clock Bella Martin arrived, to show off her new

chaise and patronise her less fortunate friend with a drive in Hyde Park.

It was there Elise spied the widow, riding in a carriage with her betrothed and his relations.

"How ill she looks. The widow," she explained as Bella peered curiously about her at the parade of vehicles.

"Oh, *her.* I expect she should. Reggie said she and the girl—that blonde dab of a thing he's so taken with, you know."

"Miss Glenwood."

"Yes. Sick in bed for two days, and the house shut up tight. So Reggie sends enough flowers for six funerals." She gave the widow another contemptuous glance. "Appropriate, I'd say. I always thought she looked like a corpse anyhow."

"Her complexion is very fair," Elise said thoughtfully, "but she never looked so ill before, I think."

"Maybe someone's been keeping her up late nights," was the sly retort.


"Lord Brandon was here?" Lilith said as she took the package from her butler.

"He said it wasn't a call, madam. He wished simply to leave that for you. He seemed to be in rather a hurry."

"Yes. Yes, I expect he was," she mumbled. She turned and headed up the stairs to her room.

She'd hardly taken off her bonnet when Mary appeared.

"There, now," the maid said disapprovingly, "didn't I warn you to keep to your bed? You're tired to death. You'd better take a nap if you mean to go out tonight."

"I'm not going out," said Lilith. "I've asked Lady Enders to take Cecily to the Gowerbys'. If you'll just undo the buttons, I'll manage the rest myself."

The abigail opened her mouth to protest, then shut it tightly, did as she was bid, and quietly left the room.

Her hands shaking, Lilith undressed and wrapped herself in an old cotton robe. Then she sat in the chair by the window and stared a long while at the package.

An hour passed before she could bring herself to unwrap it. As the paper fluttered to the floor, her lower lip began to tremble.

*Mansfield Park.* The book she'd been reading that day at Hookham's . . . and dropped, in her agitation.

"Oh, Julian," she murmured. She opened the first volume to the fly-leaf. The handwriting was black and bold, as arrogant as its owner. The words were simple: "May life with your 'Edmund Bertram' be, truly, happily ever after. Brandon."

There was something more, however. In the middle of the volume, pressed between a piece of silver paper and a note, was a small, white orchid, tinged with mauve.

The note informed her that Mr. Higginbottom had been instructed to deposit all her payments towards Davenant's debt into a separate account at her bank. Lord Brandon hoped she would make use of these funds as she required— as wedding gifts for her nieces, if she liked, or for any other estimable purpose.

Lilith lay note and orchid upon the table beside her, opened to the first chapter, and began to read.

# === 19 ===

THOUGH LORD BRANDON did not return to his town house until sunrise, he found his cousin waiting up for him. The marquess had scarcely stepped through the front door when Lord Robert burst into the hall.

"Gad, Julian, you're enough to drive a chap to Bedlam. Where the devil have you been?"

"Oh, here and there." The marquess calmly strode past him into the library, dropped his hat and gloves onto a chair, then headed for the tray of decanters. He poured himself a glass of brandy and proceeded to make himself quite comfortable in his favourite chair.

"I say, Julian, I do believe you're doing this just to punish me. I know I've lost two stone from the suspense. What's happened? Have you talked to her? Have you been talking all this time?"

"No."

"Julian!"

"I do wish you would not jump about like a frantic puppy, Robin. I am tempted to swat you with a newspaper. Really, you are very tiresome. A puppy would be less trouble, I am certain. Thank heaven I shall not have the house-training of you."

"Julian!"

"There is writing paper in the upper left drawer of my desk," Lord Brandon said, waving his glass in that direction. "You'd be wiser to occupy your time composing a letter to your father-in-law-to-be. No, on second thought, *I* shall compose it. Your grammar is shocking, your punctuation and spelling execrable."

Robert gazed blankly at him for a moment. Then he rushed to his cousin and began pumping his free hand up and down. "Oh, good show, Julian. Good show. Gad, but you're amazing. You can do anything!"

"I doubt I shall be able to restore my arm to its socket."

Robert abruptly released him. "Yes, of course. Carried away. You can't know how—how—Gad, I'm so relieved. I just kept sinking lower and lower the longer you were gone, until I thought I'd just better hang myself."

" 'Men have died from time to time, and worms have eaten them, but not for love.' "

"Well, if you say so. But I thought I *would* die. I don't know when I've spent a worse night."

"I'm tired, Robin. I want to go to bed. Can we just get this letter done?"

"Yes, yes, absolutely. This minute." Robert plunked himself down at the desk, tore out a stack of paper, picked up a pen, and waited.

"Mind you don't spoil all my pens. And no blots."

"Yes, Julian," was the docile reply.

As it turned out, Lord Robert spoiled a dozen quills, because not one but two letters needed to be written. After Julian had examined the first and pronounced it tolerable, he had gone into a queer sort of trance. Then, in an equally queer voice, he had reminded Robert of Cecily's aunt.

Though the young pair had not eloped, they had caused the widow considerable distress. She deserved a personal apology, of course, but an advance note—properly penitent— would be needed, if Robert expected to be admitted to speak to her at all.

This note turned out to be far more difficult than the first, with Julian revising every word a hundred times and ordering sheet after sheet torn up. At last the thing was done.

It was sent to the widow midmorning, with a request for an appointment in the early afternoon.

Shortly after noon, a frantic Robert received word that Mrs. Davenant would await him at two o'clock.

He arrived at one-thirty, and was left to cool his heels the full remaining half hour before he was shown into the drawing room.

"You intend to seek Lord Glenwood's consent, I trust?" the widow asked after she'd listened composedly to Robert's incoherent apologies.

"Yes, ma'am. That is, if you don't object. I know I've given you every reason to dislike me, but you must know—"

"I don't dislike you," she said coolly. "I've never disliked you, Lord Robert. That was an unfortunate misunderstanding. If you truly care for my niece—"

"Oh, I *do*. Believe me, I'd die to make her happy. Really, I would. She's the finest girl in the world!"

"Yes. Well." She paused and Robert waited anxiously.

Really, he thought, she was as bad as Julian for dragging a thing out and driving a man distracted.

"Are your parents aware of your intentions?" she asked finally.

He assured her there would be no trouble with his family. They'd be delighted. Julian had written this very day—a wonderful letter. "But he's so clever," Robert went on. "The words just come to him, you know. That is . . . well, he spoke so highly of Cec—of Miss Glenwood. And when they meet her, I know they'll love her. They can't help it. No one could," he said fervently.

That earned a small smile. "Very well," she said. "I shall ask Cecily to step down to speak with you."

"Oh, Mrs. Davenant." Robert shot up out of his chair, and forgetting altogether who she was, yanked her up from hers and hugged her. "Thank you," he cried. "You really are splendid. Julian was quite right. That is—" Hastily, he let go and blushed. "I beg your pardon."

She flushed a bit as well, but she nodded with her customary cool politeness, then turned away to summon her niece.

Lord Robert was given a very generous half hour alone with his darling, though the door to the drawing room was left open and a servant hovered nearby. When the young man finally took his leave, Cecily ran upstairs to her aunt's sitting room, hugged her a dozen times, and told her she was the sweetest, kindest, most understanding aunt a girl could ever want—even a horribly ill-bred, ungrateful girl like herself.

"I only want you to be happy, Cecily," said Lilith.

"Yes, Aunt, and I shall be," said Cecily. She dropped onto the footstool and gazed thoughtfully at her aunt. "Though I do wish you'd be happy as well."

"Naturally, I am, dear. You have been a great success, and now you will marry a very suitable young man who loves you dearly. That is all I could wish for."

"Is it?" Cecily took her aunt's hand and squeezed it. "Is it *all* you wish for? Don't you ever wish for yourself?"

The aunt's posture grew more rigid.

"Don't you ever wish to be with someone who loves you dearly? Even if he doesn't quite know it. Because they never do, do they?" she asked, half to herself. "We have to tell them *everything*."

She came out of her abstraction with a grin. "I must tell you, Aunt, this Season has been extremely educational. I had no idea men could be so confused and impractical. They will wander about aimlessly, making themselves cross and unhappy, and it never occurs to them what the trouble is. Or if it does, they won't speak of it, because it isn't dignified—or something. Do you know, Lord Robert was thoroughly astounded when I told him I cared for him?"

"Was he?" Lilith asked faintly.

Cecily nodded. "Did you ever hear anything so ridiculous? Almost as ridiculous as his not knowing he cared for me." She stood up. "Thank heaven *that's* over. He's much more sensible now."

"I'm glad to hear it, dear."

"Well, I should like to speak more with you, Aunt, but I know Sir Thomas is coming, and you probably have a great deal to discuss with him. I suppose he'll want to set a date at last, now I'm off your hands. But we can talk tonight, can't we, after we come home?"

"Yes, of course we can. As much as you like, dear."

"Downs?" Sir Thomas repeated as he took the cup and saucer Lilith held out to him. "Well, that is very good, I suppose. Excellent family, of course. He has been a bit wild, but he is young. I daresay he'll settle down soon enough. Married life is marvelously settling—when, that is, the characters are well-suited."

"And when there is deep affection."

"Indeed, yes. Mutual regard and respect—that is the foundation."

"Oh, Thomas." Lilith put down her cup and rose from the sofa.

He jumped up. "My dear, what is it? Have you qualms about the match? If so—"

"No. That is, not about Cecily." She folded her hands before her and raised her chin. "It's about us, Thomas. There's no way to work up to it tactfully, I'm afraid. I cannot marry you."

"Lilith! What is this?" Angry scarlet mounted his neck and ears.

"I cannot," she said. "I cannot be your wife. I married once without love. I shall not make that mistake again."

He was obviously striving for patience. "Come now, Lilith. We are not a pair of moonstruck children. Infatuation is no basis for a marriage—not a sound one. You know that as well as I, surely."

"I know our basis is not a sound one—not for me, at least. I'm not what I thought I was—or what you think me. I know I'll make you unhappy, and myself as well. To marry you is to injure us both."

With an effort he regained his self-restraint, and the angry colour subsided. "You have been ill," he said, more judiciously. "You are overwrought, and a few natural anxieties—perfectly natural, my dear—seem insurmountable obstacles. You want more rest. It is all these late nights, hurrying from one noisy place to another, and too much rich food."

"I have been . . . unwell," she said slowly, "but I am not so now. I have been troubled, but it's my conscience troubles me. In my heart of hearts, I knew I was wrong to accept you. I pray you will forgive me for having done so. I did not know my own heart."

"You didn't know Brandon then, is what you mean," he snapped.

Her features hardened to marble.

His hands clamped together behind his back, Thomas began to pace the carpet.

"You think I'm blind," he said heatedly. "I'm not. I'd heard enough of him. He must make a conquest of every woman he meets. Yet I saw no great harm in my future bride's cultivating one who has the ear of the world's most powerful men: Castlereagh, Wellington, Metternich, and not only our own Regent, but half the monarchs of Europe. Knowing you, I saw no danger in the acquaintance. And so I told my sister. Lilith Davenant, I told her, would never lose her head over such a man. But you have, it seems." He paused to glare at her. "Now you will throw your life away. For what? A libertine who'll make love to you at ten o'clock and lie in the arms of a ballet dancer at twelve."

Lilith let him rage on. He was entitled. She had insulted him deeply, betrayed him repeatedly. He could devise no words harsher than those with which she'd already flogged herself. Nevertheless, no words either could produce would ever change her heart. She stood, and endured, and when it was done and he'd gone at last, she ordered a bath and calmly walked up to her room to prepare for the evening ahead.

The letter was delivered shortly after Lilith had arisen

from her bath. It lay on the tray next to the cup of herbal tea Emma had prepared. The handwriting was unfamiliar. It was, however, a woman's hand.

Within a few sentences, the sender's identity became painfully clear. Lilith turned the page over.

"I tell you, Madame, for him I care nothing. If he is in misery all his days, I should not be troubled. But you, I think, suffer as well, and I prefer you did not, for you have done me so much good."

Then it came, all of it, the entire story of the "knaves' wager," as Elise titled it: Lord Brandon's efforts to keep Robert from disgrace, and Elise's refusal to yield her so-easily-managed lover. The letter continued:

"You will wonder what wicked devil inspired me to so vile a game with another's virtue. I answer, Madame, that I never believed your virtue in danger. Ah, and how I wished to see the noble marquess taught a lesson—to see him thwarted, just once. For I must tell you he was abominably insolent. To be humbled by such a man was more than my pride could bear. *Alors,* I perceive his strong attraction to you. I see as well he is doomed to fail, and so I goad and challenge him.

What would you have me do? Plead and weep? Throw myself at his feet? Beg for mercy from a man who thinks women weak and mindless, like infants?

In my place, you would have defied him. But you are a great lady—his social equal—and I am merely *une fille publique.* So I put you in my place, as my champion. And you did defy him.

Today he tells me I have won. But I see I have won more than our wager. He is not so arrogant now. This time it is the great lord who seeks mercy. Well, I have given him what he wishes— not for his sake, or Robert's, or even for the girl's—but for yours. You have given me better revenge than I hoped. I will not repay you by bringing shame upon you and your family. Also, to tell you frankly, I am paid well for my forbearance.

There is but one matter more. Not important, perhaps, for you may be happy to see the last of him. He leaves in two days' time for Paris. This time, I do not think he will return.

The room was spacious and luxurious, yet not ornate. Golden threads glistened in the green draperies and in the chair coverings; otherwise, gilt was at a minimum. Several choice landscape paintings hung in elegantly simple frames upon the walls.

Above the large marble fireplace loomed a man's portrait. Tall, stern, forbidding, he glared down his hawklike nose at the woman who stared defiantly back.

Beneath the wig, Lilith thought, his hair would be thick and raven black—perhaps streaked with grey at the temples, for this was not the portrait of a young man. The mouth was thinner, and the lines there and at the corners of the eyes were more deeply etched. The eyes themselves were not quite the same green—but what artist could capture that colour?

An intimidating figure he must have been, the late Marquess of Brandon. What would he have made of the woman who stood in his drawing room, her hair unbound, streaming down her back, her tall, slim body draped—and scarcely concealed—in slate-blue silk?

Lilith heard footsteps approaching. She turned to the door, straightened her spine, and raised her chin.

The man she awaited burst through the door, then stopped short, visibly composed himself, and proceeded more slowly into the room. He halted some distance from her.

Lord Brandon had been dressing—and was not altogether done, she thought wryly. His neck-cloth was crooked, and the knot was loose, clumsily tied.

"This is an unlooked-for honour," he said. He sounded short of breath.

"I should hope so," she said. "I don't know many ladies who are in the habit of paying late-night calls."

"Not to single gentlemen." He glanced about the quiet room. "And certainly not without escort. Have you taken leave of your senses, Mrs. Davenant?"

"I have come to take leave of you," she answered frostily. "Since you are far too busy to take proper leave of me. I suppose you meant to depart without a word. Paris, I understand."

"You are well-informed."

"Not so well as I could wish. I wanted to satisfy my curiosity."

She moved past the fireplace in a rustle of silk, and paused at the sofa. No, it was better not to sit down. She felt stronger upright. She let her fingers trail lightly over the silken embroidery.

"Women are excessively curious, are they not?" she continued. "It is a known failing of our gender. We have a regrettable need to be enlightened on every matter that appears to concern us. For instance, I have been the object of a wager."

She threw him a glance from under her lashes, and saw his colour deepen. "It is very tiresome of me, I know, but I long to be apprised of the details," she added.

"Lilith, don't—"

"Have you truly lost? You see, I have no idea how much time you had to seduce me. Perhaps you'd be so kind as to tell me the truth."

"Eight weeks," came the low reply.

"Good heavens! So much? And how odd." She calculated rapidly. "I thought you'd been in London but *seven*. Unless my addition is at fault, you might have seduced me the other day, and won your wager. I realise, of course, you

224

were anxious about the children. Yet we were already delayed by the storm. Another few minutes could not have made a great difference."

"A few minutes?" he asked with something like his customary coolness. "Please consider my reputation."

"All you had to do was bed me," she shot back. "Surely you hadn't bargained how long you'd be about it. I do not recollect, in any case, making any effort to prevent you. On the contrary—"

"Stop it!" He moved a few steps nearer. "I know well enough what I've done and what I am."

"I don't," she said. "It seems I know nothing about you."

"That's true. You knew a stranger, a man I created for the occasion." He turned away to the fireplace and took up a poker. There was no fire, but he thrust angrily at the coals laid in the grate while he went on. "You said the other day my words were always lies and easy speeches. It was worse than you know. You asked for truth. If you can bear it, I suppose I can bear to tell it."

"I want the truth," she said.

He told her. He explained how he'd employed two of her servants to apprise him of all her plans. That was how he'd happened to be at Hookham's—and everywhere else she went. He told how he'd bribed the clerk to block the aisle, ordered Ezra to ply the Enderses' coachman with drink, maneuvered their walk at Redley Park. All this and more—all his stratagems.

"I was awake to every opportunity, you see," he said. "I would have said anything, done anything. Scarcely a word or gesture escaped me but was deliberately intended to weaken you. Every wile and guile I ever learned, Lilith—and new ones I invented. Never was there such a calculated siege," he finished, his voice weary.

She had not suspected—not the half of it—and was mortified at her naïveté. Still, he'd gone to considerable lengths. Any woman must be flattered by so painstaking a pursuit.

"So *that* is why I succumbed. No wonder. What mere female could be proof against such an onslaught? My conscience is quite clear, then," she said, glaring at him. "But *you*, after putting yourself to such trouble—why did you not reap the fruits of your labours the other day?"

"I could not." His gaze was still locked upon the grate.

"Why was that? An attack of conscience? But you haven't any, as you've just explained. Was I not sufficiently eager? Or was there some other way you found me . . . inadequate?" she asked, her chin determinedly aloft.

He turned round. "Good God, woman. How can you imagine such a thing? The one matter I never lied about was wanting you. In that I was never false."

"Then why, Julian? And don't repeat your ludicrous speech about my vulnerability. Pray have some respect for my intelligence."

She waited through a long silence. He would tell her the truth. He must. And she would bear it, whatever it was, because she must.

"It was what I saw in your eyes," he said at last. "Or what I thought I saw—but that was enough."

"What was it?" He must have felt her gaze hard upon him, but he wouldn't meet it.

"I thought it was love."

She stood proudly still while hot embarrassment swept her face. "Oh."

"Naturally, I was delighted. I had only connived for your person, not your heart. Indeed, I was in raptures." He struck the coals savagely, once, then replaced the poker in its rack. "Overjoyed to discover I'd made you love a man who didn't exist."

"I can see that must have been a blow to your pride," she said evenly, though her heart lightened within her. "Still, was it worth losing your wager? Was it worth sacrificing your cousin?"

He threw her a surprised glance, then looked away again. "What do you know of that?"

"I had a letter from Miss Fourgette. I must admit there was some consolation in learning the stake was not money or property. My honour for your cousin's. Abstract, but equitable, perhaps. Why did you deliberately lose?" she asked.

He stood, one hand resting on the mantel, his gaze still avoiding hers. His arrogant, handsome face was drawn into tight lines, his mouth set, his green eyes clouded. Yes, he was unhappy, genuinely so. Perhaps that was no more than he deserved.

"Why, Julian?"

"You won't believe it. Too romantic by half."

"Tell me."

"I could not go to that woman and tell her I had won," he said quietly. "It was too precious a treasure you offered me. I would not have it debased into a common, sordid episode."

She ought to let him suffer some little for all the suffering he'd cost her. At least something for the high price she'd paid to come here: her reputation, honour . . . her pride. Yet she'd come needing answers, honest ones, and this at least was not the humiliation she'd steeled herself to meet.

"That was . . . noble of you," she said.

He uttered one short, contemptuous laugh. "Hardly. Robert was in no danger. I knew I could buy her off."

"Still, it would have been cheaper to seduce me."

"I've behaved cheaply enough, I think. I refused to admit how deeply I cared for you, because my vanity would not bear it. My heart had always been quite safe. It was insupportable to admit that you'd seduced *me,* body and soul. Gad—to admit I liked talking with you of *farming*? To admit I delighted in your quick-witted responses to my sophistries? To acknowledge I'd rather argue with you about books, music, art than hear another accept my every word as a jewel of wisdom? Worst of all was to admit I wanted your good opinion—nearly as much as I wanted your person. No, my dear—too mortifying for words," he said, his voice edged with bitterness. "I would admit none of these until the damage was done, when it was too late to woo you honestly. Why should you accept as truth speeches so like their false predecessors?"

"Why, indeed?" she returned. "I am a paragon in so many ways, according to you—yet far too stupid to distinguish fact from seductive fiction. I swallowed every lie. Naturally, it follows I must disregard every truth. Your logic is astonishing, my lord. Nearly as remarkable as your courage. You repent your wickedness—or so you imply. You admit you care for me—or so it seems. And you promptly prepare to flee for Paris."

That jolted him. His sinking head shot up and the eyes he turned to her blazed with anger and hurt.

"Did you think I'd remain to dance at your wedding, Lilith?" he snapped. "Is it not enough I lie awake nights, seeing you in Bexley's arms? Lie alone, except for the agreeable voice of my conscience. Yes, *that* keeps me company with its pleasant refrain: how it might have been *me*," he went on furiously. "How I might be holding you . . . if I had not been such a bloody *fool*."

She folded her trembling hands tightly before her. "There will be no wedding," she said. "I have jilted Thomas. I, too, lied to myself. I thought I could be a good wife to him, even after my heart was stolen from me." The knuckles of her clamped hands turned white with the pressure of her grip as she added, "You went to a deal of trouble to make me love you, Julian. I think you'll have a devil of a time making me stop."

He stared at her, his green eyes wide with disbelief. Then it penetrated . . . at last.

"By God," he said hoarsely. "By God, but you are extraordinary."

She shook her head. "Afraid, perhaps—or stubborn—I don't know. Yet I had to come—shameless, brazen as it was of me—because you meant to go away and . . ." She drew a steadying breath. "And I—I could not let you go without a fight, Julian. I can't. It doesn't matter what you've done. Don't leave me," she said, almost inaudibly. "Not . . . not yet."

"Lilith."

Strong arms reached for her and drew her up against him. "Not yet," he repeated, burying his face in her hair. "Oh, not *yet*."

His fingers threaded through her hair, stroking, soothing. With a shudder of relief, she relaxed at last in the familiar scent of sandalwood, the comforting strength of his arms, and rested her head against his pounding heart.

"I love you," he said.

"Yes."

"I can't lose you now, Lilith. I won't." He drew her head back to look at her. "You're mine. *Mine*," he whispered fiercely.

"Yes."

"You don't understand." He bit his lip. "Oh, Lord. Lilith?"

"Yes."

"I have something rather shocking to tell you. Perhaps you'd better sit down."

# === 20 ===

"AUNT HAS GONE?" Cecily repeated.

"Yes, miss. Ordered a hackney and flew out of the house— and her hair not even done up. That was almost an hour ago, and she's not back yet—and Lord Robert is downstairs waiting."

"Then you must go to Mrs. Wellwicke and help her dress quickly. I can't go without a chaperon, even if I am engaged."

"But, miss, hadn't you better wait for your aunt?"

"No, I think I'd better not. I shall entertain Lord Robert until Mrs. Wellwicke comes down."

"But, miss—"

"Good heavens, Susan. If Aunt had wanted me to wait, she would have said so, wouldn't she?" Miss Glenwood responded ingenuously as she slipped past her maid and through the door.

With Cawble's keen eye upon him, Lord Robert dared no more than drop a light kiss on his beloved's forehead. When, a moment later, he learned she intended to go out without her aunt, he was sorely tempted to shake the dear girl.

"She'll kill us!" he whispered harshly. "She'll banish me, she'll write your father and—"

"She'll do no such thing," Cecily answered. "Mary said she had on her nicest gown and her hair was all unpinned. Besides, I saw the book your cousin gave her. She's gone to him, of course—so naturally, it's absurd to expect her to return in time for the party. Thank heaven! When she came back the other day so gloomy, I was at my wits' end. I was so certain they'd have made it up by then. After all, they were on the road together at least twenty-four hours."

Lord Robert drew her farther into the room. "That was a terrible scheme, darling. When I saw your aunt this afternoon—gad, I've never felt so guilty in my whole life. And she never scolded—not once. I wanted to crawl into a hole, really I did."

"Well, we hadn't any choice, had we?" was the unrepentant answer as Miss Glenwood plopped down onto the sofa. "There's nothing like an elopement for getting the concentrated attention of one's elders, is there? And there's nothing to feel guilty about, because we didn't run away, did we? Besides, haven't they worried us half to death, the two of them? The nightmares I've had of that tiresome Sir Thomas married to my splendid aunt and turning her into a prim, fussy, miserable old woman. With her hair in those nasty coils. And a lot of bald little fussy children whining at her." She shuddered.

Lord Robert glanced at the door outside which the butler hovered, then took a seat beside his darling girl. "Don't get your hopes up about any other sort of children," he warned *sotto voce*. "Hillard said Julian was packing for Paris."

"Then he'll just have to unpack, I daresay," Cecily retorted. "When it comes to obstinacy, he's no match for my aunt."

"You don't know Julian."

She smiled up at him. "Don't I? Would you care to place a wager, my lord?"

"I think you're labouring under a misapprehension," Lord Brandon said slowly. "I *was* preparing to flee the country, like a coward—but it wasn't because I despaired of making you my mistress. I couldn't—that is, I can't—" He realised he was fiddling nervously with his neck-cloth. Abruptly, his hand dropped to his side. "I don't want you as my mistress."

Her gaze fell to the carpet and the colour rose to her fine, high cheekbones.

"Damn! That's not how I meant—By God, why must this be so curst impossible! That imbecile Bexley did better, I'll warrant," he muttered, clenching his fists and glaring at his evening slippers. "I want—I love you, with—with all my heart. I think I've loved you from the moment I first clapped eyes on you. Lord, why the devil should you believe that? Another of my confounded treacle speeches." He gritted his teeth. "Lilith Davenant, would you— Drat it! I'm a thorough wretch and I couldn't have treated you more shabbily—and I know I deserve to be miserable all my days—but I wish you'd let me try to be better, as . . . as your husband. I know there can't be a worse prospect in all the United Kingdom," he added hurriedly, "but I *swear* I'll be a good one—or die trying."

Slowly her head rose, and two slate-blue eyes fixed wonderingly upon his flushed countenance. "My hearing is failing me," she said breathlessly. "It sounded as though you just asked me to marry you."

"I did," he said, appalled at the wretched state of his nerves. "You wonder how I can have the temerity, but the fact is, I haven't any choice."

"Well. Indeed." Her gaze reverted to her hands, folded in her lap. "I'm struck all of a heap."

"No more than I."

"That's because you're overwrought. This is what comes of giving rein to one's emotions. We have descended into melodrama. Later, when you're cooler, you'll think better of it."

"I most certainly will not!" Panic abruptly superseded indignation. "Or do you mean *you* don't think much of it? No, of course you wouldn't," he answered miserably. "What a fool I am. Irresistible as a lover, perhaps, but as a husband—heaven forbid. You've already had one of my ilk, haven't you? You're hardly likely to make the same experiment twice."

"I'm older and wiser now," she said, "yet I love you."

"Yes, but what's the good of that if you won't marry me?" he complained ungraciously, scarcely heeding her through the black gloom overpowering him. "*Now*, naturally, after you've cursed me with this fiendish ogre of a conscience. Oh, it doesn't matter. I'm behaving abominably. Robin isn't half so infantile. I suppose I should take my punishment like a man."

"I wish you would not always be ramming thoughts into my head and words into my mouth, Julian," she said with a touch of impatience. "I didn't say I wouldn't marry you."

He gazed blankly at her.

"Well, did I?" she asked.

"Didn't you?"

"I was only trying to allow you time for second thoughts. I was sure you'd taken leave of your wits momentarily. Unfortunately, since you seem to persist in the ailment—"

"You wicked, teasing, *cruel* girl." He moved nearer to drop to one knee before her.

"Very likely I am. I hope you're prepared for a lifetime of it."

"I'll gladly endure all the torments of the damned," he joyfully assured her. "The question is, Are *you* prepared, my love?" He captured both her hands in his. "I want to parade you about in public and make my friends die of envy. I want to snatch you from your dancing partners and hold you as close as I like when we whirl about the room. I want to live with you. I want to rattle my newspaper at you during breakfast and quarrel with you about politics and the servants and the rearing of our children. I want to talk with you and tease you and care for you. I even want to trudge with you through muddy fields, to worry about the rain and the crops and the cattle."

"That may be your best speech yet," she said softly. Her cool blue gaze had softened too. "I'm afraid you're in a very bad way, my lord. Still, if ours is a *long* engagement, perhaps you'll come to your senses in time."

He uncoiled his long form from its position of supplication to take a more satisfactory place beside her on the sofa.

"It's true I feel rather giddy at the moment," he answered, "but I strongly doubt I shall ever come to my senses. Or perhaps I have at last. I don't know. I really am quite confused, weak, and dizzy. I had better take hold of something."

He gathered her close to him. Then his fingers crept into the gleaming, copper-lit curls framing her face. His gaze lingered on the haughty countenance that had so entranced and intrigued him from the start—the cool alabaster of her skin, the smouldering blue smoke of her eyes, the wanton ripeness of her generous mouth.

"I love you," he whispered.

Her mouth curled into a wicked smile that made his heart thump like a legion of marching infantry.

"So you do," she answered. "A costly mistake, I think."

"Indeed, I hadn't expected so high a price as marriage, madam. But what else is one to do? A mistress may be lost on a wager—or led astray by the next good-looking, sweet-talking rogue to cross her path. Marriage it is, then," he said, his voice low, fierce, possessive.

His kiss was fierce too, hungry, demanding. Yet there was at last peace of a sort within. And so, when she drew away after a moment or two, Julian quieted himself with the reflection that there would be time and time enough. Against every odd, Lilith Davenant would be his. Lady Brandon. His marchioness. The thought threw his heart crashing against his ribs.

"There's just one thing," she said, her fingers playing with the curls at his ear.

"Anything," he answered hoarsely.

"Well, actually, three things. There is Diana next year, then Emily the year after, and Barbara the next. Oh, and Claire—that makes four. But she will not be ready for a few years after *that*. Four more nieces, Julian."

"*Four* of them?" He sat back abruptly. "Perhaps I have

been hasty. I don't believe I can survive any more of your nieces, Mrs. Davenant."

"They're very sweet girls," Lilith defended. "Darling girls, just like Cecily."

He shuddered theatrically. "No, not like Cecily. Anything but that."

"You can't be provoked with Cecily. Recollect she did come to her senses in time."

"She was never out of her senses," he retorted. "Not for a moment. I've never heard of such a coolly calculating little minx as that one. If her cousins are anything like her, I shall advise England's entire male population to make for the South Seas *at once*."

"I'm sorry you feel that way, because she likes you immensely. She was taken with you from the start, you know," Lilith said. She reached up again, this time to stroke his stubborn jaw.

He brought her hand to his lips. "Was she?"

"Oh, yes. Because you were dark and devilish-looking. 'A bad, beautiful angel,' she called you—although she was comparing you to a horse at the time. All my nieces will dote upon you and make me jealous."

"Will they, just goddess? It seems the managing has begun already." He pressed another kiss upon her hand. "I see what our marriage will be like. You'll lead me about by the nose. What a pathetic prospect."

"Ah, yes, my lord, but such a *seductive* one. And poor me—I'm so susceptible to seduction."

He grasped the back of her head and brought her mouth to within an inch of his. "Indeed. Thank you for reminding me. In all my horror of impending nieces, I'd very nearly forgotten about *that*."

"Not until after we're wed, Julian," she said primly.

"Oh, no. Of course not."

"Your reformation must begin at once. There is not a minute to be lost. I am resolved."

Resolved or no, a devilish promise lurked in smoky blue depths.

"Yes, my love. And I respect you for it, indeed I do," he said. "Naturally, I can wait."

"Deceitful knave," she said.

"Yes," he breathed as his mouth covered hers.

❖❖❖❖❖❖❖❖❖❖❖❖❖❖❖❖❖❖❖❖❖❖❖❖❖❖❖

Author's note: For the story's purposes, the debut of *Mansfield Park* has been advanced a few weeks. Miss Austen's novel was published in three volumes on 9 May 1814.*

*Source: *Jane Austen: Her Life,* by Park Honan. St. Martin's Press. New York. 1988.